The Starwielder
Armageddon's Eclipse
Ian Cassidy

Acknowledgements

I am eternally grateful for the unending love and support from my wife Cat Cassidy, who has been by my side through the beginning of this entire story. She witnessed the journey, and even got involved firsthand, spending countless hours with me in all the different aspects drafting, editing, and publishing independently.

I'm also thankful for my parents, younger brothers, and those friends closest to me who have supported me along the way.

Also, with extreme gratitude—the artists I've built an amazing relationship with all over the world, their concept artwork has helped me so much in bringing my stories to life with their talented efforts and brilliant illustrations.

Pronunciation Guide/Glossary

CHARACTER PRONOUNCE:

Cyngosa (sin-go-sa)

Saaliha (sa-lee-ha)

Minax (min-nax)

Khelu (key-lo)

Dorrion (door-e-ion)

Eos (ee-os)

Stratos (stra-t-os)

Tidus (ti-duh-us)

Kerith (ke-rii-th)

Glyph (glif)

Veridian (ver-rid-ee-uhn)

Sidra (sid-r-ah)

Daxil (dax-ill)

LOCATION PRONOUNCE/Glossary:

Lycandia (li-can-dee-ah): One of the two known supercontinents of the planet, the homeland of *Lycandians*.

Perilith (peh-rill-lith): The other known supercontinent, the homeland of the *Felidaens*.

Wulftheon (wolf-the-on): One of the democratic republic countries of *Lycandia*, located just outside the heart of the supercontinent. Its southern neighbor is *Aluan*.

Aluan (aa-loo-ann): Another republic, this country made up of unified stateships, operates with a senate, congress, and separate council of judges.

Umbris (uhm-b-ris): The capital city of *Perilith*.

Port Liekos (Ly-kos): The capital city of *Edon*, the home of direwolfs.

Luminous (loo-min-noos): The capital of the *Aluan Republic*.

For even more information about the people, places, and magic of Homeworld in the *Starwielder* universe, please check out the QR code below for the compendium on the official website!

Contents

CHAPTER ONE: The Forsaken Castle ... 1

CHAPTER TWO: The Salvaging Site ... 24

CHAPTER THREE: The Weight Of Consequences ... 32

CHAPTER FOUR: An Enticing Bounty ... 52

CHAPTER FIVE: The Paladins Patriotic Revolution ... 60

CHAPTER SIX: Stepping Stones, And Self Liberation From Captivity ... 80

CHAPTER SEVEN: The Maleficent Ritual ... 98

CHAPTER EIGHT: Armageddon's Eclipse ... 111

CHAPTER NINE: Straying Into The Fringes Of Madness ... 145

CHAPTER TEN: The Satellite Siege ... 166

CHAPTER ELEVEN: A Somber Dawn ... 182

CHAPTER TWELVE: Battle Of The Bastion ... 194

CHAPTER THIRTEEN: Persistent Grudges And Unlikely Alliances ... 219

CHAPTER FOURTEEN: Out From The Cauldron, Into The Conflagration ... 248

CHAPTER FIFTEEN: The Prince Of Crows ... 263

CHAPTER SIXTEEN: Crafting The Ethereal Lattice ... 277

CHAPTER SEVENTEEN: The Corrupted Spire Of Malice — 298

CHAPTER EIGHTEEN: The Darkest Black Hole, And The Brightest Star — 325

CHAPTER NINETEEN: Treading Along The Tightrope Of Destiny — 348

CHAPTER TWENTY: Tranquility's Endurance — 354

EPILOGUE: The Reverse-Engineered Resurrection — 364

CHAPTER ONE: The Forsaken Castle

"TUMBLING THROUGH TIME AND space alongside shooting stars, it felt like falling in reverse through raindrops. What was that?" Khelu Odena says, giddily brushing herself off, after being flung out of the tear in the very fabric of reality where the normally dormant stain glass in the center of the moon gate is. With a flick of her tail she stands up wobbly, still shaky and feeling lightheaded, as she beholds the circular moon gate shaped monument in the center of the chilly unfurnished great hall, scrutinizing it with growing interest in the murkiness.

An ancient, circular shaped monument is seated in the center of the unfurnished great hall. The castle was built over the moongate monument, and appears to postdate the immovable landmark by many millennia. The faint howling of a blizzard outside can be heard, as snow and wind pelt against the thick windows. Meanwhile, inside the castle, everything lies dormant and undisturbed. Except for the start of a faint vibration, which emits from the center of the monument's moon gate made of stained glass and stone, vanishing as a tear in time and space appears now instead. A short time after, six individuals are thrown out of it.

Minax Bolide, a ten foot tall anthropomorphic dragon, glides himself to a halt using his wings to assist in braking, his blood red and black membranes sounding like flapping leather through the air. The *Starwielder's* mighty cosmic iridescent colored weapon *Alpha and Omega* disappears from one claw-like hand and the *Macrocosm Lexicon,* an unequivocally powerful spell book he was previously holding in his other claw, now hangs from a chain attached to the girdle of his armor as he moves. Now free to help catch his free-flying friends.

"I've got you, Cyngosa and Dorrion." Minax gingerly catches the two *Lycandians*, hugging them against his torso encased in the *Starwielder's* legendary boulder opal armor. Tiny inconsistent splotches or speckles of greens, blues, reds, and purples add unique visual dynamic contrasting the shiny golden brown. Minax releases Cyngosa, helping to lay Dorrion against him tenderly, who only responds with a raspy, painful grunt.

Cyngosa Maelstrom, an anthropomorphic Direwolf mercenary, is carrying a wounded comrade of theirs, Dorrion Chrisbane, during the trip through time and space and fortunately emerge together upon exiting. Dorrion clings to Cyngosa for support while Minax catches the pair gently from the wintery air. He could feel it in his extremities. Cyngosa lifts his neon green lensed goggles up from covering his turquoise eyes onto his forehead once Dorrion's full weight is no longer on him.

Cyngosa, body still pumping with adrenaline from the cosmic ride he went on, plus the events leading up to it, moves his attention around to the dark, cold and musty smelling place he and his companions abruptly land in. Flaring his nostrils as his breath is visible due to the brisk temperature, ignoring its bite, returning his focus to Dorrion.

"Dorrion, take it easy buddy, okay? I think I got something to help you." With his ears pierced with three emerald going flat against his head, he nervously twitching and jamming one of his paws into his leather vest he wears over his matte black armor plating, discovering quickly his ankhs are gone, and his totems are out of magical power from their previous fight. Cyngosa gives a brief defeated expression at the travesty before perking up toward the others with melancholy in his tone of voice. "I don't have any magical energy left for healing. I'm out of charged totems too. We got a first aid kit? Something? Hopefully anything?"

Dorrion, an older mixed breed of Timberwolf and Greywolf, indicated by his bourbon brown and gray splotchy fur colors. His normally neatly kept long silver hair is in frazzles around his shoulders, including his disheveled clothing beneath his damaged armor plating. Severely injured in their final effort to escape from relentless enemies, when Minax provided the miracle that culminated in bringing them all here, out of the reach of enclosing foes. Grimacing in pain and his ears pinned to his head, Dorrion gave a sigh of relief at the thought.

Dorrion watches as Cyngosa rummages, coughing weakly. "You did phenomenal work with the circumstances we had to face in *Port Humility*. You and I know I'm way past needing a gauze strip here."

Saaliha, an anthropomorphic cheetah, rises up to her feet, recovering from the roll she put herself into while being flung from the portal, wearing a black kevlar body suit with gold armor plates on top, covering the torso, thighs, and arms. Saaliha's pink glowing eyes, accustomed to the dark faster than those of her *Lycandian* companions, take in the decrepit state of the antechamber. Seeing no evident danger around them, she lands her sight on her severely wounded godfather.

Khelu clicks on a utility flashlight from her backpack while investigating, brushing back some of her brown dreadlocks with her other paw, the colorful beads catching the light from it. Her face still showing disbelief as she directs the flashlight around the grand room next, wondering what mysterious place this could be.

Eos, the bluish pink, flaming phoenix, however, is like a living and flying lantern with wings floating in the dim castle. Their head whips about, exploring the new surroundings, assisting the others in seeing through the dark. Eos swoops down to perch themselves on Cyngosa's shoulder, while he's looking up at the others, appearing saddened, sensing the anxiousness coming off from the others, without words being spoken frequently. The phoenix, being extremely intelligent, emits a worrisome coo in Dorrion's direction.

Saaliha Moonwane, after a brief examination of the room, also notices the familiar *Cosmic Decagon* featured in ten stained glass pieces at the center of the moongate stone monument they were just thrown through. She swiftly moves closer to Cyngosa and Dorrion.

"I lost my medical aid drone in the battle in *Port Humility*, somewhere in the town. Like, way before we retreated to the *Trinity* compound." She lets out a hesitant, painful sigh, nervously flicking at her retractable claws. "I don't know what to do. I have a first aid kit, but," she sucks in air and lets out a shaky exhale with tears brimming in her eyes, "some of these look critical, pretty severe honestly." Saaliha checks her cellphone, observing its battery life less than half, adding somberly, "No signal. Wherever we are is remote."

During the interim, Cyngosa bandages and applying pressure to Dorrion's wounds, trying his best to keep his anxious paws steady. Minax and Khelu linger closer, watching with increasing concerns of their own. Dorrion, glancing up at Saaliha with his pewter eyes wide, speaks with his breath visible in the chilly air. "We all have choices to make. This was my choice. You are not responsible for what risks I decide to take upon myself. Hiding in the aircraft like some coward was never an option for me, dearest Saaliha."

Saaliha, slouching with a sharp stinging welling inside her chest, narrowing her glowing pink eyes, but the rest of her face couldn't mask her distraught feeling brewing inside her. "Stubborn old fool. Yes, it is the correct option. I have eight lives to spare...You have one. We need you if *Trinity of Tranquility* is to succeed. With Mom, Dad, and Rhanisha dead. My brother Kerith was lost out there somewhere, probably dead soon enough." She gives a ragged sigh, adding, "*I need you.*"

The older *Lycandian* chuckles warmly, optimism in his tone. "Make those count, then. I lived a single, long and fulfilled life. I always knew my work would outlive me one way or another, but the world is in good paws. You all have everything you need. *Trinity* is not defeated. The cause is not lost."

Minax Bolide approaches Dorrion with exhaustion, crouching solemnly while his wings with golden scaly limbs and with membranes in the colors of blood red and black droop. His dark horns ablaze with tiny orange magma veins, bowing his head as he stares at his fatality wounded *Trinity* mentor. Saaliha had said it perfectly as dread weighed on Minax, like an invisible press on him. Slouching his shoulders and breathing a soft sigh that didn't bring any relief from the tension in his chest. He hovers a claw over Dorrion's fading body. "Your time to go isn't yet, not if I have anything to say about it." Minax attempts to channel a healing magic spell, which does take some hold of the more grievous injuries to Dorrion's torso and right leg.

Khelu shivers momentarily before trying to warm herself up and keep the flashlight on herself and the huddled group, who are attending to Dorrion and collecting themselves from the dazzling trip. Khelu still sees stars in her golden eyes from the nebulous tube she traveled through at light speed, the buzzing in her ears fading gradually. Thankfully, the woozy feeling dissipates, reminding her of her minor injuries. Catching bits of what Dorrion utters and mostly of what Minax says back, Khelu focuses her attention on Dorrion, snapping, "Don't you talk like that now. Minax bailed our asses out. He can save you." Khelu moves back from the monument, glancing at each of them. With a tone of concern, she asks, "Where are on *Homeworld* are we though? This castle is freezing cold. I definitely hear a storm outside."

Cyngosa gets up and runs over to a window, which is closed up behind a long, elegant curtain, probably being tied up a century ago and left as is. A gust of wind hammers against the castle as snowflakes click on the glass. He tears the whole curtain down. It's nighttime and blustery outside, pitch black and leaving Cyngosa unable to make out any lay of the land beyond the window in the seconds he takes. Moving back over to Minax in the dim castle, he wraps part of the curtain around the wooden rod it came off of. He offers the wooden rod, with the partially draping curtain at a safe distance with one arm, and a wink of his glowing turquoise eye in the darkness. "If you don't mind?"

Minax inclines his head once, taking a quick inhale of the brisk air and then exhaling a burst of flame at the cloth, setting it ablaze. Cyngosa smiles with an optimistic expression, holding up the torch they created and casting the light on the others to help their visibility.

Standing up also, Khelu swivels the flashlight around in her shaky grip. "Is there a couch, bed, or something we can lay Dorrion on besides the freezing stone floor?" With increasing light, she whips around and spots the outline of another room, down the adjacent hallway attached to the antechamber. "I'll check." Khelu reports back in a brief couple seconds, haloed by her flashlight. "I think I could make out a table, some other furniture in the other room. There are more rooms. Let's find him a bed, or something. What he really needs is a hospital."

Cyngosa scratches behind his pierced ear, nervously playing with his hair with his paw and silently agreeing with Khelu, before sighing. "Probably not the best idea, considering we're recognized terrorists by the *Aluan Republic*, considering us part of *Trinity* or something."

Minax corrects Cyngosa with a reassuring but stern tone. "You *are* members of *Trinity*. We all still have to rise to the challenges, even when problems arise and the circumstances for us to change our plans."

"Oh, I'm not suggesting we give up my dude, just evaluating the objective reality of our screwed situation here." Cyngosa scratches under his chin.

They go ahead and carefully transport Dorrion, who is fading in and out of consciousness and staying silent and still with flickering eyelids, toward the room Khelu discovered in the otherwise empty castle. Saaliha carries the torch now to light the way while Cyngosa, who is gingerly supporting Dorrion by his shoulders as they go, comments to Minax, "Well, I didn't say I was turning tail and dipping out or suggesting we quit." He now peers down and gestures with open paws at his torso. Despite his black attire, blood stains are visible in the fabric. "Some of this blood on me isn't mine only. Those *Stardust Elementalists* fought and died beside us. *Trinity's* laundry list of allies is only getting shorter."

The pungent smelling smoke generated by the burning curtain torch rises toward the room's tall ceiling, a scent familiar to Saaliha in particular while the flashes of the Moonwane Estate burning down all around here as she scrambled with her father and brother to save her already doomed mother. Emotional ache and anger come to her anxious mind now laden with Dorrion's dismal state, feeling her whiskers twitch and her lips curl. The torch provides a bit of comfort and, to all their appreciation, a better dome of lighting helping with Khelu's flashlight. The room is bigger than the shadow allowed them to see, with a beautiful brick fireplace and a gaunt brown couch. A love seat and a table are the only other pieces of furniture. Saaliha walks quickly over to the fireplace and throws Cyngosa's torch in, moving in a sprint to grab the other unused portion of the curtain to throw on the table.

Minax and Cyngosa carefully lay Dorrion on top, trying to keep his body level. Minax lingers watching over Dorrion lying still, fighting an internal sense of guilt as he furrows his scaly brow over glassy purple eyes and chews his lip. Cyngosa strolls over to the adolescent fire, kneeling to pull his spent wooden totems that he can't recharge out of his black leather vest pockets to plop them in the fireplace. Minax inhales, then exhales into the fireplace to help light it as the flames from Cyngosa's torch dance around the pieces of wood, giving off a bounteous pleasant burning odor to compete against the foul fabric odor.

Dorrion arouses and speaks to them all with his breath visible, this time increasing energy than before in his voice. "Thank you. It feels a bit better already. Gah, the pain is a bastard, though." Laying flat on his back on the table with throw pillows under him, he stares up at the gorgeously decorated ceiling, Minax quietly follow's Dorrion's gaze to stare up as well. "This *Lycandian* architecture is of very specific design for a castle such as this, and quite a chilly climate. We must be in *Wulftheon*. That tear, in reality, took us almost half-way across the world."

"I didn't have any destination in mind when I opened that portal in the *Cosmicism Monument*, I just desired someplace far away from the army trying to kill us..." Minax trails off mid-sentence, changing the topic as he contemplates, asking Dorrion, "*Wulftheon*? This country's name is familiar at least. Hostile?" Dorrion flutters his eyes shut and lets a sputtering cough out before going nonverbal, his breathing still evident as his chest rises and falls.

Cyngosa and Khelu exchange concerned expressions, Cyngosa once again digging into his bag to pull out a bare wooden cylinder and his carving knife, and starts work on a healing totem as his muscle memory formed over many years of carving, takes over. He keeps attentive to the conversation, stating, "No, this is not good. But I think we're safe for now."

"Yeah, fortunately, this place…is an antique." Khelu looks around, taking in the design and architecture of the castle's interior, having never seen a place like this before in all of her adventures with Cyngosa. "Including that room we teleported into minutes ago, I don't think any part of this place has been occupied, or even used, in almost a century by anyone. Based on the settling of dust that I can see. But there has to be plumbing and electricity installed. I noticed some light fixtures. I spy some outlets too."

Saaliha confidently grins. "Promising. Maybe we can find things like food or drinkable water. If not, we can purify snow into water to drink. Heat so we don't freeze to death. Dorrion's lost a lot of blood by now. We need to get him water. I'll volunteer to prowl around. This place can't be impossible to cover completely in a short time and see what we can make use of."

Khelu tunes into what Saaliha said, being temporarily lost in her thoughts, still lingering her eyes on Dorrion. "I'll go with you! Give you some extra light."

Cyngosa pulls out the *Elemental Magic Mastery*, a unique spell book he acquired weeks prior in *Port Liekos*, a time to him that now felt so long ago with how quick and turbulent events have been, with a gulp he utters to Khelu and Saaliha, looking up at them. "I'll stay by Dorrion's side and give him anything I can muster for healing magic as I replenish mana. Time's not in our favor, and even my skills have limits. I'll look through this, continue carving up a restoration totem or two. He bled a lot during our escape." Eos unfurls their wings, flying away from Dorrion to take flight. Cyngosa adds in a morose tone, "Go with them and help scout it out, buddy. Me and Minax will be okay here."

"Adaros and Elith would be so proud of you." Dorrion coughs, directing his attention to Saaliha. "Certainly, from what I've witnessed. I'll see you soon, kid." Shifting his position in the bed, he gazes warmly to Cyngosa, who pauses mid-walk when he notices Dorrion looking at him. "We escaped, we obliterated the Genesis Machine to keep it out of Clyde Crowly's paws, and we bought time against the true horrors his ambitions have. There isn't a basement in existence that isn't too low for him to stoop into to get what he wants."

Saaliha, already moving with a nimble pace heading for the hallway, gives Cyngosa and Minax a relieved expression, sounding genuinely indebted. "Thank you. If we're not back in five minutes, look for us. Let's do this then, hurry."

She and Khelu briskly walk down the colder, dimly lit hallway. Eos coasts above the two of them, darting their crystal sapphire eyes amidst the old ceiling architecture. Khelu and Saaliha wander from the warmth and light of the fireplace, missing it already as the castle's cold air soon clinging to their clothing and fur, their soft audible breathing marked by the hidden chill. The wind howls against the frosted glass of the hallways and antechambers as Saaliha and Khelu's flashlights keep their walk illuminated. They inspect through room after room while Eos silently flutters on with their bright wings, checking out the strange castle with them. They walk past a small library with a billiard table, offering nothing important to their mission besides visual intrigue at the dusty knickknacks left on shelves. Khelu attempts to keep pace with Saaliha while she outpaces her along the hallway. An agitated chaw of a couple crows roosting, riding out the storm rumbling outside, amongst the rafters up above spooks Saaliha and Khelu.

"Electricity would be in the basement, first aid—" Khelu starts to say, as they exit a neglected study room.

"A bathroom!" Saaliha exclaims after she shoulder-slams the door open and immediately raids the cabinet for any medical items she can find. "Painkillers, gauze...No, we need something to help fill or properly stitch wounds." Khelu pokes in with her flashlight to observe Saaliha's discovery. "However, this disinfecting alcohol is a good find. I'll meet you in that main foyer we passed, but I'm going to run this back to them first." Eos lets out an excited chirp and watches Saaliha and Khelu from above, circling around the cramped room.

"Awesome, now we're on to something." Khelu waits in the castle's hallway now. She slowly casts her flashlight's glow on the walls and the few assortments of knickknack objects adorning furniture surfaces. Saaliha disappears at a run to drop off their usual find, and for a time, Khelu is left alone—soon distracted by an oil painting hanging on the opposite stone wall a few feet down the hall. Out of growing boredom and to keep her mind from Dorrion, she inspects the detail with her flashlight moving up close.

The piece is in incredible condition considering the length of time that has passed, or what the piece has been through. The painting has a dramatic sweeping landscape and shows a group of *Lycandians* successfully ambushing a large crudely looking winged beast standing on two legs. Saaliha returns, pulling her attention away when Khelu's ears perk up in the direction of her approaching footsteps.

"Hey, Saaliha. What do you think that's supposed to be?" Khelu asks her, in a tone dripping suspiciously, that she herself already knew the **answer.**

"A *Galanexian*. There's some history connected to this place that probably relates to those *Paladins* identified, but I doubt anything has been left here."

"The more I look around this place, the more it reminds me of a museum. Minax shouldn't find this if he wanders." Fast on the draw, Saaliha yanks a sheet covering a convenient seat and in an effort throws it over the painting. Enough is covered to divert curiosity if passing by. The two journey down the castle hall.

Khelu and Saaliha walk to the basement entrance, having combed most of the first floor of the castle by now. Khelu opens the door, revealing a stairway down, being greeted by a musty aroma. Eos simply flies down, the phoenix apparently fearless meanwhile Khelu and Saaliha's feet creak on the wooden stairs. Moving with steadily increasing excitement now, the two approach the electrical breaker system after wandering the cluttered basement.

Saaliha's paw hesitates while holding the lever, her eyes darting to look at Khelu directly. The wind of the wintry storm can be heard, even from underground, Saaliha says. "If we turn a single light on in this castle, this *usually* empty place will suddenly pop up like a beacon in the middle of the night, for who knows how many miles..."

"Clever thinking, hun. But let's flip the boiler switch and warm this bitch up at least," Khelu comments. Keeping her flashlight steady in the surrounding dark, Saaliha silently bobs her head in agreement. Flipping the old analog switch emits an aggressive clicking sound. The boiler system rumbles to life after some time as the pilot light fires up.

"Perfect. Still connected to a power grid." Saaliha raises her own flashlight, directing it past and over Khelu's shoulder, mumbling, "The water valve is somewhere around here."

Cyngosa and Minax keep close to Dorrion, who is asleep but visibly breathing and still alive. He rests on the makeshift cushioned table, while Cyngosa and Minax carry a complete king sized bed into the room. The fire crackles away happily as two freshly smashed up wooden chairs now burn on top of the pre-existing embers.

"We really shouldn't move Dorrion too much anymore, but let's keep him close to the fireplace so he doesn't freeze," says Minax, easing the end of the bed he is carrying down gently as his scaly but smooth claws release the finely carved oak frame.

Cyngosa lowers his end of the bed they are moving in from the hallway. "Easy now. Hang on, old man, we'll get you nice and cozy in just a moment here."

Wandering over to quickly toss two other wooden arms of a broken up chair into the crackling and snapping fire, Minax boldly stomps down on the glowing embers to make room, the intense heat not bothering his scaly *Galanexian* foot.

Cyngosa returns to his little project of hastily carving a partially blank wooden totem, his breath visible in the air despite the fireplace being in his proximity, his eyes darting in Minax's direction. "Got a minor healing totem in the works here. That disinfection liquid Saaliha dropped off will clean any potential infection," he says with a disheartened sigh.

Cold and tired also, Minax rests his weary purple eyes on Cyngosa with an equally exhausted expression. "You do the best you can, Cyngosa. Does the *Elemental Magic Mastery* provide anything, some powerful restoration incantation, or anything of the sort?" The *Starwielder* adjusts his wings while stifling a yawn, his mind racing, despite the weariness.

Cyngosa adverts his gaze up from his carving work to answer him. "I'd need something living to sort of jump start this very strong spell I came across...while he is still alive. It would initiate a rapid tissue regeneration. But there isn't much here that would work, as we are excluded as options."

Minax raises his defined scaly brow. Cyngosa, carving away with his knife, caught him looking and could see his widened eyes. "Suggesting necromancy. I wasn't aware we were this desperate, or you knew how to use such magic. Considering he'd approve?"

Cyngosa, hearing the lack of enthusiasm in Minax's tone, flares his nostrils and lets a grumble out before explaining. "It's not entirely necromancy, and it's definitely not demonic magic. The spell isn't asking for a sacrifice, unfortunately we're in the middle of the worst place to find suitable plantlife. Do you want to save him or not?"

"Syphoning lifeforce out of plants certainly sounds like a category of dark magic. By the Creator's will. Of course I want to save Dorrion, but not with dark magical means." Minax shakes his head and adds, "I'm sorry, my friend, this is non-negotiable."

Cyngosa shrugs dismissively, frustration at their overall predicament growing and causing a rising in his voice. "There isn't much plantlife to work with, anyway." Cyngosa exhales loudly and deflates. "Wait, Minax, what about the *Lexicon?*"

Minax stares sternly but thoughtfully at Cyngosa with his piercing purple eyes, but a soft clinking sound comes from the vents as the boiler heating system tries to warm up the small but long dormant and frigid castle, distracting him for a second. He continues in a warmer tone. "You're the healing magic expert, though, shaman. There must be something we can do."

Cyngosa scratches at the wooden totem with his knife and blows the dust and shavings away, pausing his work. "All schools of magic have laws and limitations…" Trailing off, he leans over to let his turquoise eyes wander the *Lexicon* with Minax, his paws absentmindedly returning to carving the healing totem still. "And costs to bear. What kind of power does the *Starwielder* possess that can help Dorrion?"

Fanning briefly around the ancient spell book's pages, Minax licks his lips with his silver forked tongue and says, "I have not found any healing magic in here, but there are some astounding levels of magic. Commanding the powers of nature."

Cyngosa and Minax pause their conversation and glance up as Eos flaps their wings, soaring into the room. Khelu and Saaliha return just seconds after. They already feel a margin of warmth seep into the long dormant space. The wind outside moans and howls, thick snow flurries buffering the glass.

Saaliha sways her spotted tail behind her in accomplishment, offering a hopeful smile as she approaches them. "We got water and electricity on. I'll start trying to get an internet signal or maybe boost our phones somehow. We should wait until daylight before turning on any lights."

"We could try to send a signal to other *Trinity* members? Certainly, once Dorrion wakes up, we can ask if he's got anyone out there?" Minax inquires. While his attention is on Saaliha, he happens to notice Cyngosa walks over with his carved totem to the bed where Dorrion is laying.

Cyngosa places the totem on the bed near Dorrion and passes his paws over it in a rhythmic motion. Soon, the totem begins to shimmer with a soft neon glow. "Not a bad idea…" The others watching him notice the scars ebbed deep into his flesh glow the same color as the magic energy he channels. "*Blessed by the Elements*, but even my amplified magic gifts have a point where they're depleted for a time, my dudes." He blows whatever wood dust remains for good measure, then looks up at Khelu, still standing. "There was mention of a kitchen pantry."

"Yeah, why?" Khelu asks, but receives her answer faster than she can finish the question, Cyngosa passing by her and Saaliha. Eos twists through the air to follow him. Saaliha, Minax, and Khelu look at him and dismiss it. Saaliha approaches Dorrion, asleep still, and silently prays for him.

Reluctant to leave his side, Saaliha peels herself away to go to the dining room table. Pulling a router device from her backpack, she wires it up to her laptop, extracting a neatly rolled up power cord. She plugs it into the nearest outlet. The metallic purple object makes an audible hum and beeps three times before going quiet. Saaliha nods. "It's connected." Lifting her cellphone to it with a promising grin. "Weak signal, but it's something we can work with."

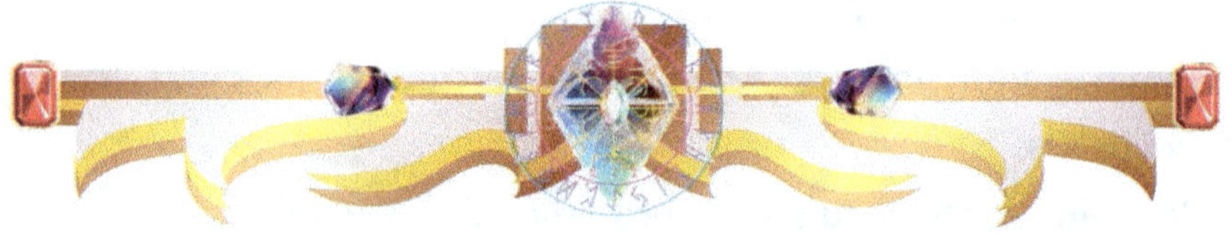

Cyngosa, having his turn now, with Eos flying along with him, wanders the chilly dark castle hallway with a mild curiosity. The unfamiliar architecture of stone archways over antique appearing wood and metal banded doors, cast iron braziers dangling from bloated metal chains. Cyngosa moving into the kitchen pantry section, Eos's flaming body and blazing wings illuminating the smooth stonework floor, the thick wood table and chairs. The room was sparsely decorated, the same stale air hovers here as Cyngosa wanders about, grateful for the few moments away from Dorrion and the grave state of being he's in. A sense of survivor's guilt washes over him, but he just as quickly mentally dismisses it. He stops in his tracks, recognizing and opening a wooden sliding hatch, revealing a tall shelving unit behind. Once the limited light with him shines on the contents within, Cyngosa discovers the shelves loaded with bottles of aging wine and bourbon, and he lets out a pleased chuckle.

"Ohh, hell yeah." He reaches up to the top and pulls a bottle of bourbon down to inspect it. "Finally, a win." Eos lightly tapping the bottle with their beak a couple times, emitting a squawk.

Cynosa hears Eos in his mind. "*Are you sure this is a good choice right now?*" Cyngosa hums with a small smirk on his visage, turning from the bottle cupboard.

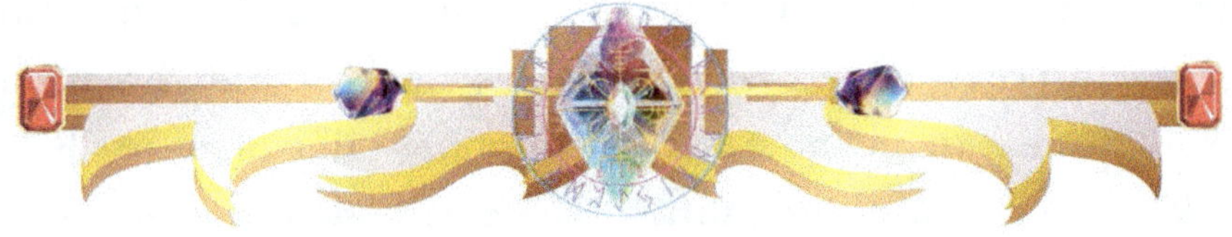

Cyngosa and Eos return to the others in the living quarters of the castle, an open bottle in one paw and two still sealed in his other. He shows off his bounty to them.

Saaliha's melancholy expression melts into an amused smirk at Cyngosa. arriving with bottles raised in the air in either paw. "You can't be serious. I didn't expect there to be anything edible left in a deserted place like this. But of course you sniffed up the booze."

Cyngosa strides from the wintry hallway into the living room they were huddling in. "Yup, pretty much empty. The two fridges in the kitchen were left unplugged, and the water coming out of the pipes is dirty looking." He beams at the bottle in his grip. "The liquor is chilled already, too. Bonus."

Khelu takes a bottle from Cyngosa and plops down on a nearby musty loveseat, sighing the whole time the wind outside buffers against the sturdy stone castle wall. "Now what? Drink and wait?"

"Yes. We patiently wait until morning and this snow storm passes, remote as this place is. I'm certain civilization may be in reach, it may just be far. We should rest and set up shifts to watch over Dorrion," Minax Bolide states to them all. Cyngosa takes a whiff of the woody scent from the bottle after opening its screw-on cap and tosses it back for a gulp. The malt-like sweetness is a surprise to him.

Cyngosa passes the bottle over to Khelu and she grips the bottle by the neck, taking a sampling swig. The extra watery syrup alcohol hits her taste buds on her tongue and she blurts afterward, "Harsh, but sweet."

Saaliha stares at Dorrion quietly breathing, uninterested in getting drunk for the time-being, waits with her right leg bouncing from intense internal anxiety as she fixates on him. Her breathing steadily increases, and an upset twitch of her tail behind her like a cracking whip follows purrs softly, "These *Paladins.* Our enemies will experience what we *Felidaen*'s have a phrase for; Primal justice."

Shifting her gaze from Saaliha to Minax and Cyngosa, Khelu says, "We're in rough shape here. So what if we have electricity and heat for now? We need a plan."

"Calling for help is obviously out of the question. We're being hunted. Especially me," Minax says back to Khelu, a thoughtful frown on his face.

"But maybe there are some *Trinity* members out there that can help us?" Cyngosa asks Saaliha, perking one of his ears upright, tossing her a hopeful smirk.

Saaliha runs a paw through her multicolored short hair, shocked to realize her retractable claws had come as she catches herself almost scratching her own forehead. "After the fighting in *Port Humility* to escape, I don't have much equipment left. Literally every last one of my combat drones got destroyed, or hit successfully. I've at least got my computer and mobile router. Once they are juiced up, we'll discover what cards we've been dealt here."

It is the middle of the night. Minax has Saaliha and Khelu cuddled up with him under a blanket on the couch by the fireplace to combine body heat, given their lack of proper insulating layers. Dorrion lay in the awkwardly placed bed nearby, underneath blankets comfortably. Khelu, Minax, and Saaliha are snorting soundly. All along, Cyngosa and Dorrion are wide awake, the older *Lycandian* billionaire stirring some time ago to discover the mercenary up and their other friends asleep. Cyngosa leans in over the fireplace, his turquoise eyes transfixed by the dancing flames with his arm resting on the hardwood mantle. Eos sits perched directly over the fire on the mantle. Dorrion lays quiet in bed, his pewter eyes glossy. The storm they arrived in has long since passed by this late hour. A calm, frigid stillness remains and the partially cloudy skies let very limited light through the snow plastered window. The alien-like castle losing its novelty to Cyngosa some time ago as he takes a swift swig of the strong alcohol in his pocket flask. Refilled recently from his earlier discovery, letting out a refreshed melancholy sigh.

Dorrion whispers, "A lot on your mind, huh?" He coughs just once, sitting up in bed.

Cyngosa blinks and perks his emerald pierced ear toward Dorrion's voice, then swivels his head and wakeful eyes up from the fire. "Oh, you know it, Dorrion." He turns and faces in his direction. "It gets very busy up there..." Cyngosa gestures vaguely at his head with one paw, then quietly proceeds away from the crackling fireplace toward Dorrion.

"A relatable feeling. Believe me, I've experienced many of those myself. I don't suppose you'd want to talk, since we're awake, or you could keep brooding over the fire. We don't have much time left," Dorrion says, an odd calmness in his tone of voice.

Cyngosa leans in closer to the bed and puts a paw on Dorrion's shoulder, grinning at him while drunk. "You always did like to talk a lot, but you're good company. I will admit I liked hearing some of the extraordinary stories you've told us. Need some water or anything?"

Dorrion lets out a short chuckle and smiles up at Cyngosa. "Heh, I do, you are right. I'm quite alright, thank you. Maybe you'll remember hearing my advice and stay focused in my absence."

Cyngosa emits a gulp quietly, and stares away for a moment, but then speaks in an optimistic tone. "You're going to be fine. Those healing totems will have you patch up in no time." He softly bumps Dorrion's arm. "Drama queen."

Dorrion laughs out and smiles. "Cyngosa, I admire your enthusiasm." His smile fades, nodding grimly as he sees it plainly in Cyngosa's watery eyes in spite of his face. "I'm finished here. This does not end here with me. Not the Creator's plan for the *Starwielder*, either. You'll need to be resilient. For yourself. And especially for them." His gaze wanders over to where Saaliha, Khelu, and Minax are slumbering. "I sense and recognize that anxiety you have."

Cyngosa clears his throat, glancing at Khelu and the others. "Everyone I ever get close to dies, Dorrion. Every person I care about. The bold and the cautious alike." He lifts the bourbon bottle to take a swig. "I don't need to go into my past again with you. Beat that dead labor-beast over and over."

Dorrion breathes deeply, winces, then says, "Does death and abandonment truly strike such fear in you? Whatever lies beyond this, heh, life. It's the Creator's Will. We are the universe and consciousness experiencing itself. We are made from stardust and matter, stardust, and matter is what we all will return to, eventually. Our time is fleeting and precious."

Without a single movement except his mouth, Cyngosa says, "Heh, getting far in the mind tonight, are we? Going to tell a fellow flawed, stoic, that it's preposterous to worry about things outside of my control next? Accept my limits, etcetera in this vast uncontrollable universe. Besides, I thought you turned your back on your faith?" His body feels like it is made of rock, unable to move his arms or legs. He finally manages to blink, anchored beside the bed.

Dorrion watches him, turning his head in the pillow underneath and says, "No Cyngosa, I turned my back on the place of worship, not my faith. But, I'm also offering a perspective you haven't yet considered, or rather seem afraid to commit to. Have trust, be open to faith, and assume a measure of leadership. You are a part of *Trinity*. Whether you love it or not, when it shines and when the storm is most fierce." His expression softens. "It's always a home. You won't be alone in darkness."

Cyngosa gives Dorrion a hard, silent study for a moment, unblinking with a glassy eye contact before answering him. "I'm just as grateful now as that night in *Port Liekos*, being invited to join *Trinity of Tranquility*. Why would I want leadership? That's naturally Minax's role. He's the *Starwielder*. After the shit I witnessed him pull off out there in the jungle, he's very much ready to lead us through what's to come." He bites his lip, pauses, and hums thoughtfully for a second. "We should be trying to rebuild the Genesis Machine. It'll take us months just to accomplish that."

Dorrion says, "Still a precise plan and a mission we cannot falter on, restoring the *Galanexians* from a wrongful extinction. Khelu is up to the task, and Saaliha's technical knowledge will help." He lets out a ragged cough. "But, in wake of recent events, it's imperative that you track down Clyde Crowly. Kill him and end whatever sinister things he's scheming with the *Armageddon Cult*. Out of survival, we have to go on the offensive now. If we truly are in *Wulftheon,* his native country, one of the hardest tasks has already been achieved. *Trinity* will show its teeth."

Cyngosa asks in a playful tone, "Still have an air of diplomacy left in you? We'll stop Clyde and whatever shadow organization working with him. All my sarcasm aside. You have my word. I've had few people give me a real chance to believe in me. You gave me that chance Dorrion, I will get this done, I promise."

Dorrion says, "Remember that the *Armageddon Cultists,* they value no living thing, only magical power and domination. They seek to accelerate doom wherever possible. They are far beyond what one would consider nihilistic, at best. Eradicator's impending arrival looms over everything and everyone. The cultists will, and have, paved the way. Perhaps willingly consulting with that angel in your dream state. Or pray for another miracle?"

Cyngosa looks elsewhere, away from Dorrion and the question, it seems, staring almost blank-faced at the fire for a moment while the alcohol continues to numb him. In a thoughtful tone, he says, "Maybe I could. Do you want me to trust others more? I don't know about that. Did you consider the perspective that my former boss double-crossed me and Khelu just before you hired us? I mean, that's just my chronologically ordered first example of why. But I trust you, Dorrion."

Dorrion replies, "You've been hurt and betrayed, and still do truly have a heart of gold and love others deeply. I've seen pieces of your true self slip through that mask you put up so often." Dorrion pauses, adding, "You have an introspective view and empathy that is unique. Don't let the darkness and ignorance of the world smolder out your fire, Cyngosa."

Cyngosa exhales quietly, licking his lips with glassy half-lidded eyes and drooping ears. "I've felt the whole world on my back before, most of my life. I'll probably still get back up, survival instincts y'know. Strength, inner and outer, has always been built in the grit of things. But why isn't it enough sometimes?" He takes another gulp of his alcohol, finding the flask empty after his last drink from it.

Dorrion smiles at Cyngosa before closing his tired pewter eyes. "Never let your integrity burn out. You'll need it in a world that's lost its own. If you don't believe in yourself, you won't see others who believe in you."

Dorrion drifts off to sleep. Cyngosa is left awake in his thoughts, the soft howl of wind blowing and the fireplace crackling his only company. He slumps down into one of the love seats and tosses the bottle back for another gulp, sitting in his thoughts until sleep takes him, eventually. Cyngosa nods off as his head dips to the right against the headrest cushion.

CHAPTER TWO: The Salvaging Site

P ENELOPE'S ARMORED SUV PULLS up to the plane crash site with an entourage of six off-road motorcyclists acting as her security detail. She exits the backseat alongside additional personnel from inside, greeted by a floral and warm temperate breeze. Penelope's secretary exits with her, out into the bright tropical sunlight, holding a flat computer device in her paws and obsessively checking it.

Penelope Briarpaw wears her usual black and white pinstripe dress suit with dozens of gold *Lycandian* paws on it. She sports an armor plating over her torso and a pair of reflective aviator sunglasses, and today chooses to traverse in hiking boots given the location's rugged terrain. The outskirts of *Port Humility*, a tiny coastal settlement on the edge of the island continent of *Ralawaith*, are surrounded by dense jungles and breathtakingly bizarre terrain formations laden with hundreds of colorful, fragrant foliage.

Regardless of all the commotion, many birds of paradise continue flying about the enclosing canopy. Penelope confidently hikes without paying the area much of her attention. Her chin tilted up, passing one purple quartz emerging out of the ground, this being one of many other different hued quartz shooting up from the mossy soil.

A couple dozen *Paladins* in uniform linger around the impressive, still smoldering crater with their *Aluan Marine* allies. Chunks of twisted metal, obliterated hardware and other debris lie scattered around. During Penelope Briarpaw's walk, field experts examine the debris amidst the bumpy terrain. A couple hundred feet away from the crash, others inspect the ancient moon gate shaped monument with stained glass windows at its core. These operations are overseen by General Sabaton, an experienced, grizzled *Lycandian* war veteran, nowadays one of *Aluan's* formidable generals.

Penelope walks over with her shoulders back and staring up. "Afternoon, General." She makes a concerned expression at the charred smokey crater and scene before them, taking off her sunglasses and chewing on the tip. She says, "This doesn't appear very promising, does it?" Sabaton tenses up, but only lets out an exhale.

Clyde Crowly exits the back of the sleek dark SUV from the opposite side, wearing a wide brimmed black hat and matching sunglasses. Ditching his usual black trench coat in the tropical heat, he wears instead a silver button-down shirt, gold cuff-links, and a gold tie clip that glints in the sun. He also sports a belt with a porcelain white belt buckle, a black skeletal *Lycandian* paw residing in the center. He strides confidently over to General Sabaton, just behind Penelope and the others. He stands atop of a grassy rise and surveys the crash site, placing his hands on his hips and pursing his lips, silently assessing his realistic options given the state of the wreck before him. While he inhales thoughtfully, the earthy and acrid scent of burned wood comes along with it.

General Sabaton silently salutes Penelope, then nods, speaking to her first. "President Briarpaw, as you can see, we've already been collecting data and material evidence." As Clyde Crowly walks up to them, the general adds, "Also, congratulations on getting the Supreme Chancellor of *Wulftheon*, Mr. Crowly."

"Slim chances that Chrisbane's machine survived the plane crash after being shot down. Of course, that possibility might have been before that meteor smashed into it after. Is there anything we can salvage?" Clyde asks, completely dismissing Sabaton's compliment, not even really looking at him as Crowly's gaze peaks from the corners of his eyes at whatever the *Aluan Marines* sniffed up.

General Sabaton sways side to side slightly, shaking his head silently. "Negative. General Cobaltfort's fast reaction shooting the aircraft down prevented them from slipping away further into dangerous wilderness. We saw what you all saw in the live battle footage. There's nothing but junk left here." He turns his attention back to Penelope and explains further. "I've already had recovery teams out cleaning this up since securing the perimeters."

Penelope impatiently watches Clyde and Sabaton with cool concern on her face. "And now what, we don't have a location on the *Galanexian*? This military operation will not go unnoticed by the world. Congress and the senate will be barking up a storm when news of what we've done here in *Port Humility* catches media attention."

General Sabaton walks past several of his workers, giving each of the *Marines* a casual nod to boost morale while they pause their work to salute. He continues to only speak to Penelope and Clyde. "No idea. Eyewitnesses saw the enemy leap into some kind of ripple in space from that landmark over there. My *Marines* secured the crashed aircraft just before that asteroid thing came down." General Sabaton gestures to a couple paltry piles of pulverized hardware, clearing his throat before speaking once again. "Here's what survived from the charred crushed metal, the bits that didn't melt into slag."

Clyde Crowly boldly approaches one of the piles and picks up a fragment of a computer motherboard, smirking as with one accord, removing his sunglasses. "Just minor setbacks is all, I believe I got what I came for...Next, the reverse engineering process, *Crowclaw Conglomerates* headquarters has a lab that will more than suffice for such a task. Box up all of these damaged electronics and waste. I'll take it all."

"Good, saving us a cleanup bill. Just know you'll have your work cut out for you, Clyde." Penelope claps her paws together before addressing the general. "Let's wrap this up. You and I need to be back in *Aluan* within two days. Congress and the senate should no doubt want a meeting in the *Bastion* for our little excursion here, and we need to brainstorm a plan to stall."

"They don't seem to possess as much enthusiasm as you and Mr. Crowly are pursuing that demonic thing, Madam President. What we've encountered here, and the resistance we met in that town, will make them rethink the matter," Sabaton says back to Penelope.

Clyde turns back to face them, contemporaneously he and the others journey back from the wreckage site to the awaiting motorcade two thousand feet away, "Ms. Briarpaw, before you hastily run off, I do have one question for you."

"Sure, I'll need to warm up with questions, I suppose." Penelope forces a laugh.

Clyde adjusts his pace with the group, walking alongside her, looking over his shoulder at General Sabaton before meeting his icy-blue eyes with Penelope's. "Did you send federal agents to capture General Cobaltfort's wife and daughter?"

The *Aluan* President stays silent for a second during their journey, chewing over thoughts before stating matter-of-factly, "Why yes, I did. Believe me, I have faith in his tenacity to accomplish the mission. I just had to make sure he would *continue* to cooperate with what's ahead of us, as many others will have too. He wasn't a special case. Others have been put in house arrest or taken in."

"You do what you feel you must, however belligerent you decide to be. Just know, he was pissed when he called me prior to your bombastic military operation in *Port Humility*, to put it simply," Clyde says, carrying emphasis on 'just know.'

Penelope narrows her eyes suspiciously at the mention of the phone call Stratos had with Clyde, a detail not made known to her. She scoffs with a tart look on her face. "Stratos will play along, or be wise enough to keep in his lane and out of our way. I won't harm his family. I haven't been given a reason." Penelope looks over her shoulder at Sabaton to question him further. "Also, how is he doing? Not killed in action yet is a plus. We can brush him off and send him after the dragon beast."

General Sabaton picks up his stride to walk on the other side of Penelope. "He's in critical condition, but he's alive and has been heavily attended by magical mending and field first aid. General Cobaltfort is now resting on the *Tempest Vortex*, in the medical bay with the others airlifted from combat. I needed the battleship's medical bay on the shore to administer medical aid and supplies to the locals under protection."

"Good work here, Silas, tidying up. Nevertheless, our grander mission continues. Reach out to your immediate subordinate lieutenant to take over command here. You're coming with me back to *Aluan* as soon as possible."

Clyde and Penelope return to the off-road SUV with their entourage and drive away from the site, squeezing Silas along with them for the ride to the coastline. *Port Humility*, with a dozen swirling pillars of smoke rising from its low skyline, has seen better days.

The crammed township of mixed stonework and metal buildings is bustling with activity from relief workers to the small grouped patrols of soldiers. Penelope, Silas, and Clyde pay no real attention to any of the scenes of the past confrontation. The electricity is still functioning. A handful of structures are in ruins, leaving a majority of the buildings left completely untouched by large munitions. With minimal damage to the streets, the presidential convoy snakes between holes in the ground.

Clyde parts ways with the President and the general, flying off of the aircraft carrier in his own private jet. A quick exchange of command onboard, and Silas soon sits beside Penelope on a separate government aircraft taking off for the *Aluan* capital.

"What is he up to? Do you think trusting Mr. Crowly is ideal?" Silas asks, while sitting down for the foreseeable future, the long flight back to the supercontinent of *Lycandia* starts. Penelope, sitting across from him, studies his suspicion.

"He has the technological infrastructure, especially now that we've allowed him clearance with our space program to help further it along."

"Yeah, a ninety-day program with no oversight that somehow needed money and expertise from the defense department. I just find those little details odd for a space expedition. He's also now a world leader," Silas says, looking back across to study Penelope.

"He is not a matter of national security. The money wasn't stolen, you know this. Clyde is working with us to restore *Aluan* to its rightful glory." She smirks confidently.

"What's he really getting out of this, being almost the single wealthiest person alive?" Silas asks, drumming his fingers contemplatively on the armrests.

"You'll see."

Luminous, the capital city of *Aluan, The United Republic of Briarhide* is a megacity reaching out for miles on the flat landscape, that is only broken up only by rivers with their sides ornately trimmed and flowered. The buildings comprising the city are a juxtaposition of structures made of hefty white granite mottled with gold, and elegantly crafted ivory towers of varying heights. The number of granite buildings vastly outnumbered that of the ivory stone skyscrapers, and these towers are found concentrated in greater commercial areas and are ornate with bronze and silver. The sun casting down from a cloudless sky as the city's ambiance of traffic, bird songs, and general bustle continues on.

Penelope and Silas emerge from the parked aircraft strutting down the gangway, and after nearly a full day on their flight, are greeted by a small crowd of shouting reporters. Including a line of intelligent agency workers tasked with security detail and the motorcade, all awaiting the president and general.

"Madam President! Is it true you've deployed special forces into forbidden, international neutral territory? Was there an executive command issued?" screams one reporter, bouncing up and down

"The terrorists responsible for the *Liekos* consulate building! Can you or General Sabaton give us some statements? Did you find them out there?" pesters another, somewhere in the crowd of roughly fifty.

"There's reports and rumors of collateral committed to the local populace of...uh, *Port Humility*," a third reporter inquires, stammering and checking a reminder note in his pad.

More questions are shouted out, the security informing the nagging reporters that no questions were to be answered as they continued to corral them. Penelope and Silas, practically encased by personnel, slink quickly and without a word, into the motorcade. The president and general roll off the tarmac in a blacked out truck, as seven identical vehicles follow.

Penelope and Silas's destination is the Central Intelligence Den, the convoy of vehicles rolling slowly after clearing the gate, the perimeter filled with watchful sniper groups perching in the trees and bushes until it sits beneath the aesthetically dull structure. A white granite dome without any windows, interconnected to this large dome, is eight smaller ones by surface tunnel enclosures connecting like legs. *Aluan's* agency for espionage and surveillance, the overgrowth on its property, being a feature and not a flaw. Silas's experienced eyes picking up numerous anti-magic devices hidden in underbrush.

Rising out of the vehicle, the personnel there move through their formalities and escort the president and general to the agency's glass doorway, tinted black to visibly shield what may be watching on the other side. The two disappear walking within.

"I'm not going to win reelection, so we won't have enough time to wait," Penelope shouts at the director of the agency standing up behind his desk.

"Things are nearly in place, Miss Briarpaw. Don't question my loyalty to the *Paladins* or my competence. I've spent months on end filtering through raw data provided by the three hundred tech shell companies under Mr. Crowly. On every citizen in *Aluan*, *Wulftheon* and even *Mirael* now," the agency director grumbles at Penelope, the gray wolf then adjusting his glasses with his fingers, hunching over while his other paw clicks speedily on his computer mouse.

CHAPTER THREE: The Weight OF Consequences

CLYDE STANDS OUTSIDE THE meeting room, separated by a wall made of gray glass with a foggy treatment. He takes a long slurp from his glossy gold travel thermos residing in one paw. In the middle of a cellphone call, he paces the silver and white receptionist lounge, communicating with someone on the other line using an earpiece. Holding his head high and roaming by the dark gray leather chairs. The room is sparse of much else decor, a faint vanilla aroma.

"I don't care. Lay off everyone that's up for a raise in all of my external shell companies across all sectors, if they've been there three. Just hire new labor from one of my several employment agencies in the regions, as needed, to fill any gaps." Clyde pauses, shifting his posture now while a panicked mumbling streams through the receiver end into his ear, but he cuts the individual off in a sharp tone. "Figure it out, regional manager. Or I'll find someone who will. You have a week to come back to me with results." Clyde disconnects the call and removes the receiver from his ear, mumbling aloud now. "Vacations...paid time off work...retirement bonus? Ridiculous, preposterous peasants."

The assistant holds her flatscreen computing device steadily in her grip and watches Clyde's scathing call with raised eyebrows the entire time and gulps before speaking. "So, um. Everything you assigned me for that project, you wanted completed by the end of today. What was it called again? 'Group Hug?' It's done, Mr. Crowly."

With an impatient tone rolling his shoulders back, Clyde flatly replies, "Fantastic. Unfortunately, there is still a loose end or two to tie up." He shoves his cellphone into his charcoal black pants pocket. He faces the assistant—a gray wolf with brunette hair in a ponytail and teal dress suit. Now with a free paw, he lifts his thermos to sip once more.

The assistant moves closer to Clyde and says, "Um, your wife, that popstar, Sally Stupor. She has been trying to reach you. She's complaining you haven't answered her texts." Her ponytail bounces as she repeatedly checks her notes on the screen.

Clyde freezes in place, but minutely shakes his head without looking at her, clasping the gleaming polished knob of the door to the meeting room, his tail and ears betraying his authentic surprise.

"Reach me? Hah, she's still on her *Mirael* tour, and has been for the last six months. Touring that whole country, pretty much." He snickers, adding snidely, "Honestly thought she would enjoy the space." He laughs. "Let Madam Stupify know I'll be free after this board meeting. Gas up the private jet that'll bring her to my estate. Then, me and her can have a riveting little chat." Clyde opens the semi-clear gray glass door and disappears into the meeting room.

"I'll relay the message. What is that?" The assistant scrunches her nose up.

"Mimosa."

The meeting room itself is plain in its decoration, a wide and flat spider-shaped table stretching from end to end of the space. A dozen *Lycandian* individuals are seated on either side of the table, adorning suit jackets with ties and matching accessories to the corporate palate shades of gray. A golden letter placard is sitting in front of each of them, going all the way from the letter 'A' through 'F,' keeping a certain level of anonymity. They sit on either side as three. Clyde quietly walks past them to the head of the table, placing down his golden thermos. A couple of the individuals present also possessing one of the gaudy things. A monitor lights up on the wall behind him as he clears his throat.

"Well…" He clicks a button and shows a graph. A green arrow appears, going straight up at ninety degrees. "*Crowclaw Global Conglomerates*, has achieved a thousand percent profit margin increase since last year. Especially in our digital space enterprises, pharmaceuticals, health insurance, and consumer products."

The *Lycandian* individual sitting behind the letter polished golden 'A' taps his pen on the table as he comments, "The *Aluanians* don't appear to be letting up any military activities in *Kranor*. There's unrest still occurring on the border between *Kranor* and *Mirael*, ever since the beginning of the coalition effort made against Snagglefang's regime a decade or so ago. We've gotten hundreds of new contracts from *Mirael* to beef up their defense capabilities. Sales are looking good."

Board Member B, also speaking up to Clyde. "We've essentially exhausted most of the underdeveloped countries around southern *Lycandia* of its labor and resources in terms of new growth." He clicks his pen nervously. "So the numbers haven't budged too much, at least on our end for the quarter. But we've maxed it."

Clyde reads over the first at Board Member A, addressing his concerns. "Oh yes, President Penelope will be ensuring *Aluan* will maintain freedom, wherever its interests may be. Herself and the *Federal Independence Party* are secure in their governance. Whether or not they win the coming election." Clyde lets his icy-blue eyes study their faces before asking, "What's the current number of our companies acquired through acquisition?"

Board Member C clears her throat and leans the elbows of her dark amber suit jacket onto the long meeting table. "Over the past year, sir? It's been close to ten thousand combined in all markets, from countries that we can participate in."

Clyde speaks to Board Member C. "These are pleasing results. The shareholders in my leasing and financing sectors have really enjoyed the upfront capital while we liquidate. This branch has performed the finest out of the thirty." Clyde sits himself at the head of the table, while the board members listen attentively. "Everyone has the same twenty-four hours, your task is to extrapolate every second of it outside of whatever sleep everyone can acquire, and generate a profit." He takes a pensive pause and drums his fingers loudly on the desk. "Ad space, luxury, and economic consumer products have been lucrative and all...But I have a new idea for our biochemical and pharmaceutical capabilities."

Board Member D speaks up now. "Oh? The previous idea was to incorporate necromancy magic...an agonizingly hard process to do in most of *Lycandia* under the radar, by the way, sir. Once we've succeeded in breaking the barrier of magical energy around *Homeworld's* atmosphere, we can achieve both deep space travel and immortality."

Clyde leans forward on the end of the desk, looking at Board Member D. "That plan is still in motion, yes, but we may be refining it based on what I have acquired in my brief excursion to *Ralawaith.* I have pieces of Chrisbane's machine. Unspeakable amounts of wealth and power to be harnessed, strewn across the cosmos, just waiting." Crowly waits and leans back in his chair, letting the board member relish in the potentiality seeing his mind churn through his expression of wonderment, turning his attention to the others around him to say, "But it is time to pivot while markets are low, by no coincidence. I have an exotic delivery coming with new opportunities in bioengineering."

Board Member B says, tilting his head, feigning curiosity. "You're going to enlighten us on what this delivery consists of?"

Clyde offers a cocky scoff and shakes his head, staring at Board Member A. "Does your personal bank account have enough commas in it to be speaking to me? Prying on my side projects? It's a special something my *Felidaen* friends and I have cooked up."

Board Member C tries to slice and dice the tension. "Didn't we have a cellular device product, or something coming out this month, from *Crowclaw Cellular?*"

Clyde stares down Board Member B for a brief second before lightening up his tone and energy, looking to the others and says, "Yes, I will be bringing a special update to the cellular services within *Silvium* from *Crowclaw Conglomerates*, for a test run. It will be going live soon from *Headquarters* right there in the city."

Board Member A ponders, "With *Aluan* pivoting so violently geopolitically, maybe it's now time to settle in *Ralawaith* further? I mean, *Port Humility* is a peasant town, five-ish miles wide. The purpose of its existence is occasionally refueling cargo ships and aircraft...maybe a pawful of times a year. Staging tropical storm relief during hurricane season. The population is literally impoverished mixed breeds, or whatever. Lepers of both continents. We'd be perfectly fine."

Board Member C points out, "The place could be bulldozed down in a week's time. Seeing the firepower, President Penelope showed up with...I'm shocked she didn't blast the place down to a molten glass parking lot in two minutes. You're close to her. Who or what was she looking for?"

"A bygone legend turned real. I don't suppose you have ever heard of the *Starwielder*?" Clyde asks Board Members A, C, and D. The other board members, and Member B, mumble and whisper to one another.

Clyde stands up again, saying, "I figured most of you have forgotten such things. But, as Supreme Chancellor of *Wulftheon*, I will now be backing any military exercises the *Aluan Republic* decides to conduct further. Do what you will, knowing this—'excursion'—and others like it, will be ongoing. I have witnessed this *Starwielder*."

Board Member B says, "So it's an overly glorified hunting trip, is it? So you can kill the last living thing of some scaly brutes long since wiped out. *Starwielder*? Hilarious fairytale, if you ask me."

Clyde Crowly drums his fingers together, grinning devilishly. "You need proof, is what I'm hearing."

Clyde picks up the remote to the computer prompter and flips it to a different browser window, displaying a video. The board members are sitting in silence now with blossoming intrigue.

The captivating recording is of a firefight battle for a crashed aircraft in the middle of some remote appearing jungle. Minax Bolide is seen amidst his comrades, who are exceedingly blurry in the shot as the shaky camera was fixated on just him at the time of recording from a chest height body cam of sorts. The board members are silent during the half minute of footage, the wobbly body cam providing a gritty point of view as the soldier advances through lush underbrush kneeling behind a mossy rock for cover. It captures the moment during a heated fire exchange, as a meteor suddenly slamming down from the sky in a spectacle.

The meteor makes contact with the aircraft, then explodes violently enough to throw debris and the *Aluan* soldier wearing body cam sent into a tumble, the video concluding.

Board Member B pipes up, staring still at the frozen screen. "I've never before seen magical powers like that, certainly not in my fifty-seven years alive. And where is this *Galanexian* now, Mr. Crowly?"

"Ah yes, the question worth multiple trillions of credits. It's evaded the *Paladins*, but I'll be putting more assets out. It'll inevitably be caught," Clyde says.

The meeting then concludes and the collected board members depart. Clyde moves closer to the individual standing up from the seat marked 'C.' A *Lycandian* Graywolf with ghostly silver fur all over his body is visible under his slate gray suit jacket. He leans in with a toothy smirk, his canine incisors peaking over his lip.

"Cravenfang, are you ready?" Crowly's arctic blue eyes nefariously bore into him as he asks in a low voice.

"Oh yes, Mr. Crowly. I've got what I need packed in my transit vehicle. I received confirmation this morning."

"Splendid, am I right?" asks another Graywolf *Lycandian*, moving from his seat behind the letter 'F.'

"You haven't seen anything yet," Clyde gloats to the pair as the remaining unassuming board members exit the room, leaving them to linger in their exchange.

Cyngosa is motionless in his drunken slumber. Unlike most occasions when choosing to intoxicate himself to numb the effects of his visions, this one is soon filled with animosity. A vivid nightmare begins; His translucent spirit floats up out of his sleeping physical body, still resting on the loveseat anchored below. Cyngosa's spirit hovers in some unknown area as the castle sizzles out of sight, unable to sense the temperature or feel anything.

Meanwhile, his physical body twists around uncomfortably in the loveseat, subconsciously twitching his ears and mumbling. He hears screaming reverberating off cavern walls that materialize before his widening eyes, catching flashes of robed individuals moving like worker ants in the near total darkness before bright red fire illuminates the dream space, forcing Cyngosa's spirit body to turn and tumble in fright, discovering he's stuck in place.

The layout of the cavern becomes more clear in Cyngosa's continuing nightmare, the screaming coming and going still. The flashing scene of a dreadful red glowing altar in the darkness passes his vision, among others, in a startling jumble. The last sustaining image is a snowy mountain peak, otherwise unremarkable in the landscape surrounding it, but this peak features a towering statue holding a sword. Cyngosa's ethereal spirit body senses a tug. In the same moment, the alpine sight before his eyes snaps away and he is back in his body, in troubled sleep.

Cyngosa is the first of the bunch to wake up, granted not a very restful sleep due to the horrid nightmare and the type of furniture he chose. Standing up from the loveseat he slept upright in his back didn't appreciate it, he catches the warm gray light of morning creeping through the snow splattered windows. The soft crackling of the dying fire and blowing wind are the only sounds consecutively happening as the others lie asleep, Khelu tossing and turning, Saaliha and Minax resting peacefully. Cyngosa stretches his muscles silently before walking over to the fireplace to salvage and reinvigorate the fire from the remaining embers.

He notices his depleted healing totem near the bed; he tosses it into the growing fire, watching Dorrion, who appears to him to be asleep, but when he inspects closer with concern, Cyngosa doesn't hear Dorrion breathing.

"Hey? I had another vision in my dream. This one wasn't an angelic messenger," Cyngosa whispers down to him. He brushes his paw against Dorrion's shoulder, his body feeling weary under his touch. Cyngosa felt a pit in his stomach form and the grogginess left him. His emerald-pierced ears go flat to his head and his tail curls down. Dorrion had passed away, possibly in his sleep overnight, from his injuries or exposure.

Cyngosa whispers, a little louder this time out loud, "No...you can't be. Not now." Letting a defeated sigh and whimper out, he slumps his shoulders, sagging his posture.

Minax stirs, rolling onto his back before sitting upright. Along with the others waking up, during the interlude in which Cyngosa is first to inspect Dorrion's bandages, he anxiously feels his pulse before accepting the grim truth. Cyngosa felt his heart stop in his chest, a tightness forming in his throat, then clenching his jaw. Saaliha yawns and stretches her arms over her head while Khelu and Minax greet everyone. "Good morning."

"I don't know what's so good about it...Dorrion didn't make it. I don't know how else to say this. I'm sorry. He died in his sleep," Cyngosa laments to Minax, Saaliha, and Khelu with emotional anguish on his face.

Minax and Khelu are visibly saddened as the news strikes them, it did not come as a shock but rather a dread Saaliha approaches Dorrion, who is laying still as if still asleep "I..." she pauses and kneels by the bed, and places her paws on Dorrion to cross his arms gently and slide the sheet's over his head, finishing her sentence after a heartbroken gulp, "didn't even get to say goodbye..."

"He was awake, and healing just fine. Just last night…" Cyngosa explains, his voice catching, sensing the weight of grief and anger settle in as the grim reality unravels for them.

Saaliha flicks his retractable claws. She scans the floor beneath the chair and raises an eyebrow at the two empty bottles. "Maybe some over-coping?" Cyngosa returns an annoyed expression to her but doesn't say a word, instead downing sanitized water from his backpack's canteen.

Khelu interjects, "C'mon Saaliha, we're all messed up here and to boot, we were running on fumes yesterday."

"I thought we were going to do this in shifts?" Saaliha inquires, turning away from the bed and gazes at Khelu accusingly.

"Are you saying this is my fault? That he died on my watch." Cyngosa stares down Saaliha, a challenge unmasked in his tone.

Minax quietly sits still in the armchair, his head propped on his fist, his purple eyes landing on each of them in turn as they argue, accuse and bicker. Saaliha snappily retorts, "Weren't you last on—"

Saaliha is cut-off as Minax leaps out of the chair violently with a gavel-like thump of his quartz tail on the smooth stone floor. "Enough. Silence! It is absolutely disgusting what has become of this world." He pauses as the others freeze. "Things were not perfect in my time. What I have witnessed myself in the last few weeks alone, however," Minax pauses as steamy smoke rises from the slits in his scaly snout, "the stunning apathy toward living things and each other…self-indulgent consumerism, narcissism…The abuse of your technology and mechanical advancements…The petty profit wars, the genocides…and by the Creator the bigotry!"

"Well, we don't live in some fantasy world. Surprise Minax. Everyone's doing the best they can in the face of their vices, corruption, and flaws," Cyngosa says, keeping his ground even if Minax Bolide tower's almost four feet taller than him.

Minax then strides past Khelu, Saaliha, and Cyngosa, who were all still frozen in place listening to his rant. He leans against the doorway to glance back at them, adding in a cooler more somber tone, "Dorrion hasn't even been dead for a day, The last wish of our friend and we fail to rise to the occasion. The tragic loss of lives in *Port Humility*, from all involved, is still fresh in my mind. I don't know about all of you? I need to pray and meditate. But continue bickering if you all must. I need silence, and out of this wretched castle."

Saaliha, Khelu, and Cyngosa gaze at one another for a silent moment during Minax's exit in the wake of his outburst. Khelu is first to speak. "Minax has a point. We can't be fighting or arguing over this." She glares at Saaliha and Cyngosa in turn, noticing the tension between the two hasn't subsided yet. Saaliha's tail erratically lashes and she folds her arms, Cyngosa grimacing with an annoyed look on his face but stares between Khelu and Saaliha.

Cyngosa says, "The nightmare I had last night was all too real. It's no coincidence we ended up here."

"What do you mean?" Saaliha says, looking directly at Cyngosa now.

"Another angelic vision?" Khelu asks, her gold eyes searching his sour expression to see the fear and slight worry brimming through.

"Much worse," Cyngosa states with a sigh, rubbing his temples with his fingers.

Now alone, Minax glides, his great wings fanned open, out of the castle's front doors, smoldering in restrained fury. He stomps his feet into the twelve inch deep snow covering the grounds with loud crunches until he reaches the thirty-foot wall, angrily leaping and flying right over it and heading up the steep mountain summit. A soft drizzle of snow flurries greets Minax on his trip.

Staring up at the gray overcast sky above him, he shouts at the dense clouds, "The *Starwielder*..." He scoffs, continuing. "Is it some cruel joke? These 'blessed' and apparently limitless cosmic powers, yet I cannot shape reality how I want it? Bend the rules even when I know it's objectively fair? I failed to stop the genocide of my people, failed to save my wife."

Minax takes four additional crunchy stomps through the fresh snow, unaffected by the cold even in his simple clothing worn underneath his *Starwielder* armor, whilst a gust whistles through the mountain summit. He mumbles to himself, "I don't suffer any self delusion of my own shortcomings, my mistakes, and my flaws, or my poor decisions." He chuckles at himself. "My judgment of all of this might have been in fact too quick, maybe flawed. These plights could befall any conscious being and their fellows, really. How can I possibly put out billions of tiny fires?"

Minax is now scaling up the mountain, giving a white wooly mountain ram with two heads asleep on a ledge nearby quite a shock as it lifts its heads up to the sounds of scraping claws on rock. The two-headed ram opens their brown eyes and observes Minax before resuming its nap, uninterested in the *Galanexian*. Minax is preoccupied with his thoughts, not even noticing the ram stirring nearby to him as he crawls vertically up toward the mountain's peak with internal determination, including the biting, crisp cold air.

Finally reaching the peak, Minax rises through the low cloud covering that breaks upon the mountain while he scans the view above and around. The sight is like laying in a field of soft orange, yellow, and gray cotton with the daylight sun beaming down from blue skies. A melodic voice fills Minax's ears.

"You have a great fury burning in your chest, Starwielder, an anger that is disorganizing your thoughts. Don't lose sight of your duties now, being ruled by emotions."

"I have not lost sight of my duties. Injustices to my own people, my allies, must not go unanswered. My anger isn't self-centered. It's fuel for the greater cause. I am more than ready to face Eradicator. It probably won't be long, given the recent activity of beings serving it." Minax turns his head about, trying to see if the voice is something he imagined, or a trick of his ears, flaring his nostrils as he inhales the fresh air.

"Turning to actions reasoned with anger will not bring you inner peace and tarnish your focus. You are also allowing frustration to fester within you from events and actions outside of your control, Minax Bolide. Resentment is poison," the harmonious sounding voice says.

Minax states, "I agree with your first statement. I still have the power of choice, and in how I respond." He pauses and closes his purple eyes. Sighing, he adds, "Including the weight of the consequences afterward."

The angelic voice in Minax's head speaks again. *"You do. The Creator gifts freewill to all sentient beings, out of a boundless love beyond mortal comprehension. The path is treacherous, Starwielder Minax Bolide. Remember that the true evil adversaries you must face are more than other mere mortals. You must continue holding your own flaws in check."*

Minax asks, "If that is so, why hasn't the Creator just flooded this world, destroy it and build anew then? If I'm truly unable to solve the world's problems myself. The *Starwielder*'s entire purpose is fighting against evil forces, especially existential doom. I spent most of my youth training, striving and preparing myself under some delusion of grandeur."

"Then perhaps consider the burden isn't entirely just for you in saving the world. Other solutions, or maybe people, require saving. Inspiring and igniting hope."

Minax sits in silence, and deep heavy thought, his face expressing the options he considered. He lets out an exhale, lowering his head with a humble grin. "I will make my case before the government of *Aluan*. If they believe the *Starwielder* has returned, then they will take into consideration the threat of *Eradicator* and his servant's nefarious schemes. I will try diplomacy." The euphonic voice doesn't give a response, the wind blowing and causing his armor to creak and clothing to flap being the only sounds.

Minax didn't rush away, his feet perching on footholds and his claws clasping the cold rock with rigid fingers. His mind wandering to his wife Tanza, replaying the memory, the wound of loss reopens itself inside Minax. Dorrion floats to mind next. Having only known the older *Lycandian* for a month's time, the loss of his friendly treatment and mentorship hits home once more, like a cold grip in his chest akin to the air around him on the peak. Savoring the isolation for a little longer before shifting around to descend back to Cyngosa, Saaliha, and Khelu.

Everyone inside the castle is separately mourning, but carrying on with determination. Saaliha is in another room in a dissociated state of mind repairing her armor using the field equipment from her backpack, tinkering and recollecting herself. In the fluid jump through the Cosmic Decagon monument in the middle of their losing battle, then dealing with her wounded godfather.

Prior, Saaliha didn't have time to take true stock of what she has left, but now with a moody hiss she meticulously counts her remaining arrows in her quiver next to her bow. Cyngosa's carefully crafted and enchanted crow shaped totems he made her from weeks ago in *Port Liekos*, laying next to her bow and quiver.

Upon looking at the three ruby colored wooden crows, infused with a magical and dangerous metal, she thinks about her exchange with Cyngosa earlier, pondering if she reacted poorly. Pulled from her thoughts to look at her mini-welder she has had in her bug out bag since escaping from Moonwane Estate, her home. It finally runs out of gas and material before it can finish completely repairing her black and gold plated armor. She discards it in the castle's basement while she curiously ransacks what she could make use of lying around the old stronghold. Her racing thoughts repeat as anger sears in her chest, using it to drive back the gnawing grief. She practically grew up with Dorrion all her life. Saaliha silently vowed when she dismissed herself from Cyngosa and Khelu earlier, moments after Minax's departure, she would set out to destroy those responsible. Cyngosa's nightmarish vision be damned. She is typing inputs into a computer program, Khelu wanders unannounced into the cramped study Saaliha has taken up to distance herself.

"You holding up, girl, you good?" she asks Saaliha, her solemn eyes noting her tense posture with hunched shoulders standing over the wooden table, the fancy candle holder and its candles thrown off the surface, left laying on the floor. Khelu bites her lip and takes two steps closer before stopping, giving Saaliha ample space.

"Khelu, you know what's crazy? *Wulftheon* borders *Aluan*, a funny detail about this supercontinent that slipped my unhinged mind," Saaliha says, the whiskers on her nose twitching on one side. She stands straight up, turning to face Khelu while her paws grab her empty backpack.

"I was kinda aware. Where are you going with this?" Khelu says and curiously takes a step or two closer to look at her computer screen.

"We are indeed in *Wulftheon*, somewhere here in this wide mountain range," Saaliha says. Khelu can see a red dot hovering on the wide satellite view being provided.

"*Aluan* is probably a day and a half away. But not on foot," Saaliha says, Khelu catching on quickly as her eyebrows narrowed.

"We should talk with Minax before deciding anything, and why go to *Aluan*?"

"I feel it's long overdue we bust the door down, and kick some ass."

"What the hell are you talking about? The five of us?"

Cyngosa sits in the cushioned old-fashioned loveseat he slept in the previous night, brooding with Eos perching above him quietly on the backrest. The sheets of the bed Dorrion lays in drawn up higher to cover him completely. Cyngosa is preoccupied carving a totem to put on the long table in the room with a clenched jaw, the mood palpable enough for Eos to sense, causing them to droop their beak. A growing assortment of other totems that he prepares to enchant on the elegant table in front of him, already chiseled with the appropriate symbol.

With a creaking of the doors, Minax returns from his mountain top trip, returning into the spacious living room as Khelu is tearing up the last portion of the smashed wooden chairs to toss into the fireplace, pulling Cyngosa's attention up from his carving. Minax's reappearance pulls Saaliha into the grand living room, laying her eyes on the crestfallen *Starwielder*. Khelu, her mouth forming but failing to find any words to say, feeling a tightness in her throat all of a sudden.

"I have given it thought, friends. But I'm going as an ambassador of *Trinity of Tranquility*. The flesh. The mind. The soul. I am the next lineage of the *Starwielder*, some of the leaders of *Aluan* or *Edon*. Maybe we can try reaching leaders from *Mirael.* Dorrion might have a relative, possibly."

"If you feel this is the best course of action, Minax," Khelu says, running a paw through her knotted hair, touching the tiny colorful beads with her fingers before sighing, looking toward the bed and Dorrion.

"I dunno," Cyngosa says, climbing up from the chair and placing his latest carving down on the cushion. Minax gives Cyngosa an expression of intrigue, his tone alluding to more.

"Really, diplomacy?" Saaliha folds her arms, shifting her weight to her right hip and silently cracking her tail behind. Slitting the lids over her glowing pink eyes. "Is this the part where you tell Minax about your vision from your dream last night?"

Minax walks closer to all of them, dragging his tail with its spiky quartz tip carelessly, his gaze going from Cyngosa to Saaliha. "Vision?" Minax asks.

"After I drifted off to sleep last night with you MInax, I had some disturbing dreams. I heard screaming, I saw robed crazies goose-step marching. An altar, underneath some snow mountain, glowing with demonic magical energy. I know that shit when I see it. What are the odds of all the snowy regions in Homeworld? It might be here."

"The *Armageddon Cult*," Minax says with an inhale. He exhales with a grunt.

"What are we going to do with Dorrion?" Cyngosa asks, casting a sorrowful glance at them, adding. "Saaliha is technically his closest relative here. The decision should be hers, I say."

"Sure thing, Cyngosa."

"Agreed, bro," Khelu says. Saaliha, though still emotionally raw, throws an appreciative look toward Cyngosa for considering it.

"Say our final goodbyes to him, but I don't want to bury him in this frozen hell," Saaliha says, her pierced ears drooping. She looks around at her disheveled companions, all bathed in midday sunlight streaming through the castle windows. Outside, the sky has cleared of last night's snow, with sunbeams shining through the drifting clouds.

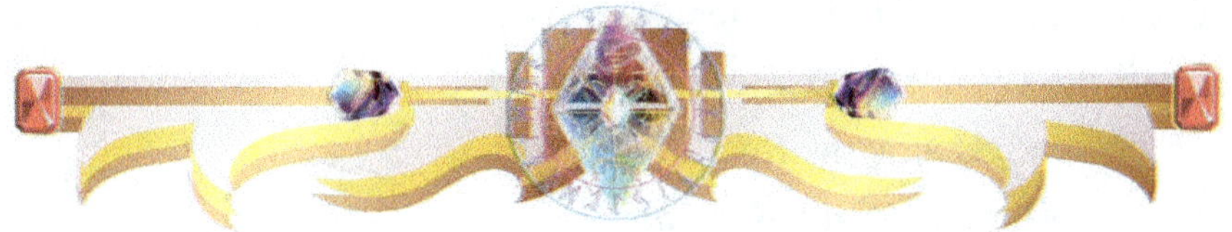

They collectively agree to hold a service for Dorrion outside in the evening chilly air, the wind not nearly as gusty as the night their group first arrived in the strange land of *Wulftheon*. Cyngosa and Minax clear and pack down the snow of their chosen spot in silence, offering on another a dull wet eyed look now and again. Saaliha and Khelu go in search of more wood before it gets too dark to see, Eos accompanying them. To their luck, tucked in the corner of the castle's courtyard, a firewood shed appears as Khelu and Saaliha wander, but stay tight to the castle.

Khelu and Saaliha return with armfuls of wood to their selected spot, informing Cyngosa and Minax. Quickly the four of them make a group trip, acquiring enough wood to prop Dorrion's body, wrapped up in the bed quilt still, off the ground two feet high evenly. It is the best they can do, the last sunbeams of dusk glimmering on the horizon as stars peak through the blanket of blackness above.

Dorrion's body rests on his funeral pyre now after they stiffly lift him up and place him down on it, each paying their silent respects. Saying their final verbal goodbyes with stooped postures, down turned facial features, and closed in limbs.

"Light it up. You living-breathing flamethrower," Cyngosa says, glancing at Minax slowly, slumping his head, tears finally showing. Minax inhales, breathing out a burst of fire at the base of the pyre to set it ablaze. The very act leaves a grief-stricken look on his face, witnessing the fire swarm through the dry wood quickly. The growing embers provide warmth in the wintry air, but it's bittersweet.

Standing in the ambiance of the crackling bonfire, the quiet moan of a soft breeze and the flames are the only noise until Minax breaks through the sounds, clearing his throat.

When the sun sets after the final battle
And the rain sprinkles Creator's tears
We will be with thee across the heavens
Hero, you mustn't have any fears.
As you walk through the valley
Great hero you can finally rest
And your name and your image shall live on
As you lie amongst the best.
Great hero, thou hast travelled far and wide
And walked throughout the land
Some battles you have fought alone
And some alongside your band.
We thank you, adventurer for the battles you've fought
And everything you have done
And in the creator's great holy game
We can finally say you've won.

"Beautiful, did you come up with that yourself?" Saaliha asks, watery eyed with a trembling chin with her whiskers flat once Minax concludes.

"No, a *Galanexian* funeral ballad," Minax answers her in a soft monotone. However, he did not turn his head away, mesmerized by the burning funeral pyre. "What is this castle called, anyway?" Minax asks, to no one in particular among his silent mourning companions. Eos perches on Cyngosa's shoulder, the blueish pink phoenix offering comfort to him the best they could.

Khelu, examining Minax Bolide's slacking wings occasionally brushed by a soft gust, says, "*Solstice Keep,* I was curious myself. I looked it up with Saaliha when we got online a couple hours ago. Don't get excited. It took over twenty minutes to load a map. The signal is," she chuckles, "horrible, to put it bluntly. It's an abandoned *Paladin* castle, from centuries ago, built on the summit of Mt. Sleet."

Cyngosa, staying nonverbal, raises his eyebrows and widens his wet eyes at the news Khelu delivers, his mind still churning his final conversations with Dorrion and deep within himself Cyngosa feels an ironclad conviction formulates. His grief muddled with anger as well. With a steely resolve, he vowed in Dorrion's memory he would get Clyde Crowly, or die.

Minax stares around the nocturnal wintery landscape, his purple eyes holding a watery sadness to them at the coincidence, sarcastically announcing with an amused expression on his face, "Heh, how fitting for the likes of us. Right?"

CHAPTER FOUR: An Enticing Bounty

P URPLE, PINK AND YELLOW neon lights cast fantastical colors on the inside and outside walls of the clubhouse styled bar within the *Porcelain Orchid* casino. Monique, bartending for a small number of patrons, is approached by a Graywolf wearing a black suit jacket and pants, his outfit making him stand out from the more casually dressed attendees present. Monique, being a Timberdire breed *Lycandian*, based on her glossy bronze fur. Monique has short black hair, and two protruding upper fangs, and wears a grungy tank top and black jean shorts, a zesty floral perfume wafting off her person. Monique acts like she didn't notice the wolf staring at her, but as she's wiping down the bar, he leans on it with his elbows and asks, loudly enough over the music and general commotion around them, "Monique Tempestfang?"

Monique's glowing indigo eyes catapulted up from her busywork and straight at this stranger, who apparently knew her family's last name, giving him a hostile and suspicious look. She replies, "Who's asking? Let me see a badge number, or zip it."

The Graywolf reaches into his jacket's breast pocket, then shows Monique a business card while also explaining himself. "I'm a contractor from a *Crowclaw Conglomerate* private defense company called *Iron Group*."

"Look pal, I don't do contract work on the record books anymore, for anyone. Now what will it be? How about a rum on the rocks? You look like you could use a stiff drink," Monique says, in the process of drying a pint glass in her paws and not even bothering to examine the Graywolf's card.

"Is that so?" He slides the card on the bar over to her, using his manicured claw. "Well, I'm certain you can still help me out. The line blurs between 'contract work' and freelance marauding. I know you and some former colleagues of yours dance all over that line around here." Monique could pick up on the slight effort to intimidate her behind the veneer of politeness.

Monique narrows her eyes, standing her ground and giving this stranger a dirty look, lifting a chrome bat.

"Alrighty asshole, humor me or I'll have to bonk your dome in with my anti-creep stick."

The Graywolf shakes his head with a bemused smirk, saying, "You've seen videos, images, probably even memes at this point circulating the mainstream of a dragon beast, attacking the *Aluan Navy* during President Penelope's special military operation?"

"Of course I have. So, let me guess." Monique playfully scratches under her chin. "You need to hire a bunch of rent'a'thugs and then are going to chase after it, am I right?"

The *Iron Group* contractor raises his eyebrows with a grin spreading across his face. "That is putting it rather bluntly, but yes. But my employer is offering substantial payouts after this beast's inevitable capture. Dead or alive," he says, making a casual gesture of a cutting motion across his throat with his thumb.

"How substantial are we talking here? Cut the vague charade, already," Monique states, leaning over the bar.

"Ohh no. Unless you agree to cooperate. Your former colleagues around, by chance? Straywolf and Paradigm," the contractor asks, shifting his tone of voice from stern to sweet.

"I haven't spoken to either of them in almost a year now, blocked on all forms of communication. Your guess is as good as mine as to what they've been up to," Monique says.

"Apparently aiding this dragon, beast, creature thing. I've got proof," the *Iron Group* contractor says in turn, not revealing too much as Monique appears impressed, or perhaps concerned, by this news.

"That's wild. Um, I guess, good for them?" Monique comments, feigning a lack of concern as she keeps her poker-face up against the contractor. She internally admits she is certainly curious what the dynamic pair has gotten into.

"Contact me if you'd like to join the hunt. Have yourself a pleasant night," the contractor finishes with a forced smile, then checks his cellphone from his pocket for the time and turns away from the bar and Monique, walking past an entranceway with a portion of the casino's large slot machine area in open view. She watches him depart without a word, but certainly not because she didn't have anything to say. Monique was just the wiser.

Watching, and keeping attentive to all the activities of the entire bar from the furthest table, sits a roguish-looking tiger. His bright orange feline eyes flash and a scrutinizing expression melts over his features, watching as the Graywolf turns to leave. The tiger stands up from the shadowed table and walks to the bar and Monique. The lights illuminate his brown leather wide-brimmed hat and black denim vest on his slim torso wearing dark worn jeans, and once he leans over the bar, he widens his smile to Monique, showing his left golden fang and a few subtle scars on his face.

"What was that about, a law enforcement detective sniffing around?" the tiger, twitching his whiskers, asks Monique, making her divert her gaze up to him as he lifts his glass to drink. Monique dismisses the thoughts of her ex and her ex's step-brother.

"No, a private contractor snooping around for warm bodies to enlist for some kind of hunt. What's up Zane, need another drink?" Monique answers him. Zane's eyes dart to the business card still on the bar and he smirks looking at it after finishing a long drink from the golden brown liquor inside.

"Nope, finishing my second round now matter of fact." Zane then asks, "A hunt, you say. After a person?" He adds an amused chuckle, continuing on when he picks up the business card without an objection from Monique still working behind the bar, flipping the small paper card between his fingers noisily. "Heh, you can almost *feel* the money."

"He mentioned it was that dragon beast thing seen flying and causing mayhem around *Port Humility*. You can deal with it if you want. My raiding, piracy and mercenary days are done," Monique says matter-of-factly.

Zane, his whiskers twitching as his mind calculates, shrugs a shoulder and says, "Hmph, THAT dragon beast? There hasn't been a bounty yet that's escaped my claws. See you around, Monique." The tiger bounty hunter tips his leather hat and turns from the bar and places his finished glass on it, plucking the sliced orange peel off it to munch on while he trailing after the contractor into the intensely vivid casino.

Zane strolls between the slot machines, paying no heed to the individuals preoccupied with gambling, or the flashing lights and many, often unbearably obnoxious sounds coming from all the machines and chit-chat. He notices the contractor heading toward one of the exits with bodyguards in tow, gaining on him before he could walk out of the doors and disappear into the city.

"Hey there, mate, hold up a sec," he calls out, not caring that two bouncers approach him. Zane then shows off the business card between two fingers of his paw. "I hear you goin' dragon hunting."

The *Iron Group* contractor turns around to address Zane, raising an eyebrow and staring down his snout at the *Felidaen* stranger. He takes in the tiger's appearance and wardrobe before replying to him, the bodyguards present keeping alert, sizing him up as well. "As a matter of fact, yes. Why? Are you a friend, or perhaps an associate of Monique's?

"Oh no, not really. We gravitate to similar social circles, mate. But I'm certainly a third party option that's interested in this," Zane replies, his golden fang aglow in the light as he gives a toothy smile, continuing on as he extends a paw to the contractor. "Allow me to introduce myself as Topaz Talon."

The contractor takes the bounty hunter's paw in a firm shake before he says, "Well, Mr. Topaz? What is it that you can offer my employer?" He folds his arms across his chest.

Zane, or 'Topaz Talon,' smiles and answers with arrogance in his tone, "I'm one of the best bounty hunters in *Port Liekos.* Ever heard of the *Golden Skull Buccaneers*?"

"Yes, a pirate nuisance against fair trade on the ocean of the southern coast of *Lycandia,* to a handful of countries. A skeevy bunch," the contractor comments condescendingly, keeping a smug on his face.

Returning his own toothy grin, Zane continues. "Yes. But I've never let my quarry escape me. Dead or alive, I bring them in. Hiring me is a no brainer. I don't have to be burdened by those pesky international or local laws, civil liberties, no due process, rules of engagement, or ethics. I don't answer to some government agency...I'm the boss..." Zane trails off to chuckle murderously, before finishing. "And I don't show mercy."

"Excellent. Will it be just you?" the contractor asks.

In sync, the group exits the *Porcelain Orchid*, preoccupied in conversation, outside into the evening humid night of *Port Liekos*. The neon illuminated towers of the megacity varied in height, but even from the bustling street level, the tropical trees growing on some of the buildings were visible enough. With a plethora of sounds washing over them, live music and ambiance of the crowds walking along the sidewalks and passing traffic. The fragrance of sweet smoking tobacco from hookahs, including an array of different street foods, wafting in the salty coastal air that strikes Zane's nostrils. His gut gives a quiet rumble of complaint. However, the bounty hunter dismisses his hunger, keeping his attention elsewhere.

"No, I lead a chapter in the South Sea pirate alliance, the *Golden Skull Buccaneers* themselves, in fact," Zane says, strolling with a swagger in his stride beside the contractor. The bodyguards encircling them along the walk, as they drift away from the pedestrian traffic to an area with no curious passersby. Still under the glow of colorful lights. Zane's piercing orange eyes notice the contractor's poker face in their verbal exchange slip for a moment upon realizing who he is as his eyebrows shoot up and he clears his throat. Zane clarifies, "I'll have a crew of muscle with me that knows how to get down and dirty, on sea, land, and air."

His initial impressed reaction fading by this point, the contractor gestures to one of his bodyguards to pass over a thin computer screen into his possession. In the same motion, he searches through the device, as he replies to Zane in a sustained condescending tone.

"Yes, yes. That's grand, mister uh, Topaz Tooth, er Talon. Whatever, I just need to know if you are in. Then we'll proceed giving away any critical information to you and your crew."

"Aye, dapper dude. I'm in." Zane nods, removing his leather duster hat.

The wolf contractor grins, showing him the screen. "I'm sure you've seen circulated images of the *Galanexian*. However, I believe this highly classified video will help you grasp the full extent of its capabilities," the *Iron Group* contractor says to Zane, not looking away. The bounty hunter is hardly intimidated by the hype up, eagerness on his face while his lips curl over his two curving canine teeth, revealing his golden implant. "Bring it on. Let's see it already, mate."

The contractor shifts the touch screen device in his paws around to let Zane see for himself, pressing the play button on a recorded video. The bounty hunter observes silently as the recording starts. Its point of view is through a helmet camera. Opening in some rugged jungle terrain, there's lots of jostling around as the wearer traverses a battlefield based on the explosive audio sounds and shouting. The video cuts to approaching some kind of crashed aircraft Zane watches, seeing the *Galanexian* emerging from it with a *Lycandian* figure.

Zane lets a soft scoff escape, recognizing two of the individuals helping the *Galanexian* escape as his whiskers fan out and his nostrils flare. Still watching the video recording from the soldier's camera, he grows silent once again when the video catches part of the moment in which the asteroid crashes into the aircraft wreckage. The recording gets wobbly and chaotic as the wearer obviously fights for their life, but portions of the last *Galanexian*, and the *Trinity's* escape through some tear in time and space, is without a doubt noticed in blips before the video concludes with snowy static.

"Something amuse you?" the contractor inquires, pursing his lips, intrigued by Zane's reaction.

"That Direwolf *Lycandian*, and that Timberwolf there…Heh, just some former coworkers of mine, that's all." Zane brushes his whiskers thoughtfully with his fingers, also scratching at his chin. The contractor's eyebrows raise right up at this new detail. No doubt his eyes were wide behind the shades on his face, but Zane continues. "So it can hurl a whole asteroid down onto your head and randomly rip open gateways in space and time? That's outside the fact I've heard talk going around. It can breathe fire, fly, and is almost twice our average height, strength threshold, and speed. Did I miss anything?"

"Nope, for now at least. The reward is currently set at five hundred million." The contractor offers the device back to the bodyguard whom it originated from and then writes down an address on another one of his business cards, giving it over to Zane. "We'll see you soon, Mr. Topaz, appreciate you doing business with us."

The *Lycandian* contractor steps away, his bodyguard entourage following in tandem. Zane raises the new business card, closer into the neon yellow and green light from above him to look at it closer. A feeling of achievement filling him as he lets out a murderous purr, unlocking a familiar thirst.

The hunt was on.

CHAPTER FIVE: The Paladins Patriotic Revolution

ONE OF THE GRANITE structures *of Aluan's* capitol in *Luminous* is a gargantuan *Lycandian* head, the visage carved into a snarling howl. The massive bust is supported by three wide circular floors underneath, with huge cylinder columns, mighty buttresses, and sturdy archways. This is the *Bastion of Benevolence*, where the representatives of *Aluan's* twenty stateships each would convene for court, congressional, and other civil matters for the entire country. Within the bland white granite hearing room, Penelope stands behind an off-center polished wooden podium while being debriefed by the congress and top security advisors.

"Is it not true! That you commanded General Silas Sabaton and *The Tempest Vortex* battle group to attack the neutral stateship sovereignty of *Port Humility* located on the coast of the restricted island continent of *Ralawaith*, Madam President?" Senator Billy 'Boogaloo' Benson, a heavyset and elderly senator and a true fan of the theatrics with long white hair draping to the shoulders of his slate gray suit. Leaning into his microphone to ask, sitting at a long table with the other inquirers assigned to the incident in *Port Humility*. In less than a full day, the government had mobilized and selected, with unbiased, its participants. To Penelope's expectancy, the hearing was a brutal bureaucratic inquisition and she alone would face the onslaught of questions to verbally bat off.

"Yes, I am commander and chief," Penelope replies to Billy Benson, tossing dagger eyes and a confident expression at him. "But I did not attack its native people directly. We acted on extremely time sensitive intel, to close in and destroy our enemies before they became more difficult to find."

"You would risk our troops' lives so frivolously? Most of the international world alliances, syndicates, hell, even some criminal organizations even know that the ancient monster-filled island nation is to be left alone." Senator Benson shoots his accusations at Penelope with his blue eyes going wide. The other seated heads present at the table quietly nod.

"Do you think I'm too afraid to crush our enemies?" Penelope snaps, with a defensive tone in her voice, having been going in circles for the last thirty minutes, grinding her patience slowly.

Senator Benson, pumping clenched fists in the air, scoffs boisterously. "A conundrum that my constituents, colleagues and I will see answered."

Senator Amethyst Alexandria speaks next into her microphone, a Graywolf sitting next to Senator Benson in her white dress suit. "Understandably, we've looked into the report from the Department of External Defense." She clears her throat and adds into the microphone, directed more toward the others assembled than just Penelope Briarpaw. "Senator Osgrin's disappearance is rather alarming. He's been missing for a week. Hasn't answered any emails, phone calls, or text messages. There has been no announced vacation."

Penelope adamantly taps fingers on the podium's smooth wooden surface before speaking. "It shouldn't be that alarming. His body was discovered amongst these 'Stardust Elementalists'—religious extremists. He was witnessed working with them to attack and kill our soldiers. These maniacs were sheltering amongst the locals and aiding *Trinity of Tranquility.* You remember the terrorists responsible for what happened in *Port Liekos?*"

"Yes, we discussed it at length during our emergency meeting after the physical and cyber attack on the consulate. We didn't agree on immediate military action. We merely met with our intelligence agencies and agreed to gather more information. This accusation of Osgrin should not be taken lightly. The officials from *Liekos* have to weigh in as well, concerning the attack that occurred on their soil. Congress didn't get to put a vote in, nor the senate on what was *Aluan's* next course of action. You took this upon yourself," Senator Alexandria announces.

"Is that so? Letting our enemies just slip away even as they've had sympathizers sabotage us from within?" Penelope asks, sounding disappointed, looking over as General Sabaton clears his throat and stands up from his seat.

General Silas Sabaton interjects, "If I may, Senator. We have significant reason to believe the late Senator Osgrin was a double agent. He wasn't kidnapped or held hostage. He was directly involved in orchestrating the attack on the consulate in the first place."

"This is a serious breach. The victims and the Aluanian people deserve severe inquiry into our intelligence agencies as soon as possible, then. These are breaches of national security level," Senator Alexandria says. Penelope smugly observes them go back and forth amongst themselves for the time being, savoring the reprieve of questioning.

One of Alexandria's aides speaks up. "I agree, Senator, and for the sake of our nation's integrity, this must become a priority. Where does the corruption stem from, and what else will we find?"

A *Lycandian* in a three piece, velvety dark purple suit, with a silver tie moves from sitting next to Senator Benson at the table, then slides up close with Senator Alexandria's aides after seating himself next to him, leaning on one elbow with a cocky demeanor.

"Nah! Don't pay attention to any of that nonsense. Hey! Look at this sports ball instead!" He shoves a shiny large golden rubber ball into the aide's face gently. The sharply dressed *Lycandian* politician continues speaking, "The *Aluan* people are doing splendidly, exactly where we have them and how they're living their lives. I don't know the source of this paranoia most of you have in your party. Just wait until we crush your state in the semi-finals next month." He pulls the ball away with a playful grin, staring at the aide with an arrogant smirk.

"Tremendous. Now we're getting somewhere. Understand?" Penelope's tone drips with sarcasm while she also folds her arms under her chest, leaning back away from the podium in front of her stiffly standing form.

Senator Alexandria chimes in, "Whoa, not so fast! You had covert sea, land, and air operations going without the government or the public's knowledge. Causing the deaths of locals, as well as some of our soldiers. Those waters and that region are off-limits, you know this. You've broken several international laws, you know this," Senator Alexandria grumbles with agitation in her tone, her ears bending forward through her black hair with the ends dyed faintly purple. We've been rolling back our global policies, as have some of the *Felidaens* in *Perilith*. The only real tenuous peace we have between our supercontinents and the great many countries it affects. Your actions stand to ruin what progress we've made."

"Good…" Penelope states, she pauses while the senators are taken-aback by her nonchalant tone, and continues on, "We've allowed those felines to dominate trade in the region, imposing tax on commerce around the islands unchallenged now for decades. It is time to tip the scale back in our nation's favor."

"Quite warmongering of you to announce. Regardless of your station as president, you will face consequences for these brash decisions for collateral on the native people of *Port Humility*," Senator Alexandria says, glancing over to the politician bullying her aide.

"It is the *Aluanian* people's constitutional right to be uninformed morons, and detached from reality, you know," says another politician seated next to Senator Benson.

Stratos Cobaltfort, wearing only a gurney, is asleep in a hospital bed tucked beneath white sheets while hooked up to monitors tracking his calm vitals. The Graywolf nurse present with him, finishes checking up on Stratos and wakes him up, delivering a cup of water and another tiny paper cup filled with brightly colored pill capsules. Stratos is slow to awaken, but stares around at his surroundings before easily moving upright to take the two cups from the nurse. Obviously finding himself in a medical ward of some kind, Stratos downs the pills in one swift motion, and drinks the room temperature water in another, finding it quite refreshing. He migrates his gaze to stare up at the nurse from his bed and offers her a smile.

"Thank you." Stratos clears his throat, inhaling and exhaling through his nostrils, smelling the medicinal and antiseptic air, then asking the nurse, "How many days has it been? Do you know where we are?"

"You don't have to thank me. This is what I do, sir. You've been unconscious for three days, but some of the doctors were able to fix you up. You are healing up great, but we recommend taking it easy for a bit longer," says the nurse, watching as Stratos widens his eyes and twitches his ears back.

"Three days? Whoa, what's happened?" Stratos shifts in the bed to refill his water cup to get a second drink. "I didn't think I was out for that long."

"Yes, the aircraft carrier is just off the coast of *Edon* now. We're nearing *Port Liekos*," the nurse explains to him. Stratos nodded his head afterward, silently understanding where he was now. Assuming internally when he came to, that he would have been placed in some emergency infirmary set up in *Port Humility*.

"Docking at *Liberty Garrison*, most likely, right?" Stratos comments after downing his refilled cup of water again, trying to keep his foggy mind off the recent battle he experienced, and repeating brief flashbacks.

"Refuel, resupply, and personnel exchange. I'll see you in the morning for your next med dose. Get more sleep if you can." The nurse then gathers her things up and leaves him, drawing the privacy curtain around his area while she goes to attend to the next patient. She leaves Stratos now awake and laying in bed. The medications and I.V. certainly work wonders to dull the pain he would otherwise be experiencing. Studying the numerous bandages around his torso through just his sense of touch, he lays still, and he becomes self-aware of his body. He still has all his limbs. He gratefully let out an exhale.

Gradually, the memories of the fighting outside *Port Humility* return to his mind, particularly his best friend Kruko's death while he himself was paralyzed by Minax's magic. Agent Danabi was also killed in action, which has its own weight on Stratos internally. Grief and anger grapple one another for control, but Stratos lays calmly in the bed silently fighting his emotions. His blue eyes remain wide open and staring through space, the soft beeping of his vitals monitor is the only sound that can be heard as he drifts back into sleep.

Strato's eyes blink open as the curtain of his hospital bed is drawn open dramatically. Natural sunlight pours in from the small glass square slits passed for windows on the ship, adding additional illumination within. The nurse from earlier approaches, with Lieutenant Tidus standing beside her. The nurse quietly checks Stratos's vitals and prepares his medicines as Tidus inspects over his colleague in arms, as he's lying in the hospital bed. Stratos takes note that Tidus appears patched up, but arguably Stratos has been in better shape than he is in currently. He places a neatly folded set of camouflage clothing on an empty chair before turning to speak to Stratos.

"Got caught up on some much needed beauty sleep, did ya bud?" Tidus asks his superior officer in a casual, friendly manner. Tidus offers Stratos a sincere smile before looking at the nurse, who returns holding the two paper cups. Stratos shakes his head with an amused expression on his face. The nurse steps up closer to the hospital bed.

"You know the drill." The nurse leans her arms, offering the cups over to Stratos as he's wincing and sitting upright.

Stratos squints up at the nurse and chuckles. "Oof, yeah, I'm starting to feel it." He takes his dose and swallows the water. Afterward, he addresses Tidus, his new friend and comrade-in-arms. "Ohh, you bet, Lieutenant."

"Solid, General Cobaltfort." Tidus clears his throat, then trails off, looking suddenly uncomfortable before adding somberly, "Just reckon

I should mention my condolences for Kruko out there before too much time passes."

"I'll give you two a minute. I have some other patients to check on." Hurrying along, the nurse leaves Stratos and Tidus, adding as she walks away, "I'll be back soon."

Stratos lets out a long, sighing exhale. "I appreciate it." He briefly, silently dwells before staring directly at Tidus with a smile and a motivated gleam to him, but with emotions failing to be hidden behind them. "You did phenomenal work. No matter what the outcome was, we took it on as a team."

Tidus emits a brief laugh, gesturing at Stratos's predicament. "I dunno sir, Maybe it was some phenomenal work. But not enough."

Stratos scoffs. "We got the sons of bitches, remember? What happened to that dragon beast?"

Tidus gives a long exhale of his own and grumbles, "Well, units converged and surrounded the crash. The enemy and person of interest survived and escaped. I was part of the group that found you wounded and down. Basically, that dragon beast brought down a meteor on top of the wreck, and also opened a portal through literal time and space from some ancient landmark thing. And disappeared."

Stratos lies with a dumbstruck look on his face, and blatant disbelief in his voice. "What?"

"Yeah, I'm still trying to make sense of it myself, really. Agreeable that it's in the realm of next level magical bullshittery, of course outside my field of expertise," Tidus says.

Stratos sits up more in the bed. "Absolutely, hmm. Did they debrief you at least?"

Tidus hums thoughtfully. "Yeah, told 'em what I saw, what I did, details of the mission on the ground. Unfortunately, I didn't have to write a whole essay on this." He pauses and adds with a disgruntled growl, "It sucks. That's the sum and truth of it, boss. Some of our best battle mages, with decades of magic study under their belts, don't have a clue to even begin to explain it themselves."

Taking in a breath of air, Stratos raises his shoulders up. "Whelp, give it a bit and I'll be back on my feet. This is far from over. I still have answers to get from Sabaton. Where's my phone?"

"I don't know. I reckon they took all your shit when you rolled into the ER, probably," Tidus says, but their conversion is interrupted.

A gray and white silvery wolf in slate colored nurse scrubs walks up to Tidus and Stratos, bringing muffins and hot breakfast food with him on a tray. This new nurse rests the tray on the counter and turns to lift the sheets off of Stratos's bandaged up body. This nurse reveals his ability to perform magic as he channels a soft soothing blue green light from his palms, hovering them over Stratos slowly. Stratos himself feels a sensation like someone pouring comfortably hot water over wherever the magical light's proximity touches.

"Morning there, General Cobalfort, looking way better today. The infirmary doctor will be by later to give you a checkup, but—" The nurse pauses to crack his knuckles and relocates to the other side of the bed, recasting the healing magic. "We'll certainly have you up and at it in no time."

The nurse cuts away the bandages wrapped around Stratos's thigh and focuses his soothing, healing light on the bullet wounds. Within a minute, the injuries shrink and most of the exposed, hairless skin heals up perfectly. Once he stops his spell. Appearing winded, as if the very magical spell was physically demanding.

"That's it for now. Channeling healing magic isn't an endless running faucet. Only so much at a time can be done," the nurse concludes.

Penelope Briarpaw and General Silas Sabaton stand side by side, facing three of their political comrades. Penelope speaks to Sabaton, and the others gather with her. "This hearing has gone on long enough. Don't you all agree?"

General Silas walks over to the table in the room they are taking recess in, as the *Aluan* congress continues on with its proceedings. He bends over and pulls up a suitcase, placing it on the table and opening it, knowingly turning the tumbler numbers for its lock. General Silas lets out a reluctant sigh and opens the case, revealing two stacks of clear plastic assault rifles, allowing the components within to be visible and made of stiffer opaque plastic. The set is complete with ammo magazines. The conspirators stare silently at each other, the congressional police officer present purposefully looking away without a word spoken staring at the wall. His paw was on his pistol, and he saluted Penelope as she passed by him.

"Is it really the best time, though?" asks the middle politician, an average-looking *Lycandian* with silver and gray fur. He proceeds to nervously tug and adjust his tie.

Penelope tugs the edge of her dress just enough to pull it off her shoulder, showing off the armor plates concealed beneath with a devilish smirk on her muzzle. "Hope I'm dressed properly for the occasion, and look at that..." She picks up one of the rifles, and loads an ammo magazine in it. She casts her icy eyes over with a smirk to her nervous colleague. "It is. Because Senator Alexandria—not to mention all of her political party—is out for my throat, and this will conclude with my impeachment. Mr. Crowly is, fortunately, a great friend."

Two congressmen were in the middle of a heated, booming argument while the gavel was clapping against the podium by the floor speaker. Penelope and her entourage enter the congress room, bored politicians who are only partially paying attention by looking at their cellphones or making side conversations are now in for a rude surprise. One congresswoman lets out a shriek and points at Penelope as she brandishes her rifle.

General Sabatan takes aim out at the crowd. "Everyone stay right where you are. If you are standing, sit your ass down. Congress is back in session!"

On queue, the doors into the congress room unlock and open. *Lycandians*, of predominantly Graywolf breed, calmly stride in, taking aim at the officers not in on the coup. There's brief yelling and a standoff before an exchange of gunfire. Causing momentary mayhem, Penelope climbs on top of the podium and takes the microphone next to the discarded gavel while the floor speaker goes to cower behind the podium for cover.

Penelope yells over the crowing commotion, "Put a muzzle on it! You insincere, money-grubbing agenda driven sellouts. You have failed your species, more specifically your breed. You've allowed disgusting impurity to be spawned in our nation! Mixing breeds...Direwolves and Timberwolves are one thing...But a feline and a wolf?"

Silas Sabaton storms on, "Hell, just scratching the surface really. It's been high time for a swift change of management. There are external threats that destroy and divide us. Add insult to injury by selling out *Aluan* for financial gain. They are selling our military secrets to the cats."

Senator Alexandria angrily yells at Penelope and her cohorts, "Have you lost your mind? What do you think you are doing?!"

Leaping off of the podium onto the carpeted floor, keeping a good grip of her rifle the entire time, Penelope keeps highly attentive. Looking in Senator Alexandria's directly, she says, "I'm what inevitably follows...the final solution."

Several congress members choose not to sit, instead calmly stepping down onto the floor to join General Silas and President Penelope. A shocked and flabbergasted Senator Alexandria says to them, "You traitors...I will have you and your conspirators locked away. You will be impeached and arrested for high treason. Mark my words, Miss Briarpaw!"

Senator Benson pokes his barrel torso up from the congressional desk he was cowering behind. He shouts to Penelope, "This is disgraceful to the spirit of our democracy...who are these rent-a-thugs?" Then he follows up to his colleagues, joining in the madness before him as he raises a shaky fist in the air. "I'm ashamed of you."

Senator Cornelius's head peaks up as well now from her desk, as the entire congress chamber stands huddled with panicked whispers and outcries. She interrupts, cutting off Senator Benson's rant before he gets going, yelling across the chamber, "Ohhhhh, put a lid on it, father time! Everyone knows you are barely conscious most of the week, and should have retired like four decades ago."

"Shut up!" Penelope shouts and bashes the gavel on the podium behind her several times. As she does so, the dozen armed *Paladins* fan out through the chamber room. "Going forward you will not speak, unless spoken to or asked a question! The more you make this difficult, the more your life will lose its already diminished value." Penelope looks around momentarily as the chaos in the congress room settles. She lands her eyes back on Senator Alexandria. "Impeach me? The irony, if you ask me, is when you launch an investigation and find no wrongdoing when it concerns yourselves...Don't make me repeat myself."

General Silas speaks into his radio. "Begin locking down the building entrances and exits. Dismiss all non essential personnel immediately! No one is allowed back inside. Give me a three-block street perimeter, copy?" General Sabaton waits to listen in on a crackly sounding response, looking toward Penelope to give her an affirmative nod.

Penelope, shifting her gaze from Sabaton, to the congress, says, "This revolution will be televised..." A couple *Paladins* lift cellphones up to record, meanwhile another operative takes control of a network camera as the unlucky crew concurrently stands by at gunpoint in the media and reporters section of the *Bastion's* floor. Facing the TV camera, she says, "*Aluan* will be saved from its enemies both foreign and domestic, and restored to its former glory. We are cleansing the weakness and corruption out." Penelope pauses the triumphant act, punching the air over her head and continues speaking. "We are going to fulfill its destiny by leading the other nations of *Lycandia*."

Stratos watches the television, which is displaying newsreels of the coup in progress from his hospital bed. He throws the cotton white sheets off of his bandaged up body. Tidus, who was previously occupied by his phone and talking with Stratos, now notices the coup happening in the capital live on the news. "What do you reckon all that's about?" Tidus asks, perplexed but intrigued to hear Stratos's opinion.

Stratos shakes his head as he speaks. "I don't care. Hell with calling Sabaton. We need to get out of here and pull my family free of that mess now. It should be almost a ten-hour flight to *Luminous* from where we're at. I'm alright."

"Woah, just one second there. Do you have a plan, then?" Tidus gets up when he sees Stratos starting. Stratos takes a moment or two to acclimate himself, swaying with a bit of vertigo. The nurses had previously declared him stable, so he was no longer hooked up to an IV or monitors. Wearing only a hospital gown, he grabs at the pile of clothing Tidus brought him the other day, hiking up the pants first before pulling the gown off.

Stratos continues. "Danabi was able to pull up files that some legendary spell book was being stored in the *Port Liekos* consulate building. It's called the *Macrocosm Lexicon*. Now Tidus, you and me both witnessed other wordly magic being used, at capacities that break even Physical and Magical Laws. That dragon beast is the *Starwielder*, and that beast needed the book for something. But so did Crowly and Penelope."

Tidus visibly slumps while he listens to Stratos, nodding in agreement before he says, "There's no denying what I saw and fought through. Whatever purpose the book has, or why this *Starwielder* matters, it's all something that the government isn't going to tell us." He glances again at the television while it displays an image of flashing law enforcement lights surrounding the building from an aerial view. "Heh, also General Sabaton and Penelope have their paw's full. I'm reckoning they won't be helping us."

"That's fine. I'm taking action on the matter now," Stratos states with finality in his voice.

Tidus and Stratos exit the infirmary of the aircraft carrier, climbing steep metal stairs out onto the tarmac flight deck level. The warm sun beams down onto them through the thin, scattered clouds as the cry of seagulls reaches their ears. Walking swiftly together, they draw no suspicion amongst the air force crew as they pass, Stratos savoring the sensation of the sunlight on him after days in a hospital bed.

They present their dog tags and rank IDs to the security posted at gangway before walking from the flight deck down to the dock of the *Liberty Garrison*. The pair clear the security with a simple greeting and salute, and walk down the steep ramp to the gray cement dock below. Tidus's brown eyes check out the two anchored up tug boats floating at the ready to help push the carrier back into open water.

The salty tropical sea breeze washes over them as it kicks up, coming off of the ocean, while the base's remaining palms sway lightly. Stratos, despite his anxiety to reach his family, takes the moment to cherish the warm sun and fresh air. Tidus and Stratos stroll from the dock and take to a worn dirt roadway that transitions to the actual base.

Before getting too close to the barbed wire fence gateway that was partially ajar, but not unguarded, Stratos comments, "We need to re-equip." His blue eyes scan the colorful sights around them.

Tidus speaks while flashing his rank card. "Since you mentioned the consulate earlier, I was the highest ranking officer, and this base is within the operating area of it." He slaps the plastic card against his palm a few times, adding, "Reinforcements were supposed to come from this very base that night to bail my ass out. The flight out, and touch down on the roof of the consulate building, is like five minutes from here."

Stratos sighs and pats Tidus's shoulder once. "Beatin' a dead labor beast, my friend. We know exactly why that went down the way it did. You think it'll work to open and check out weaponry and armor from the *Garrison's* store?"

Tidus and Stratos jaunt right past the guard, this one only taking a quick glance at the two of them before saluting Stratos, then Tidus. They return the salute and carry on, Stratos mentally taking note the coup didn't disrupt any operations. News travels just as quickly as it does in the civilian sector. The stationed soldiers here knew full well what was occurring back home in the republic.

Tidus speaks softly, a tone of concern as his lips are tight. "I reckon *Aluanian* airspace is going to be nuts with that madness unfolding at the *Bastion of Benevolence*, boss. We'll be okay flying an identified military craft of some kind. Over here," he excitedly finishes, approaching a large white cement structure reinforced with steel. He proceeds to unlock the door's scanning system, which emits a hefty "click."

Yanking the door open with ease Tidus, and Stratos walk right inside. Neatly aligned on the right wall are fifty standard issue *Aluan* assault rifles, with magazines and ammunition cases. Heavy machine guns with loaded, rolled up ammo belts fill the space underneath. The left side had torso armor plates, helmets, and other consumables for different combat operations.

"So, are we really going to be fighting our own side? What's the play?" Tidus asks uncomfortably. Stratos and Tidus don't hesitate to first select proper fitting armor, taking their time to adjust it properly.

Stratos answers him while they advance on to pick out and load two field issue backpacks. "If we must. Sidra and Vivian need me. You can love and be loyal to one's country, and hate the government at the same time." Stratos pauses, grasping at a rifle on the wall, now fully suited in combat armor over his camouflage shirt, pants, and the fresh bandages beneath those. "I'm aware I am a general of the new *Paladins*. I guess, Lieutenant Tidus, we have to decide what we toy soldiers do in these moments we find ourselves in."

Tidus nervously whistles and quakes his ears and tail momentarily, he darts his eyes to and away from Stratos. "I'm full send at this point, brother." He waves his ID over the scanner lock mechanism, then takes a rifle off the wall and, with it, four loaded ammo magazines. "We aren't fugitives. We have nothing to hide. The powers that be have done Danabi and Kruko dirty, including all my troops in that consulate building. They have cameras, so let's hurry up."

A sergeant wanders around the ajar door, but before reacting with violence or panic he first notices their rank and outfits, he salutes them with suspicion in his voice and on his face, "Morning, sirs, uhh is there a mission you are assigned to for all that?"

Tidus is closest to the door. He turns slowly and faces the garrison sergeant with a friendly grin, returning the salute with his free paw, the other still gripping the rifle by the stock. Now resting the rest of the gun on his shoulder, he answers him confidently. "Yes, Sergeant, we're needing to transport General Stratos here to the capital immediately."

"Is that so? I'm afraid to inform y'all, I have my orders from General Sabaton, higher ranking, that General Stratos is not to leave *Edon*. You should still be on the *Vortex*." The sergeant's suspicion increases beyond his tone, his brown eyes going back and forth between his superiors with narrowing brows.

"I have no reason to think they need me. Why?" Stratos asks. He glares at the sergeant with a frustrated-looking expression, but retracts his paw away from the rifle on the wall that is still left unlocked.

The garrison sergeant swiftly draws his pistol and aims it in Stratos and Tidus's direction."Under strict orders, General Stratos was not to be discharged from the carrier until debriefed by an agent of the *Intelligence Agency.*"

Tidus raises his paws up now while the rifle he is armed with remains slung over his shoulder. "Seems a tad aggressive, don't you reckon?"

Growling, the sergeant snaps, anger in his tone as he says, "I don't think so, with you two rifling around in our stockade."

Stratos scowls at the garrison sergeant and noisily clears his throat. "I'll cut the act. President Penelope took my family hostage before our mission, and she's attempting now to desecrate what our nation stands for. She is working with some seriously shady folk, but I'm no longer involved by my own choice. I will free my family, so if you want to know what my mission is. That is my mission."

The audible clicking of the safety being turning off gives Tidus and Stratos a brief sense of alarm as they stiffen up for a half-second. Stratos's face is the only one of the two not surprised. Tidus keeps arms up and still while the sergeant speaks sternly.

"Sorry. Orders are orders, and I'm sure they'll find it interesting that I found you two here like this. Drop all that shit, slowly!"

As Stratos goes to lift his arms up, he then lunges and pitches the loaded ammo magazine in his right paw. Simultaneously, Tidus falls fast to the hard floor of the structure, as the heavy cartridge passes over his prone form and strikes the sergeant square on the forehead. The garrison sergeant stumbles backward and Tidus grabs at his ankles to drag him further inside, out of any potential onlookers. Tidus reaches at the pistol the sergeant has and fights to not only keep his finger off the trigger but also dislodges the ammo cartridge inside it as they wrestle. In this same span of time, Stratos snaps to action and maneuvers behind the sergeant to grapple him in a chokehold with his biceps.

They tie the sergeant to the ajar armory door, compose themselves before then jogging inconspicuously toward the tarmac where multiple aircraft are parked. Stratos selects a jet-copter like aircraft, with a giant red paw and a white x on each door and the nose. "Medicine and EMS copter-jet. This'll do just fine," Stratos states, climbing up from the sun-baked dusty tarmac onto the metal platform, shouldering through the narrow way into the cockpit. Tidus follows right inside after a quick inspection of each propeller engine on either wing. With their commandeered aircraft, Stratos and Tidus fly toward *Aluan.*

Stratos uses his *Paladin* insignia rank to his advantage to clear their flight from the base, over *Port Liekos's* shoreline, traveling northwest inland. Putting as much distance as they can before the incapacitated sergeant is discovered.

"Full throttle, we'll be over *Luminous* in ten hours."

"Don't reckon this thing has radio on it, maybe a music app?" Tidus stares hopefully amidst the cockpit console, but keeping his eyes on the sky as co-pilot.

"Nope," Stratos flatly replies.

"Alright super soldier, let's hear it," Tidus says, giving a scan of the cloudy scenery with a bored expression on his face.

"Oh boy, hear what?" Stratos asks, physically relaxed in the pilot seat but mentally occupied elsewhere.

"You play guitar in a cover band. Nah, you must enjoy sports ball. That's it," Tidus says tossing him a cheesy smirk.

"Huh? Painting me as a cliche, asshole. What are your hobbies?" Stratos fires back, calmly playing along.

"Hunting, fishing off my boat, grilling," Tidus rambles on, glancing over at Stratos briefly before checking out the sky through the windshield.

"And you dare call me cliche." Stratos laughs, adding, "I grew up in Ferndale, basically rural suburbia."

"I don't yuck other's yums, but I stand on the business of what I believe.I grew up in Cedar Heights, trailer parks, and double wides," Tidus responds with a smirk. "Way up in the hills, there wasn't much to do for work so I enlisted after I finished school."

"I chose to serve since my father served. Military family, you probably get the whole picture," Stratos answers him without taking his sight from their direction of travel as he grips the control stick. Tidus nods. "You definitely just won father of the year, if you ask me. We're about to fly into the maw of hell, family man. I got your back," Tidus says.

CHAPTER SIX: Stepping Stones, And Self Liberation From Captivity

KERITH MOONWANE, AN ANTHROPOMORPHIC white striped tiger, stands in a cell that has indigo colored walls and pale neon light bars, which give a soft glow from the ceiling where the walls meet it. Kerith wears only a white tee and denim shorts. He has patches of missing fur with healing skin and bandages visibly covering his arms and part of his torso. He frowns at the door and floor in contemplative thought with baby blue eyes under long, dark hair. There is a knocking sound, his neck craning up in the chained collar attaching him to the ceiling.

Daxil Ovbrash, an anthropomorphic black panther, strides in with his sharp yellow eyes glaring at Kerith. In contrast to Kerith's dull garb, the panther wears a fancy black tunic with a hemmed purple robe over it covered by a forest green cloak clasped by gold rings. Daxil closes the cell door behind him while two guards peer inside, feline eyes highly attentive.

Daxil lets out a single chuckle and asks pompously, "Enjoying your stay so far?" A smug look forms on his face.

Kerith Moonwane holds up his wrists bound by steel handcuffs, flicking his tail behind him uselessly. "Not really. I'm afraid it's been a one out of five star review visit. Over two weeks of the same boring routine. Lousy food."

"I'll have to take that up with management, then." Daxil sinisterly steps forward. "There was a relic at the compound, underneath Moonwane Manor. It was not recovered from the wreckage. Where is it?" Daxil cocks his head to one side, asking his question in a serious t one.

Kerith's expression is confident as well, and he tilts his head to one side in mocking imitation. "If it isn't there, you know who must have it. The *Starwielder*. And there's nothing you can do once it's within their proximity."

Letting out a scoff, Daxil stares at Kerith. "You could also tell me the identity of any remaining *Trinity* members inside *Umbris*? One way or another, we will purge this entire mega-city of what remains of that secret society, *Trinity of Tranquility's* influence."

"Loyalty is a rare thing in this world, Daxil." Kerith shakes his head, adding, "I won't be breaking anyone's trust. Or my oaths."

A low growl escapes Daxil's closed mouth, his eyes narrowing. "Oh, so now we're bringing up loyalty and oath? *The Coven* has convened at *Ziggurat Of Eclipses* in the wake of your family's death. I recall that there have been many suspicions. Unfortunately, I have little evidence to present, other than what a little crow far, far away told me, about where the Moonwane's loyalty truly was all this time. To some international secret society."

"It has always been for the people's best interest, and serving *The Coven's* decisions, for generations. Who's the 'we' in this purge of yours? You ride in on your empty moral high horse, Daxil, who do you work for, hmm?" Kerith asks.

"I suppose you would want to know, Kerith. So you don't take all this overly personal. Some of my associates who work for me and I have come up with our own action plan for *The Coven*. There is certainly change brewing..." Daxil Ovbrash reaches a paw out and grasps Kerith by the chin to lift his gaze and continues speaking. "As if I would tell you, cooking you in anxiety is amusing. Others throughout *Umbris* will get what's coming to them for their own transgressions. Make no mistake about that!"

Kerith stares smugly at Daxil. "Careful throwing out so many consequences that you forget about yours, still on their way. Murderer. Sounds to me like you're a traitor and a poorly self explained hypocrite."

Daxil lets out a frustrated purr before he clenches his other paw into a fist and strikes Kerith hard across the face once before straightening up, leaning once again to give him a second strike with the other fist, leaving him slumped down on the cell floor on his knees, chains rattling.

"Now we understand each other better," Daxil says, cracking his knuckles, followed by his neck. Lifting Kerith up by his hair and yanking his head back, he growls, "You will be enslaved to the cocoa bean farms of the *Namel* coast, where you will live out the rest of your miserable life. Maybe someone in the future might reanimate you for additional labor. Or hopefully, a merciful and proper mummification."

Keirth—without his spirit broken—retorts with a cough, "Empty threats. If you were going to kill me, you would have done it at Moonwane Manor, when you found me barely conscious. At the scene of the crime." The thoughts of home, or what was home, brought an aching quiver to his stomach. Racing duressed memories, particularly the last moments he saw his sister and father alive. With narrowed vision, Kerith feels his blood pressure rising. Conflictions of grief and a defiant anger fill him, but he inhales loudly and points his chin up while thrashing at his steel cuffs.

Daxil leans in closer to Kerith and delivers five harsh upper cuts to his gut from close proximity. "Now..." He pats Kerith, who is groaning and coughing against Daxil briefly before being shoved to the cell floor. "I wouldn't test myself further if I were you, Kerith Moonwane."

Daxil turns around with a flourish of his dark emerald green cape. In the meantime, Kerith looks over his shoulder and spits a shiny small object out down into his palm, his paws kept restrained behind his back by the cuffs.

Stopping at the cell doorway that's held open now by the two guards, Daxil turns to look at Kerith one last time stating coldly. "I'll check up with you in a month. Maybe two or three."

Kerith slowly rises from the ground, coiling his tail, his wrist cuffs hitting the floor with a resounding clank, his paw holding Daxil's key, jerking into the lock of the collar attaching him to the ceiling. With a burst of adrenaline scraping his neck on the collar before it finishes opening all the way, Kerith dashes forward and leaps into a kick. Daxil barely has time to react as he's sent back first through the ajar cell door. He lands awestruck, with Kerith leaping off of Daxil's torso and running freely down the violet stone hallway, illuminated by obsidian hanging braziers and different shades of purple lights. The two guards give chase, firing stun guns rounds after Kerith. Furious, Daxil gets up to his feet to sprint after him. "I'm going to break every bone in your body when I'm done with you!" he shouts after Kerith. Kerith panting loudly, mentally applauding the effort of tracking which pocket Daxil routinely puts his keys in these past grueling days.

Rushing into a hallway intersection, Kerith catches the attention of three more cheetah guards, instantly pointing at him running in pursuit from the opposite hallway. Kerith is now maneuvering in a desperate sprint. This is his first, and probably the only, attempt he will ever have to break free. He pumps his legs madly, running down the hallway to his left as enemies give chase and gain on him. He passes two massive purple arches with ivy growing down from the ceiling. He takes swift notice of several small moon shaped, tinted and barred windows. Kerith dives the opposite way, running up the wall and kicking backward into a flip.

Kerith closes himself up and dives through the circular shaped, magenta tinted glass window, and discovers it is daytime as he free falls outward, his eyes sting taking in the fantastic view of *Umbris* after captivity. The massive slanted side of a black stone pyramid comes up beneath him, where Kerith hits the coarse stone hard and bounces up again, letting out a yowl of pain as it flares throughout his right shoulder. This time, he doesn't bounce as high. Instead, he rolls and scrambles against the warm, sunbaked stone, trying to push himself upright and keep his balance. His long hair, fur and ragged clothing buffered by pleasant, salty winds.

The cloudless sky opens up above, and squinting, Kerith sees the faint green and purple moons orbiting *Homeworld*. He can also make out the faint orange moon that is only visible on certain days, operating on a different orbital track than the others. Kerith savors the sunlight and fresh air. His last time outside had been the night he was pulled from the ruins of Moonwane Manor into Daxil's claws. He takes a moment to get his bearings and to take a breather, his chest heaving. But sounds coming from behind him make his ears flick backward, catching its source without having to turn his head. He immediately flees the only viable way—down the pyramid—taking notice in his haste wetlands stretch out.

Behind him, the two guards, three cheetahs, and Daxil file out and continue chasing, undaunted by the forty-five degree lateral pyramid face under them, spanning downward for a thousand feet or more. At the base, gray cloth awnings covering stone mezzanines in the distance. Kerith glances over his shoulder behind him to notice the cheetahs gaining on him significantly. One cheetah skids on the stone and then pounces, airborne, closing in on Kerith, the other two drawing dual looking weaponry; shiny golden Khopesh swords.

Kerith glimpses back once again in time to notice the cheetah leaping at him, claws out. He turns his running body backward and even opens his arms up to accept the tackling cheetah. The two now awkwardly roll down the pyramid, wrestling, biting, and kicking, while two additional cheetahs and Daxil follow behind. Daxil skids himself into a crouch in his thick sandals on the bumpy slanted pyramid surface while dialing on his cellphone, then speaking into it.

"He's making a break for it. Leaving the *Crescent Southwest Pyramid.* Let the other elite guards know."

In the middle of his rolling tussle with the cheetah guard, Kerith breaks away and kicks the cheetah guardsman off of him. He sends his attacker rolling into stone planters built into the grand pyramid, filled with hardy turquoise colored ivy growing. While the stunned cheetah guard recovers and brushes leaves off his gilded armor, the group passes him in pursuit of Kerith Moonwane, cascading downward. Kerith runs faster toward the base of the *Twin Moons Crescent Southwest Pyramid,* finally arriving at the bottom as he leaps through the fancy fabric covering the top of the mezzanine. As a ball of entangled chaotic gray fabric falls to the ground with him in the center of it, Kerith crashes through into a plant-covered patio on the platform and breaks through the decorative fence. Falling forward another twenty feet, Kerith rolls through with tons of pottery debris landing in the wetlands of the slow crawling river. In his stupor he pulls himself up in four foot deep water, before quickly wading away from the pyramid.

"Going to make this interesting, aren't you? Maybe we'll turn you into croc food," Daxil shouts at Kerith, gesturing around the mezzanine surrounding the base of the pyramid. Several firearm-equipped guardsmen present themselves over the stone railing portions of the platform, awaiting orders. "Shoot to detail him," Daxil commands.

"No clear shot, sir," one of the guards on the mezzanine cries out.

The sound of crackling magic can be heard off to the side as one of the three cheetahs chasing him reveals she is a spellcaster, Kerith a sitting duck as he wades quickly onto soggy land out of waist deep water. Two dark blue orbs of plasma-like energy swirl at her paw fingertips. Kerith, now getting cornered by multiple enemies, and a river at his back. "Don't force me to do it! You barely even have clothes on, fool...there's nothing shielding you here from bullets, let alone magic," the cheetah spellcaster warns Kerith.

Kerith keeps pushing distance between himself and his pursuers, his wide and bloodshot baby blue eyes evaluating each of his enemies while traversing the wetlands, not submerged in water, are densely packed with large flytrap plants between tall palm trees.

"Capture him, go! Go ahead and cut him off. Now!" screams Daxil at his cohorts, unfastening his green cape, letting it fall away, leaping down into the wetland that sprawls from the *Twin Moons Crescent Southwest Pyramid*. "I'll rip what I need to know from your flesh and bone!" Daxil adds with a deadly growl, now gripping two long metal spikes in clenched fists.

The cheetah spellcaster stays perched on the ruined mezzanine and throws the two crackling orbs of plasma magical energy at Kerith. Stumbling in the overgrowth to get away, the first projectile fizzles angrily toward Kerith, but misses his torso soaring into a palm tree trunk. He catches a kiss of the intense heat coming off it, though. The other projectile strikes the back of his right leg through the grass a split-second later, propelling him against a cluster of large flytraps in a painful cry. After Kerith flops on top of the bust plant, it lashes out in self-defense. His backside smoldering, Kerith pushes off the violently snapping flytraps that nip and pinch at him, rushing back to his feet to escape. Nearly tripping on the shallow pools around his feet, with a slight limp.

Daxil charges up quickly behind him. Each metal spike glows white hot at the ends as he closes in. Overzealously stabbing and flailing onto Kerith, who's only able to fend off so many attacks with his empty paws before yowling out in agony every time the burning hot metal stabs or thumps against his nearly bare body. He throws back a few desperate punches, a swipe or two of his retractable claws, but Daxil is swift to slip inches out of each counter-strike. Kerith's heel hits an upraise root, and he stumbles backward in his flinching, giving him a reprieve, as he lands flat on his back.

Looming over him, the sadistic panther grins, stepping over the same root. One of the cheetahs steps up beside him, taking in the sight of Kerith crawling backward. The guard on impulse rushes and grabs at Kerith.

"No, wait!" Daxil starts, alarmed, but in the same instance, Kerith reaches for the cheetah's two Khopesh swords at the same time as the guard's paws clasp his dirty torn-up shirt. Kerith secures a handle and draws the weapon free in his grip. The cheetah reacts instinctively to kick him in the hip, successfully landing a powerful kick that knocks Kerith back, his free paws drawing his remaining golden Khopesh sword.

"Dammit, sorry, sir." The guard mentally berates himself, keeping an unbreaking battle-ready look and posture toward Kerith wielding his sword. The other cheetahs arriving slow their approach from the overgrown wetlands, noticing Kerith and keep wary. They looked at Daxil expectantly with their eyes.

"So you got yourself a sword. No technological enhancement, no magical enchantment. A sword," Daxil says, twitching his whiskers into a sneer.

"And I know how to use it," Kerith hisses and slashes ferociously with his stolen golden Khopesh, making Daxil recoil and squirm back from the nasty sharp serration. The cheetahs close in together to overwhelm him. Kerith instead swings the sword to gain ground using his footwork, keeping them away. Even being outnumbered, Kerith fights off the four of them in an impressive display of slashes, cuts, and parries. He is still in *Umbris.*

Kerith listens carefully over the subtle radio chatter of the otherwise quiet standoff. The faint sounds of traffic come as a welcome to him. Kerith dodges a taser projectile then makes a move, preparing himself as the two closest cheetah guards near him respond. Kerith parries one sword, then blocks the other guard, continuing running free through the wetlands toward civilization.

Daxil waving his fists over himself, he casts a speed spell on his own feet and legs, racing past his allies a hundred miles an hour to literally run Kerith down on the pathway. This time, coming up on the poor white striped tiger with two fireballs in each palm, he dunks them both down onto his torso, causing Kerith to stumble. Almost losing his grip on the sword he acquired, Kerith yells out in pain, rolling with the attack and tries to whip around with a wild slash before going down. He lets out a triumphant purr as his blade gashes Daxil's side, the sound or tearing fabric followed by a painful gasp from the shocked panther.

Kerith scampers back up to his wobbly feet, feeling mild burns form along his back, shirtless also, as what remains of his ripped tee falls apart in tatters. Hearing shouting around him, he bolts away from Daxil through more underbrush, discovering a dirt pathway crashing through a heavy curtain of vines dangling from above.

Daxil, following mere seconds in his wake, summons similar magical projectiles like his guardsman, honing his sights on Kerith running down the path. Kerith now emerges into a grassy park attached to the wetlands, into a busy part of *Umbris*. Daxil's incoming magical ice javelins aimed at his back, emitting electricity from them as well, all become diffused instantly by the city's anti-magic perimeter.Kerith sprints madly from the grassy park into the bustling bazaar, traffic flowing on a street next to it.

Kerith slips out of sight, uttering out amid the shopfront crowd and pedestrians, still running, afraid to stop. "I need to lose them, quick."

Daxil and his backup aren't far behind as they fan out into the crowd from the manicured park. Daxil yells and points at Kerith with a spike, spotting him worming through the crowd, thereby drawing more undesirable attention. Cheetahs, tigers, and panthers watch one, growing wary as Daxil shouts after Kerith they all give him space.

The earlier three cheetahs in elite guard armor from the *Crescent Southwest Pyramid* descend on Kerith, from all angles in the middle of the bazaar. More law enforcement in the area was being drawn to the commotion.

Kerith, zig-zagging while crossing the street, causes several drivers to lock up their brakes and honk angrily. Daxil loses ground in the pursuit as his left paw reaches down to clench at the wet rip in his ruined robe, and at his injury. Letting out a predatory growl as he calls after Kerith, "Ohhh, we'll be seeing one another again soon, runt."

A fast moving subway train drives along the tracks near the road Kerith had previously crossed. Seizing his fortunate luck, Kerith relinquishes his stolen weapon, letting it hit the limestone walkway, jumping over the hilly, dusty median, grappling up onto the train while it's traveling along its commuter track at fifty miles an hour. Daxil stows away, his still cooling off spikes safely, while he sprints up but unable to reach the last car of the commuter train as it speeds away out of his reach.

Daxil letting out a frustrated snarl. He huffs to a stop and pulls out his phone, making a call that picks up instantly for him. Speaking between winded pants, he says, "Get me the commuter transit authority director!" As his fellow security forces catch up, Daxil directs orders to them as well with a sour expression. "Get after that train. Get law enforcement to intercept him at the next station."

Daxil then pulls a small green rock out of his pocket. He crushes it in his paw as it's deceivingly fragile. Tendrils of neon light of similar color to the pulverized gem briefly fly and wash over Daxil's injury, beginning to close the wound gradually.

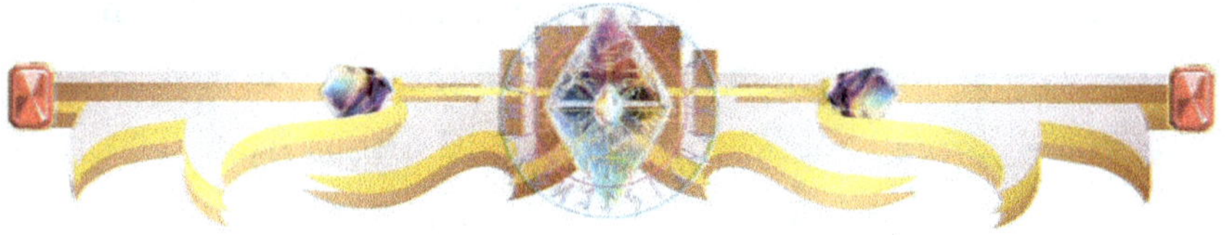

Kerith crouches low on the flat roof of the commuter trail, the gusty air around him dying down as the train slows, careful not to linger with his paws on the sun-baked metal. A computer automated voice comes through the speakers. "Now arriving at *Khopesh Edge District*. Keep tails and limbs clear of the tracks, please."

"Can't be too far now," Kerith muses while the warm wind from the moving train buffers against him, his tail flying behind him, his whiskers and long hair going wild. The train starts to slow steadily on its journey down the track. Kerith gets up as his wincing eyes identify the forms of authorities among the crowd on the upcoming platform.

Kerith observes either side of the train. One side has a ninety-degree angle barricade between it and a busy freeway, while the train's wheels whirr on the track noisily. Kerith makes a barely audible scoff of doubt. The opposite side of the train offered a promising view of a series of sprawling oases fanning out, with vibrant colorful flowers and lily pads dotting the surface. He takes a deep breath, before then leaping off the train and splashing into the warm pool.

"Ahh yes, right. Crocodiles..." he says calmly, after quickly surfacing from the shallow lime colored murky oasis pool, spitting out some of the acidic tasting water. Kerith frantically swims away as a huge, wide, frosty blue and dark purple scaly maw springs out of the water behind him. Snapping aimlessly with a splash before emitting a loud guttural hiss, the crocodile reveals its multi-horned head and sharp, glowing orange eyes. The crocodile travels with great speed after Kerith through its home in the water and lily flowers, with growing interest at the potential meal that dropped seemingly out of the sky for it.

Making it onto solid ground first, Kerith outran the now four twenty foot long crocodiles with six legs each pursuing him, flinching his tail inward to avoid one final crunching snap by an *Umbris dino-croc*. The crocodiles become bored with the chase as Kerith leaps out of the water and escapes, easily outrunning them now that they're on solid land. The agitated predators next make the nearby pink flamingos and herons take flight and clear out.

Sitting in a black chair, modeled for a computer gaming lifestyle, is Glyph. A furless, thick bodied *Sarosian*, Glyph's appearance is that of an anthropomorphic, hairless Sphynx cat but has large erect canine ears, both of which have many metal piercings, including a thick gold gauge in each bottom portion of his earlobes. Even in the dim glow of his black lights and LED light strings, the intricate tattoos of flowers and insects cover most of his visible body. He wears only a black sleeveless shirt and short leggings. He adjusts his purple framed and tinted glasses over his shining marigold eyes darting around his computer screen clicking noisily on different program windows.

Glyph puts on a pair of headphones, reaching for and speaking into a large foam microphone. "Alright folks, you know the deal. If you're new to the channel, welcome! Please like and subscribe, you know I appreciate it! So, today's content topic, pack a flashlight because we're going deep down the Jackalope hole!" Clapping his paws between words, he clears his throat while recording. "Is the *Umbris Elite* truly just a puppet state on behalf of the world banking system...well some dark money documents have surfaced y'all."

Outside of Glyph's apartment, located in one of the many identical sandstone highrises in this district, a great amount of black buttresses with violet stain glass windows are built in. Kerith, still drenched from his second dip in the oasis today, wanders erratically up the obsidian gothic style stairway that meshes seamlessly against the tan sandstone columns. The archways reaching above him have haunting neon purple lights, carefully worked into the architecture present even in the daylight hours. The memory of what floor comes back to him, after inhaling the aroma of lavender growing in vast quantities around the highrise property.

Kerith keeps his head on a heightened swivel with erect ears and wide eyes, still nursing a slight limp that only worsens as his adrenalin is close to spent. Avoiding the elevator, he hobbles up two flights. He arrives at the level Glyph's apartment is on, doors and buttresses reinforced with stone on his left, and the view of the parking lot and property below on his right. Kerith lets out a sigh of grateful relief, having run into no strangers so far. He arrives at the door labeled in neon purple number thirteen, knocking loudly several times. Kerith stares over to see Glyph's stylish chrome moped, still double chained up next to the door to his apartment.

He knocks and rings the doorbell at the same time, muttering, "Broken doorbell...Hey, Glyph? Buddy, you home?"

Paranoid stricken Kerith takes a swift gander around to check his surroundings, his heart sinking when he spots three *Umbris* police cruisers without lights or sirens on from his vantage point, rolling through the driveway and parking lot of the highrise. He has no doubt he was seen on a security camera, in a quiet panic Kerith moves and presses his face to the one window, fogging the purple glass with his exhaling, unable to determine from what he could see inside with his bloodshot eyes of the cluttered apartment, if anyone was home or not.

Oblivious to the banging and knocking, even his name being called, Glyph continues on an upbeat diatribe on his video stream, rambling on. That is, until the door to his apartment falls inward, crashing alarmingly on his floor. Sunlight pours inside the dim living room attached to his kitchen, separated by an island counter with a surface covered in clutter. Kerith picks himself up from the broken door slowly, feeling his strength finally wane. The couch and TV are next to him practically.

"Whoa!" exclaims Glyph, swiftly swiveling in his gamer chair and grabbing a metal baseball bat that is leaning against his desk. His large headphones fall off as he leaps into action. "C'mere and let me crack that skull open, dickhead! Trying to rob me." He winds up the black and chrome bat for intimidation, flabbergasted himself by the break in.

Raising his arms and empty paws up, Kerith backs away, yelling. "Wait, wait! Glyph it's me!"

Glyph, equally quick in reacting to the sudden intruder interrupting his day, recognises Kerith's face in the bright light and immediately erupts in joy. His face twisting from anger to awe, dropping the bat and closing the distance between them, hugging Kerith. Kerith lets out a pained groan from the many burned punctures and scratches he has, but hugs his friend back, smiling.

"Kerith my dude! Wow, it's been like six months since I've seen you, since The Melancholy Pit Watchers concert, actually. Man, what's new? I thought you were dead!" Releasing Kerith from his tight hug, he stares his friend up and down briefly, then takes notice of his door on his apartment floor. "Ugh, why did you have to break my door down? You could have just texted my phone. Why no shirt, by the way? Did you go swimming?"

Glyph searches Kerith over again in the light and his happy expression turns to concern, lowering his ears to his head, taking in the finer details of Kerith's appearance. "Damn, what happened? You need a hospital? But you are alive, though!" Clenching his fist with a triumphant expression, he whispers, "I knew all along the news and media lied…"

"It's a long story, but I need to get my bug out bag from you and I need to get out of *Umbris*, soon," Kerith explains, still jittery even in the presence of a friend adjusting his ripped denim shorts up. Kerith wanders to his friend's apartment window and peeks through the dirty blinds before shutting them tight and turning back to face Glyph, who speaks first.

"Go for it. Make sure to go through my first aid kit and patch yourself up some, dude. This is it, I get to go on the run with someone being man hunted!" Glyph runs over to his entire computer gaming station and grabs his microphone. "Hold up, we're going live on mobile folks. Stay streaming. Shit's going down. The risk of being deleted is real."

Kerith looking at Glyph rolls his eyes, shaking his head. "I could use some clothes if you got anything dry."

"Yeah, go right in my bedroom. I still got your old trunk. I moved it under my bed because I needed the closet space," Glyph says while he bends over, lifting the door up from his floor, leaving it propped up in its frame. Kerith gives him a grateful look and goes to his friend's bedroom, located off the main living room area in the small apartment. Kerith goes underneath his bed to pull a solid leather and metal bound trunk out. He takes the key that is stuck to the top with packing tape off and unlocks the chest.

Kerith pulls out a gold, tan, and cream camo backpack and a smaller briefcase from inside. He quickly unzips the backpack, checks its contents with his eyes and paws, then re-zips it. He moves back to the living room space of Glyph's modest four-room apartment. Glyph slips on a slate gray jean vest over his black tank top shirt, the vest laden with dozens of wild counterculture patches and band logos. His backpack is slung over one shoulder.

Kerith glances at Glyph's helmet, noticing a camera. With a surprised expression on his face, he asks his friend in disbelief, "Are you seriously filming this?"

Glyph follows Kerith out the front doorway, replying with optimism. "Ha, man! Why the hell would I not?"

"Oh, I don't know. Probably because the murdering psychotic power hungry people who were torturing me are now hunting me down Glyph," Kerith sarcastically states. Glyph stares back at him and nods once. "Okay, I mean that's fair. Audio only for some parts." Glyph reaches up to turn off the camera recorder with a bush of a button. "For now!"

Kerith shrugs, moving with his limp toward the kitchen to place his bag down. "Can I send a message on your computer real quick?

"Yeah, go for it." Glyph rummages in his closet to dig out and double check his gear, a backpack he uses for urban exploring. "I think we're good for a bit, since no one came after you through my door." Kerith's fur goes on end along his back upon hearing Glyph, and he feels his whiskers twitch with wide eyes.

"You say that, yet have no idea who's coming for me. I'm sure a camera caught me snooping up to your place," Kerith sighs as he sits himself in Glyph's gaming chair and opens a browser, composing an email without being too nosey at all the other websites. "Any minute now..." He trails off, rocking side to side nervously in the wheely chair as he works. "There we go."

"Who exactly is coming after you?" Glyph asks, leaving his bedroom but still in earshot as he pulls the door back up from the floor then adjusting it back into place on its dingy frame and hinges, then making the amusing effort to lock it. As they get downstairs, Glyph quickly moves to unlock the chains on his chrome moped. Kerith keeps watch and sighs with annoyance as a pair of officers rise into view from the stairway. Kerith gets on the back part of the single seat while Glyph fires up the moped, peeling off in the opposite direction just as the officers begin to take actual interest in them but dismiss it.

Kerith and Glyph are sitting across from one another in a cramped restaurant, Kerith in the middle of devouring a plate of deep-fried fish kabobs before noisily drinking down a full glass of water to wash down the buttery and salty. Glyph watches him, finding Kerith's pace of consumption out of the norm for him. He clears his throat. "You were held captive by Daxil Ovbrash the whole time? Why would his inquisition be interested in you—or your family—that way?"

"Because he's putting on a farce. He accuses the Moonwanes and other noble families, as well as other important figureheads of betraying the *Coven*. When, in fact, Daxil has an agenda of his own. He's not acting alone. My mom and him worked at the same place," Kerith answers, wiping his face, whiskers, and paws with napkins. Kerith pushes the empty plate with several wooden skewers left aside. While Glyph eats, Kerith continues, solemnly adding, "These are dangerous folks, Glyph. They haven't seen your face yet, or caught you with me. Just help me get out of *Umbris*. I won't beg you or guilt you into coming further than just that. Your life will be on the line, man."

"And..." Wiping his mouth, Glyph grins and continues, "You got me. I think I can offer you more than just getting out of here. I can help get us evidence on that asshole. Do you even have a plan? Or someone who could we work with and trust?"

Kerith facing Glyph directly, and with a pleased grin says, "I really appreciate it, Glyph, the only lifeline I got is in *Trinity of Tranquility*, yeah it's antique sounding, but it's a legit secret society. I don't know if there's been some kind of compromise. I sent a message to a friend in our family."

"Who's that?" Glyph inquires.

Kerith waits as a second plate of salty, savory food was placed down for them by a waitress hurrying along, speaking with boastful hope in a whisper once he and Glyph are alone. "Dorrion Chrisbanc."

CHAPTER SEVEN: The Maleficent Ritual

T HE NIGHT SKY IS clear, filled with billions of stars. The green and purple moons are visible as well, both in their full cycle appearing round in the cosmic canopy hovering above the mountain landscape. Clyde exits his completely blacked out and armored SUV convoy consisting of several vehicles similar to his, unbothered by the chill while his nostrils inhale. He wears his usual suit and attire, and unfurls a robe he is carrying. Standing waiting for him in the extremely remote dirt lot dotted with gravestones, surrounded by snow covered earthy smelling pine trees and evergreen bushes are a group of figures wearing the same style of robe Clyde holds. A cold wind moans through the summit air.

Clyde Crowly observes the others and then speaks to the group. "Wow, look how early you all are." A sinister smirk crosses his face. He wears a solid gold mask covering the upper half of his face. "Eager, I see. Shall we get started?" One of the robed wolves steps up beside Clyde while he walks. His private security and the others follow as Clyde marches forward, his eyes cast up toward the orange and yellow sphere in the night sky.

"Precisely on time, as a matter of fact. Everything is in place."

Clyde throws his black robe over himself. Everyone funnel-walks into a small tunnel cushioned on either side by dense evergreen bushes, making it almost impossible to see from the outside. The security holds up a perimeter behind the tunnel as the group heads inside a steep, jagged peak of a particular mountain. The pinnacle featuring a giant sword snapped in half at the blade being clenched by a giant, weathered stone fist residing at the very top.

Inside the dim tunnel, the way is lit with neon green glowing lanterns hanging along the stonework that the shaft is crafted from. Clyde leers over to the hooded wolf and speaks to him." Fantastic, let us be swift. The moon, *Miasma*, is full and just at the apex. Matching the others, but tonight only."

The tunnel system opens up to a wide chamber, which boasts black stonework everywhere, holding up the ceiling in a twisted fashion. Razored blades jet down from the ceiling in the millions in uneven lengths. The air is foggy and dim, cut through only by dangling gold chandeliers and their eerie candlelight. The hooded wolf speaks to Clyde while he walks away from him. "I will fetch the offerings now. The others are finishing the spell work as we speak."

"I've got the final incantations and binding spells recorded in my spell book. No easy task, might I add," Clyde responds curtly, producing a black leather tome. A hellfire glowing ruby encrusted in the center of its cover.

A helicopter flies low, loaded with a squad of armed *Lycandian* police field operatives closing in toward the remote location with the frosty pine tree-covered mountain summits. They exit their vehicles, dropping into the craggy and snowy forest environment, swiftly closing in toward their objective as the weathered headstones appear encircled by crooked iron wrought fences.

One advances upward from a snowy bush, clutching his firearm and speaking into his microphone softly. "Operator G, in position now. Signals are spotty up here. We got eyes on targets here. Ready when you are."

An ambush of gunfire catches the private security force off-guard, two drop dead from the sudden attack. Several officers converge on the lot from an opposing angle. A magical missile is hurled at them from one of the sorcerers on security, which crackles and explodes on the iron fence. Liquifying the tick metal in its radius. A chaotic standoff ensues, Operator G deploying one of his pieces of equipment, a force shield to take cover and counter-attack from. The police operatives are ultimately successful, killing all the security, no one having surrendered. Advance forward from the horrendous firefight, hearing friendly reinforcements closing in on their radios.

"Go! Move, the kidnapped have to be inside if our tip about the graveyard is accurate!" Operator G announces, rushing into the tunnel battle ready with other law enforcement operatives behind him. The dank air isn't as chilly as outside, but an eerie sensation creeps over them all. A magic using officer holding his pistol in one paw and his palm upright comments quietly next to Operator G an uneasy crack in his tone, "Something's not right about this place, sir. The aura totem on my belt is picking up very aggressive dark magic."

Clyde, ambition gleaming in his glowing arctic blue eyes in the gloom, stands around a circular purple colored circle carved into the smooth tiled floor. Silver outlines the bizarre runes against the wide black stone. An altar resides at the perfect center of the circular alien symbol. Chained to it were several younger looking *Lycandian* sacrifices in various states of panic. The hooded wolf approaches Clyde. The robed and hooded wolf who spoke to Clyde earlier outside approaches him up on the altar, whispering in Clyde's ear, "Sir, some law enforcement have arrived topside." There is a tinge of worry in the cultist's voice.

An amused expression crosses Clyde's almost hidden facial features under his own hood and mask. With a stern tone, he says to them, "Kill every last one of them if you must. The ritual begins now. We stop for nothing!"

"As you command, Grand Warlock Crowly."

Countless robed cultists grab at sub-machine guns and ammo magazines from racks lining the farthest outreaches of the spacious cavern.The law enforcement raid the area, advancing through the confusing tunnel system. The cultists storm back with fanatic abandon, and in increasing numbers. Operator G throws himself to the stone floor hard, as a body is flung overhead by an explosion right in front of him. He wildly opens fire at what he could see, but rancid smoke fills the air, cramping his visibility. Cultists run wild all around, over their own dead and wounded, unfazed in their violent frenzy.

The ritual room itself booms with loud, heavy music from an orchestra of some kind, unseen. The warlocks began to thrash in excitement around the uplifted platform where Clyde and the altar were. Clyde's paws are aglow with an inky black aura while he taps into the devilish side of the arcane further. Every hair on his person feels like it's going on end. The very skin beneath it tingling.

"Comrades, tonight, in unity, we will be unleashing an apocalyptic force!" Clyde Crowly yells, his voice rising over the music and causing an uproar of elation. The attendees numbered in the upper thousands, thrusting their limbs and fists into the air in just the ritual chamber alone, and the roars and howls of excitement now reach the same decibel of the music.

Operator G slides to cover, panting in a panic as his nerves grow more strained in the fight. A fellow officer wasn't as fortunate drops to the ground just a couple feet behind him. They advance in the tunnels enough to now hear the roaring crowd and music, like it was a concert. There is a break in the attack. He and the other officers bravely rush forward, gaining ground in the tunnel system once more.

They run up to meet nearly a cluster of a hundred cultists shoulder to shoulder from two tunnels that intersect, steamrolling toward them unabated. Operator G expels rounds from his rifle until he is hit himself, lowering for cover and to inspect his fresh injury. In turn, the officers there exchange fire, killing many cultists before eventually dying by enemy gunfire, or being overtaken. The advancing reinforcements from the surface arrive, with shields and more firepower, to meet the cultists. Operator G, bloodied up badly, is suddenly dragged behind a bulletproof shield by an ally.

Operator G, in a panicking tone, speaks, coughing. "We followed up that trafficking case into this hellhole? Who are we dealin' with? They have a whole standing army here."

The officer holding the shield was about to answer Operator G, when suddenly they were assaulted and stabbed wildly by several cultists before his very eyes, enraged and foaming at the muzzle, leaving him horrified. The mob began pushing the police back. Operator G fights for his life, and he is shoved to his knees, then onto his back, and finally up to fend for himself. The officer bashes down a cultist as the close quarter shootout and melee in the tunnels continues, cultists clamoring over the wounded and dead, throwing their bodies toward the armed officers and eventually dogpiling them. Operator G huddles and applies a first aid to himself amidst the fighting.

Back inside the ritual chamber, Clyde steps calmly to the center of the diabolical symbol while the other warlocks channel their foul magical energy into the rune. Once he places his paw upon the altar with chained and bound up victims, a powerful energy ripples throughout the chamber, putting fur and hair alike on end for all present. The very chamber, walls, and mountain shakes just once. A vile crimson beam blasts up from the center of the altar, crackling with foul orange lightning bolts. Clyde winces briefly from the sudden intense heat, warming him uncomfortably so.

Clyde Crowly, tensing his shoulders and feeling the fur on his tail go on end still, chants in a low tone before yelling out, "These seven souls of pure flesh we offer as tribute, the first price is now paid."

The crowd repeats the chant. "The price is paid."

The altar glows hotter before outright vaporizing and absorbing the poor horrified individuals bound to it. The whiff of charred and decaying flesh fills his sense of smell. Clyde stands unharmed in the proximity, but witnesses up close as the altar suddenly explodes from reality altogether. A silent black hole sits in its place.

Operator G muscles his way forward despite his injuries, as cultist after cultist with machine guns attack him and the others. He slowly makes grueling progress, but his eyes widen under his dirty goggles upon seeing the chamber firsthand. His visage under his protective face armor goes to a look of absolute terror, as a swarm of fanatics rushes up from the floor to join the trickling cultists still pushing against the law enforcement raid, whom little of remains by now. He had been and continues filming the raid with his field camera optic and now turning on his heels and a whisk of his tail joins the retreat.

"Abort mission," says one of his colleagues.

"Creator above, save us! What evil magic is that? We have to report this. Run, you fools!" Operator G yells to his peers.

The clap of a sound wave causes everyone to stumble, the massive throng of gyrating cultists tripping up on themselves while still lost in excitement. Clyde's legs wobble but he catches himself to stay upright from the rush of sooty, burning charcoal smelling breeze, but now standing all alone on the ritual spot, as the physically petrified warlocks around him who previously attached their spell energy to the summoning, now to waft away in thick cloudy ashes.

A fifteen foot tall monstrous charcoal and inky purple demon appears on top of where the black hole had once existed in space and time. Barbed wire and sharp, jagged iron is meshed and grafted horrifically into the demon's flesh on his shoulders, forearms and along its upper and lower back and wings. The fog in the room now has a crimson hue to it in wake of the ritual. Clyde takes in the demonic being's muscular towering form as it takes one loud step forward with a large glossy black hoof.

A white hot glowing forked tail whipped behind the demon mimicking hot iron. He has fiery bronze horns and glowing crimson eyes. The ritual was a success. The demon nodding with a confident smirk as the ritual symbol simmered beneath, now depleted. The demon unfurling his smoldering wings, while his wing membranes pulsate with magma veins. There is only a brief pause before cheers amongst the crowd emerge. The demon doesn't seem to even notice, or care at first, with an expression of inconvenience as it gazes around its surroundings.

The demon's fiery black eyes narrow on to the sight of Clyde, so much shorter than him in height by comparison, and he lets out a scoffing growl. "You have some great audacity pulling me from the fourth dimension, into my physical form no less. Mortal."

Operator G, in full terror, runs for his life, being chased only seconds of distance behind by a mob originating from the cultist horde. The music resumes as the demon eyes around, rather pleased at the mayhem unraveling all around before it, not noticing Operator G's escape.

Clyde, his heartbeat racing in his eardrums, smugly stares up at the demon, clenching his fists, glimmering with void like energy. "This world has been made more than ready for the conquest, but there is an obstacle before unleashing 'The Final Vision,' as is Eradicator's will. This obstacle is the *Starwielder.* You, Demon Lord Noxion Myriad, are capable of defeating it and helping usher in Homeworld's new age."

Noxion is growing a more amused expression on his visage, his eyes widening completely after Clyde finishes. "Ahh, eager servants of our lord and master. Our goals will align nicely, it seems, but make no mistake, mortal, just because you know my name doesn't mean you can command me. I'm not like a mere imp, devil, or poltergeist. Before you start to complain, I will utterly destroy the *Starwielder*, an ancient foe of ours," the demon says.

"Phenomenal, do you know when Eradicator will return?" Clyde asks, moving about and unable to stay still.

"I don't know when Eradicator will arrive, but I do know I can help expedite it. To all our benefit," Noxion Myriad answers Clyde with a sinister grin.

Clyde explains with his own diabolic smirk, lowering his hood now to look up at Noxion. "Yes, I do believe you can. I know just what you'll need to accomplish that...above ground, in the metropolitan city of *Silvium* just south of here. My forces are moving in at dawn."

Clyde Crowly moves away from his space, standing near Noxion, who remains imposingly standing at the altar. He taps a thin microphone that cancels out all music while walking to the edge of the stage to address the now buzzing and murmuring room. A single spotlight is positioned on Clyde. Claps erupt at once as he stands still. A hooded figure runs up to Clyde, handing him a microphone, his voice then blaring over speakers.

"It is time! Rise our fallen brethren upstairs, for their second chance." Clyde pauses with a chuckle, drawing a brief rise of applause. "Then invade *Silvium*, when I give the signal. Kill any and all armed resistance, including those who attack back at us with any form of magic. Blockade all highways, railways, and the airport. Capture anyone attempting to run away or hide. We cannot let them miss out. The old, the young, the sick, gay, straight...it doesn't matter. Everyone." He paces to the right, and when the fanfare dims down continues, "Once we have conquered and cleansed this city, the rest o f *Wulftheon* will follow." Noxion Myriad observes Clyde's speech approvingly. He changes direction, pacing to the left now, the spotlight following Clyde while he continues speaking. "The passage to power is death and rebirth. Most of you are Greywolf *Lycandians*. Our breed has been chosen to receive this gift, the others...not so much. We will kill them all, and with purpose."

Noxion speaks next, in a deep voice carrying far. "Blood to be spilled, yes. Some are saved, everyone else dies. Let's see this city and locate what I truly need."

Operator G is in a full sprint up to the tunnel back to the surface, drawing out his hand pistol while occasionally wiping his head back over his shoulder to see his pursuers practically on his heels. He arrives on the surface while firing several shots to put down the closest cultists behind him, even making a successful run across the snowy flat lot from the cavern entrance.

"Come on, send the video damnit," Operator G exclaims, while zig-zagging before an unseen round hits him, coming from the forest. He loses his balance on the snow as well and skids. A dozen of the cultists behind him slow their run, closing in. He growls in determination, dismissing the coppery taste on his tongue and searing pain in his right side, crawling away, frantic in his effort.

During the early break of daylight, marching and chanting in thunderous lockstep, the heavily armed and armored cult numbering in the many thousands approach through open areas, roadways, fields and from the woods into the large city of *Silvium*. Traffic comes to a stop and jams up, while citizens flee, screaming in terror, as neighborhoods and commercial districts are steadily corralled. The invaders successfully perimeter themselves around the city, creating roadway barricades on the highways and railways, also brazenly seizing the *Silvium* International airport. Local law enforcement attempts to hold a line and are shortly overrun by the sheer number of armed enemies coming at them from all possible angles. Eyewitnesses of Noxion Myriad's flight across the city result in screams of terror, the demon's aura sending those who stare too long at him into a panic.

While all this is happening, Clyde Crowly activates a program that infects the cellphone signals being transmitted throughout *Silvium*. From the safety of a windowed office overlooking the city skyline within *Crowclaw Conglomerates* Headquarters. Thousands are instantly stupefied, under some spell as they collectively group up in strange order. The cultists don't kill or capture any of these poor individuals under the spell, only those resisting or fleeing.

Walking calmly with his arms behind his back, Klaus Cravenfang stops beside Clyde and clears his throat. Clyde turns his head to look at him, saying, "Once Noxion has the *Cosmicism* monument, you must defend it until the ritual is complete. Understand, Klaus?"

"I do, Grand Warlock," Klaus says as he looks out the window, taking in the far off spectacle of the incursion, continuing with finality in his tone. "Consider it done, over my life, and the next."

Noxion flies higher above the dozen military helicopters that are fanning out over the large cityscape of *Silvium* as the cult forces close in from the mountainous countryside. The Demon Lord soars freely toward the moongate shaped monument sitting in the middle of a large recreational grove in one of the city's commercial areas. Noxion lands on the hibernating autumn grass with a loud thud, his charcoal black hooves singing the ground with an audible hiss. The unfolding chaos throughout the city could be heard in the distant background while Noxion walks closer to the ancient moon gate shaped monument.

"All too easy." He gives a scoffing snort through his goat shaped snout. Pausing to extend his right claw forward, he aims toward the colorful stained glass within the monument's arc. Noxion utters some foul sounding guttural language, his glowing red eyes flashing dangerously as several bloody red lightning bolts sparkle out and zap at the stained glass. Slowly, the ten unique stained glass images of *Cosmicism* melt away. The stained glass is now blank, like staring into a crimson mirror, and the stonework darkens as if being charred by some invisible, intense heat. Noxion extends his other claw the opposite way, a determined smirk coming across his visage.

The thirty hibernating oak trees scattered around begin to shiver and shrivel toward the demon, the awful sound of wood creaking as he drains all life from everything around him. The grass all around withers before turning to dust. Noxion proceeds to channel the terrible lightning flashing from his other claw, suddenly intensifying his evil magic spell. The monument rises out of the ground slowly, dirt and rocks displaced outward from it. "More. It needs more! Begin bringing offerings!" Noxion shouts.

CHAPTER EIGHT:
Armageddon's Eclipse

I T IS A COLD clear morning, the cloudless sky letting the sun wash over the small snow-covered castle, the white frosted fir and pines surrounding it. The majestic, mountainous landscape can be seen all around the horizon. From the outside, the castle has three floors with five towers. Four octagon towers on each point of its square base connect all the thirty-foot stone walls, including an even taller circle cylinder tower in the middle with an impressive observatory at its peak. There is evidence of modernization with electrical lines, and even antennae are seen poking up from the twelve inches of freshly fallen snow, the scorched charcoal pile with snow trodden tracks all around it eerily serene.

Staring down at the blackened mark in the snow from the window, glumly leaning against the sill, feeling cold inside like the stone under his paws. Cyngosa recalls with a blank look on his face the last conversation he had with Dorrion replaying in his mind, trying not to forget his voice. With a sigh, he pushes himself off, turning around.The sunlight making its way through the glass brightens the castle.

Cyngosa takes three steps while he's alone in the living room, stopping dead in his tracks when a beep sound hits his ear, cutting through his distracted melancholy. He didn't know where Khelu snuck off to losing track of time, leaving him alone with just Eos's quiet company while the phoenix snoozed roosted in sunlight. Saaliha is away with Minax, packing up the last of her things in a separate room, the tension between them existing throughout Dorrion's passing. Frustration still gnawing at the back of his mind about her spat with him.

Cyngosa moves to the table, looking at the folded up bloodied armor vest resting on top of Dorrion's backpack. The beep repeats itself. Wetting his lips, apprehension momentarily freezing his body in mid-reach, but Cyngosa rummages through Dorrion's belongings left on the table. Noticing that Dorrion's cellphone has a new message on it, the source of the beeping sound. He checks it with raised eyebrows, chewing the inside of his cheek. Noticing the digital message is from Kerith Moonwane under the contacts listed, issuing an SOS and requesting aid, giving his location in *Perilith*. Cyngosa exhales deeply and bites his lip, his eyes reading the message multiple times before he deletes it and then powers off the device. Burying it back in the pocket of Dorrion's discarded clothing.

Cyngosa walks away from the table and mumbles under his breath, "We can't. We must get to wherever that mountain range is. There was the demon I saw in my vision, and some kind of eclipse of the sun. I don't fully understand it. We need to stop it, somehow."

Saaliha and Minax linger together in the study room, branching off the grand living room area of *Solstice Keep*.

"Are you still able to check up on the news on that computer of yours, maybe send a message to get help?" MInax asks.

"Yeah. The range is probably limited for messages though, just this country. Whatcha thinking?" Saaliha asks, turning her head from her work to perk one ear up and cock her head to the side.

"I can't imagine what happened in *Port Humility* going unnoticed by the world," Minax states matter-of-factly, his purple eyes glinting when he looks directly at her.

"With everything happening, it never occurred to me to check. But the *Paladins* and President Briarpaw's forces were there, with countless witnesses."

Minax inclines his horned head, the red veins spider webbing through his horns aglow still despite the daylight, says in agreement, "Precisely."

Saaliha, switching from the digital aerial map on her screen to a new browser window, her fingers clicking the keys noisily as Minax watches on intently.

The first article among the exhaustive list is an image of Penelope Briarpaw cropped next to the still shot of a hectic scene. With little hesitation, Saaliha clicks the article, discovering it brings her to a live recording.

"What is all this about?" Minax watches. The recording is outside some distance away from a large wolf's head shaped structure next to the perimeter made by authorities.

A *Lycandian* reporter slips into view of the camera. "Right now, we have limited information, folks. There are reports circulating of some kind of, uh, some kind of situation unfolding. Within the *Bastion*, the senatorial and congressional chamber is experiencing some kind of, uh, hostage situation."

Saaliha and Minax dart their eyes to one another for a half-second before locking them back on the screen, listening to the reporter ramble on with uncertainty.

"Awesome-sauce, I'm sure this isn't going to complicate any diplomatic efforts you had in mind," Saaliha sarcastically comments. Minax huffs amused through his nostrils, but keeps his lips pursed, and eyes watching the live report unblinking.

Fingertips tapping along her keyboard, her pupils catch a notification on the corner of Saaliha's computer screen. The flash-drive she put in Dorrion's jet had given her access to his cellphone records, on the very night she met Minax. The very night her whole family was murdered by the crazed president sharing the screen.

Saaliha furrows her eyebrows, seeing the message become deleted. A new pit of betrayal boils in her. Minax glances away from Penelope ranting on the news report and at Saaliha with a worried expression.

"What is it?" he asks.

"A bad decision," Saaliha remarks sharply.

Minax stands resting his torso over the table, once more wearing the boulder opal plate mail armor over his regular clothes, the daylight shining through, catching a glint in the gemstone encrusted in his chest. Idly swaying his wings, listening to Saaliha.

"We're in *The Steel Peaks*, the most remote region in *Wulftheon's* border to *Aluan*," Saaliha says, standing across from Minax at the table while folding her arms. Cyngosa, sitting down at one end of the table, looks between them. Khelu stands at the other end of the table while slings her backpack over her shoulders.

"The closest city is *Silvium*, almost a hundred miles southeast of this old castle, nearest civilization to us is a manufacturing and industrial hub south, called *Thanesborough*, about sixty miles southwest," Cyngosa says, Saaliha turns her head over to him, exhaling.

Clearing her throat, Saaliha suggests, "Well, we could ask the *Trinity* operatives in *Perilith*. I believe they texted Dorrion's phone, not too long ago too."

Cyngosa stiffens up his posture, eyebrows raising up as he stares solely at Saaliha. After a second, he scratches his chin and blinks.

Averting his gaze to the table, Cyngosa says, "I don't know what you are getting at."

There is a sharp inhale from Saaliha, and the energy between them shifts considerably. Saaliha flicks her tail up, clenching the table with her open claws.

Saaliha asks, unwaveringly, "You sly piece of garbage.You actually put the thought in your canine cranium that you could just delete something under my nose. I saw it on my computer. Of all things, a distress message from my brother! Why didn't you at least give him our location?"

Cyngosa, souring his expression, replies, "WHO is on the other side of the world. We cannot afford a distraction now. How do we know for sure? And that it isn't the enemy that could be close by, trying to get us to respond to it, giving our location up in this hostile place."

"That's the excuse you're going to lean on? You could have just as easily confessed. You'd think you know a person," Saaliha retorts with growing frustration.

"You don't know my every living moment. You've only known me for like two weeks," Cyngosa argues back with throwing his arms out.

"Ohhh, act like an adult? Interesting choice of words, Cyngosa," Saaliha yells and shifts forward, continuing, "You decided to screen emails and messages on our behalf. Daxil couldn't have succeeded without Penelope Briarpaw in almost every way you look at it. She must die."

Cyngosa says, "And Dorrion explicitly told me *Silvium* is where to start. We find Clyde Crowly, we stop the global cult he operates. That Penelope and Daxil are certainly members of—at least allies—to it! I literally saw pieces of some demonic incantation they are using in my dream the other night."

Saaliha lets out an angry growl, speaking "So? Penelope's actively holding *Aluan* hostage right now out in the open. I loved Dorrion. Cyngosa, he was a second father to me, certainly in times when my own biological father felt alien to me! Her forces shot and killed him, her soldiers bombed my home, and killed my family. These *Paladins*. It was on her command, so she must pay!"

Minax chimes in, in a fuming mood, as his rumbling tone barges itself into their argument, "Agreed…"

"You're not about to do what I think you're about to do. You are taking her side?" Cyngosa glares at Minax now, frustration showing in his quaking left ear.

"My side? The side of justice for innocent blood spilled, blatant betrayal and murder. She took everything and everyone I loved. Does Penelope being *Lycandian* strike some nerve with you to defend her?" Saaliha snaps, her tail coiling and lashing behind her.

Cyngosa scoffs and replies to Saaliha. "Not at all. I'm sure she doesn't like Direwolves. But are we really going to just storm into *Luminous* and assassinate one of the most powerful world leaders on the continent? Fight her regime's army?" Cyngosa frowns, narrowing his turquoise eyes beneath his brows and exclaims. "Call this what it really is. Revenge! Petty revenge!"

Minax stretches his wings extending off the back of his shoulders, letting out a short exhale, sternly saying, "Yes."

Saaliha, an aggravated growl escaping her throat while her body was locked in a restless stance, squinting her pink eyes directly at Cyngosa. "Yes!"

Cyngosa lets out a forceful exhale through his nostrils, then covers his forehead with the palm of his paw and sighs, biting his lip with irritation as he clenches his fangs while momentarily at a loss for words. Khelu, present to their heated exchange, moves quietly beside Cyngosa, watching on.

Saaliha, her arms folding defensively, clarifies after watching Cyngosa's conflicted reaction. "Clyde isn't being spared. If Penelope is the politics, Silas is the muscle, then Clyde is the money. I'll come for him next if you don't succeed. And I'm not completely dismissing what you saw in your dream."

Khelu folds her arms under her chest and stares between Minax and Saaliha, before speaking."And? What if Crowly can't be stopped by then? He no doubt was around the area of *Port Humility*. He might have salvaged something after we escaped. He might reverse engineer what he can for use in this ritual Cyngosa saw."

Saaliha softens her look and stares at Khelu. "Salvage what? Burned plastic and molten-ized metal. We were there to witness that, so hun don't even bring that up. It's a miracle we survived the crash in the first place." Before Khelu could answer, she then addresses Cyngosa once more. "Did you actually see Clyde himself, though? We never established that. It's hard to trust what you say. I believe it could very well be one of the *Paladins* in *Aluan's* capital."

"Honestly, I did not. I saw just what I described to y'all earlier," Cyngosa replies, scratching under his chin, poking his tongue into his cheek, inhaling a long breath.

Minax looks over in Cyngosa's direction first, then in Khelu's, speaking to each of them. "We will deal with him when it's time, but I feel it in my heart that I must seek out the *Paladins*. Justice for those genocidal maniacs is long overdue, and without mercy. My obligations as the *Starwielder* depend on me setting the record straight to the people of *Aluan* and helping save them from Penelope's tyrannical attempt at dissolving their democracy."

Sluggishly scratching his paw through his messy hair, he bites his lip, saying, There are higher stakes not far from here. Penelope has already taken over. She's got what she wanted...More innocent lives will be lost, however, if we ignore Clyde."

Khelu interjects with a pinched and unhappy look but a calm tone. "I agree with where Minax and Saaliha are coming from, and although Cyngosa took Dorrion's phone without our input, we should pursue Clyde. He's the one pulling that president's strings."

Saaliha exhales somberly, but holding her chin up in defiance and speaks to Khelu first. "Then those *Lycandians* will deal with it, but I know this much as of now...I'm done with you two." She adds in Cyngosa's direction, "As if you truly give a shit about anyone or even yourself, Cyngosa."

Cyngosa scowls and takes a swig of his hip flask in dissatisfaction, turning his back to all of them. Saaliha hoists her backpack with the rest of her equipment and turns to leave the room.

"Feeling is mutual, narcissistic feline freak," Khelu utters at Saaliha in a nasty tone, crossing her arms across her chest before looking toward Minax, her tone more solemn. "You do what you think is best, hun. I'm going to *Silvium* with Cyngosa."

Minax pushes his broad shoulders back and now follows Saaliha out of the castle's living room, stopping to turn and stare at Khelu for a moment, sounding somber. "This is best. May the Creator safeguard both of you in my absence."

Khelu glances at Cyngosa when he turns around finally. He and her exchange a silent nod before moving out of the room. Cyngosa and Khelu depart, bundled up in wintery gear left abandoned in the castle, and begin hiking toward civilization in the frigid climate as the two march through the fresh powdery snow. The sky is cloudless blue, allowing the dazzling sunlight to bathe everything. No fog obscuring the scenic landscape of rippling jagged slopes all around Cyngosa and Khelu, over a million frosty evergreens peppering them. They first trudge through the vast snowy field comprising the castle's property, until reaching the dense evergreen forest a mile away.

A far less amount of snow is on the forest floor, blanketed by light brown dead pine needles. Khelu and Cyngosa cautiously trudge between the snow-dusted trees, firs, and hemlocks with more deafness underfoot. The bitter wind creaking the tallest pine's limbs overhead, and the occasional screeching of flying predatory birds coasting above were the only sounds accompanying the pair along their rough trek.

Saaliha, egged on by Penelope Briarpaw's antagonizing speech, together with Minax, takes off into the cold, crystal clear sky, heading directly south toward *Aluan* hundreds upon hundreds of miles away. The journey will take them all day.

"Well, this is bristling my whiskers, but what's done is done. There's no going back, right Minax?"

"No, we will forge our way by our own choice. That choice being, saving potential allies from a tyrannical, genocidal takeover," Minax replies in solemn agreement.

Kerith and Glyph walk along on a tan dirt pathway, exiting one of the dark brown wooden buildings with colorful neon food signs on it. Kerith's limp has subsided some. He momentarily glances at his bandages, pursing his lips with an optimistic expression. An oblivious bystander was having their cigarette that tinged the smells of hearty broth and sweet BBQ wafting in the air around them. Sprawling out on the right side of Kerith and Glyph are grasslands covered in palm trees for many miles before striking faint patchings of desert on the very horizon's edge, towering sand dunes peeking up. Glyph unlocks his scooter from the communal rack that has other different models and bikes parked with it, rolling his along to conserve gas, passing more businesses on their left. Kerith and Glyph walk away from any curious ears before Glyph breaks the silence.

"I could try breaching Daxil's private computer system, see what he's hiding. Learn the identity of who he's operating with, maybe even find addresses."

Kerith gives his best friend a skeptical look, his right paw playfully fussing with his whiskers mulling his suggestion briefly, before saying, "No, he wouldn't keep what I need in a personal system. It's not a digital file. Fortunately for us, what's hidden in the arcane can be revealed, doesn't matter if it's necromancy, shamanism or even demonic."

Glyph adjusts his backpack with his broad shoulders, glancing up the roadway. "He might have financial shit we could dig up, someone's paying him." Raising an eyebrow with the corners of his smile curling upward, he adds, sounding hopeful, "Well, if Dorrion hasn't gotten back to you, what's the plan, dude?"

"True, true." Kerith walks up beside Glyph and walks with him. "Honestly, I don't know. The *New Moon Ziggurat* wouldn't be a terribly long backtrack. It's close to this side of the megacity, actually." He lets out a disheartened sigh. "Still, it is risky trying to trace the use of demonic magic being covered up. I barely made it out of *Umbris* without being captured, but we can't run, and help isn't coming. You know what that means."

"I'm right with you then. Not just for posterity, bro," Glyph says.

"Okay, one side of this ziggurat is open to the public. The other is not." He and Glyph exchange a firm shake of their paws, moving along the sidewalk while sparse freeway traffic rolls by the strip mall.

Umbris was still bustling at street level during the nocturnal hours. The massive pyramids had lights coming from the windows from residents within. Dotting up the imposing triangle structures on the dark horizon with many little lights. Businesses are still open, including specialty shops, animal companion menageries, and other vendors producing attention grabbing spectacles along the sidewalks. Kerith rides on the back of Glyph's gas powered scooter bike whizz past the commercial area at low speeds with other bike traffic, tucking the grayish charcoal cowl of his robe over his head during their journey.

The two arrive at the *New Moon Ziggurat,* like many of the other towering black stone pyramids scattered throughout the mega city of *Umbris,* the pointy top reaching many thousands of feet from the ground. They park the moped a couple blocks away, near a portion of rural outskirts where *Umbris* folds neatly into the vast savannahs neighboring eastward. A chorus of crickets, along with other night insects, hum around them while they stare apprehensively at the pyramid.

"I've done my fair share of urban exploring in different districts of the city, but this *Ziggurat* isn't just any old abandoned building or crypt. You know, the fact that it isn't even abandoned at all. This is sorta out of my element." Glyph chuckles with a nervous grin, concurrently checking out the challenge set before them.

Kerith nods once, placing a paw on the wrinkled, tattooed skin of Glyph's shoulder and speaking confidently. "Correct. There's security, visitors, and priests performing ceremonies and what not. I've been inside multiple times before growing up."

"That's great and all. We can just walk right in, is what it sounds like to me." Glyph smiles over to Kerith in the dim moonlight.

"I know where Daxil's personal office is," Kerith says, Glyph finding this information out makes his jaw slack slightly in shock but dismisses the thought to question it.

"Lets get closer on foot then. Is his office near the top?" Glyph asks, adjusting his backpack over his shoulder as anticipation takes hold inside him, his hairless tail wags.

Kerith stares off at the pyramid and explains, "Middle level, I believe it has two window slits in its outfacing wall. The security is minimal, but still, I can't let anyone recognize me on camera."

"Should I lead with something, or you? We can try getting inside pretending to attend a ceremony, and sneak off from there. It'd be less suspicious than just climbing into the place," Glyph suggests, folding his arms across his barrel chest torso and tapping his feet.

"I'm not opposed to rolling with that." Kerith adjusts his robe again to cover the top of his head and smirks at Glyph. "As long as anyone working for Daxil is none the wiser, all the better."

Taking what they need from their backpacks, the two walk on the main path heading toward the *ziggurat* to faint noises of the inner megacity districts, and mostly the songs of crickets and the occasional shriek of a nighttime aerial raptor combing the moonlit grasses for dinner. The sheer height of the pyramid increases ever so slightly while Kerith watches it draw closer. Once more, anxiety boils lightly in his gut, leaving the fur on his back to stand on end. Kerith walks off, as they pass under a writhing, twisting tree and he picks up a suitable stick lying beneath it.

"Hey, a decent walking cane," Kerith muses. He extends his claws on his opposite paw to drag away excess bark still lingering on the branch.

After licking his lips thoughtfully, Glyph asks, "So, explain to me why Daxil betrayed your family, exactly what was being worked on? You know quite a bit about him."

Kerith inhales through his nose, closing his eyes momentarily clearing his throat in an exhale, turning his head he answers his best friend, "Daxil was working with my mom, including a team of others, who had been perfecting an antidote for *Noxium* poisoning and cancers related to its exposure. This *ziggurat* has a state-of-the-art research lab deep underneath. As above, so below. You know how it is with these pyramids, Glyph. It was extremely reserved access only. My guess is he had some shady backdoor dealings being conducted to steal the success for himself. Either way, the Moonwane Compound was destroyed by a *Lycandian* military aircraft. I witnessed the thing."

"There's still controversy over it, given the little evidence, throughout the *Coven* and the whole megacity. The case was put into a limbo ever since," Glyph comments, sharing his suspicious look with Kerith as they walk.

"Funny how that works, isn't it? I'm sure my mother's office was cleared out long ago." Kerith lets out an abrupt laugh after, his comment tone laden with sarcasm.

Glyph, suspects, twitching his whiskers, with an exaggerated scratching of his hairless chin. "Some wealthy evil *Lycandians* getting involved, now this is a jackalope hole worth diving into." He turns on the recorder for his cellphone's camera. "Getting to the root of the weed!"

Glyph and Kerith approach the entrance of the *New Moon Ziggurat*. It is well lit with purple lights, with two *Felidaen* guards posted at the front doorway under the watchful surveillance of security cameras. One is an orange tiger, the other a cheetah. Wearing magenta body-plates woven into flexible wine colored fabrics over their entire bodies, darker plum colored helmets on their heads, waxing moon-crescents rising from the visors. Kerith takes notice of the firearms holstered on the guard's belts.

The polished silver doors leading inside the *Ziggurat* just a couple feet behind. Kerith adopts a false limp, using his leg that recently had a legitimate limp to it. He wanders up with Glyph holding his free paw, the walking stick in the other. The cheetah guard smiles and takes the walking stick from Kerith, greeting them with surface-level politeness.

Glyph stops in his tracks, he and Kerith stiffening up as the uncertainty of how this would go roots in their minds. The orange tiger scans Kerith with an electronic scanner that he takes off from his utility belt, going from head to toe on Kerith, both guards ignoring Glyph, who's now breathing slightly quicker but otherwise plays off a calm demeanor. The cheetah holds Kerith's walking stick and moves to scan Glyph next from head to toe, while his tiger colleague checks the contents of Kerith's geeky appearing backpack with both paws. Carrying mana-charged crystals, a stone ankh, a generic edition of common spells, and lastly, a first aid kit. While odd, it is nothing of major concern to the guards.

With anti-magic security systems, cameras, and many other Moonstalker Forces lurking on duty, any disturbance here would be snuffed out like a candle to the breeze. The cheetah guard speaks to Kerith. "Your business here tonight?"

He clears his throat, buying a second to settle his nerves. "To get spiritual comfort from the temple," Kerith says, wringing his empty paw against his gray robe while the retractable claws of his other paw dig into the wood of his walking stick.

"Fair enough. But no *Sarosians* are allowed in the prayer chamber. He'll have to wait outside until you are finished." The orange tiger is fast to state, laced with a rumble in his throat, giving Glyph the hairless Sphinx a dirty look. Glyph feels the air catch in his lungs and a tightness inside his chest, his honey-colored eyes darting at Kerith.

"Find vitality in prayer within, sir." The cheetah guard returns the wooden makeshift cane to Kerith, who reaches slowly and deliberately to take it. The tiger takes a plastic card strung to a lanyard and presses it against an electronic pad. The smooth silvery handleless door swings inward. The cheetah keeps a wary eye on Glyph while the orange tiger ushers Kerith inside. The two exchange a wink, Glyph jerking his head upward quickly toward the left.

"Ohh, thank you! May the nebulas bless you with stardust," Kerith replies to the guard, trying to sound older, with a deep, croaking voice. For the most part, the two guards carry on their duty convinced or uncaring, Kerith breathing a muffled sigh of relief as he's inside.

"I'll catch up with you later," Glyph says, turning to walk away until he is far enough of out of the guard's vision before he carefully changes course going alongside the pyramid's perimeter as grasshoppers chirp around him and the savannah grass crunches underfoot, hardly audible over the thumping of his heartbeat in his eardrums.

Kerith hobbles into the *Ziggurat*, leaving the chorus of crickets and grasshoppers outside. Walking into a widening amphitheater, the ceiling above flat obsidian stone, same as the second floor and so on. Soft ambient purple light illuminates the ceiling, walls, and floor. Kerith's feet beneath him. The soft hum of electrical lights and the crackling of lit braziers are the only sounds now. Alert, he keeps his head swaying this way and that.

Bathed in a soft golden light, Kerith passes a series of anthropomorphic feline statues in various poses carved into the pillars. Incorporating familiar oasis plants and wildlife toward the ceiling portion in the walls. The different phases of the moons are also depicted above, all in incredibly detailed craftsmanship. He steps up a flight of stairs and walks along a hallway absent of any persons, peeking through the thin slits of the grape stained glass windows of the second floor, letting clear moonlight spill inside.

Glyph creeps adjacent, roughly twenty feet away from the pyramid, just shy of its exterior lighting, keeping to the darkness of the savannah's edge. His eyes scan the windows of the pyramid's first level until suddenly his fixated marigold orbs spot a pair of paws, one paw holding a piece of a tree branch waving in one of them.

Kerith pops his head out, not spotting any signs of a camera. He gestures for Glyph to come closer, and Glyph sneaks quickly over to the tall, sharp fence made of iron at the base of the *New Moon Ziggurat*.

Picking up a decent sized rock, Glyph wraps one end of his black, double-thick nylon rope from his backpack around the rock, before sending it as far as he could throw over the wrought iron spiked fence.

Kerith watches on nervously, his ears perking up all the way to catch the slightest sound that seems off. His wide baby blue eyes following Glyph's rock soar through the air until it lands on the forty-five degree face of the pyramid. Glyph reels the rope in until it gets jammed, the rock wedging itself between uneven charcoal black bricks. He pumps his fist with elation and a wide grin.

Cautiously, Glyph yanks himself up with his nylon rope emitting a faint stretching sound, getting his footing on the fence's first crossbar at almost twice his height up off the ground. After a few tense minutes, Glyph pulls and climbs his way to the top of the fence, squeezing himself between two large spikes, turning himself around as he descends the other side. Halfway down, he leaps from the fence onto the obsidian blocks of the pyramid, landing off-balanced and tripping over. Kerith winces, but quickly realizes Glyph is probably okay; he made it over the fence.

Glyph hikes and grabs up at the black stones, still warm from the earlier sun, grunting as he scrapes his knees and elbows, trying to keep his body low profile. Finally, reaching the window sill that Kerith is at, he hands off his backpack to him. Taking a moment's time to wedge and wiggle his body through the thin window, Glyph intentionally falls forward onto the smooth, black stone floor with a wash of purple light over it.

"Okay, we're in. Where's the stairs at?" Glyph asks, catching his breath, also a bit distracted as he observes the decorations and architecture of his new surroundings. Kerith glances over his shoulder. Letting go of Glyph's backpack as his friend reaches for it. He then straightens upright and is now moving toward a flat carpet of softly glowing green cloth.

"Here. Only way past this level," Kerith states, preparing to stand on the carpet.

Glyph walks onto it with Kerith. The illuminated carpet flashes to a neon lime green color and levitates with them on it, up thirty feet to the next floor, before lowering back down once they step off. A brass gate hastily closing off the gaping hole to the ground floor of the *Ziggurat.*

Kerith darts his eyes about. No one was on this floor with them, yet. "Watch my back. I'm just hoping he hasn't moved his office or anything."

Glyph whispers, "Oof, that would suck. I got you, dude." Despite his larger body frame, Glyph's movements are deceptively subtle, even in the near deathly silence.

Kerith speeds up his pace as memory returns to him, replenished by the surroundings and aroma. A mixture of sandalwood, pot-pourri and incense tickles his nose, heading low into a section of stone cubicles with gold tinted glass and comfortable cushioned furniture. Glyph keeps up in tow, throwing glances over his broad shoulder and twisting around to check behind him, keeping his body pressed to identical cubicles.

Kerith passes several ornate black and gold gilded offices until skidding on the reddish purple colored carpeting. Kerith inspects the number key lock to the office door, and taking a piece of parchment he has in his bag, he breathes on it, then presses it onto the keypad lightly, inspecting it in the light. He presses the matching numbers, and the office door makes a victorious clicking sound to their ears.

"Sweet revenge can often be found in just the simplest of forms," Kerith whispers back to Glyph, who has his head turned facing the hallway behind them, which is thankfully still absent from any passersby. Glyph then wipes his head back around, catching Kerith in the act of cautiously opening the door in. The pair walk inside the office, with a gothic style table and two black leather chairs placed around it.

The room's decor is black and gold like the rest of the office floor. Kerith and Glyph step on the flat carpeting. Kerith goes straight for the large, dark wooden desk, and right after a brief glance at the bare surface, he rummages through the drawers finding nothing of importance. He looks up with a sigh at his friend Glyph, slumping his shoulders and shutting each drawer in defeat.

Glyph searches around the room, spotting a coat rack in the corner behind Kerith. "I think that's his lab coat."

Kerith turns his head, following Glyph's gaze to spot it as well. He walks over and begins digging into the two pockets, pulling out a lanyard with an ID tag. "Perfect. Good eyes on that, Glyph buddy."

"Yeah, making power moves. So, uh wow, do we actually go through that high security lab?" Glyph asks, a crack of nervousness in his tone and his gauged ears twitch.

"That's the cool part. We don't have to," Kerith says, smirking and shaking his head as he tosses the lanyard tag over to Glyph, who catches it on reflex. "Log onto his computer using that and pull up whatever you can find on it. Do what you do. I can work with this." Kerith now moves Daxil's lab coat to lay it over the stooping inky black coffee table nearby.

Glyph turns on his cellphone's recording feature and walks around to face Daxil's desk and stands in front of the computer. Logging in, he types and clicking through the different programs on Daxil's office computer. "Huh…What's his lab coat good for, then?" Glyph inquires as he multitasks with excited paws.

Kerith explains as he sets up, pulling out the single ankh he has been carrying in his bag. "Demonic magic, that essence is unmistakable. Reckless, what exactly is he getting into?"

Glyph squints his eyes, humming with a curious purr before going quiet for a few seconds. Breaking the silence, he asks, "What is this 'Project Group Hug' about? It appears Daxil has been communicating with some three-piece suits from *Crowclaw Conglomerates International*. For over a month, this email chain goes back and forth, like a lot." Glyph's eyebrows arching up toward the end of his sentence.

"I don't have a clue what 'Project Group Hug' is. Those former cyber security skills of yours are becoming useful, delve in and find out more," Kerith says as he returned the lab coat exactly how it was found on the coat rack. Before then moving carefully across Daxil's office to Glyph.

Glyph admits, "You could say something like that. Saaliha was the one who actually aced the top of the class. I just barely achieved a passing grade."

Kerith nods in agreement. "She always loved building and modifying, and causing pandemonium around the manor with me and Rhanisha growing up. I've long since cried my last tear of mourning while in captivity. I will repay my family's enemy." Kerith pauses, twitches his whiskers in concert, cracking his knuckles and continuing to speak. "But we're going to need to equip ourselves properly against demonic, magical energy. It's not like elemental magic or simple arcane. I got us, though. You got this."

With a sigh, Glyph says, "Nothing about that gunship. Check out this file here though, it's blueprints for some giant laser weapon system. Delivered up to a satellite by a space shuttle. This was completed, uhh..." he trails off mid-sentence to scroll down the computer screen with the mouse, "six months ago with a successful installation in orbit." Speaking more into his cellphone mounted on his pocket, than to Kerith, "Are you viewers seeing this?!"

"Eh, just because they bolted and plugged it in correctly doesn't mean anything. I mean, in interspace, it is still an impressive task in and of itself. Any record of a test run?" Kerith asks, his curiosity getting the better of him about this satellite.

"Nope." His hairless face beams as he discovers something else entirely. "I got something even better for us, dude. I bugged his email system."

Kerith moves away from the table and is standing behind Glyph, viewing over his shoulder and creeps by the doorway on watch now. Continuing to ensure the cubicle doesn't get barged in by unannounced visitors. "Let's wrap it up and clean up any trace of our little visit."

Glyph bites his bottom lip and nods at his friend in agreement, commencing to close down the computer program he was viewing through. Taking a microfiber cloth out of his backpack, Glyph wipes down the keyboard and desk. Standing up and leaving Daxil's desk, hopefully without a trace in the aftermath of his snooping. Kerith hangs the white jacket back up where Glyph had spotted it and backtracks out of Daxil's office. Due to an immense amount of luck, their journey back to the first floor and the process of exiting goes without an incident. Glyph leaps back over the fence, and Kerith strolls past the guards as they regroup in the savannah's swaying grass.

Returning to Glyph's parked moped, which, fortunately for them, has been left in its beaten up state without further damage or tampering. Consolidating their gear with the items they left behind, Glyph starts up his moped and drives off, with Kerith on the back once more. "Where now? I got a quarter of a tank left in this shitbox."

"My dad told me once there is a *Trinity* safe house in *Vudazak*. It's probably still intact. I hope, at least, concerning the breach in *Trinity's* security."

"Awesome. *Vudazak* isn't too far, we should have enough gas. Do you have an address I can type in for my GPS?" Glyph asks as he maneuvers the moped down the bumpy dirt road back onto a main street.

"Sorry, Glyph. Heh. It's not that kind of location, it won't come up. But we can stop near it," Kerith answers.

Daylight washes over Kerith and Glyph, who notice the sun is slowly becoming dim despite its ascent in the morning sky. Kerith shields his eyes while he observes the odd solar event, which is drawing many onlookers. One of *Homeworld's* three orbiting moons covers the sun's bright rays. However, the sky has a subtle red hue to it, as the normally orange colored moon named *Miasma* is now haloed by the sun behind it, making it appear crimson to witnesses instead.

"That is no normal occurring eclipse, even with a lukewarm IQ... you can just tell," Kerith states.

"What kind of magic is capable of doing that?" Glyph asks, his gold gauged ears falling flat to his head as he cranes it up and uses his palm to break up the blinding light coming down. The rest of his posture perking up, Kerith crosses his arms.

Kerith answers his best friend with concern hinted in his voice. "Magic that no mortal being here in our dimension or reality could possibly possess, at least not without extreme conditions being met."

Glyph turns the camera back on to record again. "Hey, viewers. It's ya boy!" Holding his rectangle phone up in the sky, he pans around dramatically. Kerith scratches his chin whilst giving him a look. "I'm sure a lot of you are seeing this crazy eclipse thing...be sure to tag me in any viral threads or comment sections, if anyone knows anything! Glyph the myth, streaming live in *Vudazak*."

Kerith, swiftly running a paw through his messy long black hair, speaks up now. "Come on, buddy."

They pass an open patio café, the aroma of freshly ground coffee and sweet rolls wafting out to them. A mounted television featuring the eclipse's appearance as breaking news. Kerith and Glyph stop and wander toward the café, exhausted from the overnight adventure, a rumbling of their stomachs. Kerith sits himself on an iron and wood stool, with his friend Glyph climbing up to sit with him at the black and white tiled bar.

Kerith, keeping his gray robe made of light fabric, avoids any direct contact with any of the baristas. Glyph covers for him as he orders breakfast through a receptive, and yet hurriedly working white tiger. The barista takes the *Umbris* paper currency to the register, wiping her paws on her stained apron and moving right along to the coffee bean press that emits a hissing sound.

"I'm starving. A little breakfast won't hurt. I don't think anyone is going to recognize you," Glyph says, attempting to reassure Kerith, who finishes peeking over his shoulders and watching the sidewalk briefly.

"True, I'm hungry too. But I'll honestly feel much better once we're out of any cities," Kerith admits, licking his lips at the prospect of hot food, the freshly baked sweet rolls making him salivate. He hadn't eaten since lunch yesterday.

The news stations commenting on the eclipse immediately brought in a talking head on to explain the event, the news anchor's voice coming through the TV speakers.

"Viewers, I'm pleased to introduce Dr. Sabarren. Expert of Astronomy, and with decades of Magical study. He's joining us this morning to shed some light on this, um, lack of light."

Kerith and Glyph's attention drawn in by the TV, a panther wearing a tasteful three piece suit with a pair of glasses and appearing very academic pops on the screen from the waist up.

Dr. Sabaren is still regaining his composure as he video calls in from what could be deduced by viewers is his office, adjusting his blue-tinted glasses and smoothing his striped button-down purple and white shirt. "Thank you! What is happening is a magical manipulation of one of our moons. In this particular instance, it's *Miasma*. A tremendous amount of magical energy would be required for such a warping of physical laws. Scientists have already found the path of totality hovering somewhere over the center of *Lycandia*. That is also the source of the magical energy causing this."

"Doctor, do you or your colleagues know what will happen next? How long will this last? What, or who, may have caused this to happen?" the news anchor asks off-screen. The barista rushes up to Glyph and Kerith, placing a hot sweet roll in front of them on the countertop next to their gray ceramic cups.

"This will primarily affect the area under the eclipse's totality. Right now, invisible to our naked eyes, there is a huge vortex of raw magic energy funneling into an incarnation or spell of some sort. What the result is, I couldn't tell you. But, the indications are showing, it's dark magic in nature. It will only end once the spell has completed itself, or is somehow interrupted," Dr. Sabaren explains, the astronomer adjusts his white tie in the process of clicking through a brief clip showing how the moons and planet orbit *Homeworld*, perpetually keeping the region under the eclipse in shadow. He continues after clearing his throat, "Miraculously enough, it will not affect global tide cycles nor will the other two moons orbiting *Homeworld* collide with *Miasma* while it's stationary. But the data we are gathering from both the storm of magical energy and this sudden eclipse is mind-boggling. Who is responsible? Maybe a supernatural being. No single mortal warlock or necromancer could ever pull this off."

"This is crazy, can you believe it?" Glyph asks Kerith, nudging him with his elbow while finishing his nut and fruit infused sweet roll.

"Is it bad that I can?" Kerith says back as he sips down the coffee, appreciating the caffeine as his all-nighter's effects weigh in on him, battling a yawn.

Kerith places his paw on Glyph's shoulder, pulling him along away from the café, picking up the pace once more as they walk through *Vudazak*. The city has a skyline much lower than *Umbris*—the megacity Glyph is more accustomed to seeing—but is still bustling with urban activity. The buildings are made of hardened gray smooth clay reinforced with black metal beams and braces.

Hundreds of colorful purple, pink, and baby blue streamers attach to closely neighboring buildings of similar heights. There is almost no green vegetation in the savannah this far from the coast, especially around *Vudazak*. One single oasis on the off-center edge of the city, fed by one of the few enormous rivers flowing through the region, lies the source.

Weaving through five foot tall green stalks with silvery flowers sprouting at their tops that Kerith and Glyph have been hiking through for a couple minutes. uncover an upraised portion of land from the mud. Kerith is first to round over the hilly area, covered in growing light green grass, thousands of small purposefully placed stone markers indicating this is a graveyard. Glyph comes up behind him and halts to take in the hauntingly serene view.

Glyph, who wasn't recording as of yet, lifts his phone up and takes a single picture before Kerith gives him a very quick and stern look. Glyph gulps sheepishly for a moment. "I don't recognize these kinds of grave markings."

Kerith softens up and explains. "That's because these are the graves of *Lycandians,* who served *Trinity of Tranquility*, and perished in action far from their homeland. There is an outpost just at the end of the yard."

Glyph's eyes widen at the information and silently glances about as they traverse through the graveyard. "This all looks a bit overgrown, but this place hasn't been completely abandoned." He stops in his tracks and looks at Kerith. "*Trinity* held funerals for its members here all this time?"

"They decommissioned it six or so years ago, I think, but yes, you and I are almost there, dude. The safe house itself is still here," Kerith says, as they approach a mossy wind weathered mausoleum structure, no more than twelve feet tall depicting *Alpha and Omega*; the symbolic weapon of the *Starwielder*. Kerith leans down and places his family's locket against the sun-baked warm stone. Glyph, no stranger to magic, is still impressed, watching the stone replica of the *Starwielder's* weapon rise from the base. The base itself then lifts straight up from the ground to reveal a downward descending stairway, hidden under the now levitating stone block.

"Hmmm, I'm not convinced, my man. This safe house is more like a tomb," Glyph comments, and Kerith laughs. They climb down and inside. The stairway twists its way into the cooler deep ground, the ancient crafters taking the effort centuries ago to hone and cut the thick stone bricks, and watertight the passage with special mortar. Kerith's modern day flashlight guides him and Glyph along their way. They walk into a spacious bricked square room. The *Trinity of Tranquility* affiliates made use of every inch of the place. Shelves of non perishables, medical treatment basics, and other survival necessities are all neatly stored on various shelves throughout the room. A crude water purification machine is next to a very dated oil storage unit.

Gleaming their flashlights along the brick and steel beam reinforced ceiling, Glyph and Kerith notice a series of wire installations and they follow it to the generator in the farthest corner, flicking the switch the device sputters and it almost sparks to life, but then makes a click. Glyph wanders around, leaving Kerith to fix the battery with some fine-tuning. He clears off corrosion and restores the connection. The generator makes an awful ignition sound, but turns on.

"Can't say that thing will last for very long. We need to get a distress signal out right away. There have to be remote *Trinity* operatives that weren't caught in the attack. No matter how coordinated that attack was. We can relay what we discovered," Kerith says, watching as Glyph, who now stands by a light switch panel and flicks it on to illuminate the rest of the room. They spot one table in the middle of the room, with a pile of folding chairs and dusty looking books lazily stored on top of the table itself in stacks. Four armchairs sat around it, covered in dusty white sheets. Kerith walks over a computer on a personal sized surface nearby, pushing the power up button to no avail. Glyph moves up next, swiping the old device right off and lets it smash to the floor after first unplugging the hard wire out of the back with his other free paw.

"Screw that oversized paperweight. I think I was born right around when they stopped producing those things," Glyph says, and, placing his laptop on the surface, he plugs the cable into his own modern device with a convenient adapter.

"There might have been sensitive stuff on it," Kerith retorts, but not angrily.

"I'm positive every board in it is rotted and the data files on them are corrupted. *Trinity* knew that I'm guessing when they packed up decades ago." Glyph looks around, shaking his head and taking a momentary pause to add, "This place is just a glorified janitor's closet now, more than anything."

"It's got electricity. That'll do for what we have to accomplish here," Kerith states, unzipping his backpack, and decompressing its few contents.

The eclipse is scarcely visible through the hazy sunlight that washes over the vibrant coastal mangrove forest, broken up along the ocean by shallow sandbars and bizarre shaped deltas. The trees stand tall with lush green vines and lichen loaded with silvery white flowers draping over the snaking, slow-moving bodies of water. Their limbs sway in the sea breeze softly. The air smelling salty, yet sweet from the patches of colorful blossoming in different colors from a hundred different plant species, a particularly sandy patch in the deeper portion of an estuary has a small gray wood boat house on sturdy stilts, with several weathered mossy docks. It is a far cry from a marina port, but a single anchored steamboat sits in the outermost pier.

Veridian, an anthropomorphic lion, exits the boat, wearing battle worn silver colored combat armor, complete with broad shoulder guards, all of which featured the insignia of *Trinity of Tranquility*. He holds his helmet in one paw and his other holds his matte black assault rifle by his hip. Quietly staring around the serene area with shimmering bronze eyes, the hum of insects and songs of birds are welcoming sounds to his swiveling ears. Veridian's feline ears are prominent through his tan mane that has some streaks of snow white in it. Keeping the mane tied back are many silver rings. He walks toward the boathouse, up the creaking wooden stairs before finally going inside, the door being unlocked.

The structure is one giant room, with a radio and communication devices spread out on a solid wooden table in the middle with several empty chairs. Chairs Veridian wishes weren't bare with somber eyes. There are virtually no decorations, not even paint, the walls instead adorned with maritime charts and maps of islands, tide patterns, and coral reefs. He picks up a cellphone still plugged into a charger by all the equipment on the first table. Veridian checks to see if he has any signal at all and grins, discovering he does when standing near all the routers and devices. A satellite hotspot is available to Veridian. He decides to take his opportunity, opening his phone and making a quick call. The other end goes to an automated beep, giving his heart a flutter of excitement.

The weary lion confidently says, "This is Veridian, Operative Number 101. Stronghold has fallen. I repeat, Stronghold has fallen. I'm the last survivor." He feels defeated as the following seconds of silence dredge on.

Veridian exhales, letting his shoulders droop but keeping an optimistic smirk. His bright yellow and tan eyes take in the radio communication equipment on the table. Veridian starts by adjusting the dials while getting dissimilar static through the speakers. Refining the knob back and forth, Veridian zeros in on a new frequency. Picking up the microphone, the lion goes to broadcast.

"Hello, this is Stronghold. Operative 101, anyone on this channel frequency, over?" Unfortunately, he was met with more silence. He tries a few more times before stepping back in momentary defeat, slouching his broad shoulders while his slender tail with a brown brush tip droops to the floor.

He turns and steps back outside, leaving the door open, as the bright sunlight washes over him once more, greeted by a warm salty breeze. Standing on the tiny porch of the stilted boat house, with such a height advantage, Veridian couldn't help himself scanning the lush flowery mangroves and even out at the shallow ocean line. His nostrils flare when the next breeze that wafts by doesn't smell quite right, his left eyebrow raising up with suspicion.

A series of bleeps and clicks emit through the radio's speakers, catching Veridian's hearing over the otherwise calm ambiance. Veridian moves quickly back to the radio, catching the beeps and clicks as a form of broadcasted code. He rummages through a filing shelf above the radio equipment to retrieve a piece of paper, snatching up a pen as well, jotting down the translations. Veridian gives a deep chested laugh as he re-dials the radio and picks up the microphone again. "Hello? This is Stronghold, Operative 101. Clever transmission, whom am I speaking too, over?" There is a crinkling sound, then it clears up.

"Kerith Moonwane, I'm not familiar with Stronghold, but this is a frequency I was taught to use for *Trinity* members for emergencies. Uh, over." The voice comes through crackly sounding, but not so distorted that Veridian can't understand. His face brightens up at the mention of *Trinity.*

"Yes, I am a representative of *Trinity.* 'The Soul', 'The Flesh', 'The Mind'. A Commando. Stronghold was a garrison. It was attacked a week ago and overrun by literally thousands of black-robed mercenaries, well trained and equipped. *The Armageddon Cult.* My name is Veridian. I'm afraid I'm the only survivor of my squad that I'm aware of. Kerith Moonwane, are you Adaros's boy? Do you have a cellphone? Over," Veridian asks, and waits for a response. He notices now the croaking of frogs and harmony of insects close by have ceased, his back straightening up.

The voice of Kerith transmits once more, crackling staticky over the receiving speaker. "Yes. I'll give it to you."

Veridian scribbles down the number, then after finishing he abruptly abandons the radio and bolts upright when his ears catch the faint sound of a motorized vehicle coming from the waterfront. He puts Kerith's number into his device and stows it in a zipper pocket underneath his armor.

"Uh...Hello?" Kerith's voice carries out from the swaying radio receiver, left dangling as Veridian has long since vacated.

"Well...speaking of Eradicator," Veridian says to himself, simultaneously brandishing his firearm and clicks the safety off of his trigger. Veridian extends his empty paw down to snag his rugged, waterproof backpack that is leaning against the wall of the doorway. Using the buckles on it to hasten attaching it to his person while exiting the boathouse, staring out at the ocean with a lump forming in his throat. A formidable team of ten jet skis bounce over the waves at full speed, closing in quickly.

One of the individuals riding as a passenger extracts a rocket launcher from their backside and impressively attempts to take aim during the bumpy ride. Veridian scowls, aiming his rifle in futile effort. The attackers are just out of range for the moment, but recognizing them instantly as militants for the *Armageddon Cult*. Timing it between hitting waves to fire the projectile, the rocket launcher is released, hitting Veridian's parked steam boat directly in a fast whoosh of smoke. The anchored vessel explodes in a burst of flames and debris. Seconds later, the ski jets dispersing their occupants all across the pier once pulling up from the ocean.

Multitasking, Veridian witnesses the rocket blowing up his small boat in a boisterous boom, attempting to retaliate by shooting at the enemies that finally get into range of his gun to stall their advance. Changing his mind to escape further inland, Veridian moves around the small building. Barging into view of twelve black armored up mercenaries enclosing on the perimeter on the other side of the boathouse, he backtracks in his steps. Three take aim and open fire when they get a brief glimpse of Veridian, and miss when he flinches back for shelter.

Veridian holds his rifle close to his torso, reaching for his melee weapon slung onto his belt, a telescopic collapsible obsidian spear. The timing is perfect—two militants round the corner and barely have time to react before Veridian drives his spear into both of them. He's able to both pin them in place, and fire his assault rifle almost point blank with his foes, dropping them to the grass beneath. Veridian backtracks again, heading to the docks on the attack. Cracks and snaps of bullets whizz past Veridian, making his whiskers twitch nervously, but he maintains a stone-cold, focused expression. The *Trinity Of Tranquility* commando never blinks, shooting and zigzagging on the docks. Veridian successfully hits three of his best available targets, before running and diving into the ocean when a rocket zooms head on at him.

Above, the pier erupts. Veridian dives deeper from the bubbly force, but he's blown instead into the sandy ocean floor, scraping against the shore and feeling the air escaping his lungs. Fortunately, the depth is roughly fifteen feet or so, mercifully allowing Veridian to surface in the cover of gray smoke to inhale a gasp of air. Swimming toward the next pier coughing, unconcerned with the enemies lining it and becoming aware of him, Veridian springs out of the water with a loud roar. His collapsible spear impales the closest militant, before spin kicking the immediate enemies around him right off the pier, into the water.

Veridian grabs the damaged device off of the fallen mercenary he stabbed, then leaping next on an idling jet ski three feet from the pier, nearly slipping off as the waves make it bounce awkwardly. Veridian speeds off, ignoring the round or two that strikes his person.

"After that, *Trinity* scum! Don't let him escape and regroup with any others we may have missed!" commands one militant on his jet ski, revving the machine and starting off the pursuit, talking into his microphone he shouts, "Scorch that shit shanty down, too!"

Veridian races the watercraft up to full speed as his clenching paw squeezes the accelerator, rubbernecking his head constantly to track the *Armageddon Cultists*. Maneuvering the jet ski alongside the coastline to his right, lichen, and mossy dense jungle whipping past. On his left is a wide open ocean with waves rolling it, going on for forever, it would seem.

The *Trinity* commando swerves side to side, drifting his overall course gradually into deeper water, smirking dangerously as coastal coral reefs become visible ahead over the tide. While sprouting through the surface, the colorful reefs sprawl underneath in far greater radiuses than first assumed, concealed by the shifting depth. Veridian stares fixated on driving, going full speed into the shallow reefs, the militants chasing after him.

Finding shelter in a giant rusted out ship wreck, he takes time to study it and figure out how to operate it; it's similar to a laptop computer's outer design. Backlogging into the GPS on it, Veridian discovers where these *Armageddon Cultist* mercenaries originated from.

CHAPTER NINE: Straying Into The Fringes Of Madness

DISTANT STREET LIGHTS AND multi-colored lit up buildings can be seen on the foggy horizon as the terrain transitions from cold mountainous to hilly dense woods at nightfall. It becomes only slightly warmer outside as Cyngosa and Khelu maneuver through the gnarly, pale-trunked oak trees, towering old maples and bulbous elms that dominate the woodland flora. Their boots carefully crunch along through the dead leaves, cluttering the single-person dirt pathway. Staying alert and silent, keeping their ears perking up to any noises. The fetid aroma hits Cyngosa's nostrils of mildewing plantlife and damp fungus. Eventually, Cyngosa and Khelu creep up on the edge of a freeway, in the shadow remaining between two sleek chrome street lights just behind the roadway guard railing.

Cyngosa grows still, surveying the area, speaking softly to Khelu. "Odd, not a single trailer truck or a car and it's been like fifteen minutes just getting up to this road from the woods. There! That convenience store and gas station are across the way." Cyngosa turns his gaze to check out the parking lot, taking notice of whatever details he can. "There are three cars parked in the lot. But we need to eat something, for now."

"Yeah, and cameras to recognize our faces for the many bad assholes trying to find and get us," Khelu replies, keeping just as observant as Cyngosa, even if they are both evidently completely alone for the time being, her darting golden eyes inspect the vehicles and the dormant road.

Cyngosa shrugs with his exhaling breath showing in the crisp air, then points to a loaded up dumpster next to the back of the building. Khelu gives a silent nod and then, following Cyngosa's lead, the two walk swiftly across the empty roadway, sticking to the shadows until they are forced under the lighting of the store. Cyngosa and Khelu pivot to casual postures, strolling along the neatly kept sidewalk, until they were behind the convenience store building, out of sight from the freeway. Catchy pop music playing from the screen speakers located in the gas pumps floats onto the pair's ears. Khelu tilts her head as one vehicle is left parked and unattended at a pump station with the nozzle still inside it.

Handing off his rifle and ammunition to Khelu and readjusting his clothing, Cyngosa says to Khelu with finality, "I'll go in, get us some water and trail mix or whatever's light to eat. Ask the clerk a question or two to see what's up. I still can't get any cell signal out here. Keep an eye out."

"You got it, bro. See If they have those little gummy sharks in there. Grab those for me too," Khelu replies. Cyngosa offers Khelu a casual forehead salute and a smirk, walking away.

Cyngosa enters the shop, inhaling nervously when the doorbell beeps and the automated doors slide open with an inviting warm wash over him, uncertain what to expect. His turquoise eyes with tired bags hanging under them scan the brightly lit and fully stocked shelves, seeing no customers. The flatscreens mounted up above on the walls behind the cash register desk display an image of colored bars and emit a busy tone from their speakers, no cashier in sight.

Cyngosa, only slightly unnerved, moves through the small store while his tail fidgets from side to side. He briefly glances at a newspaper stack that has a picture of Clyde Crowly, with some politicians he can't recognize on the front page. Moving on down the snack food aisle, Cyngosa turns away, feeling a tingling chill run down his back. He locates and grabs trail mix packages, and wanders to the fridges at the back for three bottles of water. Noticing in the glass door's reflection a cashier was now standing behind the counter, eerily attentive suddenly.

The café section is empty, and not a sound can be heard coming from the store's back end, but the salty and buttery aroma of the fast food certainly makes Cyngosa's stomach growl noisily after taking a long whiff of it. Cyngosa confidently strides toward the counter, pointing his head up and nodding, clutching the smooth wrinkly plastic bags, deciding to cut his shopping short, silently greeting the Graywolf behind the counter. But be that as it may, no acknowledgement was given in return, just a blank expression, as if Cyngosa didn't even exist.

Placing his purchases on the counter calmly and looking at the cashier's face, Cyngosa strikes up conversation again. "Evening, bro. Just these, I guess. Thanks." He leans on the counter, pulling out his cash from the inside pocket of his vest, glancing at the screens once and noticing the weird signal image being displayed. "So, I don't live around here. Anything going on?"

The cashier doesn't answer him immediately, but slowly, almost with a limp reaction, reaches for the items and scans them one at a time. Cyngosa watches him move lethargically. Red and blue emergency lights flash brightly through the glass briefly as a group of law enforcement cars suddenly pass the store and down the freeway outside, speeding wildly on by. The cashier finally speaks in a monotone, remaining expressionless and standing in a zombie-like posture, staring through Cyngosa.

"Nothing's going on, patron. That'll be twelve dollars and thirty-four cents, please."

Cyngosa fails in his attempt not to openly look suspiciously back at the stupefied clerk, who he is simultaneously handing a paper bill to, representing significant value. In the frame of time, the cashier methodically takes the paper currency and opens the register and makes change, Cyngosa mutters to him, "Oh, I thought as much." He took the change when it was finally offered and added, "I don't need a bag for these, thanks!"

Cyngosa briskly walks out of the convenience store back into the cooling night air. He passes off a bottle of water and bag of trail and mix and the gummies Khelu requested, continuing his brisk walk while Khelu reunites with him. "You seem spooked, what is it?" Khelu asks, opening the water bottle as she's striding her legs in keeping up with Cyngosa, offering his rifle back to him, which he takes.

Continuing to lead, Cyngosa walks down the side of the freeway toward the city, passing a glossy metal sign labeled *Silvium*. "The cashier seemed a little off, plus all those cars and the place was completely empty except for just that one dude. I should probably charge one of my ankh's that sense magical auras." He rips open the packaging and consumes the salty, savory snack food to satiate his rumbling stomach.

"Yeah, there's something malicious and strange going on here. We'll see for ourselves in a couple more miles," Khelu states with concern in her voice, following him closely along the sleek pavement with the large city welcomingly glowing on the horizon. With his rifle slung over his shoulder, Cyngosa clenches a smooth triangle stone in his palm, channeling energy into it that tugs at his stamina and leaves him winded after it's done.

Cyngosa and Khelu soon enter the district called *Thornhide Heights* of *Silvium City*, evident by a road sign. As their journey coming off the freeway shifts into the rural section of the cityscape, they witness dozens of vehicles left abandoned—blocking the exits—and more parked on streets leading throughout. The houses are visibly untouched, at least from their vantage point on the street.

"What the hell is all this? Looks like the aftermath of a riot?" Khelu asks out loud, more so to herself than to Cyngosa. Cyngosa quietly scans his immediate vicinity with suspicious, glowing turquoise eyes.

"Very zombie-apocalypse vibe, kinda. But not. However, my ankh's glowing red. Dark magic has been used nearby."

Cyngosa looks over and inspects a parked SUV, then a car. They both walk down the sparsely settled road, the existing houses separated by swaths of hilly landscape. They notice the couple of commercial buildings around them still have lights on, but nobody is inside. This doesn't sit well with Cyngosa. "I don't think so. Nothing stolen or broken, really. It looks and feels like everyone just collectively left. Dropped whatever they were doing, even," Cyngosa says, he meanders around the down casting glow of the streetlight walking by a post office building.

Wandering quietly through the dark nighttime streets, continuing to avoid the light from the street lamps when they can, they come to a more affluent residential area and approach four torched up vehicles sitting in what remains of a hastily made blockade.

"Yeah, you say that, but..." Khelu jerks her head, tossing her braids and gestures with her free paw as they pass by the scorched blockade, the other brandishing her weapon as unease slithers down her spine. Her gold eyes picking up on evidence of a gunfight from the street under them, her tail curling up alert, seeing dispensed casings.

"These were cop vehicles." Cyngosa stops to put a bare paw on a burned, twisted piece of metal. "It's warm. It's been quite a few hours since whatever took place here. Keep your eyes peeled. We're absolutely not alone. But where are they?"

"Who? There's nobody anywhere it feels like." Khelu, on edge now, keeping a closer proximity to Cyngosa on their walk.

"The *Armageddon Cultists*," Cyngosa mutters, with a thin lip, his insides burning with determination.

Cyngosa and Khelu wander from the street heading into the backyard of a large, beautifully decorated brick house, thick hearty firs spotting the lawn. They creep up the fancy back porch of the brick house attached to a wooden deck. Getting to the first window, Cyngosa peers in. From what he could see, most of the brick house was left in darkness, except from the living room where he could see the television was the only thing left on. With the same multi-colored bar national alert image on it like the one he saw in the convenience store earlier. He moves to test the door and finds it unlocked, quietly opening it and entering, brandishing his firearm now.

Khelu frowning and lowering her ear's to her head, whispering as she follows him to the doorway, looking inside. "Uh, what are you doing?"

Cyngosa says nothing, putting a finger to his lips and pointing around him. Picking up on the queues, Khelu understands and goes off silently, checking the other rooms. The foreign scents of the household waft through Khelu and Cyngosa's noses, the kitchen still having a lingering aroma of cleaning chemicals. Catching back up to Cyngosa, now standing in the house's living room, Khelu shoots him two thumbs up. Cyngosa takes the remote control nearby and starts trying to change the channel on the eighty-inch flatscreen, discovering every channel he switches to produce the same content. The image and a soft dial tone emanate from the television.

"Odd, electricity, cable still." Cyngosa then pulls out his cellphone and checks the screen, freezing in place, rolling his lips over his fangs. "There's internet service. Should we connect to it?" His eyes aglow in the dim living room dart at Khelu. She catches the hint of uncertainty in his voice, nervously cracking her knuckles.

Khelu nods and she pulls her cellphone out of her pocket, locating the house's router right there in the living room. "This is all very eerie, but I don't see why not. We couldn't make phone calls out or to each other earlier."

Once connected, the home screen suddenly goes dark, with a burning red wolf skull in the center. Cyngosa, in a knee-jerk reaction, slaps the device out of Khelu's paw and onto the floor in a blur, kicking it away.

Khelu first lets out a painful yelp and hisses, "Ow!" She then glares at the phone, now on the other side of the glamorously decorated living room floor. The soft red light gleams off the screen, casting its light hauntingly throughout the room. Khelu gasps at Cyngosa, recognizing this "It's..."

Cyngosa finishes for her, no less bewildered or horrified. "It's like the *Corporatist Insurrection* happening all over again." His eyes studying the device from far, commenting, "I know that kind of dark magic when I see it. The whole city is saturated in it."

The faint sound of an engine is heard rumbling over the ambiance of the dial tone coming from the television. Khelu, closest to the window, peeks between the drawn shut curtains to the street. Her golden eyes went wide, gulping as her mouth went dry. In the street, bathed in the streetlights, were an organized group of dark-robed individuals and a plated up aggressive looking double-cab pickup truck with a turret mounted in its bed frame. Twenty of them, all holding assault rifles, already fanning out from their ride, combing their surroundings.

Khelu moves toward Cyngosa, eyes still wide, whispering, "Cyn, bro, we need to slip outta here." She does a double-take glance. "Like right now."

Cyngosa, also perking his ears up to the noise, quietly agrees and they move toward the back where they entered. Cyngosa bumps into Khelu, who freezes up and stops instantly in her tracks. From the backyard, seven more robed and armor plated individuals walk up to the house, three moving up the porch to the house as the others wander purposefully toward the street. Cyngosa and Khelu backtrack hastily, but make no noise other than the wooden floor making a soft squeak or two in the hallway. Trapped in the foyer of the affluent brick house, as two of the three wander into the house.

Khelu readies her rifle, throughout the time looking at Cyngosa, a painful expression on her face. "We have no choice."

Cyngosa double checks the half-empty magazine in his rifle, nodding at her with a grim look on his face, free paw moving to the array of ankhs and totems outlining his waist. He grabs an azurite stone bird statue and winks one of his eyes at her, whispering sarcastically, "Oh, happy, happy, joy, joy."

As the armed individual wanders into the living room, the pale glow of the television screen washing over them, they stand still to look amongst the knickknacks. Like a silhouetted in motion, Cyngosa comes sprinting full speed toward them and tackles the hooded figure to the ground, forcing their gun away when it's pulled up to aim and shoot. Cyngosa clenches his fist, becoming engulfed in fire suddenly as he punches the robed enemy several times before he's kicked off by them.

Cyngosa stumbles backward into the face of the large couch behind as the robed enemy stands up, part of their hood scorched away to show a *Lycandian* wolf face beneath, locked in a scowl. The commotion is loud enough to bring the other individual in the house running into the living room, where they are unfortunately gunned down from behind by Khelu taking position. Cyngosa wobbly recovers, and in a combined effort, they blast down the last one before they have a chance to retrieve their firearm. Khelu leans close to the fallen enemy's discarded gun, grabbing it up and removing the ammo cartridge from it.

"Let's leave, now!" Cyngosa exclaims, but right as they both turn to head toward the back porch, the elegant front door of the foyer blows inward as five cultists storm in. Another enemy appearing from the window. The rifle stock bursts through the glass and wood framing before. Cyngosa, stunned, halts and stutters, "Oh, shit!"

Khelu and Cyngosa open fire with their weapons, hitting nothing but forcing the newly arriving enemies to take cover. Looking toward the window freshly broken into, Cyngosa and Khelu rush at the cultist still trying to come through the window together. Outside the fire fight only worsens for Cyngosa and Khelu, as all the robed individuals are now alert, several shooting at the brick house to the silhouettes of Cyngosa or Khelu who shoot back when able. Cyngosa takes an opportunity running along the lawn to place down the azurite bird statue, which seconds later vaporizes. The ablaze blue, purple and pink phoenix swoops up into the night sky, catching the violent attention of the enemies around as the pickup truck turret begins firing at Eos. A magical ice javelin from one of the magic using cultists whistles past while Eos whirls and twists.

Cyngosa crouches out of view of the cultists, saying, "Welcome back, buddy, sorry about the rude awakening. We're in a jam here. Hooded assholes are bad, go get 'em!" Pushing on the offensive as he shoots at the exposed cultists right out on the street or lawns. Eos madly flames up their body and dive-bombs the closest enemy.

Khelu swaps her ammunition magazine for the one she took off the assailant's gun, discharging her firearm to her satisfaction at another enemy, scoffing. "Silver lining, they are using the same type of ammo," Khelu comments.

Cyngosa slings his rifle over his arm and grabs two ankhs at once from his belt, gripping two fireballs he sends on at the truck and the other at two cultists grouped up. One aims for the truck, rolls harmlessly straight up into the sky by some magical force. The other scores a direct hit on the torso of the unsuspecting, dropping them both from the shockwave. Khelu outmaneuvers two cultists in close quarter combat as they fight on the front lawn and sidewalk. The pops and cracks of gunfire echoes in the cold night air, occasional shouting piercing the night.

"More, behind us!" Khelu calls over to Cyngosa, but she isn't sure where they should go. Five more enemies now emerge from the house, and from the backyard three more on top of that make a bold attempt to try flanking Cyngosa and Khelu. Eos swoops by spitting fire from its beak and clawing with its talons at various enemies among the group, disorienting their attack effort.

Cyngosa stands still for a moment to expel full auto at an enemy before ducking down, heading toward the garage of the neighboring house now. "Go, keep moving away!" shouts to Khelu, lifting his rifle once again and dropping another cultist. A returning round cracks over Cyngosa's head into the window of the next empty house. One particular enemy standing on the fallen charred body of their own hoists up with two paws a machine gun, then took aim at Khelu and began emptying their long bandolier of round after continuous round. Khelu ducks and rolls flat to the ground as a brutal spray of rounds strikes the side of the garage she and Cyngosa are trying to get to.

Cyngosa, at the garage's threshold, crouches and huddles as bullets rain in, a dozen blasting apart the window and siding of the garage. He tries to take aim, but the uninterrupted fire rate keeps him prone to the smooth cement floor, in the interim being showered by wood splinters and drywall crumbs.

The cultists methodically close in on them. Khelu scrambles up the lawn, getting behind a thick leafless oak tree. She squirms herself together, then leans from behind the tree as bullets thump against the trunk. Khelu, having found a better position, is now discharging in retaliation, as the heavy machine gunner waddles their way closer still, relentlessly holding the trigger.

Eos, in a horizontal corkscrew, lands into the adjacent advancing cultist, attempting to flank Khelu's tree protection, razor sharp talons doing what significant damage they could to the armor but tearing apart the robes flowing about their person. The phoenix, exhibiting intelligence as it later decides to open its beak, squeaks a poof of flame into the enemy's face before relieving them of their firearm, flying off.

Left as easy pickings for Khelu, who crouch-rolls to the opposite side of the oak tree and fires her own rifle at her, would be ambusher with five direct rounds as they are partially ablaze, their body now dropping to the grassy lawn. Flapping away as bullets fly by in vain attempts from the heavy machine gunner, Eos discards the gun in its talons on the slanted shingled rooftop of the neighboring house before elevating higher, ducking behind the brick chimney, which immediately proceeds to be chipped away rather efficiently by the machine gun. Momentarily tumbles in on itself.

Cyngosa reacts swiftly during the break, holding a different ankh now. He clenches it and summons a mist filled with miniature icicles, four to five inches each. With his other paw and a flick of his wrist, he snaps his fingers and produces a basketball sized fireball. He hurls his two magical spells with incredible velocity, more so than usual magic projectiles, all at the machine gunner's hooded and masked helmet. The fireball reaches first, crashing straight on into the gunner's face mask, before a spell reducing effect shrinks the ball's size down. The shield effect ends, overwhelmed as the ice crashes into the halted fireball, causing both magic spells to erupt.

The machine gunner stumbles backward first, losing their grip on the cumbersome weapon. They lurch forward, trying to recover it, all while being viciously pelted by Cyngosa—until they fall back and finally lay still. Several more advance by, unfaltering.

From an aerial perspective, the eerie neighborhood was bustling with activity as twelve more cultists advance on Cyngosa and Khelu from near the woods. From the opposite side among the affluent houses and hibernating gardens, roughly fifty or so had now been drawn into the fight. Especially as the bright flashes of magic sparkled in the night, and the loud exchange of firearms filled the air.

Hugging Khelu tight as she leaps into the garage momentarily, Cyngosa falls in with her, hitting the hard cement with a grunt. Khelu rolls over to the other side of the garage when she notices many more enemies advancing down the neighborhood street toward the house. Tail hiking up high behind him, and his head making small jerks, Cyngosa moves upright for cover. "Creator above, damn are these dudes something else. We're drawing the whole suburb in on us."

Cyngosa places down a totem on the cement, the wooden object giving off a soft blue aura, in the nick of time too, as an enemy's magical fireball soars at the garage before being dispelled by the anti-magic projectile totem. Harmless ashes spraying them in the aftermath.

Khelu aims down her gun and, not looking at Cyngosa as she answers. "Nope, I don't think we can't keep this up. I'll run out of ammo before they run out of people to throw at us. Are these the cultists you mentioned?" Cyngosa doesn't confirm, running out of time as the fight arrives right on top of them.

The two start firing at advancing enemies, trying to hold them down in place. Four or so carelessly throw themselves at the garage in a wild run. Cyngosa guns them down but, having to flinch for cover as posted up enemies shoot at him. Khelu herself exchanges fire with one stubborn enemy behind a parked elegant sedan's front end, just on the street in front of them. Eventually, Khelu achieves a perfect shot to the enemy's head armor. Defeated, they go limp, slumping down against the car before sliding to the street. Four more take their place.

Crashing sounds and breaking glass could be heard from inside the house attached to the garage they are defending themselves inside. Eos flaps out of the doorway to them with an alarmed screech.

"Aw gee, do you hear that? Sounds to me like it's time to bail," Cyngosa says, retreating into the garage, maneuvering past a parked sport motorcycle with its kickstand out. He quickly presses the automatic garage door button, shutting the overhead door, as incoming rounds crack into it and the walls. Khelu takes a few more shots at either flank, going on until her clip is empty and the chamber is cleared with a click. The door closes, but already shots randomly pierce through and pelt it.

Khelu staring down at the bike inside the garage with Cyngosa as footsteps could be heard, muses in a melancholy tone, "This brings some unpleasant childhood memories back up. I haven't been on anything like this for many years."

Outside the garage in the lawns and from the street, a cluster group of sixty *Armageddon Cultists* march up the driveway and position themselves at the closed overhead door, all taking aim before a second later opening fire simultaneously.The concentrated gunfire shreds the overhead door, causing it to fall apart and collapse into the driveway over the course of just seconds. A buzzing engine sound echoes out, and from the doorway into the house proper, with bullets being fired after them in their wake from within, Cyngosa and Khelu skid into view on the cement floor of the garage. Khelu, strapped to Cyngosa's waist with three belts for anchoring, grasping her and Cyngosa's rifles in her paws. She opens fire the third counting second they had ripped into view of the clustered group of surprised enemies.

She sends several of the sixty cultists down and out instantly. Others sustain stunning injuries. Taking their chance, Cyngosa peels out down the driveway to the street, as Khelu actively sprays either rifle outward, catching many attempting to flee, duck, or even leap at them in some form of wild abandon. The pickup truck's engine on the street behind them roars loudly as it accelerates after Cyngosa and Khelu, on their 'borrowed' sport bike. Eos barrel-rolls down from the sky to harass the gunner on the truck, setting them partially ablaze with a screech before flipping like an arrowhead mid-air, obstructing the truck's windshield next.

Yelling over the wind and engine as they speed through the autumn suburban area, Khelu asks, "Hey, how much gas is in this thing, anyway?"

Cyngosa yells back over the wind and noise, "Just enough, I think. Hah, just the right amount, if you must know."

Cyngosa and Khelu race down the roadway at night, being pursued by the truck, which weaves around awkwardly abandoned cars, skidding noisily as Eos is pecking mercilessly at the glass. Cyngosa races up the hood of one low-trim abandoned car, flying over a chain-link fence into a ball field, heading toward the street and buildings past it. The adrenaline in his body he feels his ears ringing and heart pounding.

The truck barrels through the fence, tearing it down and rolling over it without losing any tires or speed in the process. Eos develops a new tactic as the fiery phoenix swoops into the cab after fracturing the passenger window glass, creating mayhem inside. Eos fights with beak, fiery breath, and razor talons.

Cyngosa is racing toward a group of a dozen armed cultists who point and yell, two shooting at them but forced to scatter. Cyngosa bobs and weaves the bike, creating a hard-to-hit target. Khelu holds on, while the bike skids practically sideways before swiveling through the group. The truck behind them crashes loudly against a parked car as it races to keep up, but continues the chase as more gunshots rang out.

Cyngosa's face exhibits dread, his mouth going agape upon hearing the distinct whirring sound of a helicopter closing in overhead as the chase moves down the street to an intersection and plaza. The cultists on board flashing their search light onto the buzzing, darting bike below them. Two hanging out of the attack helicopter, on either side, aim and shoot as the helicopter itself fires off a rocket too.

With Cyngosa's rifle slung over her shoulder, Khelu aims the one in her paw behind at the helicopter and shoots freely at it—to little avail—shouting, "These bastards have an entire army. Oh shit! Incoming!" Cyngosa skids the bike down a different street passing a fast foot restaurant and gas station as the rocket misses feet of their persons with an angry hiss, striking a parked taxi just fifteen feet in front of them blowing it airborne and aflame instantly to crash back down on the street upside down.

"Whoa! Little too close for comfort there!" Cyngosa exclaims, feeling the heat and squints from the flare of light but still zooming down the road at full speed, the engine giving it all it has with a constant whiny pitch. "Hang on tight."

The road he chose came into a huge open mall parking lot, with a parking garage and sprawling stores. The truck behind them skids on its wheels, trying to catch up and ram their bike, but Cyngosa's maneuvering cost them speed over grassy medians and curbs. Eos attempts to smash the windshield to disrupt the driver, but they are relentless.

Khelu spots a single sparkle flare go up, and she quickly pats Cyngosa's shoulder. Cyngosa catches it before it fades completely, and he drifts the bike toward its source from the parking garage attaching to the mall itself. A bullet cracks by and strikes Cyngosa's shoulder, causing them to drift uncontrollably but he maneuvers into a skid and recovers, the truck's grill just feet behind them as they regain ground, passing concrete pylons of the parking garage on one side and the three story mall on the other, the chase goes down the backside of the mall forcing the helicopter to cease pursuit, losing a visual on the bike.

Whipping around a corner Cyngosa and Khelu slip between two twenty foot long shipping trailers on steel chassis parked up against the loading dock of the *Silvium* outlet mall's rear end, the truck also at high speeds pressing them from behind doesn't have enough stopping distance as it skids loudly before crashing head-on into the two trailers, and crushing the front end and part of the cab into.

Cyngosa and Khelu slow the bike down before hearing a loud whistle from an open overhead door level with the ground nearby. Cyngosa guides the bike into a slow roll toward the doorway as it lifts before he shuts the bike off, Eos being swift enough to swoop in and land on Cyngosa's shoulder. When he and Khelu are off of it, he discards the bike.

Khelu, Cyngosa, and Eos find themselves now inside a brightly lit warehouse attached to the mall. Many shelves packed with boxes, two desks with computers on them, and a fork truck were all in view. A couple plastic wrapped pallets of merchandise lying about with eight Graywolf *Lycandians* in police uniforms present, the one closest to them approaches. Three had their weapons casually out with fingers in their safeties and triggers. With looks of untrustworthiness on their faces thrown toward the Direwolf and Timberwolf breed *Lycandians*, but were not aiming at them yet, Cyngosa and Khelu equally feel tingling on their fingers and toes.

"Hi? Do you understand me?" His bluish flint eyes look at Cyngosa and Khelu, hesitantly. Seeing them armed but standing completely still, the officer lowers his firearm.

"Yeah, I can understand you. What's going on? Who are you guys?" Khelu asks, staring at the officer with distrust on her face, keeping her eyes unblinking and head following his every move.

Cyngosa's turquoise eyes carefully scan the officers also, keeping his facial expression like stone, silently sizing up the situation and gulping quietly. His paws keep his weapon clenched tighter, the officer still slowly walking closer to them. "There's a whole militarized cult out taking over the city, my dude. Where did they come from?"

"I'm Officer Benedict Alabaster, police chief of the *Thornhide Heights* precinct. Yes, the entire city of *Silvium* is under sinister occupation, but there's more going on here. Who are you two?" The officer looks at Cyngosa and Khelu.

"You can call me Paradigm. Thanks for setting off that flare. They have been chasing us since we walked into the city," Khelu answers, the tension lessening as the officer relaxes his posture in front of them.

"I'm Straywolf. Crazy times, huh?" Cyngosa replies, his turquoise eyes quickly looking over the others standing in the warehouse.

Officer Alabaster, giving a nod to Khelu, stares at Cyngosa before speaking to him. "Worse. A third of my cadets began to show signs of some kind of hypnosis at the same time, thousands of citizens were too. Me and Officer Argyle here," he gestures over to one policeman sitting on the desk nearby, "were on patrol when everything changed. Then a giant pillar seemed to rise out of nowhere, in one of the city parks."

Officer Argyle bursts into the conversation, his tone dripping with accusation. "Yeah, it was like anyone who was staring at, or on their phone at a specific time, became like a zombie. Then those hooded robed maniacs attacked everywhere, all at once in vehicles and helicopters. It was unreal. Murdering those that didn't turn and resisted capture, and kidnapping everyone else." Officer Argyle sits up from the desk and walks over to Cyngosa and Khelu, coming closer to them and staring with a suspicious expression, commenting, "You two certainly aren't from around here, a coincidence I guess right?"

Khelu, narrowing her golden eyes, looks at Officer Argyle with a frown. Feeling the fur on her limbs creep up, she asks, "What are you implying? That we had something to do with all this?"

Officer Alabaster, clearing his throat loudly, steps between Officer Argyle and Khelu to attempt to diffuse the tension. "No one said either of you had anything to do with this attack..." He turns to face Khelu and Cyngosa now with a friendly expression. "There's just not many Direwolves or Timberwolves in *Silvium*."

Cyngosa pinches his bottom lip, darting his eyes at Khelu, then scoffs, asking the two officers, "So? Me and her are on vacation. We got caught up in all this running for our lives."

"Straywolf, Paradigm...Oh come on. Do you two have any ID of some kind? Our city, maybe our country, is being taken over by robed and hooded mercenaries. You two could be deserters for all we know, spies. Or decoys of some kind?" Officer Argyle inquiries, his grayish white furred forehead wrinkling, paws on his hips with fingers drumming his belt.

Khelu and Cyngosa groan, another officer from the back even chimes in for Argyle to drop it, Officer Alabaster himself throwing him a silencing glare.

With a sigh, Officer Alabaster offers Cyngosa and Khelu a sincere expression. "Sorry about that. Tensions are a little high right now...I think you two are fine. You haven't shot us on sight, or look like you're in some kinda hypnotic psycho state of mind. You'll be safe here. Take a break."

Officer Benedict Alabaster walks over to Officer Argyle and the two walk side by side, obviously talking to one another. Cyngosa and Khelu exchange curious expressions with one another. Eos perched on Cyngosa's left shoulder, keeping a cautious eye on the *Lycandian* strangers.

Khelu, a breath catching in her chest, whispers to Cyngosa, "I don't trust these guys, do you?"

Stifling a laugh, Cyngosa whispers back, "Hell no...but I'm trying to figure out what to do. Clyde is here somewhere in *Silvium*, whether these cops believe us or not. This is his doing. I have a promise to keep to Dorrion." Cyngosa pauses to let out a brief groan. "Not a lot of options, thanks to Saaliha and Minax screwing off on us. But let's not get into that here now."

Officer Alabaster and Argyle approach Cyngosa and Khelu, inviting them and Eos further inside the warehouse. They walk together calmly and speak.

"You two have decided to 'vacation' at a rather poor time, but you are different than they are. If anything, we might be able to help each other out. Especially since you have weapons and look like fighters," Officer Alabaster says, continuing to walk with them casually.

"That entirely depends. Are you after Clyde Crowly?" Cyngosa inquires, boldly getting to the point.

Officer Argyle and Officer Alabaster look at one another in surprise for a brief second, recognizing the name obviously.

"What would the new supreme chancellor have to do with this?" Officer Argyle inquires, raising an eyebrow.

Cyngosa and Khelu quickly stare at each other, then back to the officers, with Khelu showing more shock upon hearing this information.

"Clyde Crowly is the one responsible for the signal. My friends traced its origin to his company's server. Heavily wrapped under spyware, VPN protections and all sorts of tech shit...that I can't explain," Cyngosa lies to them. Khelu stares at him momentarily.

Officer Alabaster stares at Cyngosa, folding his arms over his chest, and asks, "Where are those friends of yours now? That's a serious claim, but I'd love to see what they found out with my own eyes." Eos ruffles their feathers subtly, Cyngosa feels with the phoenix perching on his shoulder, but it goes unnoticed by the officers.

Rubbing his chin, swaying on his feet side-to-side, Cyngosa admits with a melancholy sigh, "Honestly dude, by now they're hundreds and hundreds of miles away from us, maybe in the *Republic of Aluan* by now. They're mad at me over my bullshit. There isn't anything I can do about it. Besides stopping this by ourselves."

"If we were going to be mutually transparent here, we sent a group of special field operatives tracking down missing children and adult kidnappings...Since yesterday, the whole mission went dark on us the night before. Hours later, the city is overrun in broad daylight," Officer Alabaster says.

"Me and Paradigm are also after these individuals," Cyngosa states, making eye contact with Alabaster and Argyle, picking up the sheer sincerity in Cyngosa's tone and demeanor.

"So, you've come to assassinate Mr. Crowly? You know I can't just let you go and do that. But I'll be the one to cuff him for you, we'll subdue him together, I sense you are on to something and we're lacking proper detectives since, uh yeah…Your statements are good enough for me to make him a suspect until we unpack hard evidence," Officer Alabaster says to Cyngosa.

Officer Argyle comments, "Funny you suggest that. There's a relay station, up in the mountains on the northern remote part of *Silvium*. We also traced it to where this signal you speak of emits, too, but we haven't identified it. It's preventing us from getting any outside help." Cyngosa feels his stomach flip. A quick expression of astonishment crosses his features, but he shakes his head.

"Mind if we catch a ride with y'all?" Khelu asks the two officers.

Officer Alabaster stares between Cyngosa and Khelu and nods approvingly. "I don't see why not. There's only nearly thirty of us left. I could honestly use the help to take down who's responsible for all this mayhem. So if you two are in. I'll be more than happy." He offers them an encouraging smile, then continues, "I will be honest. I have no idea what we will face up there."

"We have a dozen SUV cruisers. If we encounter one of their tanks, we'll just zip by and keep racing. We're making a blitz on that station and then try to break the signal to call for help. The terrain is horrible up to and at the relay station for heavy war equipment," Officer Argyle explains.

CHAPTER TEN: The Satellite Siege

E ARLY DAWNS LIGHT CREEPS over the mountainous landscape, still cloaked in darkness. Seven SUVs speed up the inclined roadway, passing cellphone towers and power lines, but surrounded by mostly trees and a sprawling snowy mountain landscape, now on the very edge of *Silvium.* They drive toward a small relay and power hub station outside the city.

The lead vehicle smashes through a chain-link fence that was locked up, destroying it as all the vehicles accelerate even faster still on the bumpy, snowy dirt road. Cyngosa and Khelu are seated in the back holding their firearms, while Officer Alabaster drives and Officer Argyle is in the passenger seat, loading his rifle and pressing the automatic window down, taking aim, presenting the weapon's muzzle out and steadying it on the door's mirror, opening fire now and again. The much colder air from the altitude rushes inside, making Khelu shiver.

"There it is! Way up on the ridge!" Officer Benedict Alabaster exclaims, a loud cracking thunk sound is heard as a bullet strikes their SUV from outside. Officer Alabaster speaks into his radio next. "Get to the control room and shut the satellite dish down, cut the program's transmission. They know we're coming now, don't hold back. You all know the stakes here, our families and homes. Maybe more if we don't stop them."

Officer Alabaster speeds the vehicle up, running out of road as it opens to a slanted hilly dirt lot, he and the other drivers fan their vehicles out as *Armageddon Cultists* react, two of the largest vehicles the police had left drive straight on toward the building until stopped in the snow or by fanatical enemies.

Officer Argyle opens fire when targets present themselves, with gun muzzle flashes flaring up then vanishing in the waning dark. The dish was on the higher portion of the base of a rounded mountain, three of the six confined on as the others stopped to deploy the police officers seated inside.

Under the starry but fading night sky, sunlight just slightly lurking over the horizon, a fierce shootout begins on the hilly terrain. Cyngosa leaps from the vehicle just seconds before it completes its stop, with Eos flapping madly and taking higher altitude over the battle. Shots ring in as the back windshield shatters. Running toward the two story square building, Khelu and Officer Alabaster follow Cyngosa as they face a dozen cultists, and those are the ones they can see just immediately. Officers from other vehicles fan out, shooting and advancing the attack on the well lit building from multiple angles now.

Khelu gasping, her breath visible in the air, whirling into action. "It's like fifteen degrees up here." Her eyes catching Eos dive-bomb onto a robed assailant talons first before expelling flames from their body like a mini-explosion.

Cyngosa, sliding down and hurling a fireball from one of his totems hanging from his waist, at an enemy just ahead of them. "Got one! Go! I'll cover you." He looks at Khelu, then at his peripherals as the firefight picks up.

Officer Alabaster gunned down two cultists before lunging into a roll behind a metal rectangle electrical box. "Keep it up! Push for the operations building. We just need to get inside to defend a position in the control room."

A *Silvium* police officer holding their assault rifle at the ready takes cover nearby Benedict, yelling over the gunfire to him. "Sir? How do we get inside?"

The facility itself provides the answer. A wide door from the second floor opens as one single hooded cultist leads a huge group, flooding out into view from within the building.

"Ahh, so you've chosen oblivion by our doing here and now, rather than by our master, the glorious Eradicator?" one of the hooded figures yells while drawing a vile, green glowing butcher blade in one paw, and hoisting a sawed-off shotgun outward in the other. "Lord Kaiser Plagueheart loves to play rough!" Lord Plagueheart 's only distinguishing features beyond the standard cultist garb are the ornate armaments layered over his robes and a golden wolf mask that covers his face and muzzle. Serrated blades emerge backward off of his shoulder plates.

Cyngosa calls over to the others with him, "We go through them...try and break or fight our way in!"

"Would you take a look at this crazy asshat..." Khelu muses nervously, glancing at Lord Plagueheart before taking aim with her rifle.

Whilst they run making a gallant advance under fire, one of Cyngosa's shield totems dissolves a sideways-thrown fireball coming from the enemy into harmless sparkles, he remarks. "Ehh, if you've seen one evil death worshiping psychopath, you've seen them all right? Let's kick his teeth in," Cyngosa says. Summoning a twig out of thin air, it begins to grow into a quarterstaff. "Together."

Cyngosa hurls another fire ball up at the mezzanine, disrupting the cluster gathering up there to shoot down from above. Lord Plagueheart rushes down the stairway, followed eagerly by dozens of hollering cultists, with stunning advantage on the vastly outnumbered *Silvium* police as they spread out on the counter-attack to defend the array dish. Lord Plagueheart shrugs off the several clean shots Benny, Cyngosa, and Khelu make on him before he closes into the fight like some mad berserker clapping at their firearms.

A brief and bloody melee ensues, many of the cultists using knives only, police stationed by the SUV's take long shots into the fight or take down those with firearms or throwing magic projectiles. Lord Plagueheart blasts and slices his way amongst the overwhelmed, accepting returning hits all the same until Cyngosa and Khelu catch his direct attention in the thinning fray. The ambient background of bullets crack, and chaos as the fight for control of the satellite dish continues.

Lord Plaugeheart slashes down an officer that just took a shot to his skull helmet, then charges unhindered at Cyngosa and Khelu, yelling out loud, "I'm going to enjoy making you bleed out slowly, Direwolf vermin." He ducks under a fireball from Cyngosa, dashing low and forward with his horrendous butcher blade in a wide and upward moving cut.

Cyngosa leaps backward, just missing having his torso gashed across by the evil weapon, but his magic quarterstaff bursting into sparkles. He fired his rifle point blank at Lord Plagueheart with his other arm.

Khelu fires her rifle at Lord Plagueheart, safely away from Cyngosa, until her rifle's magazine is empty. Many of her shots hammer his torso armor loudly and his plated armored arm wields the sawed-off double-barrel shotgun, throwing off Lord Plagueheart's aim. Forced to reload and move as the fighting disrupts her.

Officer Benedict rushes right up afterward, crashing into Lord Plagueheart with his riot shield before striking relentlessly with a fully spiked button. "Now I got you, son of a bitch" Soon forced to raise his shield up for the butcher blade that comes crashing in against him. Lord Plagueheart sweeps his attacks from Cyngosa to Benny now. Given such an opportunity, Cyngosa exhales and clenches another ankh to summon a more powerful fireball spell.

A molten rock sphere formulates hovering in his palm, but as he goes to toss it, a cultist runs at him with a knife and stabs wildly at Cyngosa. Cyngosa squirms away and involuntarily is forced to hurl his spell right into his attacker instead, almost point blank. Lord Plagueheart glances backward as easily fending off Officer Alabaster with his hideous butcher blade, blasting his double-barrel shotgun directly at Cyngosa mid-leap at the same time. The gun's blast sends him rolling down, gasping in pain, but grateful his armor plating holds up.

Lord Plagueheart, kicking beneath the riot shield at his feet, shoving Officer Alabaster back before aiming the double-barrel shotgun at him next. "Your efforts are in vain here...this city is just the very beginning! We will reach the whole supercontinent soon!" He fires it at Officer Alabaster, whose gear and shield, absorbing most of the pellet ammunition, but sending him tumbling back alive and unharmed.

Khelu enters the close fight with a powerful twist kick, out of the blue. She sends Lord Plagueheart's outreached sawed-off double-barrel shotgun flying out of his grip. "Oh, put a muzzle on it!" she yells.

Chuckling diabolically, Lord Plaugeheart gets up, shrugging off Khelu's attack before swinging at her with this butcher blade. Growling maniacally at Khelu, he says, "You will see. You will hear..." He takes another swing at her, then another. "You will understand!"

Khelu gasps, ducking low, coming up right after the butcher blade swings past and instantly drawing two combat knives from her belt. Lunging in courageously, her arms pumping furiously with pointed ends at Lord Plagueheart's torso and underarms. Lord Plagueheart didn't let the numerous stabbings hinder him. As Khelu is on the offensive, he sweeps his leg out to try to catch her with a sideway kick, forcing her to pivot mid-attack.

Swings his butcher blade madly at Khelu, dipping back to avoid her opportune stabs. Maneuvering the fight toward his discarded double-barrel gun. "Even over my dead body, you will still fail to stop us," Plagueheart spits.

Khelu's gold eyes widen in fear when Lord Plagueheart retracts suddenly in reach of his firearm, sprinting closer in and shoulder-tackling him after he rises from finally retrieving it. "I can oblige you!" Her free arm stabbing her knife swiftly before she's physically struck by the double-barrel gun itself.

After Lord Plagueheart backhands Khelu across the head with the firearm, he raises it at her when she's thrown and shoots at her, striking her. Khelu lands hard and rolls to a crouching position, recovering herself the best she could. Plagueheart walked toward her, reloading his double-barrel and having to holster his blade to reach for slugs secured in his hip pouch. "Don't worry, even as a mutilated corpse, you'll still serve a purpose to our master—" He's abruptly cut off mid-sentence as three bullets crack in against him from afar, and more.

Officer Argyle fires his rifle at Lord Plagueheart from the rooftop of the relay building. Other officers present with him, trying to break into the building. Officer Argyle grins, firing his entire clip. Lord Plagueheart's modern armor is pelted up and cracking under his torn robes, the impact behind the barrage of bullets throwing him onto his back. Khelu getting to her feet, she and Officer Argyle offer each other a brief long distance salute before returning to fight.

During Lord Plagueheart's stumbles, Cyngosa also pulls himself up to his feet from the cold packed down snow beneath him, casting a quick look at Khelu with relief to see her alive. Bloodied up and appearing worse for wear Cyngosa checks and discards an empty rifle magazine, also a shriveled up wood carving; the remains of a spent healing totem. Rolling his shoulders as he pulls up the *Elemental Magic Mastery* book, slipping open to a page marked by a neon red sticky note, hip-firing his rifle at another attacker.

Cyngosa, with bravado and aggression in his stance, shouts, "Hold up! I didn't hear no bell!" The fallen cultist drops nearby to him, and he begins casting another spell directly from it. "Ding, ding, bro."

Khelu and Lord Plagueheart exchange attacks at one another nearby. Cyngosa's magic projectile hurls in at him in the same timeframe. A static sound erupts, followed by six spiraling iridescent lights, three in each of his palms. His magical scarred tattoos flash rainbow for a brief time as he sends these strange projectiles at Lord Plagueheart and up on the ridge where the cultists had focused their efforts to ruthlessly murder the police.

Officer Alabaster, who was previously separated in the chaos, is taking a quick observation of the many dead now and growing number of wounded still up, fighting for the control room. The two *Lycandians* bizarre phoenix fared well, Benedict Alabaster notes, but was the combined effort enough?

During Cyngosa and Khelu's encounter with the leader, the doorway inside had been broken open, inside the building, with most of the remaining officers grouping up and making desperate final efforts to shut down the signal. Benedict Alabaster sees Cyngosa's diamond shaped magic projectiles soar in, zapping the entire line of enemies. He reacts and makes a zig-zagging dash to reunite with his fellow besieged officers.

Lord Plagueheart shudders violently after the same three diamond shaped iridescent lights crash into his body, electrifying him and stripping away any magical protection he has on his person too. With hysterical laughter, he hurls his butcher blade at Khelu before falling to his knees. It gashes across her right side near her stomach before passing by. She keeps her two daggers clenched the entire time.

"Oof, damn!" Khelu hisses and, with painful determination, she drives her combat knives into Lord Plagueheart, finishing the fight but with a bittersweet victory. Running for cover now, heading the opposite direction of the facility, Khelu skids downhill, hurling her combat knives at two separate enemies as she goes. Officer Argyle, pausing in his post, gets a signal finally as his cellphone is out and recording. He starts dialing to call for help, as the effort to defend the control room from the roof and below from what remained of the cultists grew increasingly challenging.

General Sabaton stands stiffly, the corners of his mouth turned downward as he answers the call. He's standing in the defense coordination office, somewhere in *Aluan*, an oily black room aglow with screens, button panels, and a couple attentive operators. Putting on a pair of headphones, he asks into the microphone, "Hello? May I ask who's trying to reach this line?" Then, turning his head to the operator next to him, quietly asks, "How long until you trace the signal?"

Officer Argyle stays on the phone, continuing to aim his rifle at the barricaded metal door to the roof, and exhaling apprehensively. "This is Officer Timothy Argyle of the *Silvium* Police. The city has been overrun by some kind of heavily armed terrorist cult, taking citizens hostage or worse. They've hacked into the electrical grid, internet, everything! All access in and out is blocked."

Clyde Crowly, from his own location separate from General Sabaton, listening in to the distress call and spying on General Sabaton's operations. "I'll take this one from here, General, if you wouldn't mind?"

General Sabaton looks at the screen, giving Clyde a grim but silently understanding nod of approval. Unmuting and returning to the call, General Sabaton could unmistakably make out the background noise of the battle. "Just give me your exact coordinates. Officer, hold in there."

Officer Argyle—now mortally wounded—slouches against the rooftop antenna. He stares at the metal door, blown out moments earlier, and the fallen cultists in front of him. With his chest heaving, Officer Argyle speaks loudly into the receiver. "This is the spot on my signal! I'll stay on call as long as I need, please. Destroy the dish with an airstrike or something. Millions depend..." He stops speaking, having to concentrate as more cultists climb up at him from the doorway. "Send help!"

"Don't worry about it, son. It'll all be over shortly. We got you," General Sabaton calmly replies, keeping his unblinking eyes on the monitor when the operator working next to him puts the aerial feed from a satellite into view.

Officer Argyle defeats the attackers and exhales heavily, his breath seen in the cold morning air as the rising sun fills the clouds with warmer colors. A confused expression on his face by the phrasing, he glances out below from his rooftop perch as the hold out continues.

The *Armageddon Cultists* assault the remaining officers in the building entrance below.

Clyde Crowly receives a GPS signal from the phone call into his personal computer and quickly clicks around with his mouse before he types a brief command into the program. A devilish smirk comes across his face as a computer program boots up, emitting an audible musical tone.

Out in immediate orbit, the octahedron-shaped satellite with two sets of panel wings slowly floats through space close to the atmosphere, tugged by gravity and adjusting its course with small different thrusters on occasion. The octahedron's pointed end facing *Homeworld* opens. The whole face of the satellite transforms, opening like a flower in slow bloom. Fifty or so antennas aim into a focused point. A single red light beam emits from each antenna, coming together to formulate an intense column as components on the satellite rotate faster. The supercharged laser beam soars down to the planet's surface with slight lag time, fighting physics of the atmosphere and friction.

Back down on *Homeworld* at the array station, Officer Argyle lurches forward to the roof edge and starts shooting down at the enemy, until he's out of ammo, a red flash above caught his attention, instinctively through years of training he draws his pistol. The left portion of the dish array building was struck by a massive red beam from above, blowing it into fiery pieces and leveling whatever was beneath, right down to the cement foundation. The force of the laser beam's impact nearby sent Argyle flying off the ledge with debris Officer Alabaster, holding the line, is momentarily stunned by this, caught up in the fighting over the control panel as he and four officers work to shut down the system.

Clyde, cackling with amusement as he directs the beam's path using his index finger on the touch screen device, which provides him a far out bird's-eye view of the array station. Pinching the screen, he zooms the camera in closer.

Cyngosa bashes his new magical quarterstaff on a cultist, before sending his foe away with a double swing. "I got more whoop ass for you, come get some!" Then witnessing part of the dish array building explode from the red beam, he's thrown down by the blast wave, and in a panicked tone calls out, "What the hell was that? Damnit, Khelu, where are you at?"

Cyngosa fends off another wild stabbing from a new attacker, backtracking over the rough terrain with feet crunching loudly in the snow, he switches to one paw to hold his magical staff, his empty one now clenches an ankh. He smacks the cultist across the head with a hefty solid block of ice that suddenly occupies his paw. Cyngosa twists around and hurls his ice block spell at another enemy trying to charge in at him, striking their leg, taking them out of the fight. His turquoise eyes spot Khelu. Crawling her way to a police SUV, he runs and battles his way toward her. A crack of a flying bullet or two was heard over the growing roar of burning materials, followed by the screech of Eos clawing away at a stumbling, wounded cultist.

A second crimson beam from the sky above bombards the place, this time in a steady stream as it fries the collected ground snow, four officers abandoning their SUV, as its course blasts the vehicle into a fiery explosion before continuing onward. The cultists were not safe either, as some got caught in its track or were too close to its contact point with the ground, being blown away by its force, or struck by law enforcement vehicle wreckage. Fire and smoke billowing into the sky, including its acrid aroma reaching.

"I will stay to finish this. Doesn't matter if the building is destroyed. We have to shut off the program within the network!" Officer Benedict Alabaster exclaims. A third laser strikes down directly into the melee, barraging them all as it hits through the control room itself. Bodies of cultists and riot geared police alike thrown in the air aflame. Cyngosa catches the blast at what feels like his ankles, feeling his tail fur partially singe away and the heat bite the entire back of his person, before behind flung far forward and hitting the snowy ground hard. He wasn't alone as several others badly burned up, land like rag dolls around him, the scent of charred hair and clothing hits his nostrils. The orbital laser beam traveling once more in a sweeping, methodical swirl where the final stand once was, Eos darting this way and that to escape its devastating route.

Wounded, exhausted, and angry, Cyngosa snarls and hurls himself up from the ground, trying to escape the area. Internally at a loss for what to do now, his mind focuses on finding Khelu, or Eos. The bright red orbital laser beam torches everything it touches, still in the background behind him, right down to the soil beneath. A tool and groundskeeping shed erupts into pieces as the laser maneuvers through it and onward. Cyngosa's widened turquoise eyes spot Khelu on the snowy edge of the perimeter, against a chain-link fence and snow-covered fir bushes.

Khelu looks in his direction, hobbling out and trying to catch his attention, waving one arm as her other holds pressure over her injury. A single law enforcement SUV attempts to flee driving toward the road, Cyngosa and Khelu each witnessing a fresh blast from the sky above strike it dead in the center, sending fiery debris spraying outward everywhere, in the span of time that they close the distance to one another.

Khelu, grimacing from her injuries, calls to Cyngosa. They observe Eos flapping their fiery wings, coming closer. "The road is a no-go. Let's get over the fence. It's the only way out of here!"

"Lean on me, come on!" Cyngosa says, helping support her as they stagger along. Eos circles them protectively, but there appears to be no enemies or allies left. He runs to her and the two return to the fence, Cyngosa helping Khelu up with a painful groan while she cuts the barbed wire and clears the fence. Khelu gives Cyngosa assistance over the fence, exasperated due to his injuries, then finally reaching what they believe to be a relative sanctuary. The two lay on their backs on the chilled snowy ground panting with rapid exhales ten feet away from the barbed wire fence.

After a moment, the laser ceases and only the sound of crackling fire and the moan of the wind could be heard, leaving the morning empty of any birdsong. Although, arguably, Cyngosa and Khelu hear their rapidly beating hearts and ragged breathing predominately over anything else. The familiar sounds of helicopter blades whirling in the wind fill the air and are now closing the distance to the burning facility ruins. Khelu and Cyngosa keep low to the ground as they traverse the mountain side now.

Cyngosa stops in his tracks, his tail and ears twitching with shock when his cellphone rings loudly. Alarmed as he hasn't had a signal since disconnecting his device from the corrupted communications infrastructure, upon what he and Khelu witnessed earlier connecting to a house's network. He boldly takes the call, seeing no evidence of the demonic mind washing magic. Through the phone into Cyngosa's ear with a sinister chuckle comes Clyde's voice. "Hey! Look who's still kicking and screaming...Cyngosa Maelstrom. I thought I recognized you scampering around way down there."

Panting and inhaling the fresher air, smelling pine, Cyngosa still trying to catch his breath from the fight and escape, one paw still holding the cellphone to his ear and Cyngosa and Khelu wander onward. "How do you know my name? Who is this? How did you get this number?" he demands. Khelu, also shivering and wounded, follows Cyngosa as the two wander on foot through the snowy pines back toward *Silvium.* They traverse far around the relay in the rugged woodland terrain.

Clyde calmly replies, "It's Mr. Crowly. I'm sure you've heard of me. Honestly, I'm impressed you made it this far and somehow still alive, but it's time you go home now, Cyngosa. Quit while you're ahead."

Cyngosa stops to lean against a pine tree's jagged bark trunk, his breath visible in the cool morning as the sun shines brightly through the fir boughs above him and Khelu. After a moment, Cyngosa smirks. "Why Clyde, scared you're not built for this beef you started?"

Keeping his amused tone through the phone, Clyde continues speaking. "Ohh, I'd ask you the same. Are you built for it, lone Direwolf mercenary? Come on...I know you're a smart one, even for your kind. So make the logical decision, that orbital laser is just one of my toys."

"I'd even pay for the chance..." Cyngosa snaps back, moving his free paw to inspect a few burn marks on his arm, looking behind at his tail to notice the charred fur was lower and more spiky than before.

Clyde laughs. "I hear a lot of empty bravado. Why not join me? Whatever Chrisbane paid you, I could double it. I can offer you so much more than money. The *Starwielder's* capture is only inevitable. Take a good dose of some cope."

Cyngosa leans off of the pine tree and continues trudging through the woodlands with Khelu close behind. "Money isn't a thing to me anymore bro, I'd pay half of the billion Dorrion paid me, just to wreck you face to face in person. You can't buy me, or tempt me, Crowly. *Trinity* will bring justice for what you've done here, straight to you!"

Khelu wanders along behind him, sore and tired. "Who's that? Did I hear that correctly? You said Clyde."

"Clyde Crowly himself," Cyngosa clarifies to Khelu, his emotions a mixture of anger and surprise. Clyde was in the middle of speaking as he did so.

With a scoff, Clyde continues. "Well, what I have done here will soon be the fate of the entire supercontinent. Let it be acknowledged that I wasn't without mercy. Like many before you, I offered you an opportunity at true power beyond anything you could possibly comprehend, and you arrogantly spurred it instead. On what, some pathetic moral high ground?"

"You bet! I'll see you soon..." Cyngosa hangs up his phone and turns it off next, denying Clyde the opportunity to speak further. Turning to face Khelu, speaking to her after a cough. "I got some healing ankhs left."

"This gash on my abdomen is really it. I bandaged it, but it's stinging. Rest is all mostly cuts and scrapes, maybe sprained something in my leg. What did he say to you?" Khelu asks.

Cyngosa walks over and extracts two of his three remaining totems to heal Khelu. A soft greenish blue aura washes over her wound as they rest on a piece of level terrain. But Cyngosa's turquoise eyes narrow when he sees the magic wasn't closing the wound as fast as it should be. "Him and these cultists are going to unleash this insanity across *Lycandia*. I don't believe there's a country or region that could stop it." The two take a moment's pause, Cyngosa looking with heightened concern at Khelu's injury. "That's odd. Was there some kind of enchantment on whatever cut you?"

"That Plagueheart guy got me earlier in the fight, cut me pretty good. I had some time to bandage up and slow the bleeding just before that wild laser beam started cooking everyone and everything. I feel it's getting worse..." Khelu laments.

"I got something that cleanses, vexes, enchantments, and poisons." Whipping his backpack off, Cyngosa digs through it the right side zipper pocket. He pulls a vial from a secured plastic holder, similar to one that holds packaged beverages, and offers it to Khelu. "Bottoms up
"

Khelu partially smiles as she takes the vial and removes the cork cap, drinking the contents quickly and giving a sour expression from the resinous bitter taste. "Yuck, not a fan of that flavor."

"Yeah, sorry, not the most pleasant beverage," Cyngosa says, giving her a playful wink. They resume wandering back toward the road through the evergreen woods, billows of smoke rising from the burning relay station in the high distance now. The dish was still on and active, evident by red lights, and it continued to slowly readjust its position now and again.

CHAPTER ELEVEN: A Somber Dawn

OVERCAST AS CLOUDS SLOWLY twist red in hue in the sky above. Cyngosa and Khelu walk cautiously through a partially filled parking lot, the first piece of civilization they have found since trekking on foot from the failed relay battle back into *Silvium*. A massive supermarket sat next to a hardware store, sharing the lot attached to a two lane main street. More buildings and roadway lie in the distance, however, this sparsely settled nook of the large city had patches of morning fog covering some of the horizon from their view. The fog helps the pair maintain some semblance of stealth, as random patrols of cultists are soon spotted by Cyngosa and Khelu's alert eyesight.

With a nervous clearing of his throat, he whispers to Khelu, "We need more supplies, food, and clean water especially! Let's move on to that grocery store, get what we need plus whatever we find that might help us bring the fight to Clyde." Khelu doesn't offer a reply, something off that Cyngosa catches.

Khelu makes pained straining sounds throughout the walk and eventually catches Cyngosa's hearing while they step stealthily between a white cargo truck and a foliage covered hill, to their back. Expressing visible worry on his face, and concern in his voice, he says, "You okay? Feeling a bit nauseous is, in fact, a side effect of the cleanser." Khelu stubbornly nods.

A moment later Khelu hunches over, tasting bile in her mouth, as they are momentarily stopped in their journey through the parking lot between empty cars and trucks. "I don't know what this feeling is. My head hurts really bad. It's been starting to spread all over, dude." Before Cyngosa can react, Khelu collapses and rolls to her back on the coarse, cool asphalt beneath them. Cyngosa rushes over, quickly lifting her clothing to inspect the same injury from before. It has closed and healed, only further fueling his confusion.

"If it's not a vex or enchantment, or a fungal infection," Cyngosa grumbles, his face twisting with intensity as he scrambles through his thoughts. "If nothing else works, it's demonic magic, damn. But I need time to make a purifying ankh."

Khelu, sounding sickly, forces herself upright. "I...I'm losing control of myself."

"Fight it, hold on," he begs with a pleading expression on his face, helping her haunch her way between a red car and a blue van, to attempt to keep out of sight from the scattered enemies loitering about. With shaky paws, Cyngosa swivels his head around before taking in a relieved inhale. Eos, keeping a watchful eye on the pair from above, takes notice of their emergency stop and slowly descends from the foggy sky. Reconsidering it when the azure phoenix's sight sees them surrounded, but not yet noticed, Cyngosa mentally tells them to float above but not attack.

Cyngosa moved beside Khelu, hastily swings his backpack off and pulls out his carving knife from his belt. In a moment's time, also selecting a wooden cylinder, carving it madly. Finishing the piece in under five minutes' time, speaking the enchantments proper phrasing with a soft spark of light blue coming from his fingertips, Cyngosa then forcefully putting the ankh into Khelu's paws.

"Sis, you need to hold on, I need you to." Cyngosa's voice cracks, sensing his throat tighten up on him suddenly, but in the situation remains actively collected, willing himself to save her. He pokes his head up and, with daring eyes, takes a brief peek at their surroundings before dipping back down. Cyngosa places his paws over Khelu, noticing them getting cold, his jaw clenching, and a muffled growl of anguish escapes. He closes his own fluttery paws and fingers over them while Khelu shakily holds the freshly carved and enchanted ankh.

But then, the automatic doors to the supermarket open, and ten *Armageddon Cultists* walk out, two noticing Cyngosa and Khelu when they quickly stare around the lot, noticing them between and amongst the parked vehicles.

"I saw movement over there…" announces one. The cultist proceeds to close in with the others, weapons up and at the ready as their booted feet clap against the pavement.

Cyngosa raises his own firearm and prepares himself. Keeping his gaze forward, he says to Khelu in a grizzly whisper, "I've always watched out for you since we were children. You've had my back every day of life. I'm not about to abandon you now. Not like this. Why isn't my damn ankh working?"

"Kinda like what Dorrion said, *Trinity's* candlelight is still lit," Khelu says up at him, making Cyngosa's emerald-pierced ears dart in the direction behind him, reaching her paw still clutching the ankh up to his shoulder and clasps it tightly, blurting out, "Don't do it."

Khelu crawls backward toward the cultists, leaving her gear behind and looking at Cyngosa with her gold-colored eyes as they turn pale. Cyngosa's face melting to agonizing horror as notices while he tries to reach out, quietly with a pleading expression as the enemies get closer by the passing second.

Losing a straining fight with herself for control of her body, Khelu becomes dazed and almost expressionless, and soon her body stills itself even if her voice emits in strain. "It's too late, Cyngosa, they got me. I don't feel anything. Don't get yourself killed for dumb shit now, think bigger. I love you like family, bro."

"What are you doing? Me and Eos can kill these clowns easily, then we all can escape," Cyngosa says, denial dripping through in his voice, stubbornly clenching his paws on his rifle.

"Find Crowly, finish it," Khelu says back to him. The look of pained desperation wasn't there anymore, and neither was Khelu and Cyngosa knew her as.

Cyngosa, feeling his world crash around him, reluctantly drags her gear himself, and hides from view on the opposite side of the red sedan as the cultists finally approach on sight coming from the storefronts.They don't shoot Khelu on sight but move warily closer instead, inspecting her, as she slowly rises to her feet, slow and mechanical-like. Cyngosa, meanwhile, is aiming his rifle, but hesitates, watching and listening in with perked ears.

Lowering his weapon, the front most cultist, leans in to inspect Khelu's eyes. "Ahh, there's no faking it. It's a newly hallowed seer. She must have just turned, bear witness to the truth as it washes away, distracting consciousness. That cleansing totem is futile against the powers of Eradicator," he explains to the others. To Khelu, the cultist says, "Welcome."

Khelu, in her entranced state of being, starts walking forward as if by some silent command past the cultists. As if they didn't even exist, paying no heed to any word spoken to her.

A second hooded cultist speaks up next. "She'll wander her way on her own to the Spire to join the many thousands of others. I don't see anyone else here. Two of you," he points at his cohorts, "escort her. The rest come with me. We're moving the patrol onward."

Cyngosa forces himself the other way, defeated that he can't do anything about Khelu. Not with undoubtedly more enemies lurking in earshot to hear should he decide to fight. Khelu's logic makes sense. Cyngosa couldn't fight the whole city and the effort lacked a fixed goal. Cyngosa noticed that the *Armageddon Cultists* took people alive and wanted answers. Emotionally devastated, his expression sours and with wet eyes, Cyngosa strains himself, keeping it together until the enemies leave.

Maneuvering to close the distance between himself and the supermarket now, he reinforces the thought through his mind that Khelu is right. There isn't anything he could do for her now and time wasn't a luxury. Rifle at the ready now as he slips through the automatic doors, the bright light of the LEDs washing down over the colorful and attention pulling displays.

Cyngosa, appreciating the sheltering warmth of indoors, heads straight for the first aid and medicine aisle in the completely empty store. Eos flapping inside after Cyngosa, sensing their confusion over Khelu's crisis.The shelves are all stocked still, lights on, refrigerators working, but the eeriness lack of anybody present hardly concerns Cyngosa.

Now obsessively driven in a state of seething rage and grief, he flares his nostrils and baring his fangs, muttering to Eos, "There's something about that spire in the city, and the cultists keeping people alive, dark magic needs a warlock for its source. And we know who."

Snatching a bottle of isopropyl disinfectant right off the shelf as he passes by it, Cyngosa douses the liquid over his exposed scrapes and cuts. He ignores the stinging, hissing through clenched fangs while the medicinal scent fills his nose, and he winces. Then he applies basic first aid to himself to old injuries, with what he could find in the middle of the aisle.

He tidies himself up, his shoulders hunching forward over his chest and his tail drooping behind him. The full weight and shock still hasn't set, Cyngosa fought the onslaught of short-term memories he has with Khelu. moving to the back of the supermarket toward the employee break room with new supplies. He immediately swings his backpack on top of an empty table, it and the room smelling of bleach and a hint of mint.

Cyngosa laces his rifle down next to it, before he empties everything out and quickly reorganizes the contents, tossing out the used leftover trash of his field first aid kit and a couple empty water bottles. Next, with heaviness, he empties Khelu's backpack to recover her personal items that served Cyngosa no use. There was little else left for supplies.

Cyngosa sinks into the chair of the breakroom table, having a disheartened look while he forlornly inspects what remains, five magazines of ammo left for his rifle, no water, three granola energy bars, and six smoothed wooden cylinders, which were totem blanks that he could carve. He picks up his utility knife and tests its edge, afterward rummaging in a bag pocket for a whetstone to sharpen it.

"Been a long, rough week…" he mutters as he unstrap his torso vest with his armor plates inside held in stitched pockets. His shirt underneath is dirty with rips in it. He starts to dab healing ointment on his gashes, leaving the garment on and oxygen reaching them.

Cyngosa's bloodshot, but still glowing turquoise eyes linger on the physical photograph of him and Khelu when they were escaping as young adults from *Olcan*. Moving past the cleaning and home goods aisle, he shuffles along and discovers the clothing section.

Cyngosa tears his ruined shirt off, letting some of his pent up anger expel. He puts a brand new dark green long sleeve shirt with some interesting black graphics on it from the store's humble selection, the clothing features a paw fist pumping sticking his index and pinky fingers up with four halo rings going around it. Munching down on salty preserved jerky and swallowing down an entire bottle of fruit juice, moving quietly through the aisles collecting items into his backpack. Cyngosa exits the automatic doors of the market, his gold plated rifle slung on his shoulder but at the ready.

Cyngosa exits with Eos on his right shoulder, starting his trek toward *Crowclaw Conglomerates Silvium* headquarters to find Clyde Crowly. Moving stealthily through a thickly settled, upper-class appearing neighborhood near the plaza he's in. Cautiously aware of the unknown number of enemies around him going from lawn to lawn, a tank with serrated bumpers on its front and back slowly rolls along down the street right by him with ten or so robed cultists as escorts to the intimidating war machine.

Never before in his life had Cyngosa felt or seen such a concentration of dark magic. On the far horizon of *Silvium* stood a massive tower, more a twisted spire than any normal structure. It was clearly out of place, sinister. A single red beam pierced the hazy sky above. Lurking shallow beneath the surface of his anger, loss, and defeat is something more, fear. His head swivels about before taking a moment's cover in an evergreen bush next to the sidewalk.Turning away, Cyngosa recognizes the *Crowclaw Conglomerates* illuminated logo on the face of another tower, on the side of *Silvium* closest to him. Cyngosa traverses from the backyards of the outer suburbs in the general direction of this tower, meandering his course between hushed houses for three blocks, before having to leap over a tall wooden fence to avoid a clustered group of cultists.

Jogging quickly through the mechanic's parking lot he drops into, he darts across the street to another neighborhood of houses, Eos fluttering after him, flying close behind. Having a moral internal dilemma with himself, he suddenly hears familiar beeps from Dorrion's phone, just like before at *Solstice Keep*. It makes Cyngosa—who was otherwise traveling in complete silence with his burdening thoughts—drop flat to his stomach on the lawn in front of a white bay window of a house's living room, feeling every fiber of fur on his person go on end at once. Eos chirps, diving up to hide in a tree bough.

He then just as hurriedly fetches the cellphone to open it and tries to call the number, remembering it actually acquired a signal through the *Armageddon Cult's* blackout. "Sorry! Calls are unavailable at this time through your service provider to the region," an automated voice replies from the device.

Cyngosa pulls the phone from his ear to stare at the screen with slight aggravation. "Well, how rude of you…"

Looking and reading the cellphone screen, Cyngosa walks along the sidewalk left uneven by tree roots, texting whoever is on the other end without even knowing who they are, cautious to yank his eyes up to inspect his surroundings. But if their signal breaches through going unnoticed by Crowly or his henchmen, Cyngosa will risk it. He sends a text:

Dorrion has passed, I'm a friend of his and a member of Trinity. We are in rough shape, we were transported to Silvium, it's a city way up in northern Wulftheon in Lycandia. The Armageddon Cult has turned the place into a failed state, they've created an obelisk in the city that is brainwashing everyone using a specific network signal. Local resistance attempted to destroy it or shut it down, then we got blasted by some crazy sky laser.

Glyph and Kerith linger inside the old *Trinity* safe house, Kerith says. "*The Armageddon Cult*, but if this is true, that space to surface laser is operational which, not to digress, is half badass and equally half horrifying…" Kerith tugs at his whiskers pensively, narrowing his baby blue eyes aglow in the dingy lighting. "That Commando Veridian guy mentioned that name before, this cult."

"Whoever this person is, they have one shot and one shot only. That's all my auto program is good for before the satellite does a security update after manual use. It's the best I can do. It will wipe my program out completely, so they should make it count," Glyph says, staring at Kerith with a serious expression outside of his usual zany on
e.

Kerith stares back with equal concern at Glyph. "This could be an enemy that took Dorrion's phone, setting us up. Hm, I suppose ask them to tell us something only Dorrion would know." Kerith lets out a drawn-out sigh. "Dorrion's death is quite crushing news, if proven true."

Glyph leans over, reading the text with an antic laugh. "They're name is Cyngosa?" He mispronounced it horribly. "Saaliha is alive and the last surviving *Galanexian* is the *Starwielder* who is traveling with them to try and stop the cult…this person has got to be absolutely crazy. Trust me, I know what crazy looks and sounds like."

"Oh, you do? Ha no doubt, hmm…Okay." Kerith pats Glyph on his wrinkled leathery shoulder bearing colorful floral tattoos. He took a moment to scratch his own chin, a clever grin on his face. "Let's ask them something only Saaliha or Dorrion would know."

Cyngosa walks fast into a wispy wooded area after passing the final houses in the cul-de-sac, traversing the landscape that is now bumpy and laden with dead leaves and fallen tree branches. Eos fluctuates their flight path amongst the gnarly limbs. Cyngosa's fingers hammer away, sending a text message explaining:

I'm closing in on Crowly's base of operations. I can blast the building with his own satellite laser if I can get access to it somehow. Saaliha was alive the last I saw her, her father Adaros shattered his soul into nine pieces to save her from a terrible sickness when she was young. Dorrion's machine experiment, the Genesis Machine is destroyed and it's important we restore it.

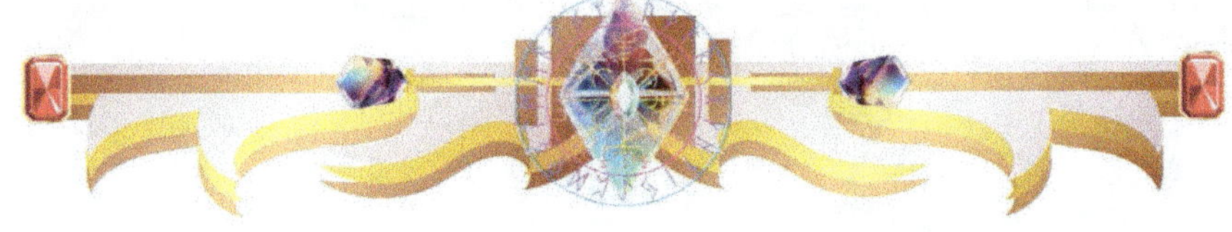

Glyph reads Cyngosa's first message verbatim. His eyes widened behind his purple tinted glasses and giving a giggle, Glyph comments, "Cute idea, Oooh, I wouldn't do that just yet. He needs to stop their building defensive system from identifying friendly targets somehow, otherwise it'll just ignore the command." Kerith hums and reads the message, also developing a look of genuine surprise. Such an intimate detail between Saaliha and their father was strictly family knowledge. Knowledge that had put the Moonwanes in hot water back then.

"That's the best we can do for, uh, Cyngosa, he knows about Saaliha's secret. But if he also knows about Dorrion's machine prototype, then he's trustworthy enough for me. Bugging Daxil's email might only work for so long. Has anything interesting popped up while we can still see his messages? Kerith asks, folding his arms across his chest now.

Glyph switches tabs on his laptop, chewing his bottom-lip as his marigold pupils go line by line. "Two hours ago, he was informed that a salvage effort from *Port Humility* provided materials. I'll take a guess that this might have something to do with that 'Group Hug' project. It was transported to the coast of *Xarus*," Glyph says.

"*Xarus?* Certainly raises my eyebrows if Daxil has to travel that far across *Perilith*. To a geo politically neutral country with an unsavory reputation, no less," Kerith comments. "Let's wait a bit longer and wait to hear back from Veridian on what you and I should do next."

Cyngosa briefly reads the screen, revealing to him each symbol and letter he had to text to the program. He closes the phone and continues on his way, stowing it back in his vest pocket. Closing in toward *Crowclaw Conglomerates,* discovering it was a skyscraper nestled on top of a wide and tall square building within the manicured landscape of a wide parking lot, all behind a barbed wire fence. Cyngosa surveys the situation and sees the security gatehouse with only a two-way road leading in, a road with no sidewalk, and many streetlights and cameras lining it. He follows the tall barbed wire fence and circumvents the gatehouse and security all together, by climbing up as Eos swoops overhead under the cover of dozens of fir trees. Cyngosa first disenchants the detection magic on it with one paw. His palm gives off a faint glow of blue, a reddish heatwave visibly comes off the fence to the naked eye as he removes the magic placed on it. He tries his best to keep cover from any potential watchers before slicing through the wire with his new pair of pliers, the store tag still hanging.

Cyngosa leaps down on the cool ground of dead pine needles, slipping unnoticed into the wide, woody acreage consisting of the company's property perimeter.

CHAPTER TWELVE: Battle Of The Bastion

SAALIHA CLASPS ONTO MINAX'S ankles whilst they drift through the clear waning night, the air growing a tad warmer leaving behind the mountainous country of *Wulftheon* almost behind. The stars and universe high above them fade away as the light pollution from large cities far below becomes more concentrated, continuing on their flight south. Minax slows his descent in the direction of a particularly overgrown grassy knoll with bulbous bushes, flapping his golden and black scaly wings quicker, as the ruby red membranes emit a leathery sound against the wind resistance. Saaliha lets go and lands upright after a brief roll amongst the colorful and fragrant zinnia flowers stretching out. Their arrival causes a family of jackalopes to flee in a hurry, Saaliha's sharp eyes barely catching their fluffy cotton tails disappear into leafy shrubs nearby.

"I need a little break, plus the *Republic of Aluan's* border isn't much farther away. It's guarded airspace and we're going to need our strength," Minax says. There's a momentary pause between them while the lingering crickets sing in the pre-dawn, walking a few steps in the cool mangled grasses underfoot before slouching to fall into a sitting position.

"Thanks again, Minax, for carrying me. Finding my own suitable ride to keep up with you AND maintaining subtly is kind of...yeah. Difficult." Saaliha pauses, studying the horizon from her vantage point on the gnoll. The plains and prairie landscape sweeps wide for many miles, broken up only by remote patches of trees and many lofty jagged rock formations that curl like copper colored talons up from the ground.

"Don't apologize Saaliha, it's probably best if we aren't in some kind of traceable vehicle or other metal death trap form of transportation. Maybe flying straight in isn't the best approach, but I'm grateful you're here to help. With Penelope's coup in progress, I'm sure they're on high alert," Minax says, sitting himself down on the grass and ferns before laying on his back underneath a towering oak tree. The boulder opal *Starwielder* armor on Minax's body melts off as he relaxes.

"Let's sneak up to a remote part of the wall, then fly directly up to the highest altitude you can. Screw it, if it's just cameras catching us, we can lose them." Now sitting herself down on a wide patch of more vibrant zinnias, Saaliha excavates through her bag and inspecting her quiver. "Since our fight and escape from *Port Humility,* I haven't had a chance to properly re-equip. I salvaged what I could from that creepy *Paladin* castle. I only have twenty arrows left. I got my swords, and I'm able to use whatever weapons I can steal from them. But I'm gonna be honest about my limited capabilities here. This is an extremely unhinged plan."

Minax gives an amused snort. "Plans crafted by us are always audacious. I've learned to expect this."

Saaliha offers her own mirthful giggle.

Exhaling, Minax stands up, stretching, looking over the horizon alongside Saaliha taking in the alien-like land before him, saying to her, "I never thought in my lifetime I'd travel this far from home, into *Lycandia,* of all places."

Saaliha turns her head to look at Minax and gives an amused chuckle before speaking. "A mutual sentiment, although *Luminous* isn't a pleasant place for either of our kind. That's under normal circumstances, too. Last place on *Homeworld* I would want to leisurely travel."

Minax stares up into the starless sky while the blazing rays of sunlight bask the hilly prairie, and beyond in light. "The sun will be up all the way soon, Saaliha. If we must face Briarpaw and her new age *Paladins* in broad daylight, so be it. Nothing will stop me. I feel the guilty weight of every one of my ancestor's souls that I failed to fight for centuries ago. Maybe I can restore my own honor."

"You feel a sense of dishonor? I don't think you are dishonored. I wasn't with you in the astral projection, so I don't know what you witnessed that was hidden by your trauma-fueled amnesia, or what your past self experienced. I just remember it upset you greatly afterward."

"Pouring salt over freshly reopened scars is basically what it feels like. Scars that never truly healed completely, and when my mind inevitably wanders onto it, the pain is renewed."

Saaliha's expression turns sour, and she nods with Minax's words, silent only a second before saying to him calmly, "I've dedicated myself to this, if I must die and use one of my few remaining lives. So be it. Penelope Briarpaw, General Sabaton and her high-ranking conspirators are not prepared."

"Did you use that totem Cyngosa made for you recently? Still have it?" Minax asks.

"No, I haven't, actually," Saaliha answers, her tone and expression solemn.

"Do you think your father, mother, or sister could provide something helpful for us in a seance?" Minax asks, his tone suggests more than asks her.

She wrinkles her nose, humming out a sigh. Saaliha then says to him, "I honestly don't believe any of my family would know anything useful for us against the *Paladins*. I wish I could say someone did."

Minax, with Saaliha wrapped around his tail, flies low over the concrete and fenced up border between the *Republic of Aluan* and

Wulftheon, selecting a spot that has minimal observance lighting on it. The distant rumble and hum of a pickup truck's engine on patrol is heard below them, continuing driving along the loose gravel roadway against the wall on the *Aluan* side. It fortunately appears no one notices Minax, as he soars up high once more.

In daytime, the blood red eclipse dims the light, the sun still ablaze in a thin ring around the crimson-colored full moon. The sky remained blue, with white clouds loosely scattered and hovering, Minax's wings flap in rhythm, maintaining their marathon flight toward *Aluan's* capital. Saaliha and Minax close in to *Luminous*. The rising sunlight reveals the start of an eclipse, tinting the sky a soft crimson red.

"Hey, uh, Minax, you're seeing this, too, right?" Saaliha asks, also taking in the strange architecture accompanying them during their flight, landscaping and other structures that made up *Luminous.*

"I do…I just hope I'm wrong," Minax says in an unnerved tone.

"What do you mean? That isn't a normal eclipse, that much I can tell. But how bad can it be?" Saaliha asks, speaking up over the blustery air as Minax's muscles in his wings, shoulders and back propel them on.

"A very powerful, global demonic spell, the totality is close by. Out of the three moons orbiting *Homeworld,* I think that's *Miasma*. its natural orbit is being manipulated. Creator above have mercy," Minax explains.

Minax gives Saaliha a confirming nod. Her paws let go of his tail as his wings flap quickly, now gaining speed. Saaliha falls through the open air, as she fans out her limbs, letting fabric wings sail under her arms. Now soaring toward the *Bastion of Benevolence*, drawing her dual swords from her hips.

"I am a vengeance incarnated!" Saaliha screams as the air bellows around her.

"I am justice in the flesh and blood!" Minax yells, summoning *Alpha and Omega* to his clenched claw as he descends downward.

As Saaliha and Minax freefall, three *Aluan* air force fighter jets spot the two above the city limits now and start closing in after correcting their flight. Penelope Briarpaw with her earpiece listens in on the same frequency from within the *Bastion of Benevolence*. She darts her angry eyes at General Sabaton, who also is hearing the alert from the pilot. "Two unidentified possible targets, closing in on the *Bastion!*"

"On it—" says General Sabaton, raising his radio to speak into it sternly. "Direct orders, take 'em out."

A fighter jet suddenly screams its way toward Saaliha and Minax, opening fire with twin gatling guns on the nose of the aircraft on the pair as they freefall, breaking the sound barrier in its wake. Saaliha is forced to bail off-course, awkwardly careening over the massive white granite wolf visage that comprised the rooftop of the *Bastion* itself. Minax's wild aerial maneuvers minimize what munitions would have hit him dead on.

"Don't worry about me!" Saaliha calls up to Minax, wide-eyed after she lands on the edge of a rooftop ledge, then leaping off.

Minax still absorbs some of the rounds, hitting him from behind, crashing hard into the thick glass window that is the right eye of the decorative roof. After two hard smashes, the glass gives away and Minax falls with his wings outstretched into the congress and senate chambers below, in a cascade of showering shards.

Saaliha, with the wind roaring in her ears and tossing her multi-colored short hair about her head, descends onto a flat rooftop, her purplish metal Khopesh swords flaring up with fire and frost on each blade's edge with the push of a button. Her pink eyes dart about, taking in a quick study of her surroundings. She is alone on a white and gold granite platform. Now bolting forward through the arch granite doorway, Saaliha encounters a group of *Paladins.*

One of the Graywolf *Lycandians* pulls up his assault rifle and opens fire at her, ceasing when he misses and she slips behind a column, out of sight. Saaliha's heart thumping in her chest, centering her breathing, evaluating her next move. Keeping her ears twitching upright, hearing footsteps while simultaneously corner checking as her cheek is against the cool granite. At last, she comes out in a sideways roll and charges at her enemies before leaping airborne into a pounce.

There is a burst of gunfire. Saaliha dashes through the air into a full run, having cut down two *Paladins* in a violent gash with her twin fire and ice enhanced blades. The remaining make reactive movements, one dropping to the smoothly polished granite floor, others choosing to maintain distance and fire their weapons. Saaliha pole vaults herself off the *Paladin* who kneels to take aim, landing in the personal space of another adversary.

Before the corrupted *Aluan Marine* could act any further, Saaliha downward kicks his firearm, forcing the following shot rounds to harmlessly hit and disintegrate against the floor. The others hold fire so as not to hit their comrade. Many others attempt to close into the melee to help attempt to take Saaliha down.

Instead, Saaliha swirls her swords wildly, simultaneously flexing and twisting her body to dip and dive, accenting her swordsmanship with deadly fashion. Fending and parrying away her enemies, she delivers harsh kicks with her strong legs.

The conflict increases with intensity as Saaliha Moonwane continues on with her lone assault outside the *Bastion of Benevolence*; the insurrectionists drawn to the commotion. In her resourcefulness, she sheaths one of her enhanced swords and skids past a fallen enemy, picking up a grenade and activating it and tossing it.

With a show of competence, one *Paladin* gently bats the grenade away from his group so it harmlessly explodes many feet away. Before shooting their rifle at Saaliha, she falls sideways as a couple rounds from the *Paladin's* rifle strike her armor plates harmlessly.

Saaliha pounces up from the smooth granite ground through the air, landing in the group of *Paladin* insurrectionists. In a whirlwind with both of her swords, Saaliha mercilessly slashing her enemies as they drop or attempt to put much needed distance between themselves and the crazed cheetah. While her swords strike two enemies simultaneously, a severely injured third attempts to throw themselves into her, Saaliha pivots on her feet as the *Paladin* twice her size barrels just past her she stood a second ago. The *Paladin* whirls himself around drawing a sword and a spiked baton, as Saaliha lifts her swords for their inevitable attack.

Saaliah, still embattled below, is unaware of Silas Sabaton exiting the *Bastion of Benevolence*, platinum metallic plates covering most of his body and limbs wearing his camouflage colored uniform underneath them. General Sabaton pulls his helmet visor over his face as he strides across the platform toward the granite stairs leading down. A bronze two handed ax slung over his left shoulder, a matte black submachine gun in his right paw held at hip-level. As soon as he has Saaliha in his line of sight and she's not near other *Paladins*, he opens fire at her at a rapid rate, forcing her to skid for cover after a couple bullet grazes and missed hits. Saaliha vanishes from Silas's view, behind a thick granite column.

While in a crazy close quarter fight with two more *Paladins*, Silas descends the granite stairs, Silas lifts the ax off his shoulder and flicks a safety switch off, pulling the trigger as a chain blade built in on the edge of the large ax-head spins up with an unnerving revving sound.

Saaliha's iridescent Khopesh swords, the two blades aflame now, whirl high and low, preoccupied with fending off multiple attacks at once. Successfully gashing the *Paladin* to her right across their abdomen in visually fluid slashes, dislodging them from the fight. Meanwhile, her swords both lock against the other *Paladin's* electrifying batons overhead, the weapons shooting sparks on contact, Saaliha back kicks with her power left leg to strike her enemy's face.

The *Paladin* twists in the direction of Saaliha's hard kick, forcing them to fall against the column, becoming off-balanced further. Merciless now, and with blood thirst in her fiery hot pink eyes and her mouth baring her fangs, Saaliha nonchalantly flashes her two swords fatally across her stunned enemy's throat, moving around the column again.

Presently standing over a couple fallen *Paladins*, extending her curved blade forward to point at General Sabaton, Saaliha lets out a murderous hiss, and even as every fiber of her being vibrates with adrenaline she feels an explosion of renewed anger boil up inside her torso and shouts at him, "Do you even know what honor is? I've come to bring the fight face to face. For my sister, mother, father, and other innocents!"

"Yes, as a matter of fact I do know what honor is—" General Sabaton ceases speaking, leaping at her with his chain belt ax, cutting down in a vicious arc putting Saaliha on the defensive immediately, then growling, "Now, allow me to give you a true welcome to the *Republic of Aluan*, kitty cat."

In contrast to his appearance and partial prosthetic limbs, the grizzled war veteran was swift. Realizing he hit empty air, he transfers his weapon's direction and clangs loudly against Saaliha's two swords. Saaliha bounces up into the air, landing on the stairs behind Silas.

The general whirls around to face her, advancing with quick powerful swings, one cutting Saaliha across her golden armor plates on her arms, forcing her to roll against the granite floor as their fight up the stairs ends on another level platform between stairways. On even footing and with Saaliha far enough, Silas switches his ax off and pulls his submachine gun still slung on his person up, hip firing the weapon in her direction, continuing to gun at her as he starts bringing the weapon up to aim more effectively.

"I recognized you, *Felidaen.* Oh yes, the surviving Moonwane girl. You're like a cursed splinter in the paw."

Saaliha scrambles sideways in a barrel roll, extracting her bow, and lets loose up to three desperate arrows at General Sabaton each time she comes upright. Eventually rolling for cover behind one of the thick supporting granite columns. She shouts at Silas Sabaton, "Alternatively, I'm more like the thorn on a perennial rose. But thanks for noticing."

Saaliha pulls her bow free from her back and notches one of her seventeen precious remaining arrows quickly. Saaliha lets loose the arrow while biting her bottom lip. After only a couple seconds, her modified arrowhead explodes, creating an instantaneous smoke screen all around General Sabaton and herself. Enveloping the area and stalling, the reinforcements trickling up to Silas's aid. General

Sabaton himself holding his ax, and keeping his other paw open inches from his sub-machines grip, his feet planted in place with a confident smirk on his weathered face awaiting her next move.

Issuing many frightened gasps from the senators and congress members themselves being held hostage, politicians from every corner of the republic. But also *Paladin* militants numbering over a hundred. Minax lands on the smooth white and black granite floor of the congressional room with a loud thud, shielding himself with his wings as the small remaining pieces of glass rain down briefly. The *Lycandians* all around freeze in shock, some with expressions of abhorrent horror on their faces.

"It's the *Galanexian* demon! Sweet Creator above, protect us!" an *Aluan* congressman shouts while covering his head with his paws, ducking low.

"Ohhh no!" exclaims Senator Billy 'Boogaloo' Benson , joining several others cowering down out of Minax's sight as he throws his round physique to the carpeted floor.

Armed *Paladins* take positions while aiming at the intruder. More than a handful of them unnerved, seeing Minax Bolide up close and personal. "Stop! Hold your fire. I come in the name of diplomacy. For justice to be upheld for Penelope Briarpaw's crimes!" he yells throughout the congressional chamber.

"The demon can speak *Lycandian*!" another *Aluan* congress member yells out from somewhere in the chamber.

"Yes, I can also understand you. I'm Minax Bolide," Minax announces. He raises his empty claws up in the air, trying to appear as harmless as he can despite being fully suited in the *Starwielder* armor. His purple eyes seeing a sea of chin lowered looks of contempt and stiff postures.

Minax tries to explain over the murmuring and agitation from those around him, "On behalf of the Creator, I come to you as the *Starwielder*! To fulfill my destiny and duty against corruption. To smite the wicked and restore order. Most important, I must warn you all about an evil force coming—"

"That's hilarious. It has a name. Those dragons were just a bunch of savage flying monsters. They've been gone for centuries. That's definitely one thing that's wicked in this world, there back now!" another *Lycandian* screams from another area in the chamber, angrily pointing at Minax with an insincere smirk.

Maintaining his composure, Minax growls but clears his throat to speak loudly. "Whether it's *Galanexian* or *Lycandian*, both can be capable of being 'savage,' as you all put it. History will now be set straight, if you hear my testimony!"

The chamber room—despite being packed so many individuals—astonishingly went quiet for five seconds.

"Go on," Senator Alexandria coaxes Minax. Snorting loudly, Penelope growls at her, including several *Paladins* tossing her dirty looks, shifting in place.

"Your ancestors ground up all the *Galanexians* for fuel, wiped us out completely in a genocide, pillaged, then destroyed what remained of our civilization in the process. Even propped up your own civilizations and furthered refined warfare amongst your own kind," says Minax, he bows his head, continuing. "My people were not meek and peaceful. We stood ready for war and fought plenty amongst our own. But we held a healthy respect for diplom—"

Penelope Briarpaw cut off Minax's monologue, and in a loud, confident tone. "The correct phrasing you are looking for is conquered." She scoffs and waves her left paw dismissively toward Minax. She gazes around the chamber, during which a dozen of her supporters jeer and chuckle, shouting to all present, "Stop entertaining this nonsense! If you recall, this happened a thousand years ago. Whatever turd you were hibernating in throughout your kind's extinction is beyond me."

Minax, flexing his fingers and arm muscles, turns his full attention to Penelope, scowling with narrowing eyes beneath a frustrated brow, and says to her, "It was your ancestors, the Crowlys and the shadowy organization you and others swear loyalty to that are responsible. *The Armageddon Cult* orchestrated these events. The evidence will be out there soon enough." He turns his attention around the chamber, physically turning in place while gesturing, speaking once more to everyone. "You claim you're a country of freedom, justice, and liberty. A democratic republic? She's actively desecrating it!"

Senator Alexandria instigates as well. "Shut up, Penelope. Let's hear him out. Why not? But I'm not surprised you don't value due process anymore, given our shared predicament. What's he going on about, anyway?" Three *Paladins* keep an uncomfortably small amount of space left between them and her, frustrated expressions now being thrown in her direction.

Penelope laughs with an edge to his, holding her chin high she yells at everyone, "Nothing but conspiracy-laden mind rot fed from wealthy terrorists such as Dorrion Chrisbane and the lot this 'Starwielder' has been in the presence of, a fact the rest of you should take into consideration. This eclipse...*Aluan*, the *Paladins*. We aren't responsible for it. But. We know the group *Trinity* was a threat to our nation's safety and security. I was right all along, you feebleminded fools. See!" She clenches her paws, angrily posturing herself as her legs plant themselves wide, stomping one foot before continuing on. "Now look at what you get for not listening. Before our incompetent politician opponents almost doomed us all, the *Paladins* took drastic measures. I took action as any strong, righteous leader would."

"Lies, ha! This stupid, scaly brute is delusional! We're saving *Aluan*," roars out one politician from the assembled onlookers, pumping his fist in the air. Several howls echo up afterward.

"Your loyalty is with *Trinity Of Tranquility* demon. I don't care what you have to say! The *Starwielder* hasn't existed in ages. Practically a legend at this point," barks out another standing with Penelope and her chief conspirators in the formation encircling Minax, staring down her nose at and pointing her finger. He growls, looking at Senator Alexandria next. "The *Paladins* will remove all enemies of *Aluan,* including corrupt politicians that led to our nation's fall from glory."

"No! I'm trying to help all of you! Eradicator, the fallen Angel of Calamity, is coming to our world. This eclipse is certainly a sign!" Minax exclaims angrily in tone, frustration growing as he curls his lips, glaring around.

"Look folks, this stuff writes itself. Yes, just like my father, I'll certainly be carrying on the legacy.The dragon beast brought one of the identified terrorists here with him. What kind of diplomatic friend is that? Plus, how do we know you aren't responsible for making the crimson eclipse? Listen, do you hear that?" Penelope announces, bringing everyone's attention to the faint noise and fighting from outside.

Penelope clears her throat and removes her large circular shield from her back, featuring the *Paladins* insignia along its face, raising her translucent plastic assault rifle toward Minax. Several politicians gasp as the time for speaking has now apparently passed. "Doomsday fear mongering. Even if the *Starwielder* returned to fight this threat.

Would it really be as a monstrous being as you?" She opens fire with her rifle right at Minax.

Minax doesn't react. His *Starwielder* armor absorbing the bullets before *Alpha and Omega* materializes into existence, floating in the air, before soaring toward Penelope's rifle to disarm her. She barrel rolls sideways onto her shield, losing the grip of her firearm but scrambles toward it. During the duration, *Aluan* congress members and senators scurry or drop for cover on the floor while Minax and Penelope attack one another. *Paladins,* however, discharge their weapons and descend on Minax like a pack of hunters, those in the far back wading their way through the chaotic chamber room toward Minax. The closest to him draw weapons, a couple pairing up behind riot shields.

"Done talking already? Pity, Penelope. I thought we were just getting somewhere! I'm not blocking the sun with *Miasma.* I have no access to dark magical powers like that. But I'm bringing the consequences of your actions to you firsthand," Minax spits sarcastically.

"Let's see what you've got. Nothing more but an endangered, completely surrounded beast," Penelope yells, climbing back up to her feet and smirking villainously, spitting, "YOU are the evil force coming to destroy us!"

"The blood of my people and millions of other innocents is on your paws! And those diabolical *Paladins,*" Minax snarls, broadening his shoulders, his tail with its quartz ball at the end waving with a jerky movement. "Everyone will see and hear the truth, with me here alive or not."

Penelope retorts over the chaos at Minax, "Dim-witted thinking, ha! Carrying on like this is all some child's story book cliché? That by killing me, suddenly all that's wrong, unfair and injustice with the world will be fixed in a flash? Surely, the real *Starwielder* isn't this naïve!"

"No, I am not that naïve. But I AM the *Starwielder*, who will no longer idly stand by!" Minax states, spinning *Alpha and Omega* in his claws before advancing toward her to attack in a series of arcing sweeps, twisting his body with fluid, experienced maneuvers. "I will deliver retribution!"

Penelope raises her shield up to block Minax's sweeping chops and quick thrusting stabs from the pointy ends of his weapon, combined with Minax's strength behind each attack, forcing Penelope to stumble back or dodge. Penelope pivots herself in a twist, after blocking at the right time with her shield, driving it along to pummel Minax in the head. He falters back a step or two, shaking his head, quickly getting his senses together to prepare for a follow up attack.

President Briarpaw holds her shield up, so it's facing Minax's direction as her upper half is briefly exposed. She glances down at a full plastic ammo magazine for her weapon and returns it to her utility belt. Dropping her assault rifle, she giggles when one of her subordinates tosses her a metal Morningstar. The bludgeoning weapon has menacing, and many studs molded into its head. Penelope attaches a chain on the end of the Morningstar with a stout carabiner hooking it to her arm, growling between her canine fangs and staring down Minax with hatred boiling in her eyes. "Let's go old school then. You haven't a clue just how apathetic so many are to your situation. I'm the hero here. *The Pantheon* is enacting the will of the Creator here. We don't need your help, monster!"

Minax stands prepared, taking notice that the *Paladins* had formed a shield phalanx around him and Penelope when they were previously fighting. He took a second glance, counting dozens standing to create a small enclosure. Penelope, being nearly six feet tall, charges at Minax, leading the way with her shield first. He is easily ten feet tall and, with a longer reach with his muscular arms than her.

Tidus pilots the commandeered medical rescue aircraft at a cruising altitude, with Stratos as the co-pilot, both of them scanning the sky and cityscape below them as they fly toward the *Bastion of Benevolence*. They notice the stark effects of Penelope's *Paladins of the Pantheon* coup on the immediate city of *Luminous*, either unsure of the wider ramifications for the country by this point in time. Protests going on in the streets far below clash with law enforcement attempting to maintain social order, all under the soft dim red light of the long-lasting eclipse.

Stratos asks into his microphone, "I don't believe there is an eclipse going on this month, but *Miasma* hasn't budged. Is it stuck in a full moon phase?"

"Beats me, brother. Anyhow, I'm more concerned with the idea of having to fight our own troops to get inside. Are we really going to?" Tidus inquires, sounding hesitant at the concept.

"We fight only who picks a fight with us in all that mess down there," Stratos states, a hint of worry in his tone.

Tidus nods his head in quiet contemplation. "That idea will result in everyone shooting at us," Tidus says, looking wide-eyed through the windshield. Stratos chuckles at his unenthusiastic blunt statement and Tidus now checks the upcoming landing zone, trying to see what lies in store for them.

"Don't overthink it. This'll be fine," Stratos says, taking notice of some of the firefights between the now two warring factions in the capital with a grim expression. Local law enforcement added to the chaos the closer they got to their destination. A round or two hit their aircraft's hull with an alarming clank sound, and they exchange the same raised eyebrow expression in silence.

"I'm good. Let's land this hovering bullet magnet on that parking garage. We'll slip through the perimeter into the *Bastion*. Are you sure that's where they are?" Tidus asks, raising an eyebrow.

"They were last when I checked the signal. It was hours ago, though. I'm hoping Penelope's paws are too full to shuffle Sidra and Vivien anywhere else. But let's not drag ass," Stratos says.

The two land their apprehended medicine and emergency response aircraft on top of a two-story parking garage, right in the center of the roof's roadway, trapping the parked vehicles. Tidus and Stratos leap out and walk briskly to the stairwell, observing on their way over that the elevators were already out of order.

They arrive on the street level of *Luminous* from the garage's concrete stairway anxiously stiff, discovering it in a state of emergency as a soft clamor of different sirens is heard. The sidewalks are bare of any pedestrians and no traffic, as the lights flash yellow in a nearby intersection. *The Bastion of Benevolence* was only a mile away. They cross the street to the other side as an ambulance and three police cruisers rush past on the empty road. They move to an uneasy stride on the sidewalk, weapons lowered but always keeping fingers near the trigger. Stratos and Tidus glance toward an army armored personnel carrier driving by them, continuing on their single mission.

"The Republic National Guard," Stratos comments after the noise of the engine subsides. The soft snaps and crackling of distant firearms reverberate off the dense urban buildings. They pass the sidewalk as it branches into neatly manicured parklands and esplanades, continuing down a cobblestone path between tall mint colored evergreens. Around them on either side is a wide open lawn with old maple, elm, and oak trees sparsely strewn out in the sea of grassy green. Tidus alternates by walking backward at times to keep eyes on what is going on behind them.

Stratos adverts his attention, even over the muffled distant resonating of combat, to a voice speaking nearby just up ahead. He keeps his rifle forward with one paw just as his other reaches back to pat Tidus on the shoulder. On instinct, they immediately advance toward it while maneuvering in a swivel formation, dutifully covering one another's blind spot. From momentary cover, Stratos arcs his head over a long rectangle earthy smelling shrub behind a pearly granite bench, finding a dark charcoal furred *Lycandian* laying out for cover and also on his cellphone, yammering to someone.

"Uh, excuse me, sir?" Stratos announces to try and break the civilian's concentration with their phone call, continuing when he notices their ears twitch right up and their tail momentarily curls. "We're not going to harm you. I need to know what's going on, though. I have a family trapped in the *Bastion*."

The *Lycandian* climbs up to his knees, the two marines noticing he's wearing a suit jacket and picks up his briefcase with his free paw, still on his phone call.

"Don't hurt me, please! I'm unarmed, some kind of civil war or coup erupting here. Police began diverting traffic and at the same time some heavily geared up looking people put up barricades."

"This has been going on for most of the day. You're saying it got worse. When?"

"The military-looking individuals have those same uniforms you're wearing, that badge looking medal." The civilian points to Strato's *Paladin* ranking. Tidus and he glance at one another silently, hastily coming to the similar conclusion with visible discomfort as they frown.

The civilian continues informing the pair he explains. "The protests only got worse when those same people arrived to violently break it up with live weaponry. Then, I think an hour ago, fighter jets closed into the city chasing that dragon thing you've seen on the news?"

Tidus's jaw slacks open and he stares at the civilian, then at Stratos. "What? Did I hear that correctly?"

Stratos has a less animated reaction and emits a disgruntled sigh, nodding his head to his own thoughts as he mulls over quietly, ignoring whatever the citizen is now saying into their phone, a loved one Stratos guessed by this point is on the other end.

"Let's stay on mission, Tidus. Believe me, your buddy Kruko's death is fresh on my mind since *Port Humility* fighting those *Trinity* bastards. But if that beast is in there. I reckon it's giving us the best opportunity to pull Sidra and Vivian out of Penelope's claws." The loud sound of a passing fire engine's siren behind on the road finishes Strato's statement and decision.

"Stay low and get to any first responders you see." Tidus instructs the citizen, before they press onward toward the *Bastion of Benevolence.* The spruced up lawns and shrubbery ends, and Tidus and Stratos arrive on a sidewalk, crossing the street right in front of them and running headlong.

Stratos lowers his rifle and stares up at the gigantic snarling wolf's head that makes up most of the structure in the process of approaching ever closer still. They notice subtle evidence of civil unrest while smoke rises through it, the flashing lights of law enforcement vehicles. Tidus suddenly yanks Stratos's shoulder pad to halt him. They both lower to their knees, becoming hyper vigilant with their ears pointing forward and eyes unblinking.

Tidus watches as tear gas canisters are shot up toward the *Bastion,* bullets coming back as a response. Stratos swivels his head and taps Tidus to follow as they hug close to concrete barriers lining the adjacent driveway to their sidewalk. A civil battle commences around them, at the foot of the *Bastion,* but at a violent stalemate.

Stratos Cobaltfort feels his fur go on end when a voice shouts at him, just ten feet behind.

"*Luminous* Police Special Forces Unit! Drop your weapon and comply now!" An officer aims at Stratos, Tidus still going unnoticed, only takes a second hesitation before he aims and opens fire. Taking the officer with a non-lethal hit, Stratos is free to roll off to the right and out of harm's way, throwing himself to the ground. The officer, however, quickly fires back at Tidus in shock before slumping down on the other side of the concrete barrier for cover and reporting into his radio.

"This is fifty-two, officer down. We have militants behind the wire. Situation is reaching critical mass down here, Sarg."

Tidus only suffers a grazing wound on his right arm from a bullet that misses him in the fleeting exchange. Letting out a painful gasp, he stumbles his way to where Stratos is now surging back to his feet with renewed adrenaline. Special forces units move in to assist their fallen comrade, three using the barrier as a shield to shoot at Stratos and Tidus before they slip out of sight.

They ascend a curving wide granite staircase. Stratos halts in his tracks as a magical ball of flame crashes against the railing nearby, right when his first foot lands. Before Tidus could even react, another *Paladin* opens fire with their assault rifle, forcing Tidus to go painfully prone still on the stairs, as rounds pelt the area above him. Stratos, feeling a short jolt to his senses, dives forward, landing on his side before shooting down all three of the *Paladin* militants.

"Clear. Tidus?" Stratos calls, rising to a crouching position as he changes out his half-spent ammo magazine for another. He glances over, seeing Tidus crawl his way up the stairs before pulling himself up. Without a word, he nods at Stratos. Stratos runs forward, Tidus giving him a curtailed salute and follows. The two ignore the *Paladins* entrenched all around the building trying to shoot at them. Stratos points out a set of windows.

Tidus, already ahead of him on this, rushes up to push his back up against it and places his paws together. Stratos leaps up with one boot on Tidus's paws. Hoisting himself up, he turns around and leans down to help pull Tidus up. An *Aluan* fighter jet screams past the *Bastion* low overhead in the act of them beginning breaking the glass of the window. Soon discovering the polished chrome bars behind the built into the window frame, lamentable.

"Still got one or two of those grenades?" Stratos asks, a smile slowly building on his face as he tilts his head and looks at Tidus.

Offering Stratos a questioning gaze, his lips part into a smile of his own. "Sure do. But I usually like knocking instead of using the doorbell." Tidus chuckles while getting out the grenades he previously took from the *Liberty Garrison* stock. "But let's do it. Fire in the hole" Tidus pulls the pins on the grenades, before gently tucking them against the bars and parts of the remaining panes of glass. He and Stratos both walk opposite ways along the thin lip of cement, before the entire window explodes in a spray of glass and debris, leaving the hefty stonework of the *Bastion* unscathed.

Tidus drops into the dry academic smelling hallway, weapon at the ready as he looks around the granite ornately decorated passage, grateful to be alone. Stratos lands behind him with his boots thumping on the smooth floor, and they move together down the hall, in no particular direction. Tidus then comments, "This place is gigantic, dude. She could be keeping them in any of these rooms or offices."

"Then we search them all," Stratos says back quickly, stubbornness seeping in his tone and already kicking in a door to a dark, empty office and moving to the door across the hall. Tidus whips behind him to keep an eye out, Stratos checks another small office, then another before they both speed walk the rest of the hall.

Rounding a corner, Stratos lifts his rifle up, aiming at the *Paladin* he sees on sight and shoots, Tidus reacting similarly. Stratos perks his ears up, feeling his tail go still. At the other end of the hallway they had previously broken into, a new group of *Paladins* shout and holler at them and start charging. Stratos opens another office, with a shaky paw's grip. Finding it empty just like the others, Tidus opens fire with his assault rifle at the corner before the *Paladins* at their flank can get around the corner and attack them.

Stratos maneuvers down the hallway of granite and marble columns, firing his rifle at *Paladins* ahead of him. In time with this, Tidus keeps more at bay from behind them, regardless of his injured arm. In between gunfights, Stratos barges open wooden doors to an office room, smaller rooms branching off behind chestnut wood doors. Using these room's doorways for partial cover as he takes down two more *Paladin* loyalists before he retreats a couple doorways back to Tidus, who by now has lost control of the group advancing on their flank.

"You can see where this fight is going to end for us, right?" Tidus asks, under harassment of incoming fire. He pins his ears poking through his hat and flinches.

"Totally. Don't sweat too much now. Sprint up and bank left in that office. I just cleared it. Right behind you"

A bright flash and a deafening bang overwhelm Stratos and Tidus's senses, but they maintain enough composure to drop flat to the hard floor and open fire from opposite positions. Bullets and a rocket-propelled grenade whoosh above where they just stood a split second prior. After the tinnitus passes and the exchange enters a short lull, Stratos yells to Tidus, "On me, Lieutenant."

The two *Aluan Marines* make quick time to the office Stratos mentioned, once taking cover inside they discover it is a small office room of six desk cubicles, Tidus peaks his head out and checks the halls, enemy bullets fire into the room after he sticks his head back inside.

"There's a stairwell, a hundred feet. There's almost fifty of them closing in, more from behind than ahead. Maybe twenty between us and those stairs," Tidus says quickly. He finishes as a mysterious canister is thrown into the office they occupy, landing right where they are crouched.

Stratos reacts quicker and hurls it back out into the hall, bouncing against the wall before a second later it explodes. A loud boom and another bright dazzling flash erupts, Stratos flinching and turning away to minimize the effect. Tidus opens fire as movement comes around the corner, toppling another *Paladin* loyalist.

Three more on either side of the doorway are at the ready as the body of their shot up comrade falls to the hallway floor. The *Paladins* emerge into the office simultaneously, intending to light the entire office up with their firepower. An office chair with a file cabinet rolls through the doorway instead. Closely following it are Stratos and Tidus. Using it for cover as they make a desperate and crafty withdrawal, they reach the stairwell before using suppressive shooting techniques to keep the impressive force on either end of the hall seeking shelter.

Relieved, Tidus and Stratos discover the stairway empty, giving them a release of tension. They emit a sigh, letting their tightened muscles relax momentarily. However, when peeking over the top, they notice additional enemies at the end of the hallway. They appear to be preoccupied with whatever commotion is occurring in the senate and congress chamber. Stratos and Tidus move up and break into the closest office on the floor landing to get out of sight. The enemies now cautiously follow up the stairway.

The room Tidus and Stratos burst into is a parlor with a dozen bookcases of bureaucratic textbooks and law books and leather armchairs and couches. A portrait of one of the republic's presidents is displayed on the bare wall between two such grand wooden bookcases, not a single window in the stale parchment smelling parlor. Tidus closes the door behind them now, and once Stratos sweeps the room and takes notice of another doorway to the parlor. Stratos's nervous paw checks the knob to find its locks, before he gives it the all clear and runs back to Tidus, helping him muscle over one of the heavy bookcases in front of the door.

In a timely fashion, as pronounced banging from the other side is heard, the door jolts in once or twice but bangs against the bookcase. Stratos and Tidus move to the locked door, nodding to one another. Tidus holds his fist up and counts down with three fingers. On the signal, they smash the door viciously until it breaks in on the third attempt. The two advance into the next room in perfect concert.

The next room attached to the parlor is similar, but styled as more of a lounge. Three more couches, a wide circular coffee table and no bookshelves. Instead, with a few amenities like a TV and an attached bathroom, refrigerator, and sink.

Sidra Colbaltfort, a Graywolf with cream and gray fur, is holding her daughter, Vivian, close by in the kitchenette portion of the room, her hazel eyes going wide and mouth going agape when she instantly recognizes her husband Stratos. "Sweetheart, I can't believe it! Federal Agents showed up at our house a week ago, I think. Vivian and I were arrested by these officers in some unfamiliar black uniforms for obstructing justice and assisting traitors. What's going on?"

"Dad?! This is not how I wanted to spend my summer vacation. These bad people kidnapped us from our house," Vivian complains, the preteen Graywolf having more cream-colored fur than gray, and with softer blue eyes than her father's deeper blue.

Stratos, sighing with relief lowers his weapon and rushes forward taking his daughter and wife in a tight embrace, while Tidus gives them a moment lingering at the broken door, his attention diverting to the increasingly violent banging at the door, cracking and splintering apart.

"I will explain my involvement in all of this, but this isn't the place nor the time, my loves. I'm getting you both out of here. Let's go," Stratos hastily explains, part of him agonizing inside, that he couldn't savor his reunion with his family just a little bit longer, but the sight of seeing them alive lifted an invisible weight off his chest and shoulder. It wasn't fear now, but anger fueling him.

"We need to bounce out of here, folks, quickly," Tidus says calmly and aims his rifle above the bookcase, the door behind it completely destroyed by this point; *Paladins* simply kick everything remaining over and storm into the room, unobstructed. One leading with a riot shield wobbles over the fallen bookcase, six with assault rifles aiming over them, preparing to barrage them.

CHAPTER THIRTEEN:
Persistent Grudges And Unlikely Alliances

I N THE CONFINES OF the congressional chamber within the *Bastion of Benevolence*, Minax carries on his fierce fight against Penelope Briarpaw and her *Paladin* cohorts in the midst of failed diplomacy. The two are forced into a closer melee by the oval shield phalanx beginning to close in.

Minax swings *Alpha and Omega* around his body with self-cautious agility before sweeping Penelope off her feet, sending her into a tumble. Minax inhales loudly before exhaling a funnel of flames from his open maw in her wake. Penelope becomes partially aflame, but smartly letting herself hit the floor and rolling to a stop against lowered shields.

Tendrils of smoke rise off her body, long hair singed off at the ends. She climbs up with a painful whine before giving a bloodthirsty growl. Going on the attack again, adrenaline and hate fueled fury coursing through Penelope now, she dips and dives through Minax's counterattacks and brings her thick Morningstar in a hard backhand strike to his head.

Instantly stunned, Minax's feet fumble back some. Penelope follows her strike up with another to his torso with a metallic clashing sound. But before she could hit him square on the face with her third vicious attack, Minax brings his spiky quartz tail tip around in a quick and powerful swing of his hips, driving it against her side, throwing her.

The *Paladins* surrounding Minax in a shieldwall enclosure reveal their spear-like weapons previously hidden by their other hand out of view. A single metal, three-dimensional fang is fixed at the spearhead. Minax gives pause in awe, when all the weapons suddenly sparkle up with electricity like an illuminating ring. Penelope, panting between breaths, giving a sadistic giggle and a wild look in her silver eyes.

"Close in and stab it to death already! Let's end this thing's pathetic misery!" Penelope commands, lunging at Minax with her brunette hair flying.

The other *Lycandians* around close in on Minax, spears jabbing up high at his torso and wings while Penelope attacks aiming low, being first to close the gap. Minax clashes with her in a series of swift parries and deflections, but he can only catch so many attacks. Once the *Paladins* close in, they start stabbing and zapping him in increasing frequency. Sustaining injuries all over and being constantly shocked, Minax attempts to fly up into the air.

That is, until a flock of nets shot by launchers soar at his swift flapping wings. Getting caught up in the net projectiles, Minax flexes his torso and arm muscles to help guide his brief fall back down, to flop on top of the closest line of *Paladins* stabbing at his legs and tail. Minax relinquishes his grip on *Alpha and Omega*, observing it fall nearby but shows no concern on his furious and pain stricken face. He bolts upright first at the ready, the five or so *Lycandians* under Minax groaning, slower to rise after being squashed by the bulky *Galanexian* abrupt landing.

Swinging his tail with a bulbous cluster of quartz at the end around like a whip, Minax writhes about. Successfully knocking the first row of the *Paladins* airborne in his thrashing while Minax fights to get on his feet from his knees. Lucky enough to duck low, one of Penelope's cohorts reaches to steal the discarded *Starwielder* weapon, only to be electrified by iridescent lightning into a wild backflip the instant his paw makes contact with it.

"I've always practiced restraint, surrender. Don't make me have to do this," Minax declares at Penelope, as one open claw reaches off to his right side to dispel a magical fiery projectile, likely from a *Paladin* mage. His left claw lowering to the *Macrocosmic Lexicon* at his waist. "There's magic in here that even I don't fully comprehend yet, but I'm ending your dark alliance's madness."

Penelope, while swinging her Morningstar up at him, shouts, "Surrender? Hah!" She also maneuvers her shield, knocking the *Lexicon* momentarily out of Minax's grip, then barrel rolling out of reach of a counter-attack. Minax dodges, by lurching backward on his heels, more iridescent lightning sparkling in his palms as *Alpha and Omega* didn't return to his grip.

Instead, the cosmic weapon quickly rises from the ground on its own accord, then spins like a propeller at full speed and cuts through the immediate *Paladins* around Minax. *Alpha and Omega* now soaring chaotically around the room, harassing *Paladins* amidst the massive congressional chamber as it gains altitude before swooping down.

Unprepared enemies failing to avoid the whirling *Starwielder's* weapon are cut down brutally, not hindering its spinning unpredictable flight around the immediate area. Buying Minax precious time under duress from Penelope and her recouping allies still. Minax exhales another cone of flames from his snarling maw at her, simultaneously getting the *Macrocosmic Lexicon* open to a familiar section. The only section he has managed to effectively study, given the circumstances of his journey up to this point.

Minax's palms flare up even more brightly when he is verbally reciting from the passage, his wide purple eyes darting from the parchment page to Penelope continuing having to put distance and flinch himself away from her ruthless assault. Despite being harried, *Paladins* attempt to close in from different angles on him as well, just as ready to impale him with their electrifying spears.

The immediate arrival of several three dimensional sacred geometric shapes in the very air and space around Minax surprises Penelope and everyone staring on in brief awe, accompanied with a loud static crackling sound reverberating everywhere. It delivers a whimsical lull in the fighting, stopping *Paladins* in their tracks. Each of the patterns glows a different color, the bright red one giving off flames and intense heat as the blue geometric shape chills all space around it.

An illuminated yellow one, hovering nearest to Penelope, suddenly negates gravity, causing her to float as well. Minax continues channeling his focus on the incantation, forcing all the semi-translucent sacred geometric symbols to converge together in close proximity with him, even as the loss of gravity affects himself, discovering himself floating upside down too.

"Sniper units. Status update?" a *Paladin* officer asks into his communication device, commanding from behind the first two rows of riot shields, keeping their glaring sights on Minax.

The frazzled politicians, and distracted *Paladins* witnessing Minax's magical feat, do so while cautious of *Alpha and Omega* continuously buzzing around still dive bombing armed enemies. Whatever otherworldly powers Minax is using didn't seem to affect anyone else for the time being.

Overlooking the congressional floor, *Paladins* have hastily taken up the balcony alcoves, six sniper positions consisting of pairs. A spotter replies into his microphone and silently taps the sniper's shoulder. The sniper instantly cocks the rifle and takes aim at Minax, floating hundreds of feet away during the *Galanexian's* unbridled magical power.

"Creator Almighty, what school of magic is that?" Senator Alexandria screams to a few of her panicking colleagues, as they watch on, others recording the extraordinary showdown on their cellphones. The *Paladins* previously encircling her are now more motivated to attack Minax, leaving her and other politicians alone **now.**

Senator Billy Benson stutters but yells back, "In all eight decades I've been alive, I have never seen any magic like that. It's not demonic magic, it's not elemental or necromancy."

"This dragon being is actually what he claims to be? The *Starwielder*?" asks the aide, crouching for cover between a rolling cushioned chair and the long desk. Senator Alexandria nervously glances all over at the chaos and sighs at the others. She ducks back down when a sniper round echoes with a sharp crack above, making her fur go on end and ears pop.

President Penelope Briarpaw lets out an angry and panicked scream, as she harmlessly flails at Minax in the zero gravity space he just created moments ago, now just out of reach of the *Starwielder*. Minax stretches one arm out at *Alpha and Omega* still far away, bringing it on a boomerang course back to him.

Penelope, releasing her Morningstar, moves her free paw to her shield bearing wrist pressing a red button as she slowly tumbles around. The armored bulky portion of her body armor near her shoulders sprouts small jet engines, blasting to life and quickly carrying Penelope straight up, leaving a plume in her wake with significant propulsion escaping the melee.

Minax watches with narrowing purple eyes at Penelope's retreat, but flinches when a couple large bullets flash into view, only because these rounds attempt to pass through the aura of the yellow scared translucent matrix floating in between. Minax avoids the projectiles and keeps conscious of where the yellow geometric sacred symbol is floating as he makes a quick study of the sniper's locations.

Penelope arcs forward, the jets on her back carrying her just feet away from the *Bastion of Benevolence's* ceiling before descending toward Minax, falling through the air now.

"Whether I live or die this day, there will be a thousand year *Pantheon.* Our network stretches quite far beyond, and our work will never cease. Now demon, I'm ending your kind's existence here and now," Penelope shouts over the shrinking altitude. Minax responds by hurling *Alpha and Omega* through the air at her, forcing her to adjust to miss nearly being impaled.

Minax, with a quick gesture and a ruby bright spark in his left palm, manipulates the glowing red sacred geometric symbol to explode into a swirling storm of heat and light before launching a storm of fireballs aiming at Penelope. Mid-plunge, a *Paladin* from the wavering phalanx tosses up his electric spear. Penelope deftly snatches the pole arm in the air. Only a hundred feet away from Minax now, she disregards the storm as the thousand or so miniature flashes hone in like heat seeking rockets into her. Penelope raises her shield and blasts through it with a primal battle cry as the stars explode.

Now on the other end of the collision, her shield has been completely disintegrated and her combat armor left smoldering, but instead jabbing straight into Minax. The two then lurch, Penelope's momentum driving forward as the spearhead of her weapon is embedded in Minax's side. *Alpha and Omega* is just now spinning on its return to Minax before it vanishes into dust, to reappear in his possession, but a second too late.

Minax lets an agonizing gasp escape his maw. Overcoming the shock of Penelope stabbing him and tackling him down on his backside, he stumbles back up to his feet, fighting, slowing her despite the aching pain he experiences throughout his side. Ripping the electrified pole from Minax's gut, Penelope plunges it in again, though less deeply this time; the nearby sacred yellow rune slows her, but her jetpack helps her advance.

Minax, with great physical effort, twists around, sweeping his quartz tail tip through two *Paladins* advancing behind him, with others in the wake of the two being bashed aside. One palm glowing bright yellow holding *Alpha and Omega*, the other empty one illuminates into a soft blue, Minax gestures at the geometric shape matching the color and guides it hovering to the center of the room.

Then the giant sacred pattern explodes from existence, in an outward burst of high speed icy wind outright tossing all the *Paladins* in the phalanx away. Penelope, under the gravity hindering effect of the yellow runic pattern, is only sent falling to her backside by the blast and slides twenty feet away. Parchments and folders throughout the congressional chamber flutter about in the wake now and leaving everyone bluster struck, Minax gives out a deep roar while staring at Penelope, drumming his tail on the floor like a death knell three times despite having momentarily wobbly limbs.

Commotion came from the very back row and doors into the chamber. The doors open and invite in a dozen *Paladin* squads from each entrance. Battle mages, also fully equipped as soldiers, with premeditated spells in their palms, rush ahead with more riot shield bearing units. Providing mobile cover, they hurl sharp icicle projectiles and molten spheres at Minax as they maneuver to retake the congressional chamber and aid beleaguering Penelope preparing to engage the *Starwielder* once more.

Wielding her Morningstar in one clenching paw and the spear in the other, Penelope Briarpaw circles toward Minax instead of charging head on this time. Minax's empty claw now harnesses the purple floating symbol, its geometric translucent shape flashing up brightly, bathing the fight in unique light, before shooting stars burst from it in fantastical colors.

The stars zoom outward, some aiming at Penelope, many filling the air around her as they soar in pursuit of the snipers' balcony positions. Minax prepares himself while just now noticing *Paladins*, who recovered from the icy blast, and with the fight still left in them, throwing themselves with furious abandon at him.

Minax commands the neon green translucent floating sacred pattern by changing his palm from purple to its matching color. Willing the sacred geometric symbol into an immediate burst of misty golden fog and a storm of irradiated green lightning bolts, filling the chamber. *Paladin* battle mages throughout the chamber with the arriving reinforcements face a tidal wave of electricity behaving as if it were an ocean wave, but a seven foot tall wave from the floor up, nonetheless. The lightning liquid wave washes against the newly arrived reinforcements, simultaneously dislodging their balance and providing an unpleasant shock.

Three *Paladins* volley over the wave, shooting at Minax with their hand pistols in the process. The purple sacred geometric and yellow symbols are all that remain now. The room, foggy from magic and gunfire, smoke filling the air smelling of arcane and munitions powder.

Minax deflects the lightning zapping spearhead, still wet with his blood from prior wounds from Penelope using *Alpha and Omega*, accepting the painful smashing of her Morningstar against the right side of his torso. Pushing the fight out of the line of fire as the pistol rounds, and more sniper rounds, rip past in his very shadow, still decelerating them from the aura of the brilliant yellow geometric symbol.

Minax pushes his weight into a sudden thrust propelling his leathery wings behind him, forcing her off balance and brings his cosmic two-headed weapon around to drive the opposite end, also with an identical spear-tip, straight into Penelope's side in the similar location she had stabbed him in. She instantly slows her assault with a painful grimace and bark.

"Heh. You should have gone for the heart," she comments snarkily, reaching back to try and puncture him once more with her spear. However, Minax's entire body shimmers purple, palms glowing the brightest primarily. The yellow sacred symbol soon fizzles out now. A tremendous cyclone of lights and colorful flame engulfs the lone remaining purple one, the tornado seeping smaller and smaller into and through Minax. Penelope lets out a shriek as *Alpha and Omega* grows white hot. Starlight cracks from her very body near her injury before exploding into millions of sparkles in a loud boom. The act visually drains Minax as he just woozily keeps his balance, the chamber getting blurry.

"From stardust and matter we originate from, to stardust and matter, we shall return, too," Minax comments, laden with exhaustive breaths.

Silas Sabaton and Saaliha Moonwane continue fighting at the front gateway to the chamber in a smoke screen, Minax in his own battle with sounds echoing from within the chamber room itself, separated by a closed magnificent metal door now only fifteen feet away. A brief booming echo of low passing jet engines passes by above.

A squad of twelve *Paladin* loyalists hike up the stairs in earnest, leading up to the even platform the two fight on, as Saaliha is in mid-flurry with her swords on General Sabaton, she quickly glances over her shoulder to catch the glimpse of more enemies.

That quick look costs Saaliha greatly.

Silas's free paw draws one of his three ten inch long combat knives from his armor plate's utility belt before delivering a burning, agonizing stab to her right side. Silas and Saaliha exchange a fierce melee. Regardless of her fresh injury, Saaliha's left sword clashes with the general's bloody dagger, sending it harmlessly away on the granite floor.

His firearm uselessly slung over his back, and also being disarmed of his combat knife as well, Silas makes a backward twisting maneuver with the last weapon left at his immediate disposal. His chainsaw ax sweeps around his person from behind. The strike from it sends Saaliha into a sideways tumble.

Saaliha feels all strength leaving her from the deep and egregious diagonal slash General Sabaton left, letting her two swords clatter to the floor as her grip fades. During Saaliha's tumble outside of his personal space, Silas frees his firearm from his shoulder, letting go of his ax to load a full ammo magazine.

General Sabaton discovers Saaliha with her bow at the ready, an arrow notched too. The very second his machine gun lines up to her, Saaliha lets loose her arrow to soar against Silas's weapon. Silas's facial expression is momentarily surprised, maybe a little impressed, as his gun is taken right out of his grip in a blink of an eye. Carried off, to be embedded in a pillar behind and above him, high out of reach, hanging by its strap.

Silas snarls with frustration, then hurls another of his combat knives he acquires from his utility belt at Saaliha, laying upright on her back still. The blade strikes Saaliha square into her chest and she drops her bow.

"Damn, that was clever," General Sabaton says, giving out an exhale and a laugh at the end, taking a slow walk toward Saaliha, who lays dying feet away now, gasping with angry growls staring in Silas's direction before feeling life finally leave her.

The general mutters, "Almost had me..." Silas mirths, facing his attention now to the *Paladins* closing in to help him. He says to them, "A couple of you hold position here, the rest of you with me! Let's take down that dragon." One of the *Paladins* reaches a paw down to check Saaliha's pulse, keeping his attention sharp with his hip supporting his assault rifle by its stock.

"Confirmed, sir. She's dead," the *Paladin* militant says to Silas, the general, and the others in tow with him, turn to rush the grand congressional chamber doors in earnest. The *Paladin* militant recovers Saaliha's swords and bow, turning around to observe the attack efforts, as he holds both swords in one paw after he awkwardly puts the bow halfway on his shoulder. As the doors open, the chaotic magic Minax Bolide is unleashing comes into view, leaving him awestruck.

The *Paladin* jolts and feels his legs being kicked out from under him, falling onto his backside as a blur of motion occurs behind. Before the distracted *Paladin* militant can even react to what is going on, Saaliha is up and alive once again and aiming straight up into the air, she lets loose an arrow with a grapple rope attached to it. The arrowhead embeds itself, just partially, into the granite awning-like structure above the doorway.

Saaliha reels herself up into the air by the grapple rope, using a carabiner and looping it on her belt. However, the weight causes the loose arrowhead to come free completely. Saaliha cuts her grapple line free with a slash of her retractable claw.

*Paladin*s still below Saaliha recuperate, shooting up at her and repositioning themselves. As gravity pulls her back down, their first shots fortunately miss her. Saaliha instead twists mid-air, notching one of fourteen remaining arrows from her quiver, strapped to the back of her damaged up golden body armor plates.

Aiming for Silas Sabaton's vulnerable back while he's dismayed by what's happening in the congress chamber, she lets loose the taut string and repeats the same process from before. Saaliah soon lands on her feet on the smooth granite floor, in the interval her arrowhead soars right on target.

Silas, pointing his chainsaw ax forward in Minax's direction, didn't notice the arrow bury into his back when it strikes his modernized combat armor from behind. A second or two later, Saaliha arrives towed along its journey. General Sabaton twitches his furry ears backward, catching the rustling of air, turning the ax around with him in fortuitous timing when he recognizes Saaliha in the blink of an eye, followed up by the distinct clanking of metal on metal.

Silas stops each of Saaliha's Khopesh swords with the blade edge of his chainsaw ax when she comes flying into him. Once planting her feet down, she drives against his block, attempting to cut him but fails.

"What feline necromancy bullshit is this! Should have figured as much. Now let's see if I chop you into a dozen pieces. Do you still come back to life?" Silas spits at her. "Let's start with carving open that skull of yours!"

"Um, in theory, yes," Saaliha says back in a winded reply as she dodges a quick series of swipes from General Sabaton's harrowing chainsaw ax, adding in a polite tone. "But I wanted to return your knife to you!" She follows up by flicking one of the combat knives Silas had previously thrown into her, through the air practically point blank, into his upper right torso. Silas, unprepared, lets out a pain filled grunt and flinches, stalling on his next attack for a moment.

Saaliha lets out a murderous yowl as she draws out her Khopesh swords, igniting both blades with fire as she delivers a flurry of successful cuts that singe Silas's armor, eventually to cut through. Silas Sabaton's eyes widen in painful terror, growling angrily and falling backward into his death throes, still trying to land a counterstrike on the mettlesome cheetah.

Saaliha Moonwane, lifting her flaming Khopesh sword to parry a *Paladin's* downward strike with a spiked baton, is suddenly buffered by intense gusts coming from within the congressional chamber. She and her enemies alike are all momentarily blown over. Echoes of shouting could be heard from within the room. Saaliha scampers up to her feet before laying her widening bright pink eyes on the immediate aftermath of Minax's otherworldly magic's afterglow, millions of small fizzling stars burning out one at a time in the air.

Minax Bolide, undeterred by the many spear-head gashes in his wing membranes, attempts a weak but still successful glide from the middle of the chamber area. Panicking politicians witnessing him lumber away into the air, after just moments ago vaporizing Penelope Briarpaw into glimmering stardust. The remaining *Paladins of the Pantheon* loyalists, not dead or wounded, stood their ground to keep their hostages.

An explosion comes off to the far side behind Saaliha. Her ruby-pierced up ears twitch behind her head, catching the sound, before she gazes over her shoulder. She discovers a dozen *Aluan Marines* maneuvering through, one of the forerunning marines yelling to his comrades, "Secure the congress folk, detain or take down any separatist you come into contact with."

Saaliha evades bewildered *Aluan Marines* and the *Paladins* separatists as they battle each other frantically. Locating and rushing toward Minax just as he barges out of the congress chamber of the *Bastion of Benevolence*.

"Time to mosey on out of here, am I right?" Saaliha calls Minax, taking quick note of her friend's injuries and battle fatigued appearance as the two reunite with a serious expression, and gulps. She definitely sees plenty of fight left within Minax, and they certainly need it as the civil conflict boils around them, with no allies. *Aluan Marines* and *Paladins* also engage Saaliha and Minax, besides one another.

"I agree, Saaliha. I don't think I can carry you out of here. My wings are torn up and I think one of my wing's limb bones is broken," Minax says, craning his neck around the thick granite column he and Saaliha are sheltering behind, surveying the skirmishing forces before continuing. "We'll concentrate on the opposite hallway that the marines didn't breach through. There are *Paladins* holding that hallway too. Be ready."

Stratos Cobaltfort, freshly beaten up with bruises on his face and panting heavily between watchful glances, leads the way down a narrow white hallway lit with golden LED lights along the floor trim. The floor itself and walls are made of granite and have no windows, forcing him and those with him to bunch up in a single file walk, rubbing against the cool, rough granite practically. Pinching his assault rifle between his arm, with one paw on the trigger, his other holding Sidra's. Vivian, sandwiched between the two adults, during the intervening time, Tidus keeps a vigilant cover at the rear.

Behind the troupe are over a dozen *Paladins* sustaining pursuit of them from the halls, ceasing fire without a clear line of sight on them. The enormous *Bastion of Benevolence* could resemble a finely carved mountain from the sheer number of pillars, hallways, and granite rooms that exist. Stratos could only hope he didn't lead his new friend-at-arms and family to capture or worse as he reaches the end of the tight walkway, which he soon discovers leads to a wide foyer area.

The next thing Stratos notices is that the foyer is an active combat area. The noise of gunshots, shouting and a magic projectile or two being set loose washes over his ears like a familiar song, combatants springing up and down from cover. The foyer has multiple staircases, accessing only two stories of the much taller structure. Stratos and the others in tow come to a halt.

Sheltering behind a granite architecture structure in a rectangle shape, and with only the two thick white pillars on either end of the doorway they all exited from, the options are sparse. The construction is identical on the opposite side of the foyer, however the *Aluan Marines* were entrenched in the granite dugout. Half the line of sight across is cut in half, but two large granite stairways leading up, broken up by three-level landings.

The main doorway of the foyer consists of an impressive bulwark built over the existing granite stonework, the *Paladins* who still occupy it presently and use it for a high ground advantage over everyone.

Stratos shouts over his shoulder. "Huh. Not sure what to do now. Tidus, buddy, hold those guys behind us back. Buy us a couple seconds."

Tidus finishes off his half empty ammunition magazine, giving their pursuers pause, not breaking concentration he reloads his rifle, calling over his shoulder, "I'll do the best I can with what I got at my disposal, General. Should we link up with that *Aluan Marines* special unit?"

"Negative. We're also hunted by them, remember? *Federal Special Forces* are present. We need to get back to that parking garage," Stratos replies, his experienced gaze scanning the skirmish for any breaks to slip through. He lifts his rifle, taking another scan through the scope this time.

Sidra chimes in, on edge by the violence unfolding before her, as she grips Vivian tighter to her torso. "Parking garage? We're going to just up and drive outta here? *Luminous* must be under lockdown by now, my love."

"Oh, I got something way cooler than that," Stratos says, smirking at his wife and daughter concisely.

"Like, a rocket ship, Dad?" Vivian nervously inquires.

The *Paladins* hold up in the bulwark, unleash their full firepower, as three heavy machine guns stream bright rounds. One line of fire aims at the slightest movements Stratos made upon first stepping into the room unawares, as the other two guns aim at different groups of *Aluan Marines* attempting to siege the congress room. In tandem, an unknown number of loyalists open fire at any targets visible and available to them, not wearing the correct uniform. An impressive force of them rising out and then transitioning down from the congressional floor, bogging down the government's advance.

"Damn! That exit is out of the equation now," Stratos comments, dipping down as the enemy's rounds crack against the surrounding granite. Pressing an arm back to keep his family out of danger, pieces of granite chip away and go flying. Stratos, with his muscles corded, holds his rifle ready but doesn't shoot back, wisely conserving his ammo in this fruitless fight. A fight that Isn't his, or his family's, and escape slips further out of reach as time passes quickly to Stratos.

Minax Bolide, both of his claws in the process whirling *Alpha and Omega* on his left side, spins the powerful cosmic weapon to deflect any potential projectiles. Saaliha is maneuvering on Minax's right side, her two swords at the ready and emitting electricity. The *Starwielder* and cheetah unintentionally move toward where Stratos is hunkering down with his family.

Unknown to Stratos, reassessing the bulwark and limited exits, as a rocket from the *Aluan Marines* zooms just above it before exploding harmlessly in the air, then dispensing sharpened metal tubes downward in a brutal rainfall effect. Tidus, by this point, lets off a couple rounds down the hall, to keep the enemy still at all of their heels down when the *Paladin* loyalists resume efforts to overtake them. One militant exchanges a crazily close firefight suddenly in a bold attack, Tidus managing to be victorious as the militant drops, overcome by their instant wounds. Stratos's attention yanked away. He aims down the hallway as well. Putting his finger on the trigger to dispense three bullets, hitting the blockade the nearest enemy is hiding behind. Granite dust and thin gun smoke begin to hover around them, Stratos silently berating himself in hindsight.

The *Starwielder* materializes from behind one pillar, acting as support for the foyer roof, running as he shields Saaliha beside him. The odd pair draw hunting enemy eyes, but vanish out of sight. Minax skids on his feet to prevent himself from crashing into Stratos. Saaliha rounds the corner to take cover behind the next granite pillar simultaneously, with her head looking back out of instinct before she even notices the three *Lycandians* standing in front of her.

"What the—what is that thing!" Sidra shouts and points at Minax, the *Galanexian* still on his backside only a mere five feet from all of them. Recognizing Minax, Stratos's breathing quickened, his grip tightening on his rifle, his fingers aching. Minax, flexing his wings out and slithering his quartz tipped tail behind him, getting up into a crouching position, doesn't divert his sights from Stratos as Tidus takes notice.

"Hold your fire!" Saaliha says to Stratos and Tidus, and once Minax stands upright, he speaks to Stratos and Tidus as well. "You! You're that *Lycandian* from *Port Humility*...are you a *Paladin*?"

Stratos eases the barrel of his rifle down slowly but, keeping his grip ready, not turning his eyes or head away from Minax still, sternly saying, "No, I'm a constitutional republic *Marine* trying to get his family to safety. But you're the beast that attacked my boys. You killed one of my best friends in battle, Squad Leader and Scouting Specialist Kruko."

Loosening up his posture, but keeping an untrustworthy glare at Stratos, he replies, just as sternly, "And this Kruko tried to kill mine. I was never standing idly by for that to happen. I take no personal satisfaction in his death," Minax says, keeping his ground. Saaliha lets out a growl, but it's cut short when Tidus shifts his assault rifle's direction to have it pointed at her instead, also still being nervously attentive to the besieged hallway nearby.

"Easy now, kitty cat. Comical to have you stumble up on us, we really should stop meeting like this. But what's going on here in the capital is starting to take on more clarity, I reckon," Tidus says to Saaliha.

"Penelope Briarpaw is gone. I killed her after confronting her and the others. Me and Saaliha need to escape here, my qualms aren't with the *Aluan* people nor is this civil conflict mine to shape the total outcome of," Minax tries to explain, his head turning between them all, listening under duress from the continued fighting close by to them.

"Escaping from here is a great idea. We'll pick this conversation back up shortly," Stratos says, darting his gaze between Minax and Saaliha. He gives them death stares each as a loud boom goes off somewhere behind all of them, adding at last, "Truce? To get out with what's left of our hides intact?" Minax gives nonverbal confirmations. Inclining his horned head, a loud burst of gunfire rumbles itself over their argument.

"Totally," Saaliha says to them, her left ear perking up and her tail taut and swaying behind her. Still untrusting of her former enemies, but she would consider herself delusional if she and Minax could escape unbloodied further, or worse.

"Go back the way we came in?" suggests Tidus enthusiastically.

Wispy maroon clouds, carried on an intermediate breeze, float high over *Luminous*, as the daytime weather becomes increasingly overcast. Daylight breaks up across the city, however one ray of sun shooting down casts itself particularly by sheer happenstance over the *Bastion of Benevolence*.

Law enforcement, military personnel, and others are in the middle of maintaining their embattled perimeter. A large couch crashes through a two panel wide window on the second story floor. The free falling furniture goes largely unnoticed as it lands on the neatly manicured grass below with a snapping of wood and a series of creaking sounds. Minax Bolide, Saaliha Moonwane, and Stratos Cobaltfort stick their heads out of the broken window to take a peek. In the interim, Tidus can be heard firing close by, aiming at their relentless enemies.

"I'll land on my feet for sure, but I think I'll break my ankles and knees. That's a hard landing," Saaliha announces while she flares the nostrils of her small nose to the fresh air, a second afterward estimating the distance down. Slipping her beaten up backpack off, she pulls out a rope. Minax and Stratos, catching on to her plan, help her tie a knot with their combined strength. Minax climbs up to the thick granite windowsill.

"How about the ten foot tall dragon beast first? I must be the heaviest, so I'll test it. Go down one at a time after me. I'll be on watch down there."

"Be careful, Minax, you're already injured as it is," Saaliha remarks, feeling her throat constrict and eyes wince, looking over his many gashes to his wings and tail.

Minax pinches the rope between his tough scaly feet and palms—not too tightly as to risk stripping the rope away—on his slide down. Letting go when the remaining fall is more harmless, he lands in a crouch with a painful grunt, as his injured wings flinch behind him. He stumbles tiredly up on his feet and grabs at the end of Saaliha's rope, giving it slight tension with one claw.

"I'm good, let's go. I'll catch you if you fall," Minax yells up to a backdrop of sirens and distorted megaphone announcements.

"Hurry up, y'all!" Tidus calls, twitching back into the room for cover as three bullets pierce the wooden and drywall portion of the wall featuring a decorative light. Sidra gasps and Vivian lets out a panicked scream. Thankfully, no one is hit. Saaliha steps back, gesturing at the *Lycandian* and her daughter to get out next. Stratos gives his wife and daughter a worrisome look and gestures in a rush, Sidra climbing up to the ledge and grasping the rope. She plunges down with a terrified whoop, landing next to Minax, who she immediately scampers away from. Vivian is next, sliding down in brief terror. Tidus follows down the rope, as Stratos swaps with him to provide cover fire against three bold *Paladin* militants pursuing them.

"Run through those bushes, two blocks down the street. Haul ass!" Stratos screams, mid-slid down the rope, hitting the ground and desperately running. He and the others barely reach the neatly trimmed towering hedge line before enemy rounds crack and snap around them as they miss.

The shots originate from the smashed window, however Stratos never looks back, he's last to burst his way shoulder first through the dense evergreen bush, reactively leaping up against the stone wall that exists just four feet behind the bushes rather than charge straight into this new discovery.

Stratos grunts as his chest hits the wall hard, but his free paw grapples an ample stone, as his other paw manages to not drop his gun in the whole process. He slings his assault rifle over his shoulder by its strap, getting each paw on the stone wall and looks directly up to notice Tidus offering his open paws down at him to grab hold of.

The group whiz down from the wall all together after a moment's reprieve, going from the sidewalk across the street and heading for the next city block as Stratos instructed earlier, no one saying a word over the pandemonium still engulfing *Luminous*, the street is empty, until discarded cardboard signs and other loose rubbish appears under them.

Emergency lights flare and flash from a head, silently looking at one another they all attempt to slip past a police barricade consisting of two sable colored SUVs blocking the middle of the street, neither Saaliha with her heightened vision nor Minax could tell how many officers.

Shouting erupts as several members of the group are spotted by police. They fully occupy the intersection, moving quickly along the cement sidewalk, framed by towering white and black marble government buildings. Stratos waves his family to take cover behind the bus stop structure they happen to be running past. A hot second later, he brandishes his rifle. The agitated officers leap down for cover, as Stratos pulls the trigger to his gun and aims relatively harmlessly overhead.

"Whoa there, my guy!" Tidus calls out.

"We're too close to that garage. Let's slow them," Stratos barks at Tidus. Sidra, Vivian, and Saaliha dart down, weaving through the barricade. The officers recouping quickly, win back in the exchange, as a great many handgun rounds thud noisily through the aluminum bus stop around Stratos.

Springing up from being prone on the warm asphalt, Stratos makes his break behind the others, letting off another shot from his rifle. Running as fast as their legs could carry them, Minax Bolide and the *Lycandians* rush past a couple random decorative boutiques.

Saaliha is first to turn the corner, surveying to find no immediate threats before dipping back around to check on her companions. The others are behind her, only by a ten second delay, and certainly pursued on foot. One of the pitch black SUVs noisily screeches its tires in a harsh turnabout.

Inside the parking garage, the hustling of feet reverberates off the concrete as Saaliha, Minax, Tidus, and Stratos run wildly through. Sidra, carrying Vivian on her back now, howls and shouts ringing at them all, not far behind. The distinct squeal of rubber echoes out, as one of the SUVs peels into the parking garage from the littered street, in the wake of the on-foot officers already gaining on the *Starwielder's* group.

Stratos and Tidus muscle ahead in the race to the concrete stairway at ground level, holding the line with Minax Bolide, which drew a surprised expression from the two hardened soldiers, given Minax sustained wounds. Saaliha checks the stairway with Sidra and Vivian Cobaltfort, all of whom let out gasps when Stratos and Tidus decide to shoot at the charging officers and purposefully miss.

"To the roof. Go, go!" Saaliha announces from the top flight of stairs.

Behind them, Stratos and Tidus return, Minax taking up the very rear of their fleeing efforts. Hollering can be heard bouncing off the concrete below as they move across the top floor of the garage, the group trailing behind Tidus and Stratos while they all weave through parked cars. With an outburst of laughter, Stratos spots the medical aircraft right where he and Tidus landed it earlier, with a stroke of luck it still remains.

"Let's fire this bad boy back up and screw off into the sunset!" Tidus whoops, presently a partial limp in his gait from his sustained injuries.

Stratos opens the side hatchway to let Sidra and Vivian inside, simultaneously turning around with his rifle at the ready again hearing heavy footsteps as Minax adjusts his wings to fit inside, recoiling his tail with its quartz head clear of the hatch. Slamming it shut behind himself, Stratos and Tidus rush to the cockpit portion of the small aircraft. In a timely manner too, as three military police spring into view from through the windshield amongst the dozen or so stored automobiles immediately after the pair seat themselves.

"Don't do it! Step out now with your paws up where I can see them. We know you're armed!" screams one cop, his voice a bit muffled by the aircraft, but the point still comes across crystal clear while he also brandishes his assault rifle into view. The other officer presently speaks into his radio to update other units.

"This thing ain't bulletproof, by the way. Me and Tidus already tested that out. Heads down!" Stratos instructs the others, as he presses the aircraft's ignition. Tidus flips the necessary switches to help stabilize and propel.

"Shut it down, or we will open fire! You have five seconds to comply," the same officer yells. He then quickly says something to his colleague, who postures up to take aim as well after swiftly pulling his gun at the ready.

Stratos and Tidus attempt a vertical lift off. The two cops right in front of them are suddenly below in a matter of seconds. However, in doing so, the officers open fire, aiming for the windshield of the aircraft primarily, taking more shots at the craft's nose and then finally at the engines until the target becomes too difficult or risky to shoot at anymore. Tidus and Stratos witness several bullets successfully pierce through the super thick glass. Thankfully, with its clever design, the windshield doesn't shatter completely, but through sheer grit jarringly level out the aircraft's trajectory flying away with gaining altitude.

The sounds of bullets piercing through metal, followed by the spray of sparks in the cockpit, make Sidra, Vivian, and the others curl up, letting out gasps as their flight is off to a rocky start.

"I think we're good." Stratos exhales, Tidus letting a grunt out and sighs. Stratos takes a brief glance at him and asks, "Did they get you?"

Wincing, Tidus replies, "Nah, I reckon this is still from before."

Saaliha Moonwane chimes in. "Besides kicking ass, I also make a pretty damn good pilot in a pinch."

Stratos and Tidus reciprocate a wordless exchange at one another, shrugging. Tidus speaks to Saaliha. "Go for it. It'll give me a break while I mend myself up better."

"Where are we going now?" inquires Minax, while also watching Tidus climb out of the co-pilot seat as Saaliha walks past to seat herself in his place, throughout the time they soar over the cityscape. Eventually, one of the five fighter jets roaming the immediate airspace takes observance of their aircraft.

"Attention unidentified aircraft, operation's call sign, please. This space is under security lockdown."

"Uhh..." Stratos drawls out over the microphone for half a moment, quickly pushing open a cabinet in the craft's dashboard as confetti of papers shower from overhead. By this point, the jet slows down to a cruise in close proximity to the medical aircraft, the pilots of the jet taking notice of any serial or license numbering on the troupe's hull they can see.

Tidus presses himself into the cold, uncomfortable internal hull of the aircraft. Sidra holds Vivian tightly huddled on one of the few cushioned benches within the aircraft, and all together with Minax, they shrink from being seen through the small circular windows.

Stratos extracts a specific paper that catches his eye before rambling on, "Five, Tank, Star, Image, Onslaught. Uhm, Over."

"Acknowledge that." Next, there is a nerve-wracking silence for a couple moments of flight as the *Aluan* fighter jet escorts alongside, before the voice comes back over the aircraft radio, "You're flying pretty far out of your operation number, FTSIO. Additionally, it appears you've taken hits."

With his microphone muted, Stratos muses to Saaliha next to him and in earshot of Tidus, "No way I'm giving this dude my *Paladin* officer number, that's suicide." Stratos unmutes his mic. "Yes, we've been conscripted to provide exclusive civilian evacuation, over."

Saaliha speaks into the headset microphone next. "Hello? This is a medical aircraft. We are extracting patients out, adults and children are on board, we're clearing out. Over."

"Affirmative F.T.S.I.O., good luck. Over and out." The radio crackles at the end, and the jet's engines shriek with intense flares as it soars away from them. A collective sigh of relief from everyone quickly follows the jet fighter's departure.

"I don't know. Is anywhere in *Aluan* actually safe for us now?" Tidus asks no one in particular, as he stands near Minax undressing his body armor. His eyes dart over the *Starwielder* and he muses, "You look pretty beat up. I assume you have healing magic?"

"Yes, I normally would, but I am exhausted of energy for the time being. Or else I'd have already tended to my own wounds," Minax says to Tidus. "*Wulftheon* is where we should go."

"Why? Is that where the other two menaces of your little group are at?" Tidus asks, grimacing when he splashes disinfectant on the scrapes that appear through his fur.

"It's where the *Armageddon Cult* has succeeded in some terrible spell. The eclipse of *Miasma's* totality gets darker the closer you get. It's over that entire country and I have this anxious sensation. My instinct, that I've been forcibly ignoring." Minax Bolide shifts his head from looking at Tidus over to Saaliha, asking her, "Cyngosa was right then? It is the city of *Silvium.* We must stop Mr. Crowly."

Stratos and Saaliha don't look back. They attentively and cooperatively fly the med-evacuation aircraft over the dwindling urban landscape of *Luminous,* opening up open plains dotted with smaller settlements. Saaliha speaks first, addressing Minax's final comment.

"Cyngosa is an ego-driven asshole, and I'm probably scratching the surface on that. Be that as it may, he never lied about those visions and nightmares before. The flight down for us took almost a whole day, Minax."

"We'll probably reach the *Wulftheon* border by dusk, then," Minax says, slouching down to rest.

"Visions. What visions?" Tidus asks, while tilting his head, looking at Saaliha.

"Eradicator is coming. Minax is the next *Starwielder,* the only one who can stop it," Saaliha says to Tidus unblinking, causing Sidra, Vivian, and Stratos to tune into the conversation.

"The Angel of Calamity. These cultists' deity, apparently."

Saaliha unzips her backpack and pulls out a protective compartment for her small computer. Opening the screen, she purses her lips. On the screen is the proof of Reginald Crowly's plot for the *Galanexians,* a bonus from *Trinity's* heist of the *Lexicon* Minax wields. Her pink eyes scan the images of written documentation, battle plans and still shots of old warplanes. Ledgers recording how *Perhileous* would be systematically looted, and what private enterprises got what. Minax see's what's on her screen, while resting in a sitting position close by. Saaliha and Minax make direct eye contact for a second. Minax licks his lips with his silvery forked tongue, letting out a soft sigh.

"Do it, Saaliha," Minax says with finality.

Upon Minax's request, Saaliha uploads it as a freely accessible document on the *Aluan* internet, breaching the censorship put in place before closing her device. All the while, Vivian is staring at Minax, inspecting his bizarre gemstone encrusted in his chest and the rest of his scaly form. The preteens' eyes linger on the *Galanexian's* horns, with raised eyebrows.

Sidra whispers to her daughter, "Don't stare at him, honey. It's rude." Vivian adverts her gaze from Minax right after. The mother's and daughter's exchange draws Minax's attention over to them; he gives them a warm smile. Vivian returns Minax's smile with a shy little wave.

"There's a large storm over that whole region of *Wulftheon* happening, so this is going to be a bumpy ride. I'm looking at satellite imagery of *Silvium* right now. The eye of the storm is hovering over the city," Saaliha says, pulling Minax's attention back and leaving Vivian to stare at him and Saaliha.

"Then there is where we must go," Minax chimes in, while a gust of wind buffers the aircraft, adding, "I pray for Cyngosa and Khelu if they are already in *Silvium*."

"I'm sorry, what?" Sidra speaks up—her head peering at them, inquisitive—before glancing at her husband. "Why would we want to fly into more danger, love?"

Saaliha shifts uncomfortably in the co-pilot seat, a restless feeling brewing inside her chest, above her stomach, hearing Cyngosa's name come up. Next to Saaliha, Stratos exhales nervously and quickly turns his head to make eye contact with his wife, saying gravely, "There isn't anywhere I can think of right now that isn't dangerous, Sidra. I don't like these two, but they make piss-poor liars."

"Thanks, I think?" Saaliha murmurs, furrowing her eyebrows and twitching an ear.

"What are you trying to say then, hun?" Sidra asks, a look of worry on her face.

"That I trust Minax, and if we go with him. Help him see this through. It might save us all," Stratos says back, turning his head forward. Minax stays quiet for now, raising his scaly eyebrows at the *Aluan Marine*'s words.

Vivian moves out of Sidra's gentle hold, over to Stratos to clamp her paws on his arm.

"You'll keep us safe, Dad, right? You promise?" Vivian's voice cracks slightly with anxiety.

"Always, no matter what, gumdrop," Stratos warmly answers, but stern.

They ride on the medical aircraft for four hours, off and on in silence. Minax naps this entire time to regain his strength, Tidus also taking the opportunity for shut-eye. The skies become cloudy while crossing into *Wulftheon*, growing much angrier until daytime appears to be dusk.

"We'll land on the outskirts," Stratos concludes.

CHAPTER FOURTEEN: Out From The Cauldron, Into The Conflagration

"THAT'S STRANGE. I'M NOT picking up any frequencies, and the radar is acting funny," Saaliha murmurs, tapping at the screen with her index finger a couple times.

The aircraft is flying toward *Silvium*, passing over the autumn landscape below, but while Stratos pilots it, he notices a reddish glow above them in the cloudy sky through his window. His blue eyes go wide in terror. Saaliha is sitting in the co-pilot's seat.

"What the…" Stratos mumbles, craning his neck forward to stare through their shoddy patched up windshield, a scrutinizing expression on his face. "Watch out!"

"Oh no!" yells out Minax, pressing his snout and face to the nearest miniscule round window. The exact same second, he also realizes the gleaming red. A distinct arc racing down through the fluffy magenta clouds. A huge laser from high above in the sky zaps through the fast moving aircraft, blasting its tail end with those onboard hardly having zero time to react. Saaliha lets out a surprise gasp.

The medical aircraft is instantly sent into a smokey and smoldering tailspin. Stratos snarls as he yanks on the controls, steering them as he still has system power left. Saaliha also pulls on her flight control sticks with all the strength she has in her upper body, even dramatically leaning in the desired falling direction.

Disaster on board unfolds elsewhere, as Sidra and Vivian are blown loose from their safety belts, fires spring to life, causing mixing with the pungent stench of burning electrical and plastic smoke.

Tidus, bonking his head against a deploying airbag, unbuckles and brushes the flopping oxygen mask out of his face to rush at Sidra just after the plane is struck, tackling himself and her both to the floor.

Minax loses balance when the aircraft is initially struck as well, woozily shaking around as the turbulence makes itself known to the unfortunate occupants, coughing as he brushes the thin smoke away.

"Vivian, grab onto something!" Sidra calls out in a terrified tone, Tidus grabbing the shaking plane with one paw and hauling Sidra to stable footing with the other. Unfolding in the span of seconds, they both maneuver to help Vivian. His wife's scream drags Stratos's attention to their predicament.

Grievously, Vivian just out of reach of her mom is flung to the other side of the wobbling plane, near the damaged emergency door that bursts open completely when she hits it.

"Vivian!" Stratos yells while jettisoning his efforts with Saaliha at the controls, scrambling to his paws and feet in a start, witnessing Vivian fall right out as the broken hatch flies away with her as well.

Minax reacts first, opening his injured wings and taking a backward leap into the open sky, the powerful winds buffing the inside of the free falling aircraft and his body as well, forcing the smoke every which way. Minax twists and flies right out to catch Vivian as she's falling, his claw massive to the young *Lycandian* child as he grasps her little arm and saves her from falling. Stratos is at the edge of the aircraft, Sidra holding on to him, but he's halting mid jump when he lays eyes on Minax, despite his injuries from his previous life-threatening fight, saving his daughter. They leap from the falling aircraft, Tidus and Saaliha follow behind in the air just three seconds, the two while they all float down by deploying parachutes.

Stratos glances quickly from Minax, holding his daughter safely in his muscular scaly arms, then to his worried and alert appearing wife, and Tidus as well. All floating down on parachutes through the chilly air, as the winged helicopter aircraft they were previously on board spirals to a fiery crash not far below them all, in open grassy and hilly countryside.

Minax follows their descent and once his feet touch ground, he kneels, closing his wings to let Vivian get to her feet. Stratos, Sidra, and Tidus land as their parachutes crumple to the tall grassy field underneath. Immediately, Stratos and Sidra run to their daughter. Tidus rolls his parachute up and surveys the others.

Hugging Vivian momentarily tight to his chest, with a trembling chin and tensed posture, Stratos utters between rasping breaths, "I'm so grateful you are alive. I felt my heart and stomach sink the moment I saw you fall out of the back."

Minax limps forward with a harried appearance, summoning *Alpha and Omega* into his already gripping claw. "Everyone, okay? What in the almighty Creator was that? Where's Saaliha?"

Saaliha brushes her already damaged armor off and checks her gear on her person with a sigh, sheepishly weaving her tail behind her. "Wow, I'm really starting a record for most times being shot down while piloting an aircraft in a single week."

"I have no clue what that red beam of death was," Tidus says, pulling his rifle up and unlocking the safety, his gaze looking over the fiery wreckage five hundred feet away from them, before adding, "But we cannot stay here...Let's get going!"

"Agreed! *Silvium* is a couple more miles east," Stratos chimes in, getting his rifle up, also handing his other pistol still in its holster from his waist to his wife. "Two's better than one." His sharp, blue eyes move to Minax and his face melts into an expression of gratitude, inhaling the fresh, chilled air. "Thank you, *Starwielder.*"

Sidra comfortably takes the pistol and checks it out before glancing at their rather remote surroundings, a yellowing prairie with sparse evergreen trees here and there. Mountains north, west, south of them on the distant horizon. "Thanks love, what do we do?" She glances at the *Starwielder*, still trying to get herself used to the alien appearance of the scaly *Galanexian*. Standing almost ten feet tall compared to her, Sidra warmly says to Minax, "Thank you for saving my daughter."

"Of course. It's part of my duty to protect and save the innocent," Minax replies, glancing at Vivian, then stares back at Sidra offering an empty claw over his chest.

The group wanders away from the fiery wreck toward a treeline and street heading east, Minax keeping up. The others keep a concerned watch on him, especially Saaliha. The sound of truck engines increasing in volume hits their ears, with neck-fur going on end. Stratos and Tidus grip their weapons, the muscles in their arms tense.

"I don't think they're coming to help us..." Saaliha announces, also reaching back to get her bow, and a specially engineered arrow ready to aim and let loose. Saaliha counts fourteen arrows in her quiver remaining, letting out a nervous purr. Tidus watches as four armored trucks drive off the road ahead of them and close in on the grassy field toward them and the nearby crash.

"Whelp, isn't that unfortunate?" He tucks his camo ball cap on his head and raises his firearm, holding the stock tighter.

"Go! Run the other way! Stratos yells to his family. He slaps Tidus's shoulder to let him know he's ready as they both crouch down, Stratos taking aim with him. Glancing at Saaliha as she's drawing her bow string back. "We'll hold them back, run for those woods!"

Minax, who was taking the rear guard on their journey across the meadowland, reaches out to take Vivian's paw and turns to awkwardly run. Sidra runs up with him, wielding a pistol in each paw, and clicks the chambers ready.

"Light 'em up!" Stratos commands and starts shooting, aiming at windshields and tires when his finger pulls on the trigger.

Tidus follows suit without a word, opening fire as the distance compared to the incoming trucks shrinks considerably quickly. Saaliha lets loose her arrow as it flies directly into the radiator of the fourth truck. It explodes and stalls the vehicle to a slow roll. Tidus and Stratos stall out another vehicle, but one breaks to a slippery stop and the doors fly open, a dozen enemies rolling out as the other remaining truck is barreling right toward them still. Just fifty feet behind, the stalled truck's occupants exit to fight, too.

Stratos and Tidus tactfully dodge the vehicle as it passes by. Tidus lands on his side and deftly reloads his rifle while turning his attention to the dozen enemies now charging at them with knives, a couple with firearms in their paws. Saaliha, judging the timing just right, jumps high up and rolls right onto the roof of the speeding vehicle, riding along as she tries to pry herself in with her Khopesh swords through the thin automobile metal.

"Incoming! Minax!" Stratos shouts over to the others, flaring his nostrils in a snarl, trying to put distance between themselves and these new hostile enemies.

Minax, already watching the speeding truck when it nearly hits Stratos and Tidus as it speeds by, has a glowing green beam in his palm and extends it forward. A bolt of illuminated green lightning zaps at the charging truck but has little effect as an anti-magic shield activates to diffuse the attack. Even as Saaliha tries to smash, open the window.

Minax reacts quickly as the truck accelerates to crash through him. Instead, Minax leaps up with a quick flap of his wings over the hood of the truck before dropping down with all his weight and striking the windshield wildly. Saaliha and Minax pivot their efforts when the armed cultists leap out of the vehicle, Saaliha reacting first as she pounces with a feline snarl and serrated curved blades in her paws, onto one unfortunate cultist militant.

Vivian and Sidra zig-zag away from the commotion, as Minax disorients the driver and causes the truck to spin out on the muddy grass to a halt. All the doors flying open, as a dozen more *Armageddon Cultists* emerge battle ready, some ignoring Minax to run after Sidra and Vivian. Vivian takes a brief shelter in a grassy knoll nearby when her mom stops running.

Sidra holds up the two pistols, yelling, "Stay away from me and my daughter!" She clicks each trigger. Holding accurately, she lets shot after shot fly at the hooded enemies.

In the chaotic fray, Stratos and Tidus maneuver to retreat toward Saaliha and Minax, his Sidra and Vivian under duress as well. They kill their attackers in their wild, open hilly field shootout, but no rest is earned. The two experienced soldiers roll and duck, about to take out the remaining enemy rifleman. Tidus unfortunately has one of the knife wielding cultists take a shot from him, and Stratos and still charge on. Leap at Tidus in a vicious attack.

"Damn!" Tidus rolls sideways. Once the cultist lands where he was moments before, he guns them before back tracking.

Minax, wincing in pain from his healing wings, glides off the smashed hood of the truck, he swirls *Alpha and Omega* in an descending arc with one end before transferring the momentum to swing the other, cutting down two cultists as loud gunshots echo around him from his friends fiercely fighting around him, not far off Sidra shot down three cultists running at her. Grimacing through his painful injuries and exhaustion, Minax was still reactive as he dodged stabs from an attacker behind him, whipping his tail to strike them with the quartz stone on the end of it. The cultist was thrown hard against the parked truck and slumps to the grass.

Saaliha remains on the roof of the smashed SUV, drawing her bow back and letting arrow after arrow into targets. It was like shooting fish in a barrel, her arms and paws working quickly. Stopping only once, it was time to retrieve what she could from her targets.

"Sidra, Vivian. Guys! Let's get in one of those trucks!" Stratos strikes down a cultist with a backhand before shooting them up, discarding the empty ammo magazine afterward. Stratos and Tidus catch up to where Minax was fighting seven enemies at once. The familiar engine sound comes from behind them as the first truck from earlier, with one driver remaining, attempts to crash through them once again. Tidus dives onto his stomach on the grassy earth, out of the way. Stratos tries to roll, but his foot is clipped by the bumper guard at the last moment, throwing him out of control to land awkwardly. The speeding truck skids to a stop, thumping with a crunch of metal against metal, into the other idling truck where Minax is preoccupied fighting his own foes. Minax himself is too distracted in his fight to even notice.

A cool rain falls from the angry swirling clouds in the sky, the red hued gray overcast above growing darker. The ground giving off an earthy wet aroma from the raindrops pattering down, Sidra taking shots from afar trying to help her husband, and the others advancing at the two groups fighting; Minax and Saaliha cluster at the two parked trucks still, and Tidus and Stratos struggling a hundred feet away with the remaining enemies. Vivian looks up from her grassy trench, easily spotting three new trucks with headlights on in the rain driving down the road from the other direction and swerving out into the grassy field, kicking up grass and mud in their wake.

"Uh oh...Hey, Dad! I think there's more coming after us!" Vivian shouts.

Saaliha Moonwane, still filling the role of a sniper, continues to let arrows fly into the few remaining enemies. However, pausing mid-pull, her eyes widened. Spotting the incoming vehicles brings a fresh sensation of anxiety over Saaliha. A couple drones flying low accompanied these SUVs as her feline ears picked up their buzzing sound.

"Watch out, there's more! They brought combat drones!"

Tidus shoots down two enemies before the gun in his paws clicks empty, the noise making every hair on his back rise and his breath catches. Rather than reloading it, he flips it in his grasp and bludgeons an attacker down savagely, then hurling the empty rifle at and moving to tackle another cultist to the ground right afterward.

"Well, shit..." Stratos says with a drawn out exhaling sigh, looking over at the newly armored trucks arriving. The doors open once the vehicles roll up to a complete stop.

Three groups of *Armageddon Cultist* militants leap out. Tidus is currently charging to greet them with a battle snarl. In the process, he leaps onto a fallen cultist's body, grabbing the discarded rifle adjacent to it and rolls forward up to his feet running. Opening fire at the new enemies with one of their own combat rifles now, until its chamber also clicks empty. Out of immediate ammo, Tidus got creative.

One cultist militant takes the brunt of Tidus's shots, dropping dead on the wet muddy grass as another tosses a device out, creating a temporary defensive force shield. Tidus spots this device and goes prone behind an upraised grassy knoll instead, going on the defensive. Saaliha catches up by now to assist them, with the last of her six of her arrows, nabbing an unaware cultist straight in the forehead before swapping her bow out for her modernized swords.

A necromancer *Armageddon Cultist* militant comes around the other side of the vehicle, holding a serrated black metal scythe in his left paw while clenching a glowing blood red orb in his other paw, launching the orb at the two parked SUVs that Minax and Stratos were in the middle of climbing into. Minax senses a tingle and he notices the magic missile. grabbing Stratos by his armor vest and tugs him out of the passenger seat he was climbing into.

"Wait! Get under me!" Minax yells. Stratos lets Minax grab and throw him. He leaps to protect Stratos from behind. A second later, the *Armageddon Cultist's* hellish magic projectile crashes into the smashed up SUV, blowing it up with a unique crimson hue. The magical spell shields wear off and the trucks explode. Stratos crawls beneath Minax, who shields him, before getting back to his feet. The heat from the explosion hardly affects Minax as the recently soaked ground nearby is scorched to the very dirt beneath.

Following his magical attack, the cultist raises a paw up. Channeling inky black tendrils that swarm and gently caress the fallen out in the field and around. The bodies rise from the ground, rigidly alive once again. Sidra lets out a panicked scream after she finishes emptying both of her pistols of ammunition. Vivian gasps and runs for the protection of her mom.

Tidus and Saaliha—fighting up close to this—look on in horror as the foul magic was being cast closest to them. Saaliha, recognizing the type of sorcery being used before her personally, her shock fades faster than Tidus's.

"Necromancy…being practiced so openly, and this far north in *Lycandia*?" she asks, multitasking.

The once defeated enemies were very much alive again, a dense crowd separating Stratos from his daughter and wife. A crowd that proves aggressive then perceived as it surges toward Minax and Stratos. The two exchange a confident but alarmed nod before confronting the risen dead. Sidra raises her fists, and she jerks her head at Vivian, concern on her face. Several of those cultists charge at them.

"Alright, Vivian, it's time to put those *Wackarack* lessons to the real test," Sidra says to Vivian. With panic in her eyes, she glances in Tidus and Strato's direction, separated by a wall of reanimated cultists lumbering their way at them straight away.

"Alrighty, Mom!" Vivian stands her ground with her mother, nervously kicking and striking down one of the advancing cultists. The macabre injuries it sustained no longer seem to bother it, but Vivian continued to execute vicious kicks and punches, growing more brave each second. Even getting an open claw strike on an exposed throat, doing an impressive cut despite her smaller paw.

"A necromancer," Minax comments, narrowing his focused pupilless purple eyes with his golden scaly eyebrows. He shouts, "Don't lose hope, my friends. I'm on it."

Minax whirlwinds twice around like a spinning top, slicing down nearly three ranks of the unarmed cultists, and those with knives once more in their grasp. Stratos checked his magazine by an open slit built into it, before emptying what was left directly through the enemies in front of him and reloading his last magazine. Minax Bolide inhales deep and exhales a breath of hot fire, bathing one cultist in fire instantly and simultaneously jabbing *Alpha and Omega* forward and backward at multiple foes at once.

"Help them! Fly over there and split that one in half. I'll be alright," Stratos calls Minax, tossing him a quick, cocky expression before resuming a close quarter fight for his own life. Minax gives Stratos a concerned expression before bowing his head at him and leaps up into the air, his partially torn membranes limiting his long-term flight as he strains to stay airborne.

Stratos soon was entrapped in vain of his fury fueled rage. He then roars with growing frustration tirelessly, beating, flailing, and gnashes in the close melee, even head-butting three cultists into unconsciousness. His body alone in the center of a crowd of twenty cultists cramming in against him, in such limited space he parries and deflects knife stabs, fists, and kicks.

The necromancer watches from the other side of the crowd surrounding and swarming Stratos, amused by his struggle beneath his wolf's skull headgear, safely casting his spells behind his electronic shield device. A devilish crimson glowing orb appears in his palm once again, and he hurls it at Tidus, this time catching him charging in from his previous hiding spot. Saaliha rushes out right behind Tidus with her swords at the ready.

He dives into a skid, but the demonic magical projectile homes in, lowering and fixing its direction and crashing into his torso. Saaliha glances empathically toward Tidus before cutting down the cultist in front of her, then twists around and hurls a grenade over at the necromancer before having to dive into a roll to avoid another undead cultist tackling her.

Minax Bolide arrives and lands as Tidus skids on the muddy wet grass into a tumble, the magical attack leaving part of his armor torched, instantly laying on his back. Tidus immediately has to wrestle with another cultist, throwing themselves on top of him with a knife in their paw.

Extending a claw, Minax zaps the electronic shield device with a neon lightning bolt. But the necromancer behind it attempts to diffuse the spell, failing to do so as it instead changes course. Minax's lightning spell leaps toward the parked truck nearby, passing the necromancer and his shield device and electrifying a different militant instead, to the point of throwing them backward off their feet even.

Minax closes the distance, easily canceling out the necromancer's next magical projectile, this time with a counter spell and simultaneously smashing *Alpha and Omega* down on the shield device to destroy it. Pivoting to chop away a cultist running up to stab him.

"Grab whoever you can, and retreat. Inform command! I think we've located the *Starwielder*!" a necromancer orders the other hooded militants, also speaking into a headset with a microphone. The necromancer raises his scythe to deflect Minax's downward cut in a clash of metal. Successfully evading the sharp back jab, Minax delivered on his glide past the necromancer. Minax corrects himself, sliding in the muddy thick grass of the field as the red hued rain picks up.

Minax summons a fireball to his right claw and throws it at the necromancer, who leaps into a sideways roll to avoid it. As the necromancer gets to his feet, Minax half spins at him before whipping his tail first. His sharp quartz at the tip of his tail whooshes over the necromancer's ducking head, forcing him to crawl further back before getting up. Minax tosses a palmful of neon green lightning once more, the flustered necromancer catching it directly to his body and is thrown to the wet ground.

Cultists overwhelm Sidra and Vivian, who thrash against their stupefied or reanimated undead captors, until a strange magical ointment is placed on their foreheads, causing them to cease their struggles. Saaliha and Tidus slowly get encircled by more enemies, fighting for their own lives now.

Tidus and Saaliha, also experienced and trained *Wackarack* martial artists, kick their way through toward the truck with Sidra and Vivian being loaded into. Tidus makes good ground until he has to stop mid-run and kick the dagger being hurled at him instead. Saaliha snarls as two enemies catch her tail from behind and drag her speed down, forcing her to twist around to kick and finally fight them.

Stratos witnesses Sidra and Vivian disappear into the truck. Upon doing so, he fills with yet more adrenaline, a furious rage igniting in his chest. He thrashes his way through the crowd to try and break free, futile as the SUV with his daughter and wife inside, captured in the grasp of a death cult, is promptly speeding away up a rainy slippery hill toward the distant road. The cultists left behind start diverting focus to attack Minax Bolide, understanding the *Galanexian's* being the ultimate threat to their devious goals. Four rush at him in a bloodthirsty growl including the necromancer.

Minax grumbles, the unnamed necromancer exchanges a series of deflecting blows with their respective weapons before Minax lunges through his torso armor with the pointy spear tip, and the top portion of the ax head of *Alpha and Omega.* While the serrated purplish iridescent ax cuts in, Minax pulls free, then for good measure repeats the same attack, impaling the necromancer with the other end, just after he has collapsed onto his knees from the first attack.

The necromancer hurls a black and purple sphere of shadow from his other paw up at Minax. The *Starwielder* dips his head back as the spell flies off into the crimson rainy sky above them, then slides his weapon free to impale the necromancer a final time. Stratos runs up the stumbling backside of a zombified cultist and flips over to land where Tidus is drop-kicking a new attacker of his own. The two share a brief, appreciative and relieved look before fighting the *Armageddon Cult's* forces, barehanded.

Adding a chant in a *Galanexian* dialect, a bright glowing light emitted from *Alpha and Omega* still stuck in the dying necromancer. His body fizzles into light. All the risen *Armageddon Cultists* and its militants drop dead once more, leaving Minax to face the next foe as he whirls around, exhaustively sighing.

Only twelve living enemies remain for a battered Minax, Saaliha, Tidus, and Stratos to handle as a soft boom of thunder is heard far overhead. Minax and Tidus team up through three. Stratos, in a simmering down fury, defeats three in efficient lethality. Saaliha and Minax finished the rest in the midterm. They stand in the grassy, torn up and muddy field with two burning trucks left crashed into one another, a couple others left stalled.

"Looks like they torched all the vehicles to strand us...Bet they'll be coming back out here with more soon," Tidus says, wiping his torso down with his paws, breathing tiredly.

"I didn't want to risk harming them in that vehicle, or causing a fatal crash trying to break Vivian and Sidra free," Minax says to the others, his spikey shoulders drooping some. "I'm sorry Stratos."

"Hey...you did what you can, after all you've been through and how messed up your body is right now. They're not dead yet. *Silvium* is only another twenty miles away. They were trying to take us alive, so that's probably where they'll be," Stratos says, panting as he catches his breath in the pouring rain still.

Saaliha steps up beside Minax and Stratos, exhaling tiredly to Stratos. "Your poor wife and daughter, out of the frying pan and into the fire." As she then checks out the very horizon line ahead of the freeway, the vehicles originated from.

Stratos snorts. "I know, it's keeping on an even level with how many times you've piloted a doom aircraft, Saaliha."

"This is fair. I did say I make a great pilot in a pinch. Just not a very lucky one," Saaliha calmly replies, sheathing her swords and folding her arms, winking at Stratos.

Stratos gives Saaliha a short-tempered glare, grumbling, but couldn't be mad for too long. There was empathy in Saaliha's tone and she fought hard beside him. Selecting an assault rifle laying on the grass among the fallen cultists, Stratos looks it over for any malfunction. Tidus in inspecting ammunition left on deceased shooters, also scavenging what they could make use of. Saaliha picks up one of the disabled combat drones the cultists were using, an intrigued smirk forming on her face.

"We'll get Sidra and Vivian back, and all the others. This is far from over. We know exactly where they're taking them," says Minax as they resume the trek to *Silivium* on foot.

"You got it Minax, let's do this *Starwielder*." Stratos grins, marching from the meadow to the road.

CHAPTER FIFTEEN: The Prince Of Crows

CYNGOSA CRAWLS SLOWLY, PRONE against the cold ground covered in a thick layer of golden brown pine needles as the afternoon overcast skies cast a dimness, providing him with additional stealth from enemy eyes. The two-lane paved road up to the headquarters had bright street lights beaming down on it, some personnel strolling along the cement sidewalk.

Eos flies in the cover of the clouds, watching over Cyngosa far below with a piercing aerial view. Continuing with his stealth tactic, Cyngosa eventually pauses at the edge of the parking lot. The lot is void of any automobiles, instead private jets and helicopters are parked all around, not left unguarded of course, as Cyngosa's turquoise eyes study the layout. He notices many more *Armageddon Cultists* roaming about, a number imposing enough that someone as impulsive as himself wouldn't boldly go on the attack.

Cyngosa speaks to Eos telepathically. *"Okay, buddy, follow my lead on this."*

Eos replies to Cyngosa with vibrant visuals instead of words through their eyes. The area around was teeming with threats. Once Eos finishes, Cyngosa stalls in place to silently assess the predicament, biting his bottom lip with his upper exposed canine fangs. An idea springs itself and he surveys the outskirts of the grand asphalt lot, carefully on the move once more, sticking close to the edge of the parking lot. Faint rumbling sounds of idling trailer trucks cause Cyngosa's pierced ears to perk up to attention. He could feel his fur going on end when a not so distant voice follows a presently closing hatch door. Cyngosa doesn't flinch, keeping quiet despite snapping a twig or two, maneuvering his boots through clusters of soaked dead leaves.

Cyngosa encounters two cultists at a portion of the parking lot where a utility box and some meters are installed on a dirt pathway, watching with concern. They stood under a bright street lamp, however Cyngosa didn't see any cameras and seized his ambush opportunity. He waves a paw over one of the neighboring tall pine tree's roots, making a crunching sound before he pulls up the root system to ensnare both of the cultists at once, preventing the two from raising the alarm or shooting at him with their firearms. Gritting his teeth from the effort of such a magic feat, Cyngosa proceeds in, knocking them both unconscious with a hard left and right hook with his fists. Eos swoops down from the air to land in proximity.

Now adorning pieces of their cult outfit to try and sneak into the parking lot in broad view, Cyngosa carries Eos inside his backpack, the phoenix capable of controlling their fiery body's effect on the flammable fabric. So far, Cyngosa, convincingly enough, hidden under the wolf's skull helmet mask and the black robes, continues walking carefully, and successfully despite his internal anxiety. His heartbeat thumping in his ears and he swallows, battling to keep his breathing calm and steady, proceeding past the security, fearing the worst.

His wide and nervous turquoise eyes could see through the thin slits of the helmet like mask, taking notice of the closest discreet entrance before maneuvering casually toward a service door by the best of his ability. He breathes a sigh of relief as the door handle clicks down and he opens it unchallenged, and no one's voice calls out to him from behind, yet.

Cyngosa surveys the area, and simultaneously Eos pops their head out of the backpack to steal a quick glance around before disappearing back inside. The service door was to what Cyngosa assumes was an internal parking lot at ground level. Cyngosa takes steps forward on the smooth concrete where several twenty foot trailers are parked, and attached to empty rigs.

The *Crowclaw Conglomerates* logo is blown up to scale on either side of each trailer. Cyngosa keeps a cool posture strolling by, grateful for his disguise as the bright lights bathe everything beneath them. He passes random clusters of *Armageddon Cultist* thugs, moving and organizing plastic wrapped pallets of gray boxes and black tote bins, by the dozens. Only gawking with his eyeballs, Cyngosa keeps his head straight forward, walking with an imaginary purpose as the others labored.

"Ayo! Coming through pal, times ticking. These trailers got places to be hauled too," a cultist, in a trance, says to him.

Cyngosa could tell by his emotionlessly facial expression as he got closer. Grumbling at Cyngosa, he steps on his breaks riding his electric forklift vehicle beeping and rolls closely past Cyngosa, with a load of more of these containers he initially noticed. Cyngosa shrugs at the worker and awkwardly slips through an exit after letting the forklift pass by loudly, accelerating with a hum, still daring not to speak to anyone.

A door opens inward to a wide area, and Cyngosa emerges past into a much darker setting. The light once spilling in from behind vanishes when he closes the door. He wanders ahead, noticing an elegant wide marble staircase rising. He doesn't see any other cultists yet. His ears beneath the disguise mask perk up to the echo of voices growing in volume. Cyngosa stops, standing in front of an empty reception desk, pretending to be on guard. He gives an audible gulp, smirking under the mask. He notices that there are cameras running.

Two *Lycandians* wearing black robes and golden arcane symbols embroidered in their garments stroll into Cyngosa's view. Carrying black trunks with them and pausing whatever conversation they were having before encountering Cyngosa idling. The two pass right by him, until after a couple of feet, one of the cultists twists back and speaks up to Cyngosa. "Hey you, make yourself useful and come carry this for me...since you are just standing around. This is fragile. Do you understand, peon?"

Cyngosa silently obliges the request, recognizing the authority structure and calmly keeps up appearances. He slings his rifle over his shoulder with his backpack, then takes the trunk from the cultist. They climb the staircase up to the first floor.

After some time walking, they arrive at the elevators. Cyngosa witnesses one of the two elites press a plastic badge strung to a lanyard against an electronic scanning pad. Granting access to the elevators, one whooshes down and opens before them. Cyngosa, with a dumb smug on under the mask, almost couldn't believe the turn of luck happening, however the sound of his heartbeat still hammers away in his head lessens. He swallows, clearing his throat. Still following the two high-ranking cultists into the elevator, quitting his nerves, almost physically feeling the multiple cameras on him now.

The higher-ranking cultist mutters, complaining as they stroll along together. "Making us carry the samples up to him ourselves, Mr. Crowly's ego seems to have escaped his own control."

The other cultist higher up replies to his fellows, "Pressing matters. The crimson eclipse is a glorious sign. Noxion's magic is working. Our bloody conquest will soon begin, like the Demon Lord Noxion said,

'We've made this world plump and ripe for the taking,' the promise of ultimate power will be given in turn."

Cyngosa steadies his breathing, hearing the two have their brief exchange, nodding with the second cultist's sentiment, but effectively keeping his lips sealed. The elevator opens near the top floor.

The building's upper floors have more modern designs, unlike the grand black marble, stone, and concrete below. The three walk through a spacious furnished lobby with square carpeting of various shades of gray and silver walls. The lights are off, but a couple candelabras placed on flat surfaces are lit and giving off a warm light, yet throwing foreboding shadows.

Cyngosa shifts his grip on the trunk. In fairness, it's heavy after some time carrying it. The two cultists walk in front of Cyngosa, leading the way as they approach a pair of grand decorative chamber doors. A camera fixates on them and after another half-second passes, the lock electronically opens.

Once the ornate obsidian doors open, they enter a circular chamber with a smooth marble floor and pillars rising to support a marble roof. The stonework up above is carved to mimic a cavern's stalactites. Cyngosa's turquoise eyes marvel at the room, before being drawn to the large marble desk at the other end of the chamber, illuminated by several television screens displaying chaos across the world. Clyde Crowly has his back to these TV screens, instead typing away on his laptop placed in front of him before glancing up, taking notice of their approach, and closing the device as they continue walking. Clyde rolls back the clean and decorated throne he is sitting on, the bottom engineered with wheels like an everyday office chair.

"Excellent. I've been expecting this for some time," Clyde greets them in a friendly tone.

"Yes, Grand Summoner, we acquired it and transported it ourselves from our operatives in *Perilith*. The beta variant of the biological virus," the first higher ranking cultist, the one that spoke to Cyngosa, says to Clyde, even stepping in front of his fellow and Cyngosa.

Cyngosa shifts and looks down at the trunk he's been carrying this whole time with a newfound combination of respect and abject horror. Clyde, even from this far distance, looks over the two elites and studies the disguise Cyngosa wears, noticing his unique firearm on his back and the odd bulge on his back.

"Peculiar, anyway. We'll need a test subject for its effect and you brought one with you." Clyde's ears perk up, and he gives a brief, apathetic stare.

In a flurry of motion, Cyngosa throws the trunk on the marble floor at the feet of the two cultist elites. Carefully putting down his own trunk with a suspicious growl at Cyngosa, "You've been quiet this whole time. Just who the hell do you—" He's cut off mid-sentence as the trunk strikes the floor near his feet. The other cultist lifts off the wolf's skull Cyngosa is wearing with a quick swipe, growling furiously upon seeing him.

"Hello there!" Cyngosa says with a big overly friendly expression, as a large red and orange glowing cylinder totem drops at his feet.

Cyngosa pulls off the rest of the *Armageddon Cultist* outfit, leaping up into the air as a burst of fire magic explodes under his feet from his specially enchanted totem. The two trunks and it are instantly gone in the violent burst, only leaving the elites smoldering and laying still in the aftermath on the granite floor. Eos lets out a battle shrill, flaring their wings and taking flight from Cyngosa's explosion.

Clyde's piercing blue eyes are only momentarily wide, a fierce insidious smirk forming on his conniving visage as he leaps on top of his black granite desk, the monitors still glowing and playing images behind him. Cyngosa leaps down from the propulsion. Wielding his magical tree branch quarterstaff, he sweeps it right at Clyde's head.

Smugly grinning, Clyde spin kicks Cyngosa right out of the air, forcing him to land on the floor in a crouch instead. Clyde then sprays a volley of jagged icicles from his palm toward Eos, forcing the phoenix to bail on their dive bomb completely or risk being fully impaled like a pincushion.

"Did you think I was just some scrawny three piece suit, sniveling behind a desk...?" Clyde mocks. He unfurls his dress jacket to pull out a shiny chrome assault rifle, turning on a bright blue laser and aiming at Cyngosa.

Cyngosa was fortunately ready. The moment Clyde had unfurled his jacket was when he placed a totem down to stop the terrifying bullet spray Clyde's firearm emits. While his totem holds back the incoming ferocious rate of bullets, he backtracks for cover behind a marble pillar. Clyde steps down onto the floor, reloading as the end of his gun's barrel smokes lightly.

"For a Direwolf, you have quite a lot of wit, and bravery, having traveled thousands of miles from your shit hole country...Too bad, you won't live long enough to see the designs I have for the rest of you sub-breeds in *Edon*. Then all the rest of *Lycandia*," Clyde shouts over to Cyngosa, not averting his focus or attention.

Peaking around the corner, Cyngosa shoots his own rifle back at Clyde, retracting for cover once more when he discovers his bullets are disintegrated in mid-air. It is a similar, but more refined, magical barrier than Cyngosa's, made out of a sheet of clear ice, yelling to Clyde, "This is for Khelu! You bitch boy bastard."

"I'm going to enjoy this." Clyde snaps his fingers, letting out a cruel cackle. Clyde explodes into an inky cloud of swirling tendrils and reassembles in Cyngosa's personal space, smacking him in the forehead with the end of his rifle, forcing him to hit the pillar behind him. Clyde is still laying in punches as Cyngosa tries to retaliate with his green glowing wooden staff, executing a satisfactory crack Clyde under the chin and then knocking his gun's barrel off aim.

Cyngosa, once able to go on the offensive, lunges forward and bonks Clyde hard on the head from above, simultaneously reaching to place a new totem on the floor beneath to channel another magical effect. Clyde extends a finger out, sending a single magical icicle projectile at Cyngosa's wooden totem and shattering it in a burst of bright sparkles. As Clyde follows up to strike Cyngosa in the head, he barely blocks the attack with his staff.

Pivoting in a blur, with the same free paw, Clyde draws out a strange-looking sword from his belt scabbard—a misshapen and long, jagged, transparent crystal blade. Clyde snickers diabolically, lunging and stabbing the neon bluish green, crazy sword right into Cyngosa's side. Cyngosa cries but before he could counter-attack, Crowly once more bursts into another inky explosion, leaving him hitting empty air. Cyngosa spins around on his heels as Clyde deceitfully rematerializes into physical form, attempting to impale him straight from behind.

The two nemesis attack and block each other, maneuvering across the room while transfixed in the heat of battle. Cyngosa ignores the cuts and gashes, savoring the times he strikes Clyde, displaying quick footwork as they compete with each other for tactical advantage across the smooth tiled floor of the grand office-room. Cyngosa exhales with his nostrils flaring, eyes narrowing and his fur on end, dodging both Clyde's weapon and his sweeping fist. Cyngosa kicks him back several feet from a crouching maneuver.

Clyde trips backward slightly, but then regains his balance. "Getting tired? How rude of me, please have a seat!" he barks, waving his empty paw at a nearby thick wooden chair with cushioned black leather resting against a support pillar. It rattles to life before becoming airborne and flies toward Cyngosa.

Cyngosa, running headlong on the attack, is unprepared for the possessed chair. The bewitched furniture strikes him from the side and scoops him up for a terrible ride, up into the air and straight into an opposite facing pillar of the room. Exploding into pieces, the broken chair leaves Cyngosa sliding to the smooth, chilly marble floor, emitting a painful groan. His free paw grips a shielding totem from his waist. Clyde's bullets harmlessly hit the magical force shield produced by the totem, keeping Cyngosa safe in a breath of time.

With an amused scoff, he unceremoniously discards his empty rifle magazine, soon reaching for another, Clyde advancing on the attack says, "I'm infusing the worthy gray wolves with demonic magic…The rest, including any sub-breeds, will be offerings. Fuel."

Clyde skids his feet to a halt, then reacts and blocks three of Cyngosa's fierce oncoming attacks as he leaps at him from the floor in a rage. Clyde deceptively teleports right behind him, then dashing across before repeating this process, but from different angles each time. Cyngosa gets cut along his back and side two times before achieving a spin-kick, his knee colliding right into Clyde's chest after he teleports close behind again. He breaks his magical staff on Cyngosa's body as he also brings it downward as a follow-up attack, paws firmly gripping it; now left shaking in empty air, as the magical wood splinters explode into dust that wafts away. Clyde is thrown into a slide flat on his back across the polished marble floor, soon twisting back up on his knees before he has even completely come to a stop.

"Oh, no…That explains the demonic obelisk in the city," Cyngosa mutters with a snarl on his face, exhaling with widening eyes under furrowed brows, walking closer to Clyde, still alert as the fight is far from finished.

Cruel laughter echoes over from Clyde, reaching for his firearm and discovering it missing, without taking his cold blue eyes off Cyngosa he says. "That is only part of the plan."

"You don't get to choose what happens to them," Cyngosa spits back, suddenly rushing the distance between him and Clyde, "or any of us!"

Anticipating Cyngosa to close, Clyde lunges with his vile, neon crystalline sword outward, teleporting out of harm's way. After realizing he missed, Cyngosa raises his eyebrows in surprise. Clyde then reappears several feet behind, almost in the center of the room, as the two grand doors into the chamber open. A dozen heavily combat armored mercenaries actively advance into the room, two throwing magic projectiles at Cyngosa right on sight and forcing him to shelter behind a marble pillar.

Clyde maliciously snickers. It echoes slightly off the pillars and walls, and he speaks calmly. "This world is mine. I own everything and everyone in it. In one way or another. Even down to the food you all eat, the medicine, the water you drink..." He trails off climbing inside his armored cyborg combat suit before continuing his rant. "The guns and technology, all of it." Black drones with neon blue lights glide in from around, Eos soars in to attack and destroy them with a shriek of fury.

The jetpack system on the back of Clyde's combat suit fires up. Clyde blasts forward like a bullet and punches down on Cyngosa with his metal gauntlets relentlessly. Cyngosa takes a couple hard hits to the abdomen, but fends off a few in return. He lets out a whistle, getting struck hard across the face. Eos corrals the fight in the air toward them, opening their beak to let a burst of fire breath bathe Clyde in from behind.

Diverting his attention, Clyde lays off Cyngosa to extend his metal gauntlet and casts an icy javelin at the phoenix collectively as Eos swoops past. Without looking at Cyngosa, Clyde also sends a freezing blast wave from his other gauntlet. Cyngosa finds himself pinned up against a pillar in a shocking instant, frosted over part of his torso as the cold bites. The enemy mercenaries take aim and shoot. Cyngosa, in a panic, breaking his arms out of the thin ice. He rolls forward, picking up Clyde's missing chrome assault rifle and fires back at the mercenaries and Clyde at the same time, crouching low, missing being hit.

Cyngosa kills the two mercenaries, but then flops backward as one of Clyde's *Crowclaw Industries* combat drones zaps him with a green laser. The laser nearly blasts a hole deep into his abdomen. His obliterated armor took the brunt of the laser. Cyngosa rolls his body for cover, smoke still rising from his burned clothing, the gnarly stench filling his nose momentarily.

Glaring on with frustration, Clyde growls at the dead mercenaries, "Useless..." He waves his fingers and, even with his metal gauntlet, is able to summon a putrid green magical light, zapping the dead with its electrical tendril. Speaking next to his A.I. computer in a stern tone, Clyde commands. "Initiate auto defense program!"

Advancing toward Cyngosa, Clyde flexes his fingers, ignoring one of his other combat drones crashing and exploding just behind him on the floor. More living mercenaries enter the room in the distance. His metallic high tech armor extends eight mechanical legs, giving him distance and height as he hurls two menacing icy magical javelins, straight at Cyngosa.

Cyngosa empties what ammo he has left to shave down the two incoming missiles. In return, he crams down one more totem on the floor and tosses away Clyde's gun far from their fighting area. Cyngosa doesn't have many totems or ankhs left by this point, wounded but still in the fight.

The fallen mercenaries that Clyde had previously struck with his foul magic rise from where they fell and return to the fight. Cyngosa takes notice with a brief expression of horror, whispering to himself.

"Necromancy~ of course," Cyngosa sarcastically comments.

A machine gun turret extends from each corner of the wide room's ceiling, including one between the haunting chandeliers, the computer program operating these turrets takes aim at Eos and Cyngosa before firing.

"It's over now, you mangy mongrel!" Clyde Crowly declares, tasting victory.

Cyngosa closes the distance between himself and Clyde, to prevent the turrets from gunning him by putting a friendly target in their line of sight. Clyde slashes at him with the mechanical limbs of his suit and his unholy magic sword.

"I got a special bag of goodies made for you!" Cyngosa yells back. In unison, he barrel rolls, extracting a leather bag from inside his vest pocket. Cyngosa then hurls the contents of the brown leather bag.

A thousand toothpick-sized totems spray out at Clyde's feet, and around him as he stumbles upright. Clyde gasps when his mechanical combat suit and he alike, are vanishing within a cluster of colorful firework like effects; Lightning bolts, sparkles of fire and starlight shoot every which way. With the hundreds of magical effects going off in the moment, Cyngosa couldn't help but be blown away, given his risky immediacy to his own trap. From outside, the very top floor of the lonesome standing skyscraper explodes with colorful flashes of lights and fireballs.

Cyngosa, in terror while airborne, his stomach flips as he tumbles over the edge. He quickly grabs hold of a thick-looking wire that holds his weight, still feeling his stomach fall through his boots. The top floor of the building, presently without a ceiling or walls remaining, is consumed from view in a fog of smoke, buffered by the high up winds. Cyngosa's turquoise eyes darted down, a poor decision he regrets right after as he realizes to his growing horror, how high up he is. He can hardly make out details of the parking lots or surrounding landscape, and is able to see the top of every tree for miles with ease.

Growing increasingly soaked by the pouring rain outside, Cyngosa, dangling with a tight grip on the wire, starts shimmying his way up, defiant of the blustery air around reintroducing its cold nip. A loud crash of thunder booms around him, with flashes of lightning rippling just overhead.

The moment Cyngosa clamps one of his shaky paws onto the wet edge of the building's floor, Clyde materializes into view, limping forward, exiting the shell of his nearly destroyed power suit as sparks and air pressure escape portions of it. Chunks of rumble still fall around them. Clyde appears disheveled but unharmed, draws his vile jagged crystal sword with a sinister expression on his wild face.

Eos dive bombs immediately, forcing Clyde to slash and cut wildly at the attacking phoenix but not ignoring Cyngosa. Cyngosa climbs over and finally is able to swiftly unzip and dig into his backpack. Conjointly, Clyde readies another nefarious spell to hurl right at him.

Cyngosa takes out Dorrion Chrisbane's old cellphone and presses the "send" option, submitting a pre-written text of digits the *Trinity* member originally sent him. He fumbles and drops the cellphone to the floor, and falls backward to avoid the jagged icy javelin aimed at his chest that Clyde sends his way with. A twitching, free paw snags one of his pack's straps to take it with him.

Swimming along between the loose gravitational pull of the planet and space, the familiar *Crowclaw Conglomerates* satellite receives a transmission. Cyngosa's text goes through and it activates once more to the backdrop of billions of stars, colorful distant nebulae and two of the planet's three moons orbiting in. Transforming, opening like a flower in bloom once again. A single red light beam shoots from each antenna after the satellite charges up momentarily. The supercharged laser arcs down to the planet's surface.

During the same time back down on *Homeworld* on the smokey, rainy exposed roof top, Crowly manages to impale Eos on his sword, ignoring the flames and talons raking him as he continues draining the life force out of them. The greenish-blue glowing blade delivers its vampiric effect once embedded in its victim. Eos shrieks and flounders free to spit a small fireball at Clyde. By this time, Cyngosa growls angrily, getting up from a crouching position, but before doing anything else, he notices a recognizable light right above them all in the red, gloomy, rainy sky. Cyngosa turns and runs, skidding at first on the soaking wet marble floor, before turning portions of the water under his feet to ice sliding for the edge of the tower.

The neon crimson colored orbital laser beam blasts down, right into *Crowclaw Conglomerates Headquarters* dead center as Clyde Crowly vanishes completely in the strike. Cyngosa slides into a leap right off the top floor into the open air, momentarily flying like a bird backward as he faces the destruction in the wake. The satellite's single laser beam, lagged by friction, finally finishes, leaving two floors beneath ablaze afterward. Cyngosa flails as the wind roars around him and the ground gets closer. His free falling body is struck by a magical bolt of lightning from above, disappearing in a blinding flash.

CHAPTER SIXTEEN: Crafting The Ethereal Lattice

CYNGOSA POOFS BACK INTO mortal existence, unconscious all, alone on his backside in the grove of a forest of mighty spruce, firs, and evergreen pine trees. Eos approaches happily, letting a chirp out. Flying low and keeping out of sight, scanning the area before landing beside Cyngosa, lying still. The smoldering tower wasn't far in the distance from where he appeared out of seemingly thin air.

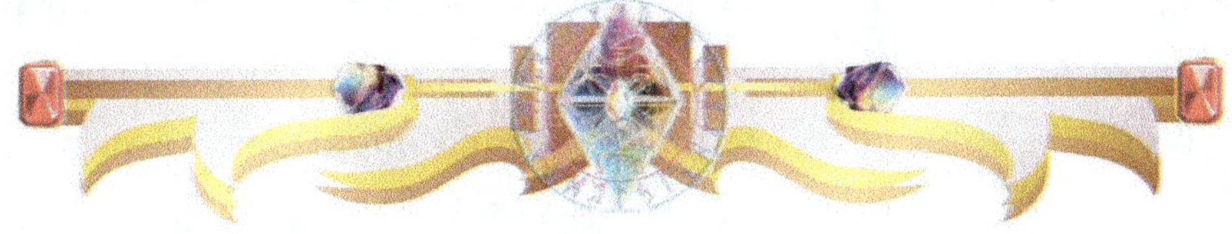

Whilst Cyngosa is unconscious, his spirit wanders inside his 'meditative realm,' a chunk of floating earth and rock floats in an endless sea of purple and blue hued nebulas. The space is odorless and without a single breath of wind blowing. A melodic echo blasts through the nebulous starry sky surrounding the floating terrestrial overgrown terrain, a white hot light rising forward. The translucent form of Cyngosa's spirit bolts upright, facing the incoming music and blinding beam, his turquoise eyes wincing shut. Shielding his face with his translucent forearm from the brightness. A mini-sun, encapsulated in rotating rings made of different precious metals, takes form from what little Cyngosa can see through his fingers. He could make out the details of thousands of lidless eyes infused into those brilliant metal rings through his wincing gaze.

"The Angel of Calamity's minions have grown bold indeed. Cyngosa Maelstrom, your virtuous actions and bravery in the face of evil haven't gone unnoticed—in spite of your faults. Take heart. All is not yet lost!" the angelic sentience announces.

"How is it all not lost? My step-sister, who I've never failed in protecting all these years, has been taken by this crazed cult, along with that entire city. I need the *Starwielder's* help, even a miracle from the Creator would be nice," Cyngosa replies, exhaling with a pause to think. "*Elemental Mastery* has nothing in it to deal with that demonic obelisk, how are they powering it? I don't have access to the *Macrocosm Lexicon*, even if I could read *Galanexian*."

The angelic sentience speaks again to Cyngosa's translucent dream form. "Correct. Without the *Starwielder* present, the *Lexicon* is of little use in this matter. Again, you've demonstrated capability, so remain steadfast! Are you familiar with the Creator's Answers, the wood of the holy tree, to print this wisdom beyond dimensions, into written word?"

"*Ethereal Arbor, yes. Am I to carve some kind of totem? I haven't a clue what symbols or shape to carve it into. What incantations should I charge it with?*" Cyngosa asks, his voice spoken in thought to the sentience.

"I will show you, mortal!" the angelic being says, then Cyngosa's transparent astral body squirms in pain. The stark image of a four foot tall round piece of pearly white wood with a smooth finish enters his thoughts with a burning sensation. He could see it crystal clear in memory immediately, engraved from the bottom up with intricate markings in a language Cyngosa couldn't recognize, let alone speak, but understood he didn't need to.

"Do you see it? Understand?" the angelic sentience asks Cyngosa.

"Yes, and these arbors are common across most of *Lycandia*. I'm sure I can find a suitable sized branch," Cyngosa's translucent dream-state replies, an invigorating feeling permeating through his molecules. The angelic sentience vanishes from Cyngosa's presence and he's forced awake.

Cyngosa's astral spirit returns to his body. When he returns to consciousness, he instantly feels the chill in the air and wetness from the rain against his body. The earthy aroma of the damp soil and pine fills Cyngosa's nostrils as he rouses with a deep inhale through his nostrils and mouth. He opens his turquoise eyes, seeing the rippling red clouds above and the rain. With a groan, he leans upright and cracks his neck before looking around.

Eos greets him with a low audible screech before spiraling around Cyngosa a couple times, a mental comment echoing in his head. *"You awake, finally!"*

Cyngosa gets up, brushing the wet leaves and not caring about the mud stains on his clothing, his head turning toward the misty woodlands next to him. His instincts kick in, and has a deep resonating feeling inside that an *Ethereal Arbor* tree could be close.

"Eos, my best little buddy. There is a certain species of special tree we need to find to help our friends," Cyngosa says, adjusting his backpack with a jerk of his shoulder. The angelic vision still left him feeling jarred, his gaze passing over his shoulder at the smoke cloud still rising from the very top portion of *Crowclaw Headquarters*. "I need a view from above, if you would please." The phoenix dips their head, making direct eye contact with Cyngosa, dilating them. Swooping their fiery blue wings, unaffected by the drizzling rainfall, Eos then takes flight.

Wandering the rainy woodlands with soft squishing sounds coming up from his boots, Cyngosa's eyes are at this time a soft ghostly white, half of his vision was now shared with Eos.Trudging forward through the dead leaves and uneven rocky terrain, once again finding himself on the outskirts of *Silvium* and into its encompassing wilderness. In the shallow fog creeping low between trees, the squawk of crows and rustling of critters reminded Cyngosa he wasn't entirely alone. He took a strange comfort in it. His worrisome mind wanders to Minax and Saaliha, curious if Minax made it and plead their case before the *Aluan Republic's* leadership, maybe stop the *Paladins*.

Mentally disheveled from his fight with Clyde Crowly and the visit from a powerful angelic being, Cyngosa hikes along over the exposed roots and damp, mulch-covered ground. He never for a second stopped worrying about Khelu, but couldn't afford to let fear or anxiety derail his task, desperately wanting answers before planning any attack. The phoenix coasting over the woodland's sparse canopy, given the season *Wulftheon* was in this time of year, with impeccable eyesight barring from above in the cool air.

Cyngosa's communal vision with Eos scans the hilly landscape while dismissing bare elms, oaks. Ignoring firs and evergreens, *Ethereal Arbor's* shed their burned bronze colored leaves every autumn, before growing them anew in spring as golden buds, forever in a cycle.

Aided with keen eyesight, Eos's head swivels to the right, Cyngosa identifies the distinct slate gray bark of one *Ethereal Arbor* nestled among some white polars and a century-old birch tree. Cyngosa extracts his mind and willpower from Eos and focuses on making double-time on reaching the *Arbor*, only a couple miles he could estimate from the phoenix's vantage point from up high.

Eagerly, Cyngosa hikes uphill, getting further into the rugged wilderness; the wind's faint roar can be heard coming from some of the lower altitude reaching mountains at the beginning of *Steel Peaks*, not far from him now. Unable to see any of the glorious distant peaks through the lithe, crawling clouds that continued to dump a drizzling rain, Cyngosa grew oddly accustomed to the unnatural crimson tint in the clouds.

All of this—the eclipse currently concealed behind the weather included—is the *Armageddon Cult* and Clyde Crowly's fault Cyngosa reminds himself, inhaling and exhaling occasionally as his anxiety and racing thoughts fluctuate. Khelu wasn't dead—yet. The more Cyngosa mulled it over, he began to figure the cultists have ulterior motives rather than just killing everyone they happen to encounter, a chill creeping under his fur on his skin throughout his body. Clyde mentioned the horrifying truth. Cyngosa clenches his fists in a blend of anger and anxiety, remembering that captives were being offered as fuel. In the exact magical meaning of how the cultists are achieving this, Cyngosa couldn't figure it out.

Maneuvering over surfacing roots and exposed giant rocks from the forest's soil, to where the old birch tree and *Ethereal Arbor* are, Cyngosa gets closer up the slate gray tree feeling a tingle of excitement bubble inside him. The bark of the *Ethereal Arbor* is bumpy and has a visually drastic swirling pattern to it. Coarse in texture compared to the bark of the birch trees neighboring it, he brushes a paw along it. Climbing up to select a perfect limb branching from one of the boughs, Cyngosa chops at it together as Eos claws and fractures the wood. The pearly white wood underneath was soon exposed as he went about stripping the bark in the effort to also break the large branch off.

Dropping from the tall, old *Ethereal Arbor* tree, Cyngosa holds his work in his paws close to his chest, with smaller sticks falling with him. The branch was roughly four feet long and almost matched up with what the angelic vision had essentially scorched into his recent memory. Cyngosa's eyes linger on some of the thicker sticks laying on the ground. He picks one up and smirks to himself.

"Hmm, maybe I'll carve up a flute with this extra piece. For Minax, if I ever see that big scaly goober again," Cyngosa says to Eos disheartened, but mostly himself, as the phoenix cocks their head looking at him. Cyngosa places a paw on the arbor and silently thanks it, turning around to backtrack his trek toward *Silvium*, seeking proper shelter to carve it.

Taking up a brief refuge inside a garage attached to the nearest house, Cyngosa encounters exiting the woods. He closes the door behind himself carefully.

Saaliha Moonwane caresses the short, multicolored pastel hair from her eyes. Her fur and hair soaked from the dusk rain, her ruby pierced feline ears are perking straight up, detecting the slightest sound as she prowls through the western side of *Silvium*. This part of the foreign city had clusters of strip malls and outlets, and with fewer skyscrapers obstructing her sharp eyesight, she could make out the devilish evil looking monument on the distant horizon. The spire is a harsh shade of crimson, and reminds Saaliha of a massive pricker thorn, the base of it shrouded by city infrastructure. "Oh, how delightfully dystopian," Saaliha says with an amused purr.

Tidus, Stratos, and Minax aren't far behind her, holding a hiding spot nearby, waiting for her to report back what she scouts out from the top of a deserted parking garage. She looks through a pair of binoculars to check out what challenges are ahead of them.

Squads of *Armageddon Cult* mercenaries and cultists are on patrol, some with armored tanks supporting them, or large pickup trucks rolling along the streets. Saaliha took note of these enemy groups, narrowing her eyes while nibbling on one of her retractable claws. The cult couldn't possibly cover every nook and cranny of *Silvium*. There has to be a stealthy route, she concludes. Saaliha makes quick work of the flight of stairs back to the street level where the others waited on alert for her return, their backsides pressed up against the building and facing the strip mall. Seeing Saaliha return, relief melts onto their faces.

"It's like a full-scale military invasion of the city. There isn't any evidence of any major combat. I recognize them, familiar armor and clothing to the assholes who assaulted us, after that laser thing zapped us out of the sky," Saaliha says to them.

"Fantastic," Stratos starts, pauses as a boom of thunder rumbles over them. "Obviously, our best choice of action is to slip through, cut the head of the snake, and save our people. Getting all of us out alive would also be an optimal outcome."

"Sounds good to me boss, heh." Tidus throws Stratos a thumbs up, his head swivels to look at the others. "Let's commandeer a ride in one of their vehicles, roll in clean."

"I don't know if I can just fly after you, running into that recurring problem, that I'll draw too much attention again. I could fly head on toward the spire, stop this myself," Minax says to Tidus, even puffing his chest out to add bravado to his confident statement.

Saaliha chimes in, twitching her whiskers, asking, "And do what? Have this entire army attack you as you 'figure it out.' We'll have to do better than that, hun. Besides, what if they want you alive and capture you?"

"Good points to bring up. Nah, we go on foot and we all stick together for now. We have the advantage of going unnoticed. We still need answers. Let's keep it moving," Stratos says to Minax and Saaliha.

"Can't argue with that reasoning, but let's seek out their leader, if anything. You've done enough and should focus on finding your family," Minax comments. Tidus gives Minax a soft pump with his free paw and says to him, "We stick together."

Looking at Tidus and inclining his head in a gesture, Tidus raises his rifle, creeping to the edge of the cold, soaked concrete wall. He peeks around the corner, surveying the street, buildings, and, more importantly, any enemies. Stratos, Saaliha, and Minax form a line behind him. Tidus turns his head around and smiles, saying, "No vehicles rolling. I believe it's clear. I reckon we make a sprint across the street, slip between that barber shop and that random building. Tight alley." Stratos peeks over the corner for a half-second and nods in agreement with Tidus. Together, with anxiety gripping each of their insides, they stiffly run across the wide open street before filling into the five-foot wide alley. Moving along, they shuffle out onto a tiny parking lot with four spots and a dumpster before walking onto the sidewalk through a vacancy.

Sticking to the shadows and being conscious of point of view, Stratos and Saaliha lead now, staring ahead, with Minax and Tidus watching behind them. Moving fairly coordinated, staying quiet as the rain patters noisily enough to mask their steps as they wander through the cityscape of *Silivium*. Crossing the street and arriving in another strip mall, this one distinguishable with futuristic LED lights and flashing advertising boards acting as guard railings when they cross from a deserted car dealership.

The *Silvium* shopping center has a low skyline, Stratos and Tidus see the demonic spire for the first time, far off in the distance, but in greater clarity. In the face of all his experiences fighting magic-using foes in wartime, Stratos feels something new clench in his chest, fear. His wet fur on the nape of his neck going on end regardless, Stratos stares unblinking at the strange neon beam for a second. What if that is where Sidra and Vivian are? Minax keeps his feet firmly on the wet ground and his still healing wings folded, cautious not to let the quartz-ball at the end of his tail accidentally bash against something.

Her alert eyes catching the flashing front of a toy store, Saaliha raises an eyebrow, her lips curling over her fangs spotting a remote control monster truck in the display window.

Several restaurants and stores lined the structure, but not a soul could be found wandering about. Worming away from the glow of streetlamps and some of the glimmering ad screens, Saaliha and Stratos guide Tidus and Minax. Minax kept an extra watch on what was behind them.

Saaliha and Stratos are first to spot Cyngosa and Eos in their peripheral vision. Witnessing the phoenix and Direwolf slip down for cover off to the left, across the street separating the strip mall from a roadside business. Saaliha's face beams briefly, a combination of relief and anxiety growing inside her. Saaliha also finding her arms and tail tensed up,

"It can't be?" Saaliha pauses, contemplating, and asks Stratos with a skeptical look on her face, "Was—or is—that Cyngosa?"

"I was about to ask you the same thing. I thought I saw movement, too. Cyngosa?" Stratos whispers to confirm. Now using the magnifying lens on his rifle scope, he can easily spot Cyngosa taking a break behind a cement parking barrier behind the sidewalk.

"Well, there's one of your other buddies. What the hell is he doing out here?" Stratos asks Saaliha, not peeling his gaze from the rifle scope.

"Probably hunting that Crowly person he's been going on about. Honestly, I couldn't tell you exactly. Let's signal him over here?" Saaliha suggests.

Stratos turns over his shoulder and emits a whistle, drawing Tidus's attention while he and Minax Bolide are busy chit chatting, supposedly keeping watch behind them. Once Tidus repositions himself closer, Stratos says to him, "Keep alert. There is nobody coming to help us, so keep it tight. I'll be right back." To Saaliha, Stratos says, "Follow me, but be my eyes. I'll try to draw Cyngosa's attention."

"Sounds good. I'll watch our perimeter. Careful Stratos." Saaliha prowls up beside the *Aluan Marine*. Stratos puts his index finger over his lips, then takes several steps out from behind the parked box truck they were using for cover. Crossing the street in a swift sprint, before crouching down against a concrete evergreen bush planter. Saaliha replaces his position and holds her bow ready. She only has four arrows remaining, but she notches one of them, nonetheless.

Eos, spotting movement when Stratos finishes his sprint, swoops down from the air to land on Cyngosa's shoulder just as he moves away from the concrete barrier he hid behind for a quick break. Singing out an upbeat and downbeat tune, the phoenix's unique song puts Cyngosa on alert and he lifts his rifle up to be ready for whatever may be coming next, slumping against a parked car to cover himself.

Stratos peeks from his new position. During this frame of time Saaliha lifts her bow over her head into Cyngosa's view. Peering through his own rifle scope, Cyngosa spots Saaliha's familiar bow poking up from the concrete planter a couple acres away. Stratos even leans into view when Cyngosa freezes up, causing the Direwolf shaman's eyebrows to become frozen in shock. Stratos gives him a thumbs up, then gestures impatiently for him to run over to their location.

Seeing Stratos's features in more detail makes Cyngosa tense before swiftly crossing the street to him. The last time he was getting this close to the *Aluan Marine*, they were murderously at one another's throats in the besieged *Trinity* facility. Never in a million years did Cyngosa guess he would run into him again. Keeping his footfalls soft and his ears perked straight up for any odd sounds or movement. Crouching low behind a parked blue SUV, his mouth going agape upon discovering Saaliha, with Stratos huddling up for cover.

"What's up, buttercup?" Saaliha asks Cyngosa, unable to truly hide the relief, and a half-smirk on her face discovering him alive, and in one piece, but also still feeling the sting of betrayal inside her from him.

"You two are literally the last people I'd thought to run into, way out here," Cyngosa says in a tone of confusion, joining Saaliha and Stratos behind the concrete planter.

"Hey, it's clear. We're all good, C'mon lets get with the others," Stratos says to the two as they traverse their way back, he cover's behind and then takes notice of a group of familiar trucks driving down the very road they were regrouping on. Stratos skids outside, to the rumbling sound of thunder.

"Caught you wandering. Judging by the shape you're in, I'm assuming you found Clyde Crowly," Saaliha remarks, twitching her whiskers, she then asks, "or have you been battling his crazy mercenary cult army this entire time?" She, Cyngosa, and Stratos move cautiously on the sidewalk toward where Minax and Tidus are posted up, at another corner of a concrete building.

"Oh I did," Cyngosa says, but pauses, seeing Saaliha and Strato's shocked expressions before continuing. "Honestly, I wouldn't have been able to do it without help. I momentarily hacked this crazy space laser and blew him up with it, using some kinda software. It gets worse, my dudes. The *Armageddon Cult* got Dorrion's Genesis machine after all. Whatever they'll do next, I have no idea."

Stratos stays silent, leading them, but screws his face up, recognizing the machine and the laser that shot their aircraft out of the sky being mentioned. Everyone freezes in place as a bright flash of lightning and a rumble of thunder briefly. At the same time, the convoy of trucks he spots passes behind them all on the road, search lights panning outward through the red gloom, but Saaliha and Cyngosa are out of sight as Stratos is flat on his stomach and still on some muddy, grassy terrain. One truck pulls into the strip mall parking lot as the others return to traveling speed.

"That's impossible. Well, specifically that part where the small meteor Minax dragged down from space should have left nothing but itty bitty fragments left. Hacking the software of a giant sky laser weapon, more probable. How'd you pull that off?" Saaliha says, perking her ears through her matted hair, but Cyngosa can see she recognizes the laser he was referring to.

"I'm just the messenger on this one," Cyngosa grumbles with frustration, adding, "I lost Dorrion's phone. It's how I was able to get control of Clyde's laser. But Kerith gave me the location of where the salvaged material was being sent from our crash. I'm sorry. I saved the number he was texting Dorrion's phone from in my own phone, if you want it. I've gotten nothing back when I try using it, though."

"Perhaps, but right now I believe we do have a bigger crisis on our paws," Saaliha says, gesturing in the direction in the sky of the swirling mass of clouds, hovering over the far off sabotaged *Cosmicism* monument.

Clearing his throat, Stratos comments with his lips curled up, "I can give you two a second. The others are a little ways over here. I'll let Tidus and Minax know. We need to structure a plan. But we should get going." Hearing Minax's name mentioned brings a warmth of relief throughout Cyngosa's torso, his shoulders still tense from earlier, slack ever so slightly.

Cyngosa and Saaliha exchange eye contact, left alone while Stratos puts significant distance from them. For a brief moment, stand in silence when the *Aluan Marine* is far away. Cyngosa speaks first. "It was inconsiderate of me to withhold information, and when we were all fighting, acting how I did."

"I let my emotions get a hold of me, my discipline slipped. Where is Khelu? Please tell me she isn't…?" Saaliha didn't want to utter the rest of the words to her question, feeling her mouth suddenly dry up and throat tighten.

Cyngosa turns his head to face her and makes eye contact with a serious expression and a heavy tone. "She's alive, but now one of those hypnotized. They have knives and swords coated with a demonic virus that turns the infected."

"I can't imagine what you two went through to get here. So," she places a paw on his shoulder, "you did the best given the situations? Dorrion would say something like that. If we're still alive, then Khelu has hope. Right?"

"Right…" Cyngosa says, in a forlorn tone as he glances away, then down at the *Ethereal Arbor* totem, mulling out loud after, "The *Elemental Mastery* had less than three paragraphs of text explaining how this thing functions. The angel had to show me a mental image of what it's supposed to look like. It was challenging to carve this kinda totem."

"It'll cleanse the *Cosmicism* monument of demonic magic, basically?" Saaliha asks, her pink eyes scanning the parking lot as the truck with cultist militants slowly cruises around, oblivious to them. Stratos silently keeps watch as Tidus and Minax watch from the distance, growing nosey from the holdup. Minax, having particular interest, perceiving a familiarity with the *Lycandian* speaking with Saaliha with watchful eyes, but remains standing with Tidus.

"What's still unclear to me is the cost it'll have," Cyngosa replies, but keeping his tone curiously optimistic. He quickens his walking pace to regroup with the other's finally, stopping to give Saaliha a tight embrace in the rain before staring directly at her. "But I'll bear the cost alongside all of you. I'm not going anywhere."

Saaliha gives him an uncomfortable look but nods—silently grasping with the unknown Cyngosa now struggles with—following him back. Stratos gives them a welcoming nod and a grin, walking alongside Cyngosa and Saaliha as they collect themselves. Reuniting with Tidus and Minax, Cyngosa and Minax gasp seeing one another.

"Cyngosa? I suspected that was you. You are alive, after all," Minax says, eyes wide and his wings unfurling as his whole body tenses up. Cyngosa didn't have much time to react before the tall *Galanexian* wraps him up in a hug. An embrace that Cyngosa oddly found himself subconsciously moving his arms around to hug Minax back in, like returning to the arms of a long-lost friend.

"Yeah, I'm a scrappy guy," Cyngosa says, smiling after Minax releases him.

"Where's Khelu? Is she alright?" Minax inquires, his voice growing with concern.

Frowning, Saaliha looks over to Minax but doesn't say anything. Cyngosa feels a sickening sensation as the fur on his neck goes on end.

"She was taken alive by the cultists. What they'll do to her, I can only imagine. I'm afraid it might be the same fate as everyone else in this city," Cyngosa informs Minax, the melancholy in his tone is not missed.

"Well, Cyngosa, my friend, we're going to put an end to this tonight," Minax states matter-of-factly, making sure his unblinking gaze meets Cyngosa's.

Cyngosa explains the special totem he was instructed to craft by the angelic vision he had.

"I can break that demonic obelisk easily. End all of this now with a *Macrocosmic Lexicon* spell. Fair warning the drawbacks and costs to these magic forces get severe," Minax states, confidently keeping his posture upright and in his armor.

"Without severing the victims hypnotized and linked to it, destroying the obelisk could likely kill everyone affected. This totem," Cyngosa explains while he pulls it from his backpack into view. "Made from *Ethereal Arbor*. I can disenchant them, disrupt the portal opening."

"Awesome, more crazy magical bullshittery," Tidus comments as he folds his arms across his chest, leaning against the yellow painted brick wall, jerking his head at Minax. "I reckon let him drop another space rock on 'em, if all else fails."

"*Ethereal Arbor*? I don't doubt what you claim to be true." Stratos clears his throat and continues solemnly. "If you got this chance. I'll move the sky above and the ground below to get us to that monstrosity, and take it down! Save my wife and daughter, and all those trapped people."

"Yes, it can be done. I can drop you right on top of the obelisk while they are least expecting it, if you want to hold on to my ankles, or I can carry you," Minax Bolide says to all of them, after thoughtfully scratching his golden scaly chin.

"Absolutely. Whatever it takes, we can do this together. I'll swallow my dignity, brush off my bruised ego. They got my sister," Cyngosa enthusiastically states, his shoulders pushing back and chest puffing out. Eos backed him up with a musical squawk, spitting fire from their beak

Minax stretches himself out and is quick to comment in a firm tone. "However, that demon will be fierce. I can already sense it." Tilting his horned head at Cyngosa, Minax's facial features show a mix of apprehension and determination.

"Yes, Demon Lord Noxion. I heard it spoken amongst the cultists. He's spellbound to it too," Cyngosa sighs, scratching his right cheek then brushing his chin.

"There's also the whole sitting army distributed across *Silvium*," Stratos says, folding his arms across his chest with an apprehensive expression on his face.

"Most of us are also low on arrows, or ammo, if you prefer. Let's ambush a small unit for their equipment. We'll need more powerful weaponry, anyway. I can try to put a virus or disrupt whatever communications are being used," Saaliha suggests, casting a hopeful look at the two *Aluan Marines* while she paces, whisking her tail behind her.

"I like her proposal," Tidus says, lifting his camouflage ball cap to scratch his head.

Cyngosa, keeping his chin high, lowers his neon green goggles with black radioactive symbols on the lenses over his eyes. Running a paw through the rain matted dark furry hair on his head. "It'll allow us to get closer."

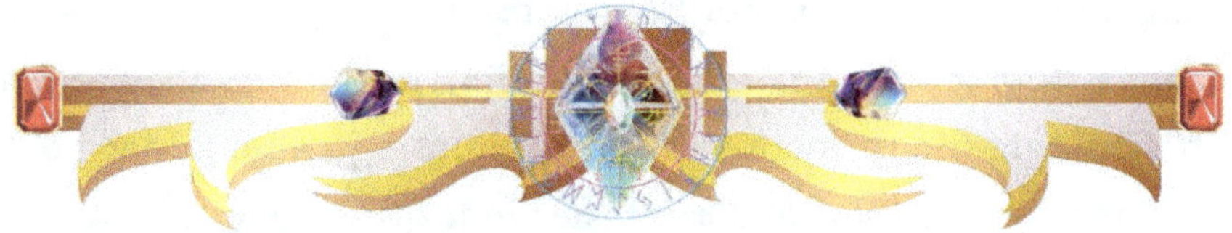

A group of six *Armageddon Cultists* take position upon the rooftop of a long, pitch black multipurpose office building, only one story tall from street level. Saaliha, Tidus, Stratos, and Cyngosa ambush the group at once from all four angles. Tidus and Stratos each tackle a separate cultist down on the soaked flat rubbery rooftop, meanwhile Cyngosa and Saaliha are left with the remaining two. One raises their weapon in an attempt to shoot the nearest of these resisting fools of Eradicator's will, but leaping up from the other side of the building's ledge comes Saaliha in an airborne dropkick. Cyngosa's wooden totem with lightning bolts chiseled in it scatters and bounces underneath the remaining cultist instantly, in a timely manner. It quickly emits a web of painful electricity as the magical energy stored within the enchanted carved totem releases outward, buying Cyngosa time to shoot them down instead.

They check out the limited resources available to them, still keeping hyper aware of lurking enemies. Saaliha inspects the field laptop without any contest from the others. Tidus and Stratos look at the compatibility of ammunition with their rifles before moving on to other things. Cyngosa holds up an RPG. "Yeah, these'll do some damage. Only a few rockets. Who wants it?"

"Oh hell yeah, allow me." Tidus eagerly reaches out with his free paw. Stratos rolls his eyes, shaking his head, amused.

Saaliha's attention piques as she types away on the field laptop keyboard, using one finger on the touchpad to click and guide herself through the programs displayed on the screen, saying to Tidus and

Cyngosa, "This'll take a few minutes I think, my dudes." Saaliha sighs, closing it and tucking it under her right arm.

Saaliha stops, seeing the random building next to the alley they all shuffled single-file through, is in fact a hunting and outdoor hobby shop. She raises her paw and raises her index finger while cautiously approaching the illuminated storefront. Minax, Tidus, and Cyngosa watch Saaliha advance to the translucent glass door as Stratos keeps watch ahead of them. "What is she doing? Can this crazy damn cat just pick up a gun already?" Tidus complains quietly. Twisting his face up, he turns his torso to face Cyngosa and Minax, expecting an answer. Minax and Cyngosa look at each other quizzically, then simultaneously shrug back at Tidus.

Noticing the gnarly garnet sky briefly light up with a streak of lightning followed with a boom of thunder, Saaliha then opens the door to the storefront at the same time, ringing a little bell dangling from the frame.

Committed, Saaliha steps quickly inside, looking around wildly, discovering the store's front end to be empty of any customers or staff. She feels her throat tighten up, and her ears twitch, her back tensing after the door shuts, but Saaliha stands in the brightly lit store unbothered for a moment. With her paws clenching at the handles of her sheathed swords, heading toward the archery section, alert pink eyes scanning the counters, aisles of camping supplies, tents, and other such essentials. With her nostrils flaring, she inhales the smelly scent of seasoned firewood, plastic, and the delicate aroma of chemicals. The only sound is the shifting of her clothing, and her footsteps underneath her, including the soft clicking buzz coming from the ceiling lights above. This gradually lowers Saaliha's thumping heartbeat as she steadies her breath, keeping her person swiveling on the ready, familiar with how sneaky these cultists are.

Outside, Cyngosa, Minax, and Tidus watch Saaliha exit the sportsman shop with her quiver packed full, with a bunch more arrows clutched in her left paw.

"If you took any longer, I would have gone in after you," Cyngosa says to Saaliha with a smirk.

Sticking her pierced tongue out, and souring her face at Cyngosa, giving him a genuinely snarky response. "I can handle myself, fine. I'm saving Khelu. You, on the other paw, need to regain my trust, dickhead."

Cyngosa maintains his cheesy grin and emits a sheepish chuckle through his teeth. Minax makes a surprised face while Tidus catches second-hand embarrassment for Cyngosa, wincing.

They return to their temporary shelter, keeping watch in a church-like structure while they get supplies. Observing their potential attack point from the highest vantage point on the tallest steeple, Cyngosa walks up to stand next to Minax while he's looking through a lancet window of the church.

"I grabbed up a stick of *Ethereal Arbor*. You and Saaliha came to mind when I was out hiking to find the tree. I planned to make you a flute, since you lost yours, way back when," Cyngosa says, looking up with a sincere expression. He lifts his left paw up, holding a crude wooden flute, evidently a work in progress.

Minax blinks his eyes rapidly, turning his head, a tone of surprise in his voice. "That's thoughtful of you. I appreciate it, my friend."

"I don't know how to make any instruments, by the way. It's gorgeous, uncommon wood, so I figured why not," Cyngosa sheepishly admits. Minax places a claw on Cyngosa's shoulder and offers a smile.

"Can't wait to see when you finish it," Minax says warmly, pushing down the chill of dreadful uncertainty lingering inside himself.

Saaliha sitting sideways on the windowsill with her attention going outward to the eerily quiet city and the *Armageddon Cultist* laptop she acquired in their little raid. It's possible she can hack into the network the cultists are using, but she discovers it will take time. She gulps with pursed lips and fanned out whiskers, Saaliha feeling the press of the clock against them.

"Cool, now we fixate on a point of entry and concentrate our attack effort," Stratos says to them. Cyngosa, Tidus, and Minax stand nearby, finalizing their personal gear and preparing to spring their attack.

"What about the Demon Lord?" Minax asks him, bringing up the demon flying openly in the rainy skies above *Silvium*. They all have caught a chilling and unnerving peak at him in split passing, but have not interacted with this winged demon as of yet. Minax switches his focus to stare at each of them for a second longer, before stating, "The more I've evaluated here, the more I have to admit that he may be an extremely powerful enemy. He's not alone either, with a squadron of fighter jets patrolling the skies everywhere."

"We could infiltrate close enough to that spooky obelisk on foot, I reckon" Tidus says supportively to Minax.

"I can see this working, up to a point. Saaliha and Cyngosa can meet us, get as close as they can before we inevitably make ourselves known. Let's face reality, we'd need a miracle to get in there unnoticed. So, Minax flies up to keep most of the enemy occupied while he takes on that demonic beast thing," Stratos says.

"Eos could scout the skies above to give us an ideal spot to assault them from," Cyngosa chimes in between the two *Aluan Marines*.

"How about splitting up into smaller, unnoticeable pairs to reach the demonically corrupted monument from separate angles? If caught, force the *Armageddon Cultists* to also split their attention?" Cyngosa suggests.

"Perfect. Maybe I wait. Or give a signal? I can take a few of their aircraft by surprise, release the virus to hack into their combat drones, too," Saaliha says as she holds one of the offline surveillance drones up to show them. Tidus, Cyngosa, and Minax smirk mischievously at Saaliha, excited at the potential mayhem that'll create in their imaginations.

While shaking his head with a grin, Stratos says, "The signal will be the second the *Starwielder* is spotted. We'll gain as much ground as we can as they're scrambling after Minax."

"If need be, improvising is what we do best, Stratos, my dude." Cyngosa bumps him with his elbow and chuckles.

Momentarily nipping on one of his finger's knuckles, Stratos replies sarcastically, "Yeah, this plan will totally work. When you turn your brain off and don't try to think about it too hard."

CHAPTER SEVENTEEN: The Corrupted Spire OF Malice

THE NIGHT SKY IS a frenzy swirling mass of towering black cumulonimbus thunderheads, with some stretching miles in an outlying diameter, high above the pine forests, browning fields, and the craggy landscape surrounding *Silvium*. The eye of the supernatural storm is orbiting around a single monument's permeance while hovering over the metropolitan city, permitting the eldritch crimson moonlight from the still ongoing eclipse to pour down from it.

Smaller wisps of gray and red stratus clouds hauntingly twist around, floating beneath the much larger cloud formations. Steady blood red rain coming down all around in rhythmic bands, accompanied by lightning and booms of rumbling thunder. Winds buffer dead leaves as trees are left bare but glossy from moisture, greenery withering up even as the wine red rains soaked the ground.

The *Wulftheon* city had clusters of averagely dressed, or suited citizens of different ages, standing in file. long groups, all in a hypnotized stupor in the pouring rain around the towering corrupted ziggurat. Spared from the early bloody massacre of the cult. Their modernized fighter jets and attack helicopters occupy the air space with vigilance, while below aggressive tanks with serrated spade bumpers on either end were rolling about the streets on patrol. Artillery and anti-air craft positions were even made on ideal rooftops of one-story buildings.

Multitudes of *Armageddon Cultists* in hooded robes of red, black, and silver patterns, adorning slate gray combat armor on top of these robes, are out en masse. They patrol the dead streets, littered with trash and abandoned vehicles, the empty and dark homes left deserted in the suburban neighborhoods.

Cyngosa creeps about in the middle of it all, with rain matted fur, crouches behind a burned out police SUV sitting on its rims and melted tires, careful to not make a single sound to disturb the natural ambiances of the conquered city. The acrid aroma stung his nose being close up to the SUV. An occasional boom of thunder over the soft clapping of rain on the metal and asphalt is the predominant backdrop noise. Cyngosa picks up the constant chanting and hears phrases such as, 'Eradicator's Army Cometh' and 'Grand Final Vision' coming from cultists grouped up in revelry. A flash of lightning illuminated the dark streets with crimson light abruptly, causing Cyngosa to flinch flat to his stomach and roll under the tighter space beneath the sunken SUV amidst accumulated paper rubbish.

A collection of a dozen cultists with belt-fed machine guns, and excessive bandoliers snaking around their torsos, halt right in the proximity of Cyngosa, who is beneath the SUV. Cyngosa mutes his headset, his finger on his rifle, but doesn't dare discharge his weapon, even if his senses are tingling. Instead, he waits, accumulating anxiety, going completely still to the point of hearing his own racing heartbeat in his ears.

A single cultist steps closer before leaning his gun on the charred wrinkled hood of the SUV, bloodshot eyes scanning beneath his face armor. "Eyelids peeled. Kill all infidels you find still resisting Grand Summoner Crowly's blessing. First here, then the glory from beyond will be unleashed for the rest of the world to experience, soon! Demon Lord Noxion will lead us, crippling whole armies by himself."

The *Armageddon Cultists* meander away while Cyngosa watches their passing attentively until they are far away enough for him to roll out. He crawls slowly around the SUV and up onto the sidewalk. Back on his feet and hugging his back against the cold and wet brick wall of a building, cautious to avoid being illuminated by the street lamp as he steps jittery, in and out of shadow.

Slipping into the alcove of a dark four-story building's doorway, he looks around before turning his mic back on. Unmuting his device, Cyngosa whispers into the small microphone, "It's Cyn. I'm getting closer to that demonic spire thing, from the south side. There's a lot of those militarized cultists bunched up forming roadblocks. They have tanks blocking the streets, keeping closing in on foot. We need to hurry."

A low rumble of thunder follows Cyngosa's message. He peaks his dilating turquoise eye through the scope of his gun. Sighing as he shakes his head, evaluating his upcoming obstacle, as his heart races and his body courses with energy. An attack helicopter with its searchlight beaming down on the street hums low overhead suddenly.

Cyngosa leans away as the aircraft flutters angrily by. He speaks into their secure radio channel once more. He swallowed the lump forming in his throat somehow. "Remember, don't let those enchanted blades of theirs stab you directly. It got my sister." He keeps pushing Khelu from his mind. Lingering on 'what ifs' only spelled certain failure, Cyngosa reasons with himself.

Saaliha, with her short-cut multicolored pastel hair and fur wet from the rain, lifts her pierced feline ears straight up. Detecting the slightest sound as she prowls on the slanted shingled rooftop of a tall building, her sharp pink eyes could make out the devilish corrupted spire just a couple blocks away.

Carrying a duffle bag, she skids down the roof in her gashed up golden plated armor. Saaliha leaps onto another rooftop with an awning below, pouncing down on an enemy cultist and taking them out. Saaliha pops up a second later, unslinging her backpack with her quiver attached to it.

She unzips it and pulls free her laptop and the *Armageddon Cultist's* combat drone she recovered. She says into the radio frequency they're sharing, "It's Saaliha. Cyngosa, we're probably just a couple miles from the corrupted spire." She takes her binoculars out and, giving the next mile or so an effective look over before speaking to the others. "There's numerous blockades getting up to the open field. They've made a fortified ring using excavating equipment around the spire. I can't see anything beyond that. Anyone got a visual past it?"

Stratos peeks his head from behind the wall, peering through the stained glass window to observe the street below, his brow furrowed and chewing his bottom lip. A four-way intersection with four abandoned cars sat under flashing yellow traffic lights. He doesn't immediately scout out any movement, leaning his head back inside as a distant boom of thunder rumbles overhead, mixing with the constant tapping of rainfall.

Minax, in silence, kneels on the stairs to the top mezzanine of the church he and Stratos were inside. With *Alpha and Omega* firmly clenched and on the alert, he stares at Stratos with an expectant expression and alert purple eyes. From the ground level below, keeping his full attention on the street, Tidus keeps guard from the church's partially opened doorway, firearm at the ready with a silencer on the muzzle.

"It's looking pretty clear so far, but I don't trust it. These cultist psychopaths could be lurking almost anywhere. The closer we get to that freaky obelisk thing, the greater their defensive efforts. We can't go on from here unnoticed, so be ready," Stratos says quietly while he approaches Minax, taking notice and acknowledges he was in a pensive state of mind by his slumping broad shoulders and wilted wings.

Minax, perking up, departs from the stairs and closes the *Macrocosm Lexicon* he was reading, and moves over to climb the nearby ladder to the roof of the church building, speaking to Stratos, "The others know what they have to do, get to the ceremony and disrupt the warlocks feeding the obelisk. Remember, getting Cyngosa and his totem is the only way to save those brainwashed Stratos."

Stratos, still underneath the ladder and looking up, watches Minax on his way up to the roof. "I've seen you fly into some crazy situations, but are you really sure of this one? Just a couple seconds flying openly out there, and this whole occupied city is going wild."

Minax crouches low to the roof, getting his recently healed wings unfurled for flight. "You'll do what you do best, then." Minax stops and points to Noxion flying up high in the foggy distance. "I have to fight him."

Minax boldly stood up and leaps into the air and spread his wing span out to gain a higher altitude.

Tidus glances up, noticing Minax flying openly in the sky and passing above him, adjusting his *Aluan* camouflage ball cap on his head as he mutters, "Oh shit."

Minax achieves more speed, building courage too as anxiety grips him, rapidly flying through the air on determined wings toward the Demon Lord just as a dreadful distress siren wails from all around. All hell breaks loose across the occupied city of *Silvium* as the *Starwielder* charges through the air. Like swarms of angry ants below, the cultists unleash their war machines and form attack groups. Noxion Myriad casually drifts through the crimson rain on smoldering infernal gray wings, sounding like wrinkling leather, paying the commotion no attention.

He senses Minax, and the demon surges forward into a one hundred and eighty degree corkscrew to face the *Starwielder* in the open skies. Noxion raises up his hideously jagged, nicked up two-handed 'sword' at the ready. "Finally! Finished hiding, have we, you winged-worm?! Ready to witness the impending demise of this world up close and personal?" Noxion asks arrogantly.

Minax yells at Noxion as he continues closing distant in the sky with *Alpha and Omega* gripped in one claw. "Over my dead body, demon!"

Easily feints off Minax's first attack; a swift swing of *Alpha and Omega* as Minax charges past and circles around in the air. "I'll happily oblige you. Don't you see the obelisk way over there, *Starwielder*?" Clenching his infernal claw, summoning a molten metal, twisted appearing spear, he continues, "Already now radiating with the power from over a hundred thousand doomed souls! With more seeping into it as we speak! You cannot possibly stop us!" He hurls the spear after Minax with fierce strength.

Minax bats away the incoming demonic javelin with mocking ease, sending a beam of bright green lightning from his own claw at the demon, electrifying him as he descends with feet, claws first to kick him downward toward the ground below. Noxion, illuminated by the *Starwielder's* painful lightning spell, lets out a grunt when Minax thrusts feet first into him, but the Demon Lord is quick to parry his cosmic *Starwielder* weapon from impaling his torso.

Equally descending, Noxion twists himself free from underneath Minax and upper cuts at his head with vicious speed. Forcing Minax to parry the hellish two-handed sword away. Noxion follows the attack by charging right into Minax with his sharp body, bashing into him with incredible strength to knock Minax backward through the air, forcing Minax to correct his flight for an instant, before being body slammed again repeatedly. A missile shot from below explodes right into Minax, sending him tumbling away, tragically losing his grip on his cosmic paragon weapon in the event.

Finally, Noxion surges through the misty air with great speed from a sudden jolt, and passes by Minax in his vulnerable tumble. The Demon Lord kicked *Alpha and Omega* away further with his foot through the air, simultaneously cutting Minax against the torso in a shower of bright sparks. The demon's brutish physique was deceivingly agile.

Minax's tumble was made extra turbulent by the attack, his special armor protecting him and absorbing most of the attack's impact besides the raw force behind it, sending pain surging through his side and shoulder. The fight descends closer to the ground level of the crowded city by this point in time. The growing roar of hundreds of machine guns firing at Minax increases from the occupying *Armageddon Cultists*. Slowing the arrival of another molten javelin from the demon, using his gravity manipulating magic, batting it away afterward again.

Shaken up, Minax recovers and soars aloft once more, being pelted briefly by bullets. In the same space of time, summoning *Alpha and Omega* back to his claws. "Ha!"

Skyrocketing higher in the sky, Noxion waits for Minax in the pouring rain, hovering with his two-handed sword held in only one. Flapping his smoldering smokey wings quickly, Noxion hurls another twisted molten metal javelin at Minax and flies down after it to also attack him. Minax deflects the molten javelin and the two-handed sword, before Noxion then sweeps in with a fist, a powerful right hook catching Minax in the head, just as breathes fire into Noxion's face up close. Minax is thrown through the air sideways. Noxion summons another molten gnarly spear and hurls it. Repeating the process wickedly fast, sending a total of six at an unprepared Minax.

Noxion gives a fiendish snort, yelling at him, "Fighting an already lost war…futile. Your death is going to be slow and magnificent to behold." Noxion swings his two-handed sword and glides slowly, watching as his six projectiles crash into Minax's body, disoriented as he gets himself together. One tore a hole in his right wing membrane, three hit his torso having two disintegrate upon impact against his *Starwielder* armor. One succeeded in impaling itself in Minax, sneaking through the magical armor. Minax gasps out in pain as his entire torso burns, but only having a couple seconds to react as Noxion swoops in to wickedly barrage him again with another overhead chop.

"I got more in me than you think! And there exists resistance from this world greater than you assume. Victory isn't yours yet," Minax retorts, willpower emanating from him even under the brutal strength and power delivered behind the demon's attacks, sparks flying away as he deflects.

Minax casts magic from his empty claw, blasting Noxion point blank repeatedly with neon green lightning, causing the demon to snarl in discomfort and seize up. Jetting into physical reality with a loud snapping sound, into his very palms *Alpha and Omega* appears as Minax is mid-swing at the Demon Lord. Noxion growls in painful aggravation, jointly blocking Minax's weapon in time, however accepting the painfully tingling lightning magic against his infernal body the entire time.

Being electrocuted with neon lime lightening spider-webbing all over him, Noxion sweeps away the first swing from Minax with a loud metallic clang, only to be then afterward struck hard by the other identical end of *Alpha and Omega*. The demon shudders and regains his balance, spatting a bloody cough. "You're going to need to do way better than that. Where is your real power, *Starwielder*?" Noxion mockingly goads him.

Noxion spins wildly into a monstrous whirlwind in the air, driving Minax back on the defensive as he wobbles in the air, and striking him a couple times in the process, forcing painful gasps out of him. Noxion ceases his spin and clenches his free demonic claw, aglow with a foul black, crimson, and neon yellow colors as his other claw holds his sword.

From the ground below their fight, a huge rain soaked asphalt and dirt chunk of a street intersection rises, dropping and bumping away abandoned vehicles and separating from pipes. Bursting into reddish hellfire as well, before the entire mass zooms up toward Minax with acceleration.

Unaware of the fiery earth projectile rising directly beneath him, Minax swiftly cuts, slashes and finally accomplishes impaling Noxion in the torso off-center. Sending a blinding white ray of magic into him from the portion of *Alpha and Omega* crunched into the Demon Lord's torso. Minax loses his grip and is violently thrown as the flaming chunk of ground strikes him from underneath. Noxion is freed and flipped backward mid-air.

Minax tumbles toward the ground, smashing through the translucent glass wall of a car dealership's office before coming to a hard stop as his body strikes the side of a rotating display vehicle, toppling it off and forcing the breath to escape his lungs. His purple eyes looking up in the rainy air, Noxion gesturing his free claw at the huge fiery earth projectile diverting its course from up to down, with frightening speed.

Lurching himself up into the sky as quickly as he can, Minax rolls sideways as the huge flaming chunk of ground and asphalt soars past him, crashing into the office building in a burst of destruction underneath him. Minax throws *Alpha and Omega* up at Noxion, impaling the demon and throwing him momentarily off-balance mid-air. Minax follows his attack upward against the demon, with dual streams of neon lightning from each of his outstretched claw palms.

Minax ignores the machine gun fire, hitting him from random cultists scrambling all about on the streets far below and some outside, and others from in commercial buildings. His *Starwielder* armor absorbs one of the cultist's magic projectiles from one of their spellcasters as well, but Minax keeps focused on his foe. He has witnessed Noxion's more lethal sorcery strength.

Noxion, still being fully electrocuted and snarling in pain when he touches *Alpha and Omega* lodged in his gut, making his claw burn white momentarily as he yanks it free before throwing it away through the wet air. "I will easily rip this pathetic world apart with my own two claws myself!"

Minax continues zapping Noxion until he's mere feet away from him. Calling the cosmic weapon *Alpha and Omega* back to his possession, he swings in with all his might again, then again. Making satisfactory, crunching sounds of metal and flesh with each successful hit.

"Not if I tear YOU apart myself first, fiend!" Minax declares and spins around, letting the bulky quartz ball on the end of his tail full on strike Noxion in the head, cracking the Demon Lord straight backward through the air with limp wings. Lightning flashes around them illuminating the aerial brawl from the bloody tinted clouds. Minax dives through the red rainy air after Noxion, forcing the demon to react swiftly in his parry and counter-attack as he recovers from the stunning hit.

The two land on the ground together mid-fight somewhere in the middle of downtown *Silvium*, massive LED screens everywhere displaying commercials and other such advertisements. The *Starwielder* and the Demon Lord fiercely face each other off in epic exchanges. Nearby cultists boldly open fire at Minax even with their infernal master Noxion in such proximity.

Noxion knocks aside an empty car with part of his torso and hip, completely occupied with pushing off one of Minax's hard and fast downward arching chops as they battle down the main street. The rancorous sound of bullets hitting metal and glass echo as Noxion's minion's open fire with impunity now, Minax flinches from being hit.

Minax maneuvers the fight toward cover behind a nearby city bus, glass pieces spraying him from the smashing windows. He reflects Noxion's onslaught before leaping back and unfurling his wings for takeoff. Jumping up and far over Noxion, and the bus to land amidst the dozen cultists shooting him, Minax mercilessly slices them all down in a rapid frenzy. When Minax finishes his cluster of foes, Noxion shears the city bus in half, simultaneously flying through it, soaring forward horrendously fast and sounding like the rumbling of a rocket engine.

Noxion Myriad catches Minax in a deep uppercut with his sword and straight onto his backside against the street, sending the ten foot tall *Galanexian* bouncing with the clanking of metal echoing out, and a painful yelp. Noxion leaps up into the sky like a missile before landing straight down on Minax, crushing him into the wet asphalt, spraying rainwater everywhere. Right as Noxion goes to ruthlessly drive his two-handed sword right through Minax's chest, where the gem in his torso is, Minax struggles to open his maw and blast the Demon Lord in the face with flames. Catching the blade with his own, Minax even uses his feet on the pole arm portions of *Alpha and Omega* to assist in repelling the demon off of himself.

Coughs a couple times, and gives out a hissing growl. Standing up in the shallow crater, back on his slightly wobbly feet, Minax grumbles. "I will stop you and this *Armageddon Cult.*"

Minax whips himself to fly forward at Noxion in the chilly air, getting struck by an RPG twice from different angles, but continues his ferocious lunge with tendrils of smoke trailing behind him in his wake and a ringing in his ears. Noxion blocks Minax's first and second attacks, letting out a metallic howl when the third attack strikes his enemy so hard Noxion staggers to keep his balance upright. Minax follows up with a roundhouse kick to the Demon Lord's torso, momentarily sending him falling backward into the dining room of a fast-food restaurant just off the street. Noxion surges back up to his feet, crushed wall and glass falling on top of the smashed up tables at his hooved feet, and then charges at Minax from the damaged building's hole.

"This has been amusing, but I'm growing bored of this, and the spire is almost charged enough," Noxion Myriad states vindictively, staring down Minax. Noxion parries and deflects each one of Minax's fierce attacks this time, before generating another molten spear and jabbing it into Minax's gut. Minax, with a look of agonized horror on his face, attempts to back off as he yelps in pain, but the Demon Lord reels him back in close with ease. Noxion causes the molten jagged spear to suddenly explode, harmless to himself. Minax however, wounded and left stunned, finds himself suddenly struck up into the air from a harsh uppercut.

Stratos and Tidus, renouncing stealth at the same time, rush out together through the doorway of the church and onto the street as the siren wails. *Silvium* is buzzing with new and foreboding activity all around them. Together they make their way toward the demonically corrupted monument, running up the sidewalk of a main street and soon catching the unfriendly eyes of *Armageddon Cultists*. Opening fire on the first cultists coming into view, then forming a defensive position behind an abandoned city bus as the enemy advanced through their bullets with little concern. Several dropped, but the crowd grew out of control and gained ground on the two soldiers.

Stratos taps Tidus's shoulder. He's busy emptying the last of his first magazine into the enemies, making full use of his silencer.

"Through this way!" Stratos says before going quiet.

Tidus hastily reloads his rifle and backtracks with Stratos through the building adjacent to the parked bus, entering an expensive store of jewelry and clothing. Setting off an alarm while the two freely sprint past the mannequins and display cases toward the fire exit glowing at the other end. Stratos and Tidus burst into an alley from the emergency fire exit doors, and sprint across a parking lot, immediately being shot at from enemies at different angles.

"Everyone, close in at their fortified ring. We'll concentrate our way through," Stratos commands sternly, trying to be heard over the noise, both near and far.

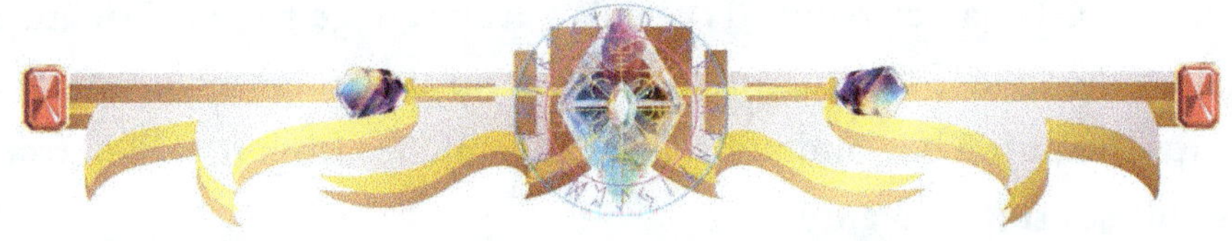

The siren commences its piercing wails. Cyngosa rises into a sprint and makes his courageous run through the streets of *Silvium* toward the corrupted monument. It's less than a thousand feet before he ends up encountering a large group of hooded robed *Armageddon Cultists*.

Three of the militants shout and take aim at him. Cyngosa, with adrenaline charging every fiber in his being and sensing this is his only time, maybe even his only chance to save Khelu, doesn't stop. He hurls a scalding fire and ice projectile that he materializes in his palm out of thin air at the group, his magical scars visible on just his forearms flashing bright orange and milky blue. Cyngosa's scalding magical projectile rockets right into the closest enemy before it explodes into a wide cloud of hot steam, engulfing them all as well. Sprinting past the checkpoint, ducking and zigzagging through abandoned cars, Cyngosa continues down the street, fixated on the mission.

"On it, Stratos," Cyngosa says into his microphone.

Saaliha quickly types into a computer program and then shuts her laptop, putting it away, and slings her backpack on again. The drone device activates and starts hovering up now into the sky. Saaliha's signal virus began causing all the cult's drones to go haywire and turn against them, self-destructing or simply turning themselves off. She unzips the duffle bag and pulls a rocket launcher from it, stolen from the cultist army's inventory.

"Time to start the party with a couple fireworks. Nothing over the top." Saaliha giggles to herself in a gleeful tone, the tension throughout her.

Saaliha sneakily relocates to the rooftop ledge and takes aim at a passing attack model helicopter before letting the propelled grenade whizz off with a cloudy hiss, striking the cultist's aircraft right in the tail and blowing it into an instant fiery tailspin. Crashing on the city street below, the enemy scrambled in reaction, but was not concerned by the wreck. With a flood of adrenaline now, Saaliha—already loading another grenade and traveling to a neighboring rooftop—perks her ears up to the cracks and snaps of near miss bullets before going fully prone.

Flat on her stomach on the hard surface, she rolls on her side, taking aim at another attack helicopter five hundred feet away in the sky, hovering above another street block, before pulling the trigger. The rocket misses the *Armageddon* militant's helicopter as the war machine swivels around and passes through empty air, instead her missile harmlessly exploding in the distance. The attack helicopter surges forward, as another alarmingly maneuvers in as well, the pilot within made fully aware of Saaliha's location on the exposed rooftop. She rolls sideways, and once getting purchase rolls up into a full sprint for the edge of the rooftop.

A dozen haywire drones belonging to the *Cult* buzz into view from the streets below and collide together into the second attack helicopter's rotor propeller system and effectively send the aircraft into a freefall crash on the street below. The leading helicopter fires one of its rockets at the building Saaliha is about to leap off from before having to disengage and continuously maneuver away from the remaining bugged drones.

While Saaliha is mid-air, the building ledge behind her explodes from the missile, the force coming from changing her trajectory and forces her straight out, debris following. In a partial airborne panic, she notices Cyngosa running toward a section of the city with taller buildings a block over from her current vantage point. Only two rows of buildings are currently separating them. Before she can react any further, her attention snaps ahead at a fast approaching wall.

Bracing herself, feeling her heart stopping in her chest, Saaliha crashes against the smooth concrete, sending a shock of pain throughout her, bouncing off the building to fall straight, with the ground less than a couple hundred feet now. Her reflexes acting in a twitch, her feet and bare paws scratch at the surface, twisting and angling her fall while one of the building's stories is externally embellished with art made of stonework.

With a quick vibrating purr of relief upon catching the chiseled ledge, and a determined smirk on her face, Saaliha hoists herself up, saying into her radio, still trying to escape the level of heat still weighing on her mind.

"Cyngosa, I just saw you running by. I'll meet you at that intersection coming up," Saaliha says as she scales the track along the building's architecture while blinding spotlights dance in her pursuit. Taking notice of a fire escape built into the structure after rounding a corner, Saaliha makes a brief stretching of her limbs in preparation while still running and jumps at it.

On the street level, a couple cultist militants rush around after her, finding Saaliha just in time as she's sprinting down the metal fire escape. Leaping off the last flight of stairs on the attack, she pulls out her curved serrated blades from their sheaths on her utility belt and gives the cultists a bloodthirsty growl, cautiously knocking the lead militant's firearm off aim in a timely manner.

Cyngosa discovers another commercial district with dozens of illuminated ad screens on three and four story tall buildings all around, flashing images of new cars, gadgets or other trendy advertising. He wasn't alone, as new militants serving the cult are stationed all about, but to his advantage, there is something causing a distraction. Cyngosa, inhaling his lung with the cool evening air, then runs up and slaps a fistful of a magical fireball into one such distracted cultist point blank from behind. Four malfunctioning drones at the next roadblock checkpoint appear to be the cause. A crack of thunder rumbles above, and a flare of lightning is muted by the overall bright buildings as Cyngosa fights close-up with the remaining three.

He quickly turns around to summon and throw an icicle projectile at another enemy, trying to close in on Saaliha from behind. Saaliha comes to a brief halt to fire off three arrows at once, leaving a single one left in her quiver. Saaliha recovers two of the arrows she spent, then they are then back on the move.

"Unfortunately, they know we're coming!" Cyngosa exclaims to Saaliha.

"Yeah, we just embrace the suck." Saaliha pauses, drawing another arrow and letting it loose into an enemy rushing at her. "Go, we're almost at the spire!"

Battling the scrambling enemy forces, Saaliha and Cyngosa continue, driven to reach the monument as fast as possible. Stratos and Tidus converge at the same location as Saaliha and Cyngosa, pulling in tow a score of agitated enemies behind them.

Eos soars through the gloomy sky. Cyngosa is able to peer down from such a grand aerial view at the trepidation of those under the hypnosis. Dozens of everyday dressed folk simply walk right up to the monument and suddenly burst into fiery ash as a single neon white light is extracted from their disintegrating person. The sight made Cyngosa feel physically ill all of a sudden, his mouth going agape in horror. Eos gives off anxious feelings into his subconscious at the diabolic ritual. This ritual fueled the obelisk, obviously, but Cyngosa notices the process isn't fast, but it's steady enough. Far, far on the outskirts, Eos's keen predatory eyesight could make out Khelu, Vivian, and Sidra Cobaltfort among the newest additions to the *Armageddon Cult's* sacrificial throng.

In defiance of the tanks parked up at the *Silvium* park's outer perimeter, the four charge at the corrupted spire up front anyway, under enemy fire from the front while also being chased by the *Armageddon Cultists* still pursuing them from the rest of the occupied city behind them. Dodging projectiles and slipping for cover whenever available, during this moment explosions from the tank rounds crash in, creating further threatening mayhem to contend with.

Time was not on their side, but with inspiration, Cyngosa yells to them, "I can purify the monument and cleanse the brainwashing!"

"Let's see it then. I'm with you, brother," Tidus says to him, chasing after Cyngosa, traversing the landscape. "I'm right behind you. Hell yeah!"

"You saw my family is still alive?" Stratos asks Cyngosa, who gives him a swift thumbs up as they all charge from the sidewalk into the ravaged park. "We can still save them, and many others!"

The pavilion, fixed with multiple heavy caliber machine guns in a fortification directly under the spire, a particular cultist leader spies with binoculars across the acres of no-man's-land between the three trench rings circling the cursed monument he's guarding. Observing *Trinity*'s remaining members and the two outlawed *Aluan Marines* assault, the cultist leader's radio crackling up to life as the local entrenched forces are engaged by these same individuals.

"Lord Klaus Cravenfang, we got four assailants at the first fortification line!" the cultist leader's radio single blares into his ear. Lord Klaus replies into his headset's mic underneath the golden wolf's skull shaped helmet he adorned over his head.

"I have already alerted the Apocalypse Knights, they and more reinforcements are en route from around *Silvium*. Demon Lord Noxion is concentrating on the *Starwielder*. Keep those infidels back!" Lord Cravenfang reaches his black gauntleted paws around the pole arm of his two-handed serrated scythe. The evil possessed monument hummed and crackled, on the verge of bursting open a new dimension, and unleashing whatever horrors Noxion has schemed up for their world.

Stratos, Saaliha, Tidus, and Cyngosa leap into the deep fortified ring surrounding the once blooming *Silvium* city park, now a formidable bulwark of three trenches encasing the demonically corrupt monument further on up.

The four attack side by side with whatever they have at their disposal, shooting at the enemy with guns, arrows and, in Cyngosa's case, magic. Saaliha leaps ahead of the others, drawing her dual serrated Khopesh swords, climbing up the next trench. One blazing blade slashing across one cultist, setting them aflame with ease as she engages the foes awaiting them, Saaliha whirls backward out of any enemy marksman's view, using the muddy earth bulwark's defensive network to her advantage.

Tidus, now close by, a couple meters away from Saaliha and selecting his own next route while under duress from an enemy sorcerer, pushes himself against the nearest trench wall as a purple fiery ball with a glowing wolf skull in the center of it smashes then explodes. The diabolical magic projectile causes a violent eruption of dirt and mud, before engulfing the immediate impact site in crimson hellfire.

Cyngosa hurls a magic projectile of his own from one of his totems, a lance made of ice that bursts over some of the hellfire, trying to snuff it. Not reacting fast enough, as one *Armageddon Cultist* dives high from a pile of sandbags and barbed wire down on top of Cyngosa afterward. Stratos quickly sideways kicks, then guns down the stunned cultist, seconds after grabbing Cyngosa by his free paw and yanking him up back to his feet. They exchange a confident nod to one another, working together to slog through the seemingly hundreds of enemies hunkering in.

The *Aluan Marine* shoots down the trench walkway behind them before then struggling to fight and defeat another enemy in close combat, more joining shouts at Cyngosa. "Gahh!" Stratos smashes aside one before dropping another. "Don't wait for me! Get your ass up there!"

"Nah, I'm not leaving no one behind again!" Cyngosa replies in the act of swiftly summoning a magical icy javelin and barraging the enemies on and around Stratos with precision.

Eos dive-bombs from the misty sky like a shooting-star of purple, pink and blue with their talons outstretched to pin a cultist, setting their body ablaze in the process before savagely clawing away. "*Exactly. Save Khelu,*" Eos mentally shouts into Cyngosa's head.

Saaliha and Tidus face one flank of attacking enemies, putting the sticky hell flame and the first ring of the cult's defense behind them. Synchronously, Cyngosa and Stratos watch each other's blind sides on their own front. Their defensive position was a small shrinking fifty foot square, assaulted all around from demonic projectile magic, firearms, and other weapons of modern warfare. Assisted by a steady stream of knife wielding fanatics rushing headlong with bloodlust, sprinting at the troupe from all angles with no self-preservation left in them. The four frantically have to alternate between close quarter combat and sudden enemies at a range, attempting to snipe or blast them away. Lightning from the stormy sky flashing bright above now and again, lighting up the chaotic battlefield below.

"What's our strategy here? Losing ground and time is ticking," Saaliha comments, under duress of their attackers, of course, as the cult shows up in full force to defend the demonically corrupted *Cosmicism* monument.

"I need to get right on top of it. They have all the hypnotized people at the base of the monument. They're sacrificing them to power that thing. A little too late to hitch a ride from Minax, I think. You got a jetpack?" Cyngosa comically asks, trying to lighten up the predicament.

Saaliha lets out a single scoff as she finishes off a foe she is fighting to answer. "Nope, where do we concentrate?"

"I'll draw their fire. Let's finally end this nightmare. Follow my lead!" Stratos yells, taking a nervous inhale.

Stratos, with his chin held high, zig-zags from his position, running with strategic intent up toward the enemy. Cyngosa and the others follow Stratos while they continue to fight their way forward. Explosions and projectiles flying all around them, throwing up dirt and debris. Stratos dives into an enemy fortification, pinning an unaware cultist between him and a stack of sandbags, before disposing of his foe. Saaliha, Tidus, and Cyngosa aren't fat behind Stratos, as they're fending off assault after assault.

The corrupted spire looms closer over them now, almost imposingly so. The bloody, fiery energy emitting from its peak into the sky humming louder, almost audible over the other chaotic sounds. It was not much further, but the four find themselves in the middle of a horde of *Armageddon Cultists* straining their capabilities to simply advance, without death certainly guaranteed. The cultists have little regard for their own, throwing themselves with abandon into friendly fire and other unknown harms alike.

"It's at least another three hundred feet, maybe more," Tidus says, adjusting his service hat before releasing the last rounds of his ammo magazine and discarding the rifle altogether. "I can almost make out the folks hypnotized and captured. The entrenchment dips down, I reckon, a couple acres."

Nearby, Saaliha cuts and slashes wildly at multiple enemies in front of her, Stratos on her right side shooting down incoming foes from afar. "Say when. We'll move together!"

Unflinching as a burst of earth and rocks spray him from an explosion and throw him onto his back, Cyngosa grabs onto a metal ankh shaped like a lightning bolt from his belt and clenching it in his palm. "Cover me, and stay alive!" he yells, standing up and rushing onward suddenly, to the other's shock reactions.

Momentarily focused on fighting three enemies at once, Stratos barely notices Cyngosa charging toward the spire all by himself, despite facing yet one more fortified trench to the monument itself. "Whoa! Wait—" Stratos is interrupted, looking at and yelling after Cyngosa as he's struck off-balance by an enemy assailant.

To Cyngosa's advantage, the cultists didn't expect to see him simply running at them all crazy like, with a delay of surprise and lagging reaction. Cyngosa shoves and strikes his way through the horde, but his valiant dash ends in way less than a minute's time. Fear closing his throat in a gulp, Cyngosa gasps once as he's finally pressed and yanked down by a number of them now, before he's completely pulled down flat on the ground. Numerous cultists were going to stab him simultaneously with their corrupted knives, but Cyngosa thrust his paw up into the air, holding the ankh in the sky.

Stratos, Tidus, and Saaliha couldn't do much as they fought to survive in place. But a unique bright blue lightning bolt arcs down from the cloudy, rainy sky above the battlefield, dancing itself over the wiggling dog pile wrestling on top of Cyngosa rapidly. The lightning has a chain effect, zapping and leaping from one body to another before throwing an electrified throng of cultists right up into the air and tossing them away.

Cyngosa barely has time to get his bearings together before new attackers are already close in right on top of him. He blasts another enemy off their feet with a fireball before dropping the spent wooden totem on the wet muddy ground at his feet, on the move. Saaliha lets out a deadly purr, taking her bow out again. She leaps out of the besieged rut they were holding up in, over both Stratos and Tidus occupied with shooting at opposite flanks.

"Now guys!" Saaliha announces, releasing arrow after arrow loose into a cultist, each arrowhead emitting beeps before exploding, giving the two soldiers reprieve as their foes spread out.

Tidus and Stratos climb over the rut and onto the flat land, running in Saaliha's wake. Saaliha sprinting up to almost her full speed pounces instead, taking one cultist and the four grouped up behind it down. Drawing out her dual iridescent Khopesh swords again, she cuts at those around her in a valiant effort to keep her ground.

Perching over a dip in the ground, Cyngosa sees below what remained of the hypnotized crowd of *Silvium* citizens, his hopeful yet panic filled eyes picking out Khelu. Cyngosa kneels and jams the totem made of magical wood down and the uniquely carved markings in the wood shimmer.

Cyngosa hovers his paws in its proximity, channeling the direction of the powerful magic at the same time being shot at from enemies in unknown locations. Not stopping his magic spell's progress, as a bullet goes straight through his plate armor, he yelps out, fortunately still alive, after the hit.

Saaliha, Stratos, and Tidus do their best to protect Cyngosa during his efforts, but *Armageddon Cultists* soon increase their concentration solely on him. Saaliha fires six arrows in two quick volleys, Stratos himself reacting and, on alert, and closes in where Cyngosa is, shielding him with his own back facing the enemy. Stratos takes the heat, buying Cyngosa time as his unique totem's spell weaves into the grim air, casting away the eerie reddish fog with beams of light. Tidus wasn't far behind, arriving to help protect Cyngosa's other flank seconds after Stratos, skidding on his side in the wet muck, gunning down two enemies chasing him combined.

Cyngosa's *Ethereal Lattice* magic radiates a glittering mint green wafting aura over the masses that are still slowly shuffling toward the corrupted spire one at a time. Causing them all to stop in their tracks as the totem magic nullifies the hypnotic effects of the mind washing demon's curse.

"Almost...I think it's working! It's honing in on the obelisk. This'll take a sec." Another round rips through him and lurches him forward onto his knees. His spell crackles, almost sounding like electricity shorting out, but regains focus, not losing the magical channel.

"Oof, gahh! That stung, damnit" Stratos and Tidus their eyes forward, shooting consistently into the horde of cultists rushing in, but now both holding concern with raised ears and tail for Cyngosa, wounded but still fighting in the gloomy battle.

Changing tactics, Saaliha charges out into the mass of enemies, assisting in stemming the flow and creating chaos with whatever gadgets she has left, out of arrows and only two swords. Meanwhile, the outside of the ring has multiple tanks approaching, a number of blacked out off-road trucks weaving over the mutilated grounds surrounding the corrupted spire. Scores more militants free running, careful not to be run over, while charging at the three.

Cyngosa grits with a painful expression, shakily extending his paws as he continues his spell work, but then he, along with Stratos and Tidus, is abruptly thrown airborne. A whizzing fireball smashes the ground near all their feet without a chance to react. Stratos is flung forward along with Tidus in a splatter of mud. Cyngosa is sent falling down into the presence of the dazed *Silvium* citizens, oblivious to all of this mayhem conducting around them, still under the curse.

His special totem survives, the *Ethereal Lattice* landing nearby with a spray of dirt chunks and wet rocks on the ground. The arbor it was crafted from certainly proving its durability on this day. Cyngosa pushes himself up to his feet and clamors over to the totem, setting it straight up once again and recasting the incantation needed.

A dozen cultists spill over the hilly edge behind him presently, ready to mow Cyngosa down as his spell channels once more to break the corrupted magic. They are also sent flying through the air from a random explosion, Saaliha emerging through the fiery wake of it in an elegant pounce, finishing into a roll at Cyngosa's aide. She completes her acrobatics, coming up into an attacking pounce on the nearest, stumbling up enemy.

"Don't have much time left. That beam is stabilizing more," Cyngosa shouts, a hideous death knell fills the air, seemingly coming from nowhere. Following it is a crimson ring flashing out. The blazing ring harmlessly expands out from the monument and Cyngosa's squinting eyes grow wide, his jaw slacking in horror, witnessing the swirling reddish hole forging itself in the sky right above.

CHAPTER EIGHTEEN: The Darkest Black Hole, And The Brightest Star

NOXION LANDS WITH AN audible wet thud on the outskirts, dismissing the fighting nearby. He lifts his free claw up toward the spiraling red hole in the sky high above the *Cosmicism* monument. Clearing away all cloud cover, and exposing the moon, *Miasma* still eclipsed, a molten red light flares in Noxion's upraised claw while he tenses his extremities. Letting out a snarl as if physically exerting himself, tugging on something invisible, Noxion pulls his tensed arm back with a triumphant laugh.

Then, leering at Cyngosa Maelstrom, then at his cleansing totem with murderous intent painted on his visage, Noxion puffs his muscular chest out with razor blades protruding from it. He swings his twisted looking sword in his claw using his wrist, emitting a heavy whooshing sound as he's striding forward, gloating in a sadistically gravely tone. "You puny mortal insect. Give me your soul, I have much better use of itl—" He's cut off mid-sentence as a cluster of meteors from straight above pelt him, forcing him to lurch forward to the ground on his claws and knees, dropping his hideous two-handed sword in the outcome.

"Don't give up, we can still stop it!" Minax Bolide yells to Cyngosa. He soars in like a righteous bolt of lightning through the bleak rainy night, rushing forward to try and impale Noxion from behind after he was pelted by meteorites and left disoriented. The Demon Lord flings around to kick at him instead with a powerful obsidian hoof. Minax is instead knocked back by a snarling Noxion. Minax felt the air leave his lungs momentarily from the kick, but he remained upright after staggering with buckling knees and blurred vision.

"If you are this world's heroes, then there was never any hope for it," Noxion says, swirling his spear-tip tail glowing white hot behind him. He points up at the sky. "Behold, you have failed!"

Curving blades stretching from trembling tentacles dig at the dimensional membrane of the sky above them, a misshapen fleshy form protruding itself out of the pulsating red hole.

The presence of the Demon Lord made Saaliha, Tidus, and Stratos unnerved all of a sudden, but they took a brief glance at the twisting red mouth in the sky, uncertainty gnawing at each of them. Together they approach Noxion despite his magical hysteria effect on them. They have come this far, and this was all or nothing. Saaliha, fighting a growing panic attack induced by the spell, slashes at the taller demon's torso and legs with wild knee-jerk attacks with her serrated blades. Saaliha is still in cooperation with the two *Lycandian* soldiers unloading their assault weapons, all of it harmless against their mutual demonic foe. The dreadful feeling still weighs in on Tidus and Stratos with increasing anxiety, more adapted from training and experience to give in to the physical responses of Noxion's cursing aura.

Minax exchanging jabs and evading tactics with Noxion, keeping the barbarous demon occupied and away from his besieged friends,

Saaliha's iridescent swords merely scratching the demon with unsatisfactory results aside from a grotesque hissing, giving off a putrid sulfur smell.

"Our weapons might be useless against a demon this powerful!" Cyngosa shouts to his embattled friends, daringly he fixes the channeling spell from one paw, using the recently freed other to hurl a magical ice javelin and fireball at Noxion, discovering both having minimal impact either. "Even most of our magic!"

Attempting to aim her slicing and dicing higher under the duress, Saaliha's fur goes on end and her body feels like it's ablaze from some kind of invisible hellfire. Tumbling backward in agony, Saaliha's vision turns into a vivid delusion right before her panic-filled pink eyes, her mouth agape momentarily.

Everything and everyone around her suddenly vanishes from her view, except the ground and sky, still feeling the nip of cold. Spectral figures of her deceased family appear right on top of her as Saaliha writhes in pain. Her father, Adaros Moonwane, kneeled closer to her tauntingly. "Weak..." her father says, the ghostly face looking straight on.

"Can't even beat a lone demon. You always know how to fail spectacularly, little sister," teases the lucid phantom of Rhanisha, her haunting facial features twisting into a laugh, a laugh that even in her pain saturated stupor isn't familiar at all. Saaliha knew this wasn't real, but somehow that didn't matter or make sense.

"Stop!" Saaliha hisses in pain, while fluttering her regular eyes her mind's eye catches glimpses through her torment at what is really occurring, seeing herself in simultaneous reality writhing on the ground as well, but with other voices and mere blips of sound.

"Such a disappointment," says the apparition of her mother, Elith Moonwane, sneering at Saaliha, still suffering under Noxion's powerful spell work.

As Saaliha writhes about in madness, Tidus and Stratos cover her while a few ambitious marauders of the cult try killing her in her vulnerable state. Panic starting to crack on their faces, but holding steadfast.

"What do you reckon is wrong with her?" Tidus snarls, his chest noticeably heaving. Growling, Tidus sways his head. "Damn, everything's hurting now."

Stratos, having opaque images of his friend and service comrade Kruko, flash before his eyes, doesn't answer Tidus. Trying to keep his attention and focus, as even the crisp sounding voice of Kruko fills his head, deafening over the surrounding mayhem.

"Why? Why did you let me die back there, buddy?" Kruko's phantasm form asks, three *Armageddon Cultists* rushing carefree through him, as if he didn't exist. Stratos angrily shakes his head before viciously swiping his rifle across one of their masked faces.

"No!" Stratos defiantly howls, feeling every nerve in his body ache similar to Tidus's complaint. Kruko's ghost slips from his vision and reappears behind him as Stratos backtracks toward Saaliha. Stratos's rising anger fills him, but the demon's grief and unbridled rage attempts to twist it.

Tidus shaking in pain, finally earning them all a reprieve from attackers kneels three feet from Saaliha as she's getting a control of her senses again. He taps her shoulder.

"No, don't touch me !" Saaliha grips at her discarded swords before she leaps away, flinching away into a roll and bolts upright.

Tidus recoils while Saaliha leaps up. He clears his throat, pointing up at the sky momentarily, and yelling. "C'mon, let's get to shut that doomsday door."

From above, three fleshy blobs fall from the hellish ring in the sky hundreds of feet up, six limbs writhing outward flexing their three-foot long blades at the end of their hideous appendages, unknown to those fighting below.

Minax maintains the demon's attention in a heated close up sword fight. With this opportunity, Cyngosa returns his full attention to channeling the *Ethereal Lattice* totem to continue its purifying aura, with the others doubling their efforts at keeping bay the steady trickle of *Armageddon Cultists*. The tide eventually lessened further as the defeated enemies began to litter the ground profusely. Gulping audibly as one of the otherworldly horrors lands nearby, whirling itself up on its sharp limbs and scampering toward him, Cyngosa materializes his enchanted wooden staff into existence and prepares himself.

With the instincts of an insect, the fleshy monstrosity rushes up on Cyngosa, despite the shaman bashing it repeatedly with his staff one-handed. Eos descends with a shriek, and with an open beak spits a cone of fire on the freakish flesh demon from behind.

Minax Bolide hurls *Alpha and Omega* at an advancing tank from behind their attacking position on the demonic obelisk, neutralizing it upon impact despite its defense mechanisms in a fantastic bursting plume of sparks. Minax notices Cyngosa battling back a many-limbed hellish monster, and yet more enemies mobilize, moving to finish his friends off. With a swift pivot, his purple eyes lock in on Noxion and with a flash of iridescent light from them, Minax twists his empty claws toward the Demon Lord.

Streaking down from high in the crimson sky above them all, multiple fiery stars glowing white hot smash down on the *Armageddon Cultist* combatants, and utterly obliterating one of the fleshy demonic horrors in a gush of organic matter before it could reach Tidus. Six off-road armor plated pickup trucks that are now less than a couple hundred feet behind Tidus, Stratos, and Saaliha, moving forward in an attempt to aid Cyngosa, who is still wounded, and is keeping his cleansing ritual going. Minax's meteor shower brings a sense of relief over Cyngosa and the *Trinity*.

Other cultists are not as successful in the endeavor, becoming fiery airborne wrecks from Minax's star barrage, skidding out or flipping to a halt. Arcing from different angles, hissing through the rain, a great many of Minax's blazing stars only collide against the Demon Lord Noxion this time.

Consecutively hammering Noxion down, in a newly created crater in the rain soaked dirt beneath. In the immediate aftermath, the crater is ablaze with iridescent flames and radiating intense visible heat, providing a bright beacon in red dim night. Noxion Myriad slowly strides out of the colorful fiery and considerably deep crater, his presence cooling the flames and whisking them away whereas the rain could not, his vile weapon ready in one hand.

To the others, ignoring Minax, Noxion states, "I could make pincushions out of all of you, insects. But I want this to be entertaining!" He snaps the lengthy fingers of his free hand, generating an aura of ugly ink hued energy around it. Noxion Myriad whips his aglow hand outward, gazing at the mesmerized crowd. Minax, widening his wing-span and tensing up, goes to charge at the Demon Lord, but Noxion teleports out of thin air.

Cyngosa, Tidus, Saaliha, and Stratos witness the massive throng of slowly swaying, hypnotized captives abruptly twitch and tense up, then feeling a new icy dread sink in. Like a living hive mind, the crowd of tens of thousands rips their mystified gaze from the diabolical obelisk and instead stares directly at them. A half second later, the crowd stiffly surges forward with arms and paws reaching out, snarling like starving beasts in unison going absolutely feral. The horde of zombified citizens interested in Tidus, Stratos, and Saaliha fan out, meshing chaotically into the cultists forces. The *Ethereal*

Lattice totem in Cyngosa's possession wards off most of them, to the other's misfortune.

Crinkling noisily into existence again, Noxion unfurls his barbed wire encrusted wings and leaps airborne backward, now far behind where Minax currently is. Noxion Myriad, while cackling, aims his foul and potent demonic magic in the direction of a line of greenhouses and foggy crop fields a ways off on the far left of the mutilated city park, where the city starts to transitions to pitch black rural neighborhoods with only street lights on. The inky black magical energy slithers over the patches of bulbous orange pumpkins, the gourds instantly vibrating and uprooting themselves from the muddy ground all on their own accord. At least twenty pumpkins bloat up twice their 'natural' size, sinister and maniac faces burning themselves into the cursed plantlife with glimmering hellfire. The demonic squash army, carrying itself on countless writhing vines and roots, marching amassing across the street from the greenhouses, chittering audibly.

Minax swings in at Noxion while also in the same action countering-spelling a destructive projectile that is being thrown at Cyngosa's *Ethereal Lattice*, dissolving it instead in a shower of harmless orange sparkles. The Demon Lord offers Minax a sinister snicker as he parry's the *Starwielder's* cosmic weapon in a brief spray of sparks. Noxion then disengages from the battle for the corrupted spire whooshing off. Minax stays hovering in place, exhaling with unblinking eyes at his main opponent. Noxion isn't finished with the foolish mortals yet. Deciding that Minax proves to be more than a growing nuisance, wholly motivated by the *Starwielder's* destruction.

Noxion baits Minax to fight him with a taunting gesture. Minax begrudgingly goes on the attack, having to desert his besieged friends. Grimly and with an ache in his chest, he gives them a glance below. Surging forward through the rainy sky, Minax Bolide starts cleaving upward and downward with *Alpha and Omega* clenched in his tight-knuckled claws, growing in anger as smoke slithers from his nostrils. Pursuing Noxion, off into the stormy night air, fighting once again.

Saaliha's weary pink eyes surveyed the fresh hell awaiting them now. While finishing off a cultist, she utters sarcastically, "Ohh, how spectacular this is going to be." She notices the skittering horror of bewitched jack-o'-lanterns coming at them, including the Apocalypse Knights who emerge from the vehicles surviving Minax's barrage from above.

Each individual knight draws out to wield a fearsome-looking sword, an inky black aura and red glowing electricity buzzing off each of their blades. Donned in an intimidating combination of modern armor and steel plates, over their usual suspected *Armageddon Cult* robes. Tidus, Saaliha, and Stratos, while embattled with what lingers from the existing forces, observe the arrival of these new foes with calamitous apprehension on their faces.

"Oh no, you don't—" Stratos Cobaltfort gasps as he quickly reacts. Unfortunately, being the closest to the mob of hypnotized citizens, he's forced to jerk into motion. He grabs a cultist attempting to attack him by the chest, halving the distance remaining of their stab attempt, before Stratos headbutts them brutally and converts them as a living shield to separate himself. The crowd pushes against both of them.

Cyngosa continues channeling the exhaustive spell from the *Ethereal Lattice* totem, Eos flying in now again to ambush an enemy from above, with sharp beak, talons, and fire-breathing. Ten mint green rays of light now pierce outward from the *Ethereal Lattice* to hit the demonic crackling obelisk far away, over the swell of a huge zombified crowd coming to tear them apart limb by limb still. Lord Klaus Cravenfang walks nonchalantly amidst the crowd toward the second ring fortification, particularly in the direction of the stubborn and meddlesome shaman.

Stratos deploys two force shield devices nearby, shouting to Tidus and Saaliha, "These are my last, group up or get stampede to death. I don't know how strong those assholes are, but they look mean. Keep going, Cyngosa," he encourages him. Hope breaks through his normally stoic appearing war-face. He doubts Cyngosa could hear him over the action.

The *Armageddon Cultists* are hesitant to blow up their sacrificial cattle just yet, and are also caught up trying to reach the *Starwielder's* comrades to kill them by more optimal means, the cultists are too now engulfed in the brainwashed horde from one front and forced to shove their way through. The melee is tame, as nearly every victim of the cult had virtually no weapons and fought with little spirit in them, still dazed by the demonic spell; Stratos fend off effortless punches and kicks that slip through the shield.

Noxion's haunted pumpkin army is unstoppable, wiggling vines acting as spider legs propel the cackling fiends through the dazed crowd with frightening speed. Saaliha readies her swords, while a bright flash of lightning and a roar of thunder emits from above, crouching low on the attack on one of the scary squashes and dicing its limbs in a wicked spin-twist. Saaliha bounces off the shrieking monster, still attempting to snap at her feet, now pouncing down onto another to fatally attack it.

In the interim, Cyngosa, pinning his pierced ears to his head from the consistent pain that his wound emits, he yells, "It's ready." He pulls the totem up in one paw and sighs, we—" He stops and clears his throat. "No. I do. I need to get the *Ethereal Lattice* right against, or on, the obelisk!" His eyes hopelessly survey the throng before speaking directly to Eos. "Special airdrop delivery."

Eos now flies overhead with an acknowledging series of chirps, and Cyngosa tosses the charged special totem up into the air for the phoenix to catch mid-flight.

The cleansing magic has a calming effect on the possessed, like one would apply a special smoke to an agitated beehive. However, it did not break the trapped person free of the demonic spell completely. Hopelessly surrounded, the *Trinity* group and their *Aluan Marine* comrades wrestle with the still bewitched citizens on one side facing the corrupted monument, the full brunt of the cultists from the others. The sizable swarm of possessed pumpkin monsters facing Saaliha and Tidus, leaving Stratos shooting at the Knights and enemies all around as he finds it more logical to keep the overwhelming forces locked down by suppressive fire at this point in the fight.

The Apocalypse Knights strode their way to the actual fight, waving their paws at the dead and fallen close around them, slowly restoring them back to the land of the living. The repulsive, dark purple and red necromantic magical energy glimmering as it washes over the bodies, lifting them upright.

Stratos now maneuvers out and in front of the force shield device, Tidus and Saaliha are surviving their fight with the majority of the skittering squash horrors.

He anxiously glances back at Cyngosa with the *Ethereal Lattice*, twenty or so feet from him in the mess before him, his bloodshot blue eyes going wide. "Well, shit." Stratos scowls, discerning suddenly being engulfed in a sea of undead cultists, plus the tragic soul-drained citizens too late to rescue.

Eos, with a determined screech, soars straight for the obelisk, but soon must contend with cultists shooting rockets, ammunition, and magic at the phoenix. Eos executes swift rolls and dips through the air. Once reaching the corrupted obelisk drops from the air amidst the last line of enemy fighters, holding the totem with each set of talons gently, the phoenix places it against the demonically corrupted monument. The wooden totem absorbs into the stone as if it were a liquid, emitting a single magnificently bright emerald hued light ripple throughout the evil possessed structure.

The moment that the magical furrow finishes passing, the eldritch opening in the stormy sky above the corrupted monument closes up, cutting the hideous red beam off, the powerful aura radiating from diminishing. The radiant red hole in the sky piercing through dimensions shutters before flickering from existence, including the writhing limbs of an endless army of horrors from beyond. Eos twirls around on their journey back, turning their head side to side, trying to locate Cyngosa.

Cyngosa, prone on all fours on the wet gnarled up ground, stares up, wincing from his gunshot wound combined with the strenuous amount of energy the *Ethereal Lattice* demanded of him. For the first time, his enchanting birth scars are completely out, leaving just his hairless dark flesh exposed beneath. His face a victorious grin, the hypnotized masses halt momentarily around Cyngosa, and elsewhere with the ritual finally interrupted.

Then, a peculiar figure approaches from the docile horde of cultist captives, crushing Cyngosa's smirk and his turquoise eyes widened with a crashing wave of fear coming over his whole person. Klaus Cravenfang, raising his two handed scythe, speeds up his stride, a swagger in his gait.

In an adrenaline fueled reflex, Cyngosa rolls sideways as the edgy blade whips by where his kneeling head and torso was a second ago. He tugs on his assault rifle's leather strap in the same motion, coming up into a crouching position and opening fire at the backside of this new enemy without worry of hitting a dazed bystander. Cyngosa's rounds hit home with ease in such close range, against the impressive armor on their target's person, however the force behind each bullet still pushes Klaus off balance further.

Lord Cravenfang slides in the mud, turning to face Cyngosa. Still in the act of emptying his weapon's entire ammo magazine, Klaus hurls a cluster of shuriken stars that hum with electricity. Cyngosa, in turn, attempts to keep firing his gun and get out of the way, painfully yelping out upon being sliced by one of the flying razors, to his terror discovering it also applies a stunning electrical jolt once embedded. Cyngosa feels every muscle in his arms and torso seize, managing to keep his legs functioning, but his uncontrollably twitching fingers almost fumble his firearm out of his possession.

"Aww, out of magic? No charged up totems and ankhs left? It does not matter, you may have canceled out the corrupted spire's connection beyond our dimension. But this is just the beginning!" Klaus taunts, not bothering to hear any reply from Cyngosa, struggling to get upright from the shock as he charges again with his two-handed serrated scythe, sweeping wide across at his abdomen. Cyngosa is left with no time to reload his spent gold plated assault rifle and instead uses it to block the scythe.

Pushing into and forcing Lord Cravenfang's weapon toward the ground and trying to get in closer to him, his free paw reaches for a combat knife on his belt. Klaus turns his person in the opposite direction instead, then kicks his right leg at Cyngosa in a hard roundhouse, landing him near his golden rifle. With a couple of feet separating the two now, Cyngosa pounces onto his rifle and rolls to his back. The gun clicks noisily, with a sinking feeling forming in his gut. Instantly, Cyngosa frees the empty magazine out of his firearm, letting it fall away. Attempts to reach at his vest pocket for more ammo, unsurprisingly coming up short, given previous events. He lets out a painful, exhaling laugh, drawing the combat knife still holding his empty gun.

Klaus circles him slowly, now more apprehensive and aware of Cyngosa's competent combat potential, continuing to advance nonetheless. He sweeps his two handed scythe across from the right, then from the left with efficient speed, almost gashing Cyngosa's chest severely on the second swing. Instead, to Cyngosa's turn of fortune as he finches in reaction, the scythe only shreds his vest as it falls away.

Cyngosa only has on his body plates and his dark pine colored long sleeve shirt underneath now, his scarred up arms and shoulders visible to the naked eye. He flicks his ears down to his head, his tail swishes with agitation behind him while crouching.

"What. You think you're some hero?" Klaus, turning his person for half a second at the dazzled crowd, still recovering before facing Cyngosa once more.

"Nah, that's just my luck, though." Cyngosa scoffs, cracking his knuckles.

Klaus's snide voice rings across to Cyngosa. "No one gives a squirt of piss. Look around you, you die for nothing. This was but a tasting sample of what's coming, sub-breed. The *Armageddon Cult* has just started its true siege for this world." He lunges again with his scythe. Cyngosa slides forward, getting cut viciously but punching both of his knuckles into Klaus's knees, forcing him to tumble with a yelp.

Cyngosa cries out, feeling warm blood running down across his body. He doesn't bother to even look at how bad. It was oddly refreshing over his pre-existing bullet wounds ache. Klaus rolls up to his feet, a murderous chuckle escaping him.

A buzzing sound emits itself. Klaus and Cyngosa hear it over their heated fight. They each avert their gaze from one another for only a couple seconds as the noise reaches a high pitch. A sizable remote control monster truck races right at Klaus, recognizing the danger for what it is.

"What the—" He attempts to scamper backward, while swiping his scythe at it but too late. Klaus and Cyngosa are thrown to the ground, Klaus taking the absolute brunt of the explosion as the toy monster truck vanishes six feet from them in a loud boom. Klaus is first to recuperate, smoke rising off his body with significant damage done to his *Crowclaw Armaments* body-armor.

Saaliha Moonwane sprints over the brim, wielding her swords set to emit flames from their iridescent serrated edges, with a hunter's yowl coming from her mouth, baring her feline fangs with her eyes wide, short hair blowing crazily.

Swirling his scythe around, Klaus cackles and sweeps at Saaliha. Forced to drop herself into a heel-driven slide, Saaliha's flaming blades clang noisily against the scythe over her head. Writhing her wrists, Saaliha works the curvature of his blades to hook the staff portion of Klaus's weapon, attempting to yank it free while her leg lashes out.

Klaus matches Saaliha's kick by throwing his armor shin up to stop her, summoning all the strength in his arms to maintain hold of his scythe from the tricky and agile cheetah. Saaliha lets out one painful gasp, then another as Klaus butts the end of his staff against her forehead.

"We're done here. But this isn't over," Klaus snaps at Saaliha. He backtracks in his steps to put some space between them, before desperately reaching at his belt. Before Saaliha could get her wits and focus together, Klaus retrieves a jagged piece of inky colored crystal from his person; she tries to leap at him this time but he explodes in a cloud of slithering fog with a painful gasp.

Seeing her cowardly foe gone, Saaliha whips her attention to Cyngosa, softening her expression from a fierce visage of battle to a look of teary-eyed concern, and a pout to her lips. She kneels down and grabs hold of Cyngosa, finding him laying on his back, and breathing heavily.

"You saved me. You came back for me," Cyngosa says weakly. His eyelids flutter shut, becoming motionless as his head leaning against her.

"You bet I did. I will be so pissed off if you die on me now," Saaliha replies with a tone of determination. She glances up, taking notice of Stratos and Tidus, closing in hurriedly.

Noxion backhands Minax with a clenched obsidian metal gauntleted fist, before punching him straight on once again directly in the face. Minax falters only briefly in the air, mustering himself now bloodied up. Corkscrewing through the foggy red air, Minax drills *Alpha and Omega* into Noxion and impales the Demon Lord again, and then again. He kicks into him repetitively before breaking away in a back flip and pumping his wings to put distance between himself and the now disoriented demon.

Noxion lets out a metallic echoey cackle from his open snarling snout, soaring after Minax, ready to strike. The two exchange deflections with their weapons, and tumble through the air as a flash of lightning brightens up the gloomy red rainy sky, with a boom of thunder over the intense fighting. Noxion's barb wired wings flapping wildly as he barrels into Minax, tackling him and following it up with casting a demonic spell.

The *Starwielder* pulls himself upright in the air, desperately blocking Noxion's hellish two-handed sword many times. Minax is sent flailing back through the air, crashing through a wide stain-glass window depicting the *Ten Truths* of *Cosmicism*. He rolls uncontrollably and devastatingly through the pews within the familiar empty church.

Groaning in agony, he shakingly rises to his feet again, from the smooth stone floor amongst the pile of wood splinters. The face of the building is blown away into fiery debris, knocking Minax on his backside, as Noxion descends in an intimidating fashion, with his barbed wire wings outstretched.

"Your all mighty Creator has no power here! Your friends have either died by now, or abandoned you...This is almost too pathetic to endure." Noxion lets a diabolical chuckling goat's bleat before scoffing. "Almost."

Noxion raises his fiendish claws out, creating a cluster of pulsating purple and black orbs of energy. He then unleashes this unholy barrage downward, the projectiles hone in on Minax like heat seeking rockets. Minax fruitlessly tries to roll out of the way, being painfully singed and stung by the magic missiles.

The opposite end of the church building explodes outward into the parking lot, with Minax flailing through it all as he attempts to take flight, on a severely re-wounded wing, but ultimately crash landing. Noxion pursues the stumbling *Starwielder*, leaving everything in flames in his wake as he also ignites the entire lot in an inferno, with an impish expression of glee.

Noxion, less than twenty feet away from Minax now, suddenly experiences the bite of *Alpha and Omega* as the powerful *Starwielder* weapon materializes between the two of them. Noxion impales himself, but barrels onward nonetheless, not even losing speed in the act. Minax grabs hold of his cosmic weapon, the pair flying down toward the ground now, struggling with difficulty to evade Noxion's trashing and pressing weight.

They land once more on the ground somewhere in *Silvium*, disjointly separating before immediately resuming the fighting, surrounded by the presence of towering buildings once more in the crowded city, including hundreds of *Armageddon Cultists* as well. Noxion relishes it with a metallic cackle.

"You have failed, *Starwielder*. I am victorious, and Eradicator will surely bless me as the champion slayer of this world!" The whole time, *Alpha and Omega* sizzles noisily at his demonic physique, as it is still punctured in his torso. Noxion, finally shocking himself painfully in the process, dislodges and throws *Alpha and Omega* at Minax, letting it bounce with several clanks on the asphalt street, before it stops to lay a couple feet from where Minax stands this moment.

Minax shakily raises his claws up to the sky and channels a white light that expels from his person. Originating from his palms and the gemstone encrusted in his chest, soon his entire body becomes completely white hot. As Noxion responds, a brilliant iridescent and white beam flares straight up into the sky. Simultaneously, a bright sonic boom brushes him and the cultists with a single tempest, disorienting two of the cultists' aircraft hovering around. Vaporizing the rain all around him, including throughout the sky, Minax manages to disintegrate the redness in the clouds and reveal brilliant iridescent colors glimmering down from a hole in the cloud masses. The *Starwielder* squints at the dastardly demon with a confident glint in his purple eyes, before closing them and praying.

"You're correct, on my own I have failed, but all is not lost yet!" Minax Bolide screams out, gazing with a trembling chin straight up into the sky.

Unexpectedly, an immense spout of clear water pours down just from the wide illuminated hole searing its way through the still angry cloud masses high above. Consuming Minax as it washes everywhere in a thunderous roar. The sheer amount of water, in seconds, has the streets of *Silvium* flooding in three feet or more of water, and rising as the spout continues like a giant faucet.

Thousands of cultists now swim, being dislodged by the strong flood current as some snag onto streetlight poles and automobiles or attempt to get inside buildings. Minax lifts higher into the sky inside the spout, unaffected by the unfathomable force of the water pouring directly on him.

With a guttural bleat, Noxion bursts out of the raging flood waters and soaring furiously toward Minax, four cultists nearby to the Demon Lord bail out of their tank as the water continues rising higher still, filling the personnel cabin. Noxion Myriad continues shrinking his distance to the spout, that is until a tornado drops out of the sky directly in his flight path.

"No!" he howls fruitlessly against the gale it brings with it, sending the Demon Lord sideways in the powerful wind, tumbling like a rag doll headfirst into a capsized car's front end as it floats along the street, smashing loudly and crushing halfway through it.

All across *Silvium*, multiple tornadoes cascade down on the city with annihilating strength from the gray and black stormy heavens, accompanied by hundreds of lightning bolts zapping madly as a brightly lit introduction to the cyclone's terrifying arrival. The cyclones, in complete formation, begin ripping up debris, such as existing rubble, abandoned vehicles, or trash and leaving the city's numerous structures unaffected first.

The *Armageddon Cultists* standing army throughout *Silvium*, including those still assaulting Minax's friends stranded at the spire's high ground this very moment, discover to their horror these storms will primarily affect only their forces, with merciless zephyrs twisting, howling everywhere.

Stratos, Tidus, and Saaliha are huddled with Cyngosa, who is now fighting to stay conscious from his injuries, with Eos perching close to his head for shelter. Khelu, exhausted and wounded, lies on her side, staring up at the frenetic sky of black and gray storm clouds. All bear witness to the extraordinary supernatural weather events unfolding before them.

Two of the many twisting cyclones wind their way close to the recently disenchanted spire, pulling numerous panicking and flailing enemies straight up into the turbulent skies. Leaving the stunned, dismayed citizens remaining completely untouched loitering around the *Cosmicism* monument all the while.

These tornados make swift, obliterating work of any helicopters and jets remaining, including anything making a desperate escape effort, but ultimately being thwarted as chaos takes over the skies above *Silvium*. Conveniently for *Trinity's* newest cadets and the rogue *Aluan Marines* huddling in place, the brunt of the cultists forces had closed in on Minax and the corrupted spire prior to whatever supreme sorcery the *Starwielder* is currently unleashing before them.

"Creator have mercy, keep down and stay put!" Stratos tries to be heard over the howling gusts, Sidra and Vivian in his embrace, both of whom are petrified in fear. But miraculously only being buffered by the whirlwind as their feet remain firmly on the wet ground.

Saaliha's pink eyes widen with astonishment on her face as her whiskers ripple in the wild breeze along with her feline tail and colorful short hair, never seeing such awesome weather forces. She sees the decimating floodwaters bogging up the tanks, trucks, and artillery equipment of their foes all around them, and yet left the small plot of muddy battle-scarred ground they hunkered down on alone. Tidus watches in shock and awe, his jaw slacking while prone on his stomach and propping himself up on his elbows as the flurry of fiery debris and aircraft wrecks whip by. Anything smaller than those objects couldn't be seen by the naked eye, being carried at the terrifying speed by the twisters.

The pulverizing flood waters continue rising to twelve feet deep now, sweeping the streets with a loud gurgling surge. The combination of multiple extreme weather forces ultimately paralyzes the *Armageddon Cult's* army. The massive waterspout concludes and Minax, exhaustively exhaling, sinks toward the ground, unaware of the level of turbulent water residing on top of it. Minax flutters his scaly eyelids open and twitches his whole body, as if waking from a nap, taking a moment to gather his surroundings.

Concerned about his injured wing, he couldn't stay airborne for long. The antigravitation magic sustaining him was starting to fade. Before he can even finish reaching for the *Macrocosmic Lexicon* slinging by its chain on his girdle, Minax is struck by a silver car with its front already destroyed. Together with the sedan, Minax crashes into a flooded building behind him.

Flexing out his tattered-up and barbed-wire-infused-wings, wounded and cut up all over his demonic physique, Noxion approaches Minax yet again. Despite the smashed metal portions of his body, and punctures to his chest, Noxion is flying in a smug-looking descent slowly, showing no concern of the twisters roaming the city. Inside, Minax strains himself up to his feet, disjointedly finding himself now waist-deep in the floodwaters pouring in from outside the revolving glass door he crashed through. He wobbles forward, regaining balance with a look of determination on his face, defiant of the fear coursing through him, the new and old wounds agitated. Minax winces, facing Noxion.

"Is all lost now, *Starwielder*?" Noxion Myriad taunts Minax, admiring the increasing disaster all around with broad shoulders and a chin held high.

Coughing, tasting metallic wetness, Minax turns his horned head to the side, spitting blood out and smirking confidently at the Demon Lord. Minax swiftly opens *The Macrocosm Lexicon*, exhaling. "Nope, never. Drastic measures. For dire situations!" Sensing defeat imminent, he channels his *Starwielder* power through the *Macrocosm Lexicon*, a black tab marking a special spell he studied up on during the night in *Solstice Keep*.

A miniature black hole forms in the sky, tugging the numerous cyclones up and inverting them. The violent winds shift direction toward it as well. Noxion, fighting the tug of the gusts, raises his hideously jagged two-handed sword to behead Minax but loses ground. The mammoth forces overtaking the Demon Lord as he, entire portions of *Silvium* and the battered remains of the cult army, are all vacuumed into the pitch black void, hallowed by blinding white light.

The black hole remains for less than a full minute before it disappears, leaving the city leveled in its wake.

Minax Bolide, his *Starwielder* armor crunched all over and still catching glints of the morning sun on it, bloodied and bruised, limps forward adamantly with his sore feet within his metal boots shuffling against the ruin. Falling to his knees and claws as the sunlight above combined with the illuminated multitudes of stars from galaxies far beyond the planet's positioning. Minax exhales loudly and painfully groans, wincing beneath the glimmering lights brilliantly shining through the fast fading clouds. His broken wings cling to his body as he exhales and inhales with a triumphant chuckle while his breath is visible in the chilly air, grimacing in pain.

Minax, feeling his body overcome with exhaustion, whispers with wide purple eyes staring up into the milky galaxy. "Glory goes to The Creator. As a stalwart servant I upheld my duty, the demon and his shadow army are undone, completely." Minax inhales before exhaling with a slight ragged sound.

Minax felt all time and space around him slow to a halt, a lustrous pearly white beam of light cast down onto Minax. As if it were a heavenly stage spotlight. Minax slowly floats up, not of his own accord, into the air before an abrupt flash travels down the light beam and crashes into Minax's body in a vibrant color burst. Feeling intense warmth spill through his aching injured body, Minax closes his eyes, savoring it before he is slowly lowered to the damp cold ground.

Time resumes its normal passing once again, as Khelu, Stratos, and the others approach Minax, laying motionless. Saaliha and Tidus carrying Cyngosa.

CHAPTER NINETEEN: Treading Along The Tightrope Of Destiny

MINAX OPENS HIS PURPLE eyes and discovers himself on his back in a large bed propped up on two mattresses, his body frame and wings too large for any other. He discovers his armor had been taken off sometime after blacking out. Now his scaly torso is strewn with medical tape and gauze, however Minax is feeling rejuvenated enough to propel himself upward in bed. His legs and arms feeling sore and stiff, and the painful throb of healing injuries all over makes Minax groan quietly, inhaling the odorless air.

A quick survey of the room he was apparently laying in recovery and he finds *The Starwielder* armor laying on a table nearby, shrunken down but still visibly damaged in the aftermath of Minax's battle with the Demon Lord. His eyes widen. Taking notice of Cyngosa in a smaller bed nearby, Minax scans the rest of the room and guesses it must belong to a hospital, spotting a gurney against the white wall across from him.

Cyngosa silently observes some of the currently healing injuries Minax has and comments, in a sympathetic tone intending to lighten the mood, "Now you have some scars like me," Cyngosa says while he observes some of the bandaged up injuries Minax has, "but those are inflicted from a powerful demonic weapon. I'm impressed that the foul magical energy didn't infect you."

"Oh, trust me, Cyngosa, it felt like fire in my veins. An evil venom, the aura. I was fighting for my life, externally, internally." He takes a brief pause to gulp and exhale. "Even spiritually."

"Dude. I don't have words to express right now how happy I am to see you alive, Minax. Since reuniting, I didn't get the best opportunity to apologize to you, parted bitterly at the castle. I should have taken diplomatic action when I could have. Some sober thinking and time, stubbornness, and anger overtook me then," Cyngosa admits to Minax, ducking his head in a humbled bow.

Minax grins warmly, looking over at him. His pupilless eyes did have an inner glow to them. "The totem was a brilliant, selfless act, Cyngosa. Quite impressed and proud of you for that. We still have much to learn. Apologies are not needed anymore for what's behind us. To err is mortal, to forgive is divine."

The two fist bump and grin at one another as Cyngosa says to the *Starwielder*, "I have my moments." He grimaces from his healing injuries.

"I don't think I've ever had a *Lycandian* best friend in my life before reawakening. You'd be the first. You make frustrating life choices, overly headstrong sometimes," Minax says, putting his right claw over the gemstone in his chest cavity, near his heart.

"Thank you."

Cyngosa and Minax are now out of their beds and reuniting with the others in the sunshine and daylight outside a small medical clinic building on the remote edge of the ruins of *Silvium*, in a debris strewn plaza. Disaster and relief efforts are underway throughout *Silvium*, the *Trinity* group going unnoticed.

The welcoming warm rays hitting their bodies bring on an invigorating feeling, after spending days under cloud and rainfall with a breath of fresh air. Cyngosa especially takes delight as he lifts his head up and closes his eyes, taking a second to bask.

Khelu lays eyes on Cyngosa, and with elation she charges at him from her stationary spot, leaning against an upside down school bus. She attempts to carefully hug him, as the others watch on walking over. Cyngosa returns the embrace with an overwhelming sense of gratitude washing over him. He couldn't hold back the few tears dripping their way out of his eyes after releasing Khelu from their hug. "I never leave family behind." Cyngosa gives a genuine smile to her.

"Bro, Minax and Saaliha filled me in on some of the wild shit that happened," Khelu says to Cyngosa, her face beaming with happiness.

Stratos, Tidus, and Saaliha approach them now, the two soldiers giving Cyngosa smirking expressions of approval on their faces and delivering soft punches to his shoulders. "Hell yeah brother! You did good," Tidus says, in a rare fashion providing Cyngosa a compliment

"Glad you're awake cupcake, we rushed out as soon as that unnatural storm passed, including Minax's black hole in the sky," Stratos says to Cyngosa, darting his blue eyes over in Minax's direction and giving the *Starwielder* an unrestrained grin, knowing him to be the creator responsible for these forces. Stratos Cobaltfort speaks at Minax with an appreciation in his tone.

"The area around the *Cosmicism Decagon Monument* was shielded by this liquid light. Best I can describe it. The survivors witnessed all of this, by the way," Saaliha says, looking at Cyngosa with lingering bewilderment on her face, "we picked your unconscious ass up and took one of the bad guy's vehicles, and bailed."

"Minax wasn't too far. There was this single iridescent light casting down over him. Eos helped too by hovering over where he was just laying there. We assumed the worst, but you still had a heartbeat."

"You all survived. Your family's safe. We saved who we could and defeated the *Cult*," Minax states warmly.

"If you two are ready. We need to get on the move before relief efforts find us. There were people who watched us escape from the monument afterward," Stratos says, gesturing the way to go with a jerk of his head. Everyone meanders carefully over the scattered rubble, giving off a soggy wooden smell.

Minax and Cyngosa nod, walking with him cautiously off to the side of the debris-strewn parking lot.

Stratos enters where they are and says, "I secured us an escape craft. We can fly south east toward *Edon*. I'm dropping my wife and daughter off with some trustworthy friends on the way."

"Are you two continuing with us? It sounds like you are to me at least," Minax Bolide asks Stratos. Minax fails to hide his eagerness. During the first meeting up in *Aluan* and battling their enemies, he has since built a kindling comradery with Stratos and Tidus.

"Indeed, it's personal now. And Me and Lieutenant General Tidus are still actively wanted fugitives by the *Aluan Federal Government*. So I will be acting on my own orders to clear our names," Stratos explains to Minax.

"Fugitives. Funny feeling, isn't it?" Cyngosa looks up, offering the two *Aluan* servicemen a playful expression and shrugging a shoulder.

"Not particularly, man. I reckon it sucks," Tidus says matter-of-factly to Cyngosa before glancing at Stratos and crossing his arms.

"We'll clear our names, on principle," Stratos says to Cyngosa, looking around at the others as he adds, "We'll have to chart a course across the ocean, or refuel for sure. There's no way we can board an aircraft, or fly one unnoticed on a single trip."

"I have a trustworthy relative to hide Sidra and Vivian. In the meantime, we'll be taking two separate aircraft once we're out of *Wulftheon*," Tidus says.

Zane walks along the concrete slipway, flicking his wide-brimmed leather hat up with his thumb, while a smirk curls on his scarred face, seeing a familiar speed-boat parked in the elegant marina. *Port Liekos* has an abundant amount of piers, without crowding its pristine black sandy beaches. This particular marina has other fishing boats and motor craft parked up, but nothing quite like this. The speed-boat has armor plating on every face, with a Plexi-glass windshield. Under the shade of a cluster of palm trees, three *Felidaens* are spotted sitting on the boat, out of the salty smelling, muggy sunlight. A different *Felidaen*—another tiger—comes up, and jumps feet first into the shallow, crystal clear water, only coming up a couple feet.

"Aye, boss. We're ready," the tiger says, wearing an unbuttoned light blue shirt with purple lotus flowers imprinted, upon closer inspection the tiger also wears a bullet-proof vest underneath. Zane the whole while is still closing the distance to the boat, slowing down to kick his leather boots off, and carry them by a couple claws in one paw, and entering the water barefoot. Zane, his brows rising over the gold lenses of his aviator sunglasses, exchanges a tight handshake with the tiger, the two coming close to bump one another.

"I appreciate the pickup, my mates. Let's get to the cove, then rally up with the rest. We're setting the whole fleet off to *Xarus*."

The tiger crewman and Zane unceremoniously stroll through the warm water and coarse rocks on the ocean floor underneath his bare feet, then climbing on board where Zane is greeted respectfully by the other crew. The speed-boat operator gasses up the idling motor, and they sail out of the narrow marina into open water, leaving the coastal megacity on the horizon behind.

The speed-boat banks left and keeps the coastline of *Edon* in sight, passing emerging rock formations featuring rotted old shipwrecks, some overgrown with plantlife. Returning inland toward a miniscule craggy cove with no beach, where over twenty boats of similar design, the one Zane rode in idle in the water or were docked up along one of the weathered wood landings. Zane keeps his hat tied to his head tightly, as the brim bounces wildly from the briny wind, his boat closing in quickly to the others.

Zane keeps one foot up on the rim of the speed-boats port side, as it slows down, leaping right on the rickety wooden dock before the boat completes its stop, and walking with swagger along. The couple dozen pirates on land eagerly move toward Zane, seeing him approach, combat boots thumping on the damp tropical grasses. A few remove their sunglasses, all of them bow their heads to him, Zane in return offering them a genuine grin, and gestures for them to go at-ease.

He brushes his whiskers. "The *Golden Skull Buccaneers* have a new contract with *Crowclaw Conglomerates*. Inform the other sub-captains, the rest of the fleet will assemble here in Emerald Cove, then we'll probably be sailing for *Xarus* in a couple days."

CHAPTER TWENTY: Tranquility's Endurance

VERIDIAN DRIFTS OVER, CAUTIOUS of the rocks lurking just beneath as he bobs up and down on the ocean's sapphire surface, the fuel tank of his hijacked jet ski from the cultists was essentially empty, in the settling sunlight Veridian's eyes can clearly make out the tiny arrow hanging damningly over the E, inhaling the salty smelling and tasting air, then exhaling with a sigh. Near to him is a towering pillar of stone, earth, and tropical foliage. A dozen similar natural formations dotted the coastline area he stops his escape effort at. The fleeing *Trinity* commando had no choice in the matter.

Hidden from view by unwanted onlookers from some of the fishing schooners nearby, amongst the geological spears reaching hundreds or thousands of feet in height, Veridian feels a sense of gratitude resting over his shoulders like a comforting invisible touch. More importantly to Veridian, presently floating on the tide toward the city-like marina built along and up one of the landmasses at slow speed, is the probability of having a superior satellite signal for his phone and electricity, now low on battery power.

Dusk settles over the region, slowly darkening the pinks and oranges in the sky like a bleeding inkwell. He still maintains hopes of reaching out to Kerith Moonwane with his critical update. The marina has eight docks that Veridian can make out from his current point of view, including multiple piers, with some stacking two stories tall. Once the jet ski bounces upon the tide, bringing Veridian close enough to one of the wooden structures, he climbs off the jet ski into the illuminated dock. He walks inland, passing a couple fisherman catching whatever nocturnal specimens would bite while sipping from a bottle.

The *Felidaen*, next to the first fisherman, slowly reels their line in to pull a bulbous fish out with shiny teal scales. Veridian strolls unsuspectingly from the dock to the dirt and rock area where four docks converge. He looks up to see a roadway leading further into this marina city he's stranded in. Overhead, street lights blink on as night descends completely. The sound of crickets and frog croaks could be heard between the densely packed stone and wood square and circular structures. Veridian noticed all the roofs are flat, and made of a bronze colored tin.

The phone dial rings while the lion *Trinity* commando abandons the jet ski at the dock heading in the direction of a large, mostly deserted plaza. Except for some preoccupied *Felidaen* chefs with their grills, minding only their business with a few lingering patrons standing in line. Self-aware he is still donning his armor identifying him, he keeps subtle and speaks to no one else, Veridian dismisses the hungry grumbling in his gut, smelling the lemony seared fish.

Kerith's voice answers Veridian almost the second the call connects."Finally, I thought you died out there or something happened." Veridian can hear the relief in Kerith's tone through the receiver, passing one of the chefs, rapidly slicing a bundle of seaweed on a cutting board.

"Heh, no. Just had to take a lengthy detour, I was ambushed by some unwelcome visitors." Veridian inhales the warm sea air carrying on it a hint of the tide, replying on the exhale. "I'm in some mega marina, likely off the coast of eastern *Xarus*, by the cultural decor I'm seeing. I wouldn't know the exact name."

"I had someone who claims they are traveling with the *Starwielder*, and is a *Trinity* operative. They reached me by Dorrion Chrisbane's own personal phone number. They have it because he died in action. This is all occurring in the northern central part of *Lycandia*," Kerith explains over the phone. Veridian is attentive to the conversation but also keeping his eyes and ears elsewhere.

"Wow." He screws his face up momentarily. Not recognizing the region, Kerith says, "Sounds like they are very far away. I can't reach their cellphone network. Give these individuals with the *Starwielder* coordinates to a rural coastal wetland area, known as *Brackish Bay*. It's also off the coast of *Xarus*, however I'm currently a thousand or maybe more miles from that side. Together we'll unite and converge there, have them get in touch once they can get connected to *Perilith's* satellites."

"Understood," Kerith replies confidently, then adds more humbly, "I wish them the best and hope they've made it out. Whatever the magic causing the eclipse originated from, is where they're at."

"So, that is what was making the sky that odd color? I had no idea an eclipse was occurring. Anyway, information from this Daxil person's email you provided me is legitimate. There is, in fact, an *Armageddon Cultist* complex."

Veridian continues instructing Kerith through the call, keeping his attention behind him while two jet skis ride up, arriving at one of the marina docks. The *Trinity Of Tranquility* commando waltzes his way on to a new street between two vendor fronts, offering vibrant porcelain cupboard ware, colorful woven quilts and crafted driftwood baskets. His ears pick up the noise emitting from a tavern not far now while Veridian's feet continue strolling the solid land of the island. The mega marina uses the island as a natural anchoring point. With a better vantage, Veridian could see dozens of piers branching toward another neighboring island close by, gleaming colorfully in the night from lighting, TV screens, and firepits.

The citrusy aroma is potent enough to sour Veridian's taste buds without ever taking an actual sip. He stops mid-stride, his tail shooting up right behind him.

"I'll try contacting you again after I charge up my device," Veridian tells Kerith.

"Understood. I'll give them a message," Kerith replies, before the conversation continues further, Veridian hangs up, the phone giving him an annoying battery alert. He grumbles, aggravated, and moves in the direction of the well lit and heavily occupied tavern.

Kerith, flicking his whiskers while glancing excitedly at Glyph seated next to him "We're going to meet up. I'm going to text the location to Cyngosa's phone now."

Glyph nods, scratching his plump right cheek with his fingers adorned with peculiar rings. Each ring has one stone of every primary and secondary color per finger, saying. "*Brackish Bay*, in *Xarus*. Ironically, this Veridian guy is saying those other folks are far away, but like he's almost three countries away from us himself." The *Sarosian* Sphinx gave an amused chuckle, adding jokingly, "Should I start looking for some economy flight tickets?"

"No, no. Evidently, this adventure of ours is bringing us very far from home, my dude," Kerith Moonwane comments heavily, but with a smile. Kerith grabs his backpack up by one of its straps and swings it over his back, looking at Glyph with a smile.

"Cool, so off to *Xarus* we go," Glyph says, compressing up his gear into his bag. Side by side, Kerith and Glyph rise out of the decrepit *Trinity* hideout into clear night, greatly enjoying the fresher air, moving back toward the city of *Vudazak*.

Seated in the apprehended SUV from the cult's militia forces, Cyngosa is with Saaliha, and Khelu closely pressed in the back seat, leaving Strato's wife and daughter seated with Tidus in the middle, a giant uprooted stop sign is lodged through the windshield and partially impaling through the front passenger seat. Minax hitches a ride holding onto the back, standing almost as tall as the vehicle if his feet were flat on the ground, holding onto the roof rack with one claw and the other hanging sideways, keeping as a watchful sentinel on their bumpy drive.

"There's an airfield nearby, by that satellite dish. It might have something we can work with. Just to escape *Wulftheon*, maybe even make it across the border near *Aluan* and get Sidra and Vivian into hiding," Stratos says, turning the steering wheel rapidly crashing through trash and rubble bits on the mutilated roadway, avoiding the larger hazards. Until rolling past the last cluttered, disheveled cul-de-sac, the roadway clears itself of obstructions. The asphalt is cracked and splintering, but improves in quality once reaching altitude and distance from the epicenter.

"Reaching *Port Liekos* from all the way up here, think it's possible?" Cyngosa asks Stratos while bouncing up and down in the seat, as the vehicle banks a hard left turn onto a dirt road. He feels a sudden tightness in his gut recognizing the evergreens on either side and the roadway, a recollection of the drive up when in the presence of the police he Khelu teamed up with.

"Very possible, but I reckon it'll take us time," Tidus says, catching sight of the torched ruins of the array building and general ground around it, letting out a whistle between his lips in dismay.

"Yeah, this was where things definitely went south for sure, for me and Cyngosa," Khelu comments, not lingering her gaze. Outside, holding onto the roof rack of the vehicle still, Minax looks solemnly at the scenery of destruction. The blackened beams, scorched concrete and ash are all that remain, the charred scent catching his nose.

"The actual laser weapon itself is in space, huh? Does it need to be close to dishes to work properly?" Minax asks into the SUV cabin from the partially opened rear window.

"I don't know. Never found that detail out," Cyngosa says forlornly, still packed in with the others, craning his neck back to speak directly at Minax, through the window.

Stratos doesn't slow down as he drives over the torched, charcoal colored ground, returning to and following the worn dirt road to the airfield many thousands of feet away. The continuous clicking and crumbling of the little rocks being kicked up against the SUV. The massive satellite dish sits completely stationary on the snowy ledge overlooking the burned away array building, as if awaiting to find a signal, or receive a command. The narrow road crests alongside the summit before leading out to a sprawling smooth plateau.

Stratos presses the brakes and slows down on a bumpy patch of ground. Once at a halt, they all exit eagerly into the fresh mountain air. Cyngosa and Khelu stretching their arms and legs, and twisting themselves. Vivian, still shy amidst a sudden group of strangers, stays beside Sidra. Minax slides off the roof, making a metal on metal scraping sound before his feet hit the dirt.

"If we have the coordinates and location of this *Armageddon Cultist* hideout in *Perilith*. We should meet with Glyph and Kerith," Minax says, glancing around at the carpet of evergreens blanketing the mountainous scenic area before looking head on at the aircraft hangar.

"Yeah, it'll take us a couple days to reach the coast. Then flying across the ocean? Wonder what Saaliha's brother must be like?" Khelu asks, walking next to Saaliha and Cyngosa.

"Heh, extremely unhinged, like her," Cyngosa suggests, playfully throwing Saaliha a smirk with a raised eyebrow.

Saaliha, in kind, offers a giggle and shrug of her right shoulder. "Yes. But with the addition of magical gifts, and an obsessive knack for sleuthing where he shouldn't."

"I doubt we wouldn't have enough fuel to make that whole journey. We could cross by boat too," Tidus says, jostling his bag over his shoulders and following alongside the others toward the hangar. The metal structure is overgrown on its backside, facing the forest. Parts of its roof and sides feature many rust spots where the cherry red paint rotted away. No vehicles are left around outside, only a pile of old wooden pallets and barrels of junk. Stratos, Tidus, and Cyngosa are first to poke inside the hangars wide bay, discovering a helicopter. Another similar aircraft sat next to it, partially covered under a dirty blue tarp.

"I'll bring over the SUV. Grab the thickest chains you can find," Stratos says, smiling confidently to Cyngosa and Khelu. By now, Saaliha is opening the door to the pilot seat and inspecting it, she says. "Keys shouldn't be an issue if you can't find them."

Tidus speaks to Saaliha, chuckling. "What, you going to hot-wire it? Does that flying metal death-trap even have fuel?"

Veridian enters the tavern, only succeeding in getting a few of the closest patrons to ignore him as he walks through being washed over with the ambiance of different voices. The sharp alcoholic scent wafting more frequently while he steps past crowded tables, some abuzz with dice games and cards. Those that take a glance at the newcomer hardly linger their attention for long before returning to whatever conversations or nursing a drink. Taking a quick look around, the establishment is made completely of broad wood panels with steel supports and braces, Veridian notices.

Loud acoustic music accompanied with flutes and musical chimes fills Veridian's ears, combining with muffled conversations. The walls are adorned with various trophies from the sea, including massive shells. The *Trinity* commando meanders his pace, running his paws along the smooth wooden bar surface, making quick eye contact with the bartender approaching him. The tiger wears a brown apron over his silky black pantaloons, with a puffy creamy white and orange shirt.

Veridian leans in over the bar and asks the tiger, "Good evening. I was curious where I am? Just came in off the dock."

"Evening, you're in *Sapphire,* mister," the tiger answers him, giving pause and Veridian's person a glance up and down before adding with an amused scoff, still sounding friendly. "You certainly aren't from around here."

"Correct you are. I was hoping I could charge my cellphone here for a bit?"

"Absolutely. If you need a drink, just come on up. A table over there has an outlet." The tiger wanders off to his busy work, leaving Veridian turning around. He locates the table and moves toward it, finding it packed with a group in the middle of conversation and drinking.

"Mind if I snake my phone charger in there, friend?" Veridian interrupts them. They simply nod in approval and wave him off, eager to return to their friend's boastful story. Plugging his phone into one end, he let one of the strangers fish his charging block into the outlet rather than awkwardly lean over them. Then he waits, standing with his back against one of the tavern's support beams between two booths full of patrons.

One of the bar patrons, inspecting Veridian for some time, slides up from the bar, giving up their seat and heading in the direction of the *Trinity* commando.

Veridian notices the silvery stars embroidered into the individual's robe, and furrows his eyebrows with curiosity while he lifts his chin up from his charging device, impatiently waiting for it to charge enough to power back on. The cloth style is familiar to him, and up closer the person carries a soft musky aroma akin to incense and reminds him of the interior of the *Cosmicism* churches of his youth.

The person withdraws their purple bluish, silky appearing hood to show off their charcoal dark fur and sleek feline face. The panther offers the lion a friendly smile.

"I'm one of the few remaining *Stardust Elementalists*. From *Port Humility*."

"Oh, I've been there once or twice. That's an international sanctuary city. What happened? A powerful storm washed you out?"

"Worse, my steadfast *Trinity* commando, the *Aluanian Navy* pursuing the *Starwielder*, arrived. Did you know, or remember, Zireth Osgrin?" the panther inquires, offering Veridian, her elegant features offering a solemn expression.

"Yeah, he was one of our own," Veridian confirms, excitement growing in his eyes for a moment.

"I'm sorry to inform you of his death, then. We fought against the invaders to help Minax escape," the *Stardust Elementalist* panther says to Veridian. The hearty lion commando takes in the disheartening news, lowering his broad shoulders.

"Well, things are looking bleak, aren't they?" Veridian halfheartedly scoffs, then after his rhetorical question a second later gives her a double take, "'Minax?' Is that the *Starwielder's* name?" he asks, sounding serious.

"Yes, that is his name. It is not all bleak. I have found a couple others wearing that same insignia you have, wearing similar armor too," the panther says, indicating with a finger pointed at the *Trinity of Tranquility* crest residing on Veridian's chest plate. While looking closer, the panther's bright yellow eyes catch sight of the scruffs, dents, and cuts in the armor and his clothing.

"Where are they sheltering up around here?" Veridian inquires, more cautious sounding to not let himself emotionally sprint into feelings of false hope so soon again.

"The *Elementalism* temple here in *Sapphire.* Out of all the mega marinas named after gemstones scattered around, this is the closest one to *Ralawaith.* Come," she says, with insistence in her tone.

EPILOGUE: The Reverse-Engineered Resurrection

THE LOW-HANGING LIGHT OF the setting sun casts itself over the briny, vast foggy marshlands, islands of thick old trees heavily laden with mosses growing amidst the shallow murky water with large vibrant bioluminescent lichens draping down. A black stone ziggurat structure resides in the muddy clay landscape, reaching far above water level, a small ceremonial procession of robed *Armageddon Cultists* crawling its way between the soft pink glowing mushrooms sprouting on the ends of their pathway up, some of these mushrooms are growing up to a foot high. The torches cast unsettling shadows against the hanging moss clinging to the ziggurat.

As the procession flies quietly into the blackness of the entranceway, a supernatural magical effect cancels the light from outside reaching into the lair, including the transparency of individuals walking inside and disappearing into an inky void.

The abyssal entrance goes down a steep flight of stairs made from thick and crudely carved stone, now brightly illuminated by gently crackling torches, the air musky and cooler than the warm humid outside. The leader of the procession brings the others toward an underground cavernous system, the distant dripping sound of water trickling and the shuffling of shoes on smooth rock are the dominant sounds aside from the soft groan of the cave. Reinforced with pillars built around, or into, the stalactites and cave walls.

Drawing down his charcoal black hood, the leader reveals the ivory feline skull on his head, the voice of Daxil Ovbrash emitting with a victorious purr. "The *lithium* and *noxium* fusion charged battery is primed, warlocks take your positions around the circle! We are ready."

Daxil gestures outward before him with arms out wide, his tail rhythmically swaying behind him with anticipation. In the center of the cavern room was a giant black metal rectangle machine, sleek in design despite its shape. Dozens of tubes, relays, and circuit boards built into it. Resting beneath the machine was a large purple and red glowing circle drawn onto the smooth stone floor. Upon further examination, it was a large and archaic altar.

The procession breaks up, as *Armageddon Cultists* withdraw to stand six feet apart all around the fiendish glowing circle. Hexagrams glimmer into sight, forming beneath each of the cultist's feet, giving off a ghostly neon purple color once standing in position. A portion, primarily those armed, march to guard the mouth of the cave complex, turning their backs against the unfolding events behind them while on watch.

One such cult member, wearing tinted black goggles over his eyes and a slate gray lab coat over his body, reaches one trembling paw to a control pad to type in several code commands as his other paw carefully turns a dial. Carefully clicking it into the desired position, wetting his lips before announcing, "Three, two, one..." He pulls downward on the ignition lever of the machine, the dynamo gears grinding to life, the humming sound of electricity surging throughout the cavern amplified by the acoustics. "Standby!"

The cultists and Daxil observe with contained excitement as the roar from the machine increases in volume. Bright blue fluid flows through the tubes. The scientist lets out a cackle from his agape maw upon the sight. With the beat, Daxil announces, "Now! Channel your life forces. Go to the very brink if we must!" Together, he and the others extend their paws at the machine. In tandem, the aura coming from the venerable altar becomes static.

Lightning zaps through the empty air around the altar, harmless to the *Armageddon Cultists* as they continue on at bold ease, unabated in the face of the wild magical backlash. A hatch door in the middle of the machine now has a foggy glass window obscuring what, or who, was inside. The ritual extracts so much energy that all the cultists are on their knees straining from the effort.

Daxil snarls, gnashing his feline fangs with determination and battles to keep himself upright as his entire body feels like it's suddenly on fire, his robes billowing on his shaky person from the forces being channeled all around him. Smirking now, as the Daxil watches while the center of space and time that the machine occupies at last glows bright red.

The mad cultist scientist checks a flat diagnosis computer screen. Briefly his crazy expression leers away to the others, and yells over the noise, "Yes! We've actually achieved it! I'm receiving vitals!" The sickly sweet stench of warm plastic, hot metal, and other material fumes fills the air momentarily.

The hatch on the top of the machine bursts open violently, still on its sturdy hinges, coincidentally a billow of noxious red and shimmering purple steam rises out from within it. Then, taking careful but confident strides up and out of the coffin sitting inside the machine's chamber, the same coffin he was previously laying deceased inside of, Clyde Crowly emerges and climbs down from the four foot tall machine.

Clyde's sumptuous designer shoes clapping against the stone altar underneath. The assembled cultists, including Daxil, stare expectantly at Clyde without making a sound for the time being.

Shattering the anticipation with a sinister laugh, Clyde speaks. "Salutations, folks. Presenting the Genesis Machine, new and improved by *Crowclaw Conglomerates*. I have grand designs to unleash with it."

The scientist, still wearing his goggles over his eyes, presents an empty wine glass to Clyde, who takes it in waiting fingers upon his approach, also carrying a corked bottle, which he makes subtle work to pop off. The scientist pours the crimson fluid with pride, then steps back with a gleeful cackle. Clyde inhales the floral scent before raising the glass, toasting those assembled before him who clap, howl and cheer as he takes a victorious drink.

Afterward, Daxil steps from the outer ring over to Clyde, saying, "Welcome back to the mortal realm, Grand Warlock Crowly."

Clyde passes off his half-drunk wine glass back to the cult scientist, facing while crossing his arms, speaking to Daxil amusedly. "I wasn't gone too long, was I?

Daxil scratches his black fuzzy chin, his edges of his lips curling in a frown before he says, "No you weren't. But the eclipse disappeared. There's been no updates or responses from *Wulftheon*. It's all gone black. We don't know why."

"What? How can that be? By now, the corrupted monument should have torn open a portal to the demonic abyss in the sky," Clyde says, sounding baffled for a moment, the celebratory atmosphere around them all dying. Daxil gives him a slight head shake looking blank. The scientist also squishes his eyebrows over the goggles at Clyde, biting his lip nervously.

Clearing his throat, Daxil continues with a confident tone, "It took two shuttle trips, but the base is prepared. My inquisition's work is still underway, but we have uncovered a relic. We can open another portal. Here."

With a brief cackle, Clyde says with a fangy smirk. "Splendid, then the best is yet to come."

The End

To Be Continued!

N. Thalahasi
Galean
Empyrean
Seland
Thalahasi
Wulfheon
Antique Proxima
Neo Proxima
Aluan "Republic Of Briarhide"
Edon "Direwolf Dominion"
Mirael
Eluin
Ayanor
Cynthali
By I.C.

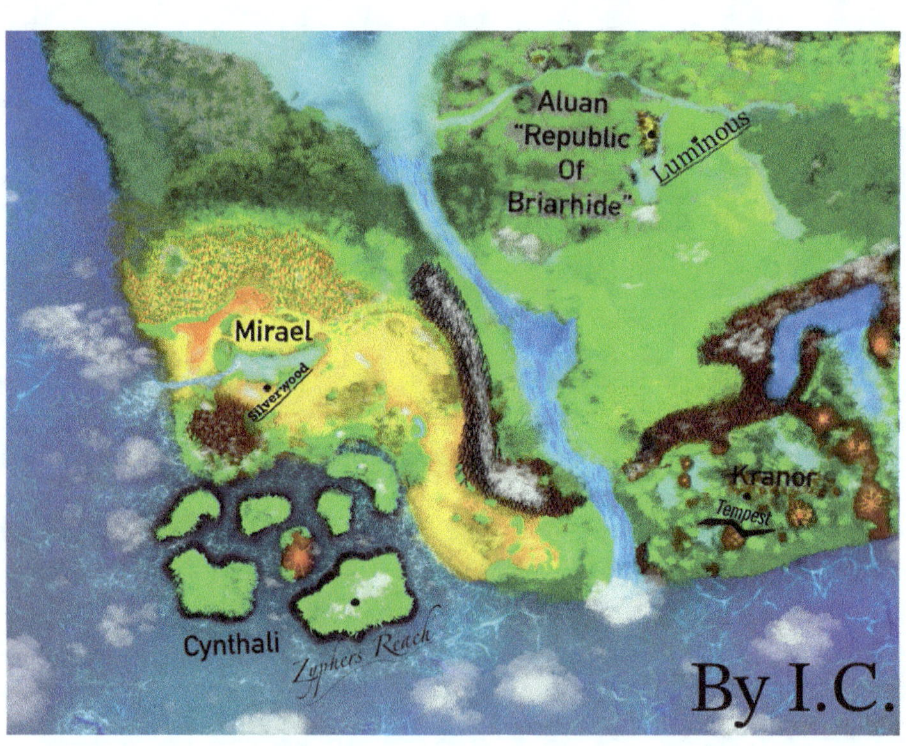

Aluan
"Republic Of Briarhide"
Luminous
Mirael
Silverwood
Kranor
Tempest
Cynthali
Zuphers Reach
By I.C.

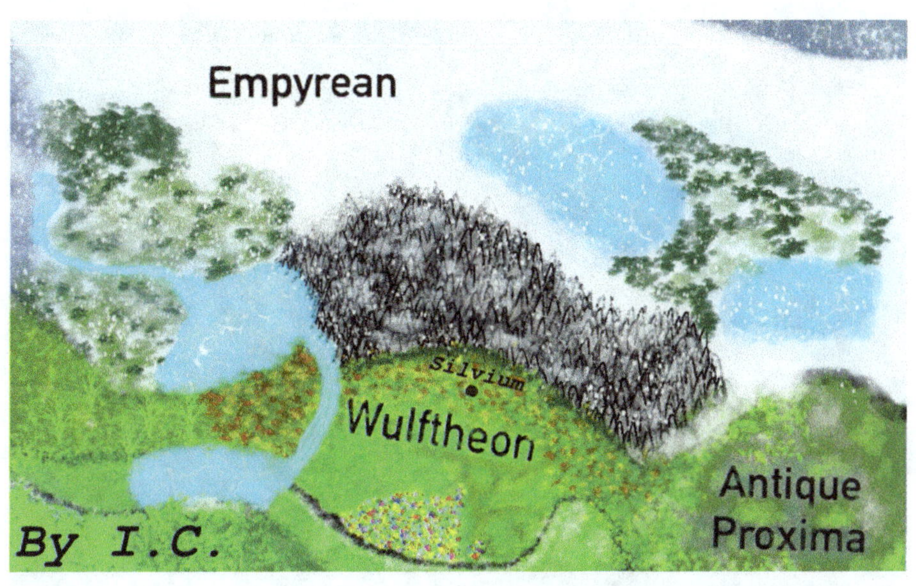

Empyrean
Silvium
Wulftheon
By I.C.
Antique
Proxima

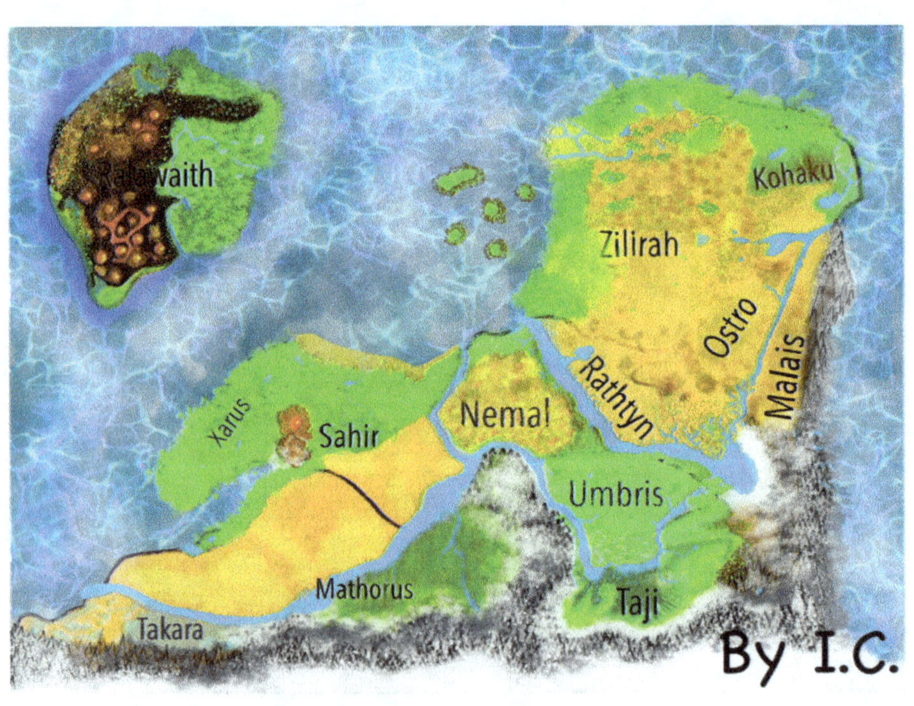

Ralawaith
Kohaku
Zilirah
Ostro
Malais
Rathtyn
Xarus
Sahir
Nemal
Umbris
Mathorus
Taji
Takara
By I.C.

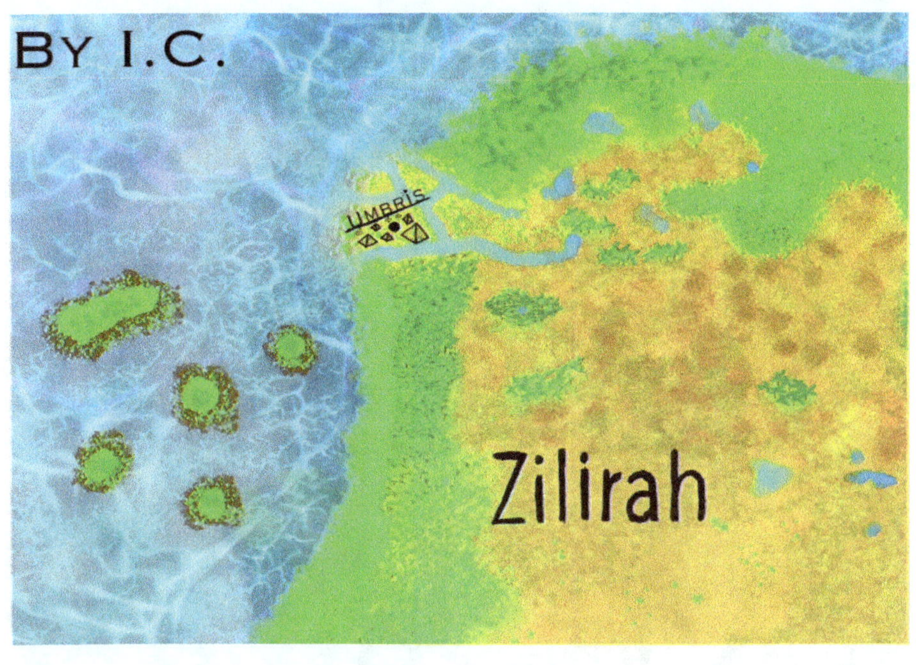
BY I.C.
UMBRIS
Zilirah

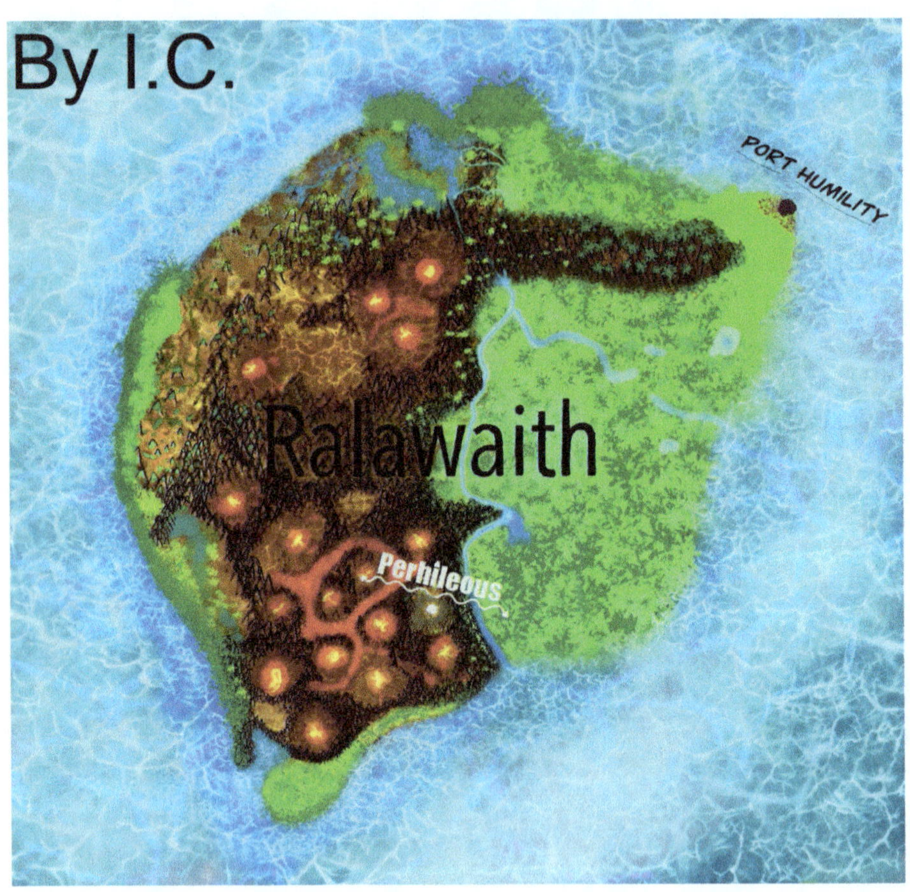

By I.C.
PORT HUMILITY
Ralawaith
Perhileous